FOAL

Redemption Song

The Beginning of the Rynn-Human Alliance

Henry Burns

ARCHWAY PUBLISHING

Copyright © 2017 Henry Burns.

All rights reserved. No part of this book may be used or reproduced by any means, graphic, electronic, or mechanical, including photocopying, recording, taping or by any information storage retrieval system without the written permission of the author except in the case of brief quotations embodied in critical articles and reviews.

This is a work of fiction. All of the characters, names, incidents, organizations, and dialogue in this novel are either the products of the author's imagination or are used fictitiously.

Archway Publishing books may be ordered through booksellers or by contacting:

Archway Publishing
1663 Liberty Drive
Bloomington, IN 47403
www.archwaypublishing.com
1 (888) 242-5904

Because of the dynamic nature of the Internet, any web addresses or links contained in this book may have changed since publication and may no longer be valid. The views expressed in this work are solely those of the author and do not necessarily reflect the views of the publisher, and the publisher hereby disclaims any responsibility for them.

Any people depicted in stock imagery provided by Thinkstock are models, and such images are being used for illustrative purposes only. Certain stock imagery © Thinkstock.

ISBN: 978-1-4808-4791-0 (sc)
ISBN: 978-1-4808-4789-7 (hc)
ISBN: 978-1-4808-4790-3 (e)

Library of Congress Control Number: 2017908668

Print information available on the last page.

Archway Publishing rev. date: 07/05/2017

Contents

Chapter 1	Exile	3
Chapter 2	Three Blessings	10
Chapter 3	Torque	22
Chapter 4	To Ride a Unicorn	36
Chapter 5	Close Encounters	51
Chapter 6	Outward Bound	65
Chapter 7	Leap of Faith	72
Chapter 8	Impatience	88
Chapter 9	Forest Cabin Clan	95
Chapter 10	Baby Steps	107
Chapter 11	Chain Reaction	111
Chapter 12	In Other News	118
Chapter 13	Core Brothers	125
Chapter 14	Press Corp	132
Chapter 15	Tide	144
Chapter 16	Haunted by the Past	148
Chapter 17	California Dreaming	158
Chapter 18	A Good Core Is Three	162
Chapter 19	Interesting Times	166
Chapter 20	Discord	173
Chapter 21	Civil Actions	176
Chapter 22	The Oligarch	192
Chapter 23	Brothers in Arms	202
Chapter 24	Armageddon	207
Chapter 25	Graz'to	217

Chapter 26	Time Is an Illusion That Only the Dead Do Not Share	227
Chapter 27	Revolution	238
Chapter 28	Disciples	240
Chapter 29	The Truth Is Like the Sun	244
Chapter 30	Zenpathy	248
Chapter 31	Pact	252
Chapter 32	First Blood	261
Chapter 33	War Paint	268
Chapter 34	Bugs	272
Chapter 35	Alsoo	276
Chapter 36	What Was Intended	286
Chapter 37	Maker	294
Chapter 38	Snake Squad	303
Chapter 39	Wobble	305
Chapter 40	3D3B and Burl	320
Chapter 41	Trojan Horse	329
Chapter 42	To Be Tall	350
Chapter 43	War Paint and War Drums	354
Chapter 44	Jamal	362
Chapter 45	A New Student	368
Chapter 46	Battle Lines	383
Chapter 47	Hatchlings	386
Chapter 48	Sad Soul	395
Chapter 49	Centurions	402
Chapter 50	What's In a Name?	406
Chapter 51	Zaski	412
Chapter 52	The Ophelia Winslow Interviews, Part One: The Terrible Three	429
Chapter 53	The Ophelia Winslow Interviews, Part Two: Warriors Go to Hell	434
Chapter 54	The Ophelia Winslow Interviews, Part Three: Rocket Man	440

Chapter 55 The Ophelia Winslow Interviews, Part 4:
        Redemption Song 444
Chapter 56 And in the End 458
Epilogue 470
Glossary of Rynn Terms 473

Year 1

1

Exile

Small Snow Flower of the Hot Springs Clan beat her fists angrily on the door of the cell that held her. "Let me out right now, offal eater!" she trilled as her feathery head crest flared out. "This is *my* ship. *Mine.*" She kicked at the door when there was no response. The pad of her booted foot impacted uselessly against the metal of the door. "*My* ship!" she repeated.

Underneath her outward anger, Small Snow Flower was frightened. It had been three days since her chief of security, Sun-Warmed Boulder of the Dwarf Forest Clan, had staged his mutiny. She had been stripped of her Torque and thrown into this holding cell.

Small Snow Flower was a Rynn. At a little over four and a half feet in height, she was tall for her species. She had the cinnamon-colored, finely scaled skin common to Rynn. Her face was triangular in shape with large dark eyes, an almost nonexistent nose, and a tiny mouth that, taken together, evoked her avian-like heritage. She could almost pass as a human if you ignored her paw-like feet and her long-fingered hands with their vestigial claws. However, the cockatoo-like head crest would be difficult to ignore.

The Rynn were a highly intelligent spacefaring species and had been exploring for over two hundred Earth years. Yet for all their intelligence and technology, they suffered the same failings as any less-advanced being. They were quarrelsome, ambitious, and vain. In short, despite their being an alien race, they were most human.

Small Snow Flower ran her long-fingered hand through her pinkish feather-like head crest nervously. She had been there three days without being able to contact anyone. "Someone should be negotiating for my release. Someone should have objected," she repeated to herself over and over.

She walked over to the circular concave sleeping kip and curled up into a ball of worry. "I have allies, I have friends," she thought fiercely. "Surely Gnarled Root or Dancing Water would have protested." She curled into a tighter ball as she thought of her friends and frequent sleep mates. She swallowed, her throat suddenly tight. "But what if they didn't?"

Small Snow Flower had good reason to doubt. She was the youngest Rynn ever to be given command of a trading ship, even if it was the smallest in her father's fleet. She was untried and untested, and Gnarled Root had often scolded her for her tendency to act aloof and detached. "You have to socialize more, Small Snow Flower. At the very least, invite some of the younger associates to share our kip."

"Morning Mist is cute," Dancing Water had added helpfully. "And I heard Sun-Warmed Boulder is very interested."

"Anyone but him," Small Snow Flower had chirped in disgust. She remembered replying, "There is something about that male that bothers me."

"I should have listened to myself," Small Snow Flower chirped again, this time in distress. "What was it the First Teacher said about listening?" She grumbled. "No one can make you listen," she recited and briefly covered her eyes. "I should have listened to myself."

Sleep was fitful and, for the first time in her life, lonely. By Rynn standards, Small Snow Flower was somewhat introverted and shy. Rynn spent most of their lives surrounded by friends and family. It was a rare Rynn who would voluntarily sleep alone. Most Rynn had multiple bed partners, and not just for sex.

Small Snow Flower having only two partners was therefore

problematic. The fact that she, Gnarled Root, and Dancing Water were not yet a breeding group just added to her problems.

Small Snow Flower spent one more miserable day in the holding cell before the door finally opened, revealing the imposing bulk and gloating face of her former security chief. If Small Snow Flower was tall for a Rynn, Sun-Warmed Boulder was, at close to five feet in height, a virtual giant.

"Rejoice, Small Snow Flower," Sun-Warmed Boulder trilled nastily. "You will not die today."

"Die?" Small Snow Flower squawked in shock.

"Why yes," Sun-Warmed Boulder returned cheerfully. "As the law states, incompetence deserves death or exile." He smiled. "I despaired on finding a suitable place for exile, but the spirits smiled upon me." His smile widened. "Of course, you still could challenge."

"Some choice," Small Snow Flower chirped despondently. Sun-Warmed Boulder was an accomplished duelist. Her father had selected Sun-Warmed Boulder as her chief of security for his skill with the blade. Her father had assumed—incorrectly, it was now apparent—that Sun-Warmed Boulder would serve as additional protection, but instead ...

Small Snow Flower's thoughts stopped suddenly. "You didn't?" she gasped in horror.

Sun-Warmed Boulder's smile widened even further. "They challenged." He shrugged. "They lost."

"Eater of week-old offal!" Small Snow Flower screamed. She launched herself at the security chief, only to be stopped by a well-placed foot. She fell to the floor. "They were my family," she gasped. "My core."

"And a better core than you deserved," Sun-Warmed Boulder sneered. He waved a hand, and two crew members entered the cell. They roughly pulled Small Snow Flower to her feet and dragged her away.

Learning of the deaths of her core broke whatever resistance remained in Small Snow Flower, and she sobbed as they dragged her to a shuttle. She continued to sob as the shuttle left the docking bay. When she found herself being chained to a partially laden supply pallet, Small Snow Flower began to scream.

"Don't let it be said that Sun-Warmed Boulder of the Dwarf Forest Clan failed to provide a chance," the chief of security laughed. "The air is breathable; the animal life might be edible. And should you escape from your bonds, you might live a long, long time." He paused. "Still." He punched Small Snow Flower in the jaw, rendering the former expedition leader unconscious.

The pallet containing the limp form of Small Snow Flower and her supplies was lifted out of the lock and onto the local short green plant life, in a clearing surrounded by tall green-topped growths. Sun-Warmed Boulder barely registered his surroundings as he checked the bonds holding Small Snow Flower. By law, the bonds were designed, with some effort, to be escapable. "We can't make it too easy, though," Sun-Warmed Boulder reflected. Seeing Small Snow Flower beginning to rouse, he started to beat his chained former commander.

Suddenly, there was a loud crack. Sun-Warmed Boulder turned his head. Approaching at a shambling run was a monstrous creature. It held a metallic object in one paw. There was another crack, and something ricocheted off the side of the shuttle.

"Oh, too bad, it looks like you will not see the morning," laughed Sun-Warmed Boulder. He quickly returned to the shuttle. In moments, it was a pinpoint in the sky, and then it vanished.

Jeremy Blunt drove his black Ford F-150 several miles deeper into the woods before running out of dirt road. Every day, he'd drive the truck along a different dirt road. In a place like Knox Gulch, there were a lot of dirt roads. It had rained the night before, and there was a chance it might rain again. Jeremy had considered postponing his walk to the next day, but old habits won. He got out and started walking. It was less exercise than it was looking for a place to die.

At the age of eighty-two, he had reached the end of a hard-worn life. His heart was failing, and recently his walks included frequent stops to catch his breath. He supposed he should head back to the city and check himself into a hospice or at least his own bed, but something—those same old habits, he supposed—would not allow him to give up and quit.

The path he followed opened into a large clearing, and he was considering turning around when he saw it. At first, he thought it was a military helicopter. The vehicle had the same general shape, but after a moment, he realized this one did not have rotors. The craft landed with a rumbling hum.

Jeremy stopped in his tracks, ducked behind a nearby tree, and watched in fascination as a section of the craft slid aside and a pallet with a tiny figure bound to the side floated out. Jeremy fought back the urge to growl. Another figure emerged from the craft and addressed the bound figure. By the gesticulations and the tone, Jeremy sensed the second being was gloating. When the second alien punched the bound one, Jeremy had no doubt.

"Why that cowardly bastard …" Jeremy snarled. He pulled his firearm from his jacket pocket and started running toward the craft, firing as he went. Aches, pains, and age were forgotten in his rage. The distance was too great for any accuracy, but based on the alien's reaction, he had gotten close. By the time Jeremy had reached the pallet, the alien ship was not even a dot in the sky.

Jeremy turned toward the pallet and almost fell as a wave of dizziness swept over him. "Not now," he growled angrily, and he used that anger to force himself to remain conscious. Still, he fell to his knees. Many minutes passed before he felt strong enough to stand and several more before he could check on the bound being.

His first thought was how tiny the creature was. *I doubt it's more than four and a half feet tall*, he thought. He vaguely remembered reading of supposed close encounters. *I thought they were supposed to be gray.* He frowned. *And with big black eyes.* This creature was the color of cinnamon, and while it did have large eyes for its size, they were barely larger than a human's. The mouth was tiny, though very human-like, and its small nose seemed more of an afterthought. The creature even had recognizable, though somewhat cup-shaped, ears. A large greenish bruise discolored the reddish-brown flesh around the eyes.

He carefully touched the creature's face, and the creature gave a slight whistling moan. "Well, it's alive," he muttered. He examined the creature's chain-like bonds, and after a little experimentation, he realized that they were just draped around the creature's body. He spent several long minutes untangling the bonds before he was able to free the alien.

Jeremy had to again stop and regain his breath. He knelt down and, with a grunt, lifted the alien into his arms. "You're a lot lighter than I thought," he said to the unconscious being. He set his jaw and started carrying the alien back to where his truck was parked. Despite the lightness of the alien being, he still needed to stop and rest several times before he finally reached the truck.

Jeremy carried the alien to the passenger side of the truck and, after placing the creature on the ground, opened the door. He grunted as he bent down, and he grunted again as he stood with the alien in his arms. With a final grunt, he shoved her into the passenger seat. Again, Jeremy took the opportunity to regain his strength. Then he retraced his steps toward the clearing. He made the trek back and forth four times before the back of the truck contained all the items that were on the pallet. He dragged the pallet to the truck as well.

It was well after dark—in fact, nearing midnight—when Jeremy finally drove the truck into his garage and carried the alien into his cabin. *Still out*, he thought in concern. He carried the creature into the spare bedroom and placed it on the bed. After some fumbling, he was able to remove the alien's boots. He stared at the paw-like feet for a moment before attempting to remove the alien's jacket.

Aliens used something very like Velcro, he noticed. The alien wore a cream-colored shirt underneath the light blue jacket, and the two mounds straining against the fabric were the proper size and position for breasts. He decided to leave the jacket in place.

He placed the boots next to the bed and covered the alien with a blanket. With a final concerned look, he left the spare bedroom and closed the door behind him.

Jeremy went back to the kitchen, made a cup a tea, and walked out onto the porch to think. He sat down and shook his head. He reached into the front of his shirt pocket and removed a pack of cigarettes. He lit one and returned the pack to his shirt pocket. "I think I've earned one today," he said, and he lit the cigarette and slowly smoked it down. When the cigarette was done, he carefully stubbed it out and placed the butt into an old beat-up coffee can that was half full of cigarette butts from previous evenings.

Jeremy stared at the night sky. "Calling today strange would be an understatement, Mei," he said to the sky. He chuckled. "There is an honest-to-god alien sleeping in the guest room."

2

THREE BLESSINGS

Small Snow Flower woke in darkness, surrounded by unfamiliar odors. She flailed around, trying to free herself from the heavy bonds holding her down, until she realized there were no bonds and she was wrapped in a blanket. After a minute or two, her racing heart slowed down, and she was able to get a better look around. It was still dark, but light was seeping in through what, despite its shape, could only be a window. It gave enough light that her eyes were able to discern some of her surroundings.

The room was roughly rectangular instead of the more familiar circular, as was the lone window. What she assumed was a door was also rectangular instead of arch-shaped. "If that's a door," she whispered nervously, "then these creatures must be giants." As if the thought acted as a summons, she heard a loud rapping on the door. Then the door opened. Small Snow Flower screamed in terror as a monstrous apparition filled the entranceway.

Small Snow Flower flung herself off the pallet and scrambled as far from the creature as possible. She searched desperately for escape, but there was no way out. Small Snow Flower cowered in a corner with her vestigial claws extended to their fullest and her crest raised to its highest extent. Her brave display was marred by the fact that her eyes were tightly shut as she waited for the end.

She heard an oddly gentle grunting and hooting and then silence. It was another minute before Small Snow Flower opened her eyes. The entranceway was again blocked, and the room was dark. *I still live*, she thought in relief. Not that she thought she was safe. For all she knew, the creature had been fooled by her bluff and was waiting for her to fall asleep.

But you were asleep, she reminded herself. *It could have killed you then.* She slowly lowered her arms and retracted her claws. Her eyes had adapted more to the gloom of her surroundings, and she began to take in more details. Wherever she was, it was bare save for a large boxlike construction against one flat wall and the soft pallet she had been lying on.

As Small Snow Flower slowly stood and walked over to the pallet, her eyes kept darting toward the blocked exit. She considered putting on her ship boots but instead padded over to the exit and pressed her ear against the flat barrier. She could hear the creature as it moved around. "What do I do?" she asked herself. "Spirits, weep for me," she chirped as visions of being eaten alive invaded her overactive imagination.

It wasn't an unreasonable fear. The Rynn had encountered three technologically advanced life-forms in their two hundred years of exploration, and two of the three considered Rynn to be nothing more than food. The Rynn weren't sure about the third, as they had become more cautious about contacting other species after their earlier experiences.

Small Snow Flower huddled in the corner of the strange boxlike room. *I won't cry, I won't*, she told herself, even as tears ran down her cheeks. *Stop it*, she commanded herself. *You may no longer have your ship, but you are still Bright Sunlight's daughter.*

She raised her head and looked at the panel covering the exit. *Spirits protect me, but if I am going to die, then I want to die on my feet.* She stood and walked over to the exit. The panel was made of some brownish substance that Small Snow Flower suspected was vegetable in nature. She noticed a round knob and tried to turn it. At first it didn't budge, but then she tried turning it in a different direction and the knob turned smoothly. She pulled on the panel and it opened.

Small Snow Flower peeked out into a brightly lit room. She blinked several times as her eyes adjusted before taking a tentative step out. At first she didn't see the creature, but the musky scent from earlier became more pronounced.

She swallowed as she realized the creature was perched on a wide fabric-covered structure no more than a handful of strides away. She straightened. "If you're going to kill me, do it now and get it over with," she chirped in false bravado.

The creature tilted its massive head in response but did nothing else. To Small Snow Flower, the lack of activity was almost painful. "Well?" she chirped angrily as the silence stretched out.

The creature's mouth turned up at the corners and then it hooted. The sound reminded Small Snow Flower somehow of laughter. The creature stood.

"Spirits protect me," Small Snow Flower trilled in shock and fear as the full height of the creature became apparent. Her crest extended to its fullest. Small Snow Flower was tall for a Rynn, yet she doubted the top of her head would reach the creature's absurdly wide shoulders. Small Snow Flower fought the urge to run back into the other room.

The creature raised one massive hand and pointed to a round construction near what seemed to be a table. The round construction was covered in a pad and looked, to Small Snow Flower, to be a smallish kip. The creature barked softly and pointed to the object again. "I'll stand," Small Snow Flower said defiantly.

The creature tilted its massive head again and then rocked its head up and down. On a Rynn, this would have been a nod of agreement. It turned, walked through a doorway, and returned several minutes later carrying a tray with a large transparent container and two smaller ones. The large container appeared to hold a colorless liquid. The creature placed the tray on the low table and gestured with one large paw.

Spirits, is it offering me water? Small Snow Flower thought in disbelief. Among the Rynn, offering water unasked was considered one of the three blessings that the First Teacher had set down thousands of Rynn years before. "The spirits bless those who, unasked, offer food, water, and clothing or shelter and require nothing in return," she had said. "From these simple courtesies, all great works begin."

Small Snow Flower looked at the creature, covered her eyes with her hands for a second, and then lifted the large container. It took both of her hands. She carefully poured the clear liquid into the each of the smaller containers, picked up one of the smaller containers, and waited. The creature hooted softly and picked up the second. The creature deliberately drank first and drained the small vessel of liquid. It lowered the container and waited.

"You do realize, our metabolisms are probably not the same," Small Snow Flower couldn't help remarking. She raised the container and drank. The water was cool and sweet. In the back of her mind, she realized she was probably exposing herself to a number of pathogens, but she was really too dehydrated to care. *Besides, I'm dead anyway.* Her crest drooped. *Or will be soon enough.*

The creature hooted and grunted to get Small Snow Flower's attention. It patted its stomach and pointed to its mouth and then at Small Snow Flower. For a brief terrifying moment, Small Snow Flower interpreted the creature's motions to indicate that she was about to be eaten. Then the creature stood again and walked into the connecting room. When it returned, it had another tray. This one had bowls containing various substances.

I think that's food. She swallowed and nodded. *The second of the three blessings.* She covered her eyes for a second and then looked at the bowls. The creature obviously had tried to give a wide sampling of different foodstuffs. *Spirits, I wish I had my Torque.* Several of the bowls contained what appeared to be animal proteins. Others contained various vegetable items. *So, they are omnivores, just like the Rynn.*

As she sampled the different food items, she again realized she was probably ingesting pathogens and toxins. If she had her Torque, she'd know for certain if she could even metabolize the food. *Not that I have much choice.*

Most of the food was somewhat bland. One white chunk had a texture that made her spit it out in disgust, and one she approached cautiously. It was orange/red in color, and on her home world, any vegetable of that color would invariably be spicy. Like most Rynn, Small Snow Flower liked spicy foods, but as part of a meal—not as the meal itself.

She cautiously nibbled off a very small amount and was surprised when the vegetable was sweet instead of spicy. A larger bite revealed that the vegetable was crunchy as well as sweet. "This is very good," she chirped. There were only a couple pieces of the orange vegetable, and she held up one of the remaining pieces and looked inquiringly at the creature. The creature rumbled a grunt in response.

"Krit?" Small Snow Flower repeated.

"Kurrut," repeated the creature.

"Kurrut," echoed Small Snow Flower. "I think I like kurrut very much," she added.

The creature hooted and again walked into the adjoining room, returning a few minutes later with a bowl filled with "kurrut." It wasn't until she was leaning back in the kip-shaped platform and sipping the last of the water that she realized she had, indeed, sat down. It was a bit of a shock to further realize that she no longer feared being eaten. She didn't think she was safe, but that particular threat no longer seemed probable.

For the first time, she looked, really looked, at her monstrous host. The creature was huge, true, but even that no longer felt threatening. *It's amazing how similarly we are constructed,* she mused. *Two arms, two legs, two eyes, two ears.* She chirped in amusement, *Assuming those great flaps are ears.* She took another sip of water. *But, spirits weep! That can't be its nose, can it?* Rynn noses were small, almost nonexistent, and barely rose above the plane of their faces.

Oddly, except for its size, the creature's mouth was the most normal looking thing. The most unusual feature, outside the oversized nose, were the white filaments, thickest over its eyes and the top of its head, that covered the exposed parts of its body. Yet despite the differences, there was one thing she was sure of. *It's definitely a male,* she thought. Why she thought that she wasn't sure, but she was certain it was true.

While she wouldn't have minded some more of the "kurruts," another need was making itself known. *Spirits weep, how do I get it to understand this?* she squirmed in discomfort. She looked at the creature and noticed it had tilted its head again and was looking at her. "What?" she chirped.

The creature stood and beckoned with one massive hand. Despite her growing conviction that the creature didn't plan on eating her, she still was going to be cautious in dealing with it. Even so, she stood and followed the creature. It led her to another blocked passageway, opened the barrier, and pointed. Easing cautiously past the creature, she looked into the room. Her crest fluttered in both surprise and agitation. *It looks like a sanitary,* she thought. *But how did it know?* She briefly covered her eyes and entered the room. The creature closed the entrance behind her.

Small Snow Flower panicked for a second and then realized that the creature was giving her privacy. She looked around and found what she took to be an elimination system and lifted the lid. She squawked in annoyance. *I'll fall into that,* she told herself.

There was a soft rapping on the barrier. After a moment, the barrier opened, and the creature walked in carrying a construction. It walked over to the elimination system and placed the construction over the opening. The construction had its own opening. The creature turned to Small Snow Flower and raised one filament-covered strip over an eye.

Small Snow Flower blinked. The construction made the sanitary usable. She nodded, and the creature left and closed the door behind it. *But how did it know?* she asked herself. The Rynn had stories of people being born with unusual mental gifts: making things move, starting fires, and reading minds. Only the most gullible took such stories seriously, yet ...

He, it, he ... Small Snow Flower thought. *He somehow knew I needed water and food and a sanitary and ... and privacy.* She shook her head. *Either he reads minds, or ...* She looked at the closed entranceway. *Or his species is way more perceptive than the Rynn.* Both options were disturbing.

Pondering the latest puzzle presented by the creature would have to wait until after Small Snow Flower finished using the sanitary. For a primitive system, it was remarkably efficient. Small Snow Flower looked around and noticed a large freestanding trough against the wall. She walked over to it. "That can't be anything other than a bath," she chirped in recognition. After a little experimentation, she figured out how to fill it with warm water. "I still may die, but at least I'm going to be clean," she declared.

Small Snow Flower removed her ship's uniform and grimaced when she realized how dirty it had become. She debated washing it first, but the warm water looked inviting, and she quickly removed the rest of her clothing. Soon she was neck deep in warm water. *They may be primitives, but they're sophisticated primitives*, she thought and lay back against the side of the trough.

She must have fallen asleep and slid down too far, because the next thing she knew, she had inhaled a lungful of water. She squawked in panic as she flailed around in the trough. Before she could recover, she found herself being pulled out of the trough by the creature.

Being so close to the creature temporarily paralyzed Small Snow Flower with fear. *Is this it?* she thought. But instead of killing her, the creature quickly wrapped her in a large square of fabric. The creature hooted at her for a moment. For the first time, she found herself looking directly into the eyes of the creature.

Whether it was the loss of her core, the loss of her ship, or just fear held back too long, something broke inside Small Snow Flower and tears began to flow. "Why?" she trilled in despair. "Spirits help me, why is this happening to me?" Her trills became a pitiful piping. "I can't ... alone. No core ... no family ... alone." She started beating her fists against the creature's broad chest. "Kill me, why won't you kill me?" she screamed. In response, the creature just held on to her tighter and started crooning soothingly.

Small Snow Flower buried her face against the creature's broad chest and wept. She barely felt the creature stand with her in his arms. He carried her into another room, placed her on a soft pad, and covered her with a thick blanket. Small Snow Flower rolled away and curled into a ball. The creature continued to croon soothingly and rubbed the small of her back. Small Snow Flower's chirps of distress slowly faded as sleep overcame her.

When the little alien finally fell asleep, Jeremy Blunt stood and left the bedroom. Why he had put her in his bedroom and his bed he wasn't sure, but he trusted his instincts. He always had. He walked out of the cabin, sat down on his favorite chair on the porch, and lit a cigarette. He smoked the cigarette silently and then, when it had burned down, lit another from the stub.

He looked at the night sky. "She cried, Mei," he informed the dark. "I don't know who that bastard was that abandoned her here, but he couldn't have been crueler." He took an angry drag on the cigarette. "The poor thing is scared out of her mind," he declared. "And trying not to show it." He shook his head. "And failing." He took another drag. "I must look like a monster to her." He exhaled a plume of smoke. "For all I know, she may think I'm keeping her alive because I like my meat fresh," he said moodily. "I know I'd think that."

Jeremy finished the cigarette and carefully stubbed it out. He stood and had to catch himself as a wave of dizziness threatened. "Shit!" he grumbled. "I can't die yet." He gasped angrily and inhaled deeply. "Not yet." He took another deep breath, and the dizziness passed. "Better," he muttered. An owl hooted from the surrounding woods. "Why me, of course," the old man said and laughed. It was an old joke and something he and his long-dead wife would say every time an owl hooted.

He walked back into his cabin and brewed himself a cup of tea. He would have preferred coffee, but he intended to sleep at some point that night. He was just finishing his tea when he heard his bedroom door open. The alien walked out with a blanket wrapped around her body.

Jeremy pointed to the other chair and then went and made a second cup of tea for the alien. He waited until the alien sat before leaving the kitchen. He returned several minutes later carrying a bundle.

The alien was sitting and sipping the tea. From the expression on the alien's face and the rippling of its feathery crest, he surmised that the alien found the tea enjoyable. He walked slowly back toward the alien and made some soothing sounds in the hope that she wouldn't get frightened. The little alien tracked him with her eyes but continued to sip her tea.

Jeremy placed the bundle on the table between him and the alien girl and pointed to it. "Some of Mei Lin's clothes," Jeremy smiled. "She was almost as tiny as you." He sat down and picked up his cooling tea.

The alien girl looked at the bundle, and her crest trembled.

"It's just clothing," Jeremy said quietly. The alien girl put down the cup and picked up the top item on the bundle. She shook it out to reveal it was a large t-shirt with a dragon on the front. "Mei Lin used to wear those as pajamas." Jeremy said.

The alien looked at the shirt and then looked at Jeremy. She pulled the shirt under the blanket and then looked at Jeremy again. "Oh yeah, right," Jeremy said quietly and turned away from the little alien. He heard some rustling and then the alien chirped and twittered. "I'm going to assume that means you're decent," he quipped and turned around to face the alien again.

The alien girl had put on the T-shirt and was looking at him.

"That looks good on you," he said. He pointed to the rest of the clothing. "Feel free to wear any of those," he said. "I think Mei Lin would approve."

The little alien's crest fluttered, and then she covered her eyes briefly and chirped and whistled. "You're welcome," Jeremy replied and repeated the eye-covering gesture. The alien chirped in response.

Jeremy could see that the alien's crest was no longer shivering. "And you don't have your claws out," he noted. He pressed his hand against his chest. "Jeremy Blunt," he said. He pointed to the alien. "And you are?"

The alien stared at him blankly. Jeremy pressed his hand against his chest again and repeated his name. He gestured at the alien.

He was about to repeat the whole thing again when the alien's crest rose. "Germyblunkt," chirped the alien. Then it pressed a hand against its chest and trilled.

"Kasumer-chirrr-chirp?" Jeremy pursed his lips and tried to repeat the whistles at the end. The alien repeated the trill. "No, I don't think so," he said after trying again. Jeremy raised a finger. "I know." He again tried to repeat the alien's name and pointed to his mouth. He shook his head. "I hope you understand that means no," he muttered then pressed a hand against his chest. "Jeremy." He pointed to the alien. "Kasumi." He repeated that several times.

The little alien stared at him for a long time and then its crest rose again. She pointed to Jeremy. "Germy." She pressed a hand against her chest. "Kasumi."

"Tell you what, if you're willing to be called Kasumi," he said in good humor, "the least I can do is be called Germy." He sat back. "Hello, Kasumi," he said.

"Helu, Germy," the alien replied.

The princess walked through the shining city. She did not look left. She did not look right. She did not look down. All made way for the princess.

The princess came upon the Temple of Light. "Open for the princess," she commanded, but the doors remained closed. "Open for the princess," she demanded, but still the doors remained closed.

Angrily, the princess was about to turn from the door when she spied an old monk sweeping the steps. "Monk," the princess said in a cold voice. "Why are the doors closed? I am the princess, and all doors open for me."

"All but this one," replied the monk calmly. She leaned the broom against a wall. "This door will only open to those who walk the path."

"Path? What path is that?" asked the princess.

"Why, the path home, of course," replied the monk.

"Home?" the princess asked in confusion. "What do you mean? I am home," she stated.

The monk laughed. "Look around you," she said. "Do you know this place?" she asked. "Look now," she ordered sharply.

The princess looked around and gasped. Except for the temple and the monk, she was surrounded by nothingness. The city she had walked through was gone. "Spirits help me," she chirped.

"Have you ever been thirsty?" asked the monk. "Truly thirsty?" the monk continued. "A thirst that dries the mouth and cracks the lips?"

"Of course not," replied the princess.

"Have you ever been hungry?" asked the monk. "With a hunger that twists your guts and bends your spine?"

"Never," replied the princess.

"Have you ever been naked?" asked the monk. "Have you ever had the cold wind blow against your bare body, the sun burning your skin, and the dust of the road covering every inch?"

"I am the princess," declared the princess. "I do not thirst, I do not hunger, and I wear the finest of clothes."

"That is why this door will not open for you," replied the monk. "That is why you are alone," she continued. "That is why you cannot go home."

"But ..." the princess chirped in protest.

"To find the path, you must first lose everything." The monk picked up the broom and started sweeping again. "You will start with your name."

Small Snow Flower bolted awake. Her head crest opened and closed in agitation. "Spirits," she chirped. Once she had calmed down, she remembered what had awakened her. "That was … I was the princess." She swallowed nervously. The Rynn may have been a technologically advanced race, but they retained a core of the primitive in their culture. Dreams were part of that.

"I never thirsted, never went hungry, and wore the finest of clothes," she whispered in realization. She looked down at the garment she was wearing. "He gave me water, he gave me food, and he gave me this to wear." Her crest fluttered. "And he gave me a name."

The little alien got up from the soft pallet and walked to the panel that closed the room off. "It's just a door," she said. She turned the knob and opened the door. She padded over to the room that contained the sanitary and walked over to the basin. There was a mirror above the basin. She looked at her reflection. "Small Snow Flower is no more," she said to her reflection. "I am … Kasumi."

3

Torque

Jeremy woke early, as he normally did. Not that he slept all that much anymore. Body aches, a congested nose, and the need to pee frequently saw to that. He lay in bed for several minutes before getting up with a grunt.

"Well, at least I woke up," he muttered quietly. He threw on a robe and exited his bedroom. His first stop was the bathroom. He noticed that the toilet seat attachment had been removed and placed against the wall. A closer examination indicated that it had been washed as well. "I wonder when she did that?"

After using the toilet, he took a quick shower and shaved, and then he went back to his room to dress. When he exited his room, he found the little alien waiting for him. She was wearing a red Chinese-style pantsuit that had a gold and green floral embroidered design. "Good morning, Kasumi," he said in greeting. "You look very nice," he added in approving tones.

"Gumonning, Germy," replied the little alien.

Jeremy raised an eyebrow. "Not bad, Kasumi." He waved a beckoning hand. "Let's have breakfast, and then I have a surprise for you." The little alien covered her eyes for a moment then followed Jeremy into the kitchen. "I wonder if you like eggs." He looked at the alien. "You can't live on carrots." He shrugged, "Well, maybe you can, but it seems kind of boring."

He went to the refrigerator and took out eggs, bread, and milk. "French toast," he decided. "Kasumi?" The little alien walked over. He handed her a slice of bread then mimed taking a bite. The little alien nibbled experimentally, then nodded. "Smart little thing, aren't you?" he commented softly.

He broke several eggs in a bowl and started whisking. He stopped when the alien girl chirped and pointed to the bowl and then her. "Sure, you can help," he said and handed her the bowl and the whisk. "Eggs," he said and pointed to the contents of the bowl.

"Ecx," repeated the little alien.

Jeremy held up the bottle of milk. "Milk."

"Mil-kah," repeated the little alien. She clumsily whisked the milk and eggs together. Jeremy added some cinnamon and salt to the bowl and let the little alien continue beating the mixture. Jeremy put a kettle on the stove to boil.

While the alien girl mixed the eggs and milk, Jeremy started heating the stovetop grill. When the grill was hot enough, he took the bowl from the girl, dipped slices of bread into the mixture, and placed them on the grill. He turned the slices and let them grill on the other side. The alien girl watched his every move.

The teakettle whistled, and Jeremy paused in cooking to pour the hot water into a teapot. He placed a mug and the smallest teacup he could find on the table before returning to the cooking toast.

Soon he had a decent stack of French toast piled on a plate. He handed the plate to the alien girl. "Here, put this on the table." He pointed to the table.

The little alien nodded and took the plate to the table while Jeremy returned to the refrigerator. He took out some butter and syrup. "And a couple carrots, just in case," he said.

He sat down at the table, placed the carrots on the alien girl's plate, and added a couple slices of French toast. He put a couple slices on his own plate. He looked at the alien girl. The little alien was staring back.

"I know that look," he said. "Mei Lin used to give me the same look." He sighed and then clapped his hands together twice and bowed to the table. "Thank you for the food."

Jeremy looked at the alien girl. "Even though she was Chinese, Mei Lin grew up in Japan," he began. Jeremy stopped. "Never mind," he muttered. "Go ahead and eat."

The little alien looked at Jeremy for a moment and then clapped her hands together. 'Tan'ka forta foo," she said. She took a bite of the French toast. Her crest fluttered as she chewed.

"Good, huh?" Jeremy said. He rubbed his belly.

"Gut-ha," agreed the alien around a mouthful of toast.

"It's better with syrup," Jeremy said. He raised the syrup bottle. "Syrup." And he poured some on his toast.

"Syrapuh," repeated the alien girl dutifully and poured some on her toast. Her crest extended, and her eyes widened. "Syrapuh, gut-ha." The little alien poured the syrup on the carrots as well. "Syrapuh, gut-ha, gut-ha," she declared. Jeremy laughed. The alien girl chittered in response.

When the meal was finished and the tea drunk, Jeremy started collecting the dirty dishes. The little alien jumped up, collected her own dishes, and followed Jeremy to the sink. "I'll wash." Jeremy handed the alien a towel. "You dry."

"Germy wass, Kasumi der-eye," declared the alien girl. When Jeremy handed the alien a dish, she wiped it with the towel. "Kasumi der-eye," she repeated. With two people washing and drying, the dishes took little time.

Jeremy beckoned with a hand. "Come, Kasumi."

"Kasumi gum," agreed the alien.

With the little alien girl following, Jeremy walked out of the house. The alien girl paused on the threshold of the doorway for several seconds. "It's okay, Kasumi," Jeremy said. The alien girl's crest fluttered for a moment, and then, with a deep breath, she followed.

Kasumi blinked as her eyes adjusted to the bright morning sun. For the first time in two sun walks, she left the relative safety of the creature's home and stepped out into an alien landscape.

Surrounding the dwelling on three sides were tall brown and gray cylindrical growths, each one topped by a mass of greenery. She inhaled deeply to sample the air, and her cuplike ears rotated slightly, bringing the sounds of the surroundings to her senses.

Kasumi followed the creature as he continued walking. He stopped at another building. It was smaller than the dwelling, and Kasumi did not see any rectangular panel-like doors. The lack was explained when Jeremy pulled up the entire front of the building.

Inside the building was a large four-wheeled construction that had to be some kind of vehicle. It had a large open space in the back end. The creature gestured toward the space. Kasumi looked and almost fainted in shock and joy. Her supplies lay neatly stacked in the back, and right on top was her Torque.

Despite her fierce desire to immediately pick up and don the Torque, she held herself back and looked at the creature. To a Rynn, being indebted to another was a shameful thing, and right now Kasumi felt indebted to the creature. *Whatever I once owned belongs to him to do with as he wants,* she thought. *Whatever I receive must be from his hands.*

"Germy." She gestured toward the supplies then toward the creature. She pantomimed picking up something and offering it. She only had to repeat it once before he hooted and reached into the back of the vehicle. To her astonishment, he picked up the Torque, looked at it for a second, and then held it out to her.

Spirits, now I'm sure he reads minds, she thought. She covered her eyes for a moment and then held out her hands. The creature gave her the Torque. Kasumi looked at the Torque and then at the creature. Slowly she placed the toroidal Torque around her neck.

Instantly, her vision became overlaid with information about her surroundings. "Torque, self-check," she trilled.

"Self-check initiated," chirped a pleasant voice in her ear. "Hello, Small Snow Flower."

"Torque, update name reference to Kasumi," she chirped back.

"Update completed. Hello, Kasumi," intoned the Torque. "Self-check completed." There was a pause. "Power cells depleted to critical levels." A display appeared in the corner of her field of vision.

"Offal-eating offspring of …" Kasumi choked off her curse. She checked the power display. "Torque, reduce all functions to standby except translation, threat, and pathogen checks unless directly requested."

"Executed," replied the Torque.

Kasumi looked at the creature. He was watching her with evident curiosity. "Torque, the creature approximately two pedin to my left is sapient and sentient," she said. "Germy," she said. She pointed to his oversized mouth. "Syrapuh, gut-ah, helu, than-yu-forta-foo."

The creature looked puzzled for a moment, and for that moment Kasumi's worry that he was a mind reader diminished. However, that worry returned in full measure at his next words and actions. He started pointing to various objects around the square space and naming them.

"Analysis indicates a high correlation between the sounds and objects," the Torque said in pleasant tones. "I have also detected microwave transmissions," the Torque added. "Apparently, the beings on this planet have developed a very sophisticated file- and data-sharing network." The display changed. "Accessing data network."

"Kasumi?" the creature grunted.

"Your new designation translates to 'mist,'" the Torque reported. "In a language locally termed 'Japanese,'" the Torque added. "However, the words spoken belong to a language locally termed 'English.'" The Torque chirped for a moment. "Translations online."

"Torque, English translations," ordered Kasumi. "Can you understand me?" The Torque grunted and hooted.

The creature raised an eyebrow. "Yes, I can," came the translation. "Do you understand me?"

Kasumi almost danced in joy. "Yes, yes, yes!" she exclaimed in glee. "I can understand you," she exulted. "Spirits rejoice, I can understand you!" She walked over to the alien and took one of his massive hands in both of hers. "May the spirits sing your name forever," she chirped fervently.

The creature hooted. "I'm sure your spirits have better things to do," he said. "Nifty little gadget you have there." He tapped the Torque with one massive finger.

"My Torque did not translate 'nifty,'" replied Kasumi. "But I think I understand." Her crest rose. "The Torque is one of the greatest creations my people have developed," she said proudly. "A child is presented with her first Torque when she learns to speak." Her crest fluttered.

"Is there something wrong with the Torque, Kasumi?" asked the creature.

"How do you do that?" protested Kasumi.

The creature chuckled when Kasumi's chirps and trills were translated. "You're pretty easy to read, Kasumi," he replied. "Your crest is very expressive, you know." He shrugged. "Right now, you're not sure if I'm telling you the truth." He hooted when Kasumi squawked in outrage. "Am I lying?"

"No," admitted Kasumi.

"I was trained to observe things," the creature continued. "I learned to spot the smallest clues in a person's behavior." He knelt down until he was eye to eye with the little alien. "Don't feel too bad. I do it to humans too."

"Do they ever accuse you of reading minds?" Kasumi chirped back.

The creature twisted his mouth in a manner that indicated humor and nodded. He pursed his lips. "I'm surprised your ... Torque can't do the same."

Kasumi's crest rose in surprise. "I don't think anyone has ever considered that possibility," she admitted. "I suppose it would be possible," she chirped musingly. "If I could ... read ... people the way you do, I don't think, no, I *know* I wouldn't have lost my ship."

"It really isn't that difficult," the creature replied. "What's wrong with the Torque?" he asked bluntly.

Kasumi's crest fluttered for a second. She gave a long chirp. "It's very low on power," she admitted reluctantly. "If I don't find a way to recharge it ..." Her crest flicked in a shrug.

The creature hooted. "We're not that primitive, Kasumi," came the translation. "At least I don't think we are," he amended. "Come to think of it, maybe we are that primitive." His mouth twisted slightly.

Kasumi's crest flicked again as she chirped and twittered. "You don't seem to use a lot of electricity," she said. "You don't even use it to heat your home."

"That's me," replied the creature. "I live mostly off the grid," he explained. "That means I don't use public utilities," he explained further after Kasumi appeared confused. He beckoned, "Here, let me show you."

He led the little alien farther from the house. "The house is heavily insulated and designed to capture as much of the sun's heat as possible." He pointed to a freestanding construction. "That's a passive solar heater for hot water." He pointed to another large rectangular construction. "And that's ..."

"That's a solar energy converter!" Kasumi said in excited chirps.

"Yeah," the creature agreed. "It supplies enough for most of my needs. What I don't use, I store in an industrial capacitor."

Kasumi looked at the solar array in growing excitement. "Torque, using the available resources, can we increase the efficiency of the solar converter in front of me?" she demanded.

After a few moments, there was a chirp. "An efficiency increase of 328 percent can be achieved with minor adjustments," came the response. "Greater efficiencies are possible but would require substantial modifications."

Kasumi turned to the creature. "You store the excess in a capacitor?" she asked. "May I see it?"

"Sure," he said and pointed to a metal housing next to the solar array. "It's in there," he said and opened a panel.

"Torque, analyze," she commanded. "If I get the estimated increases in power generation, can this store it?"

"No," came the response. "Recommend using the available standard accumulator."

Kasumi turned to the creature and began to chirp and twitter. "If you will allow, I can recharge my devices," came the translation. "But I will have to modify the solar array and use a different accumulator." Her crest fluttered for a moment. "In exchange, I will provide the specifications for whatever I do," she said. "I'm sure it would be worth something."

"That's not necessary," the creature replied.

Kasumi's crest fluttered again. *And now he refuses compensation.* She looked at the creature. "Are ... are all Earth beings like you?" she asked hesitantly.

"Like me?" Jeremy asked. He looked at the alien and noted the trembling crest and the wide-eyed stare. "I'm no saint," he stated. "I'm helping you because it's the right thing to do."

"I know!" exclaimed the little alien. "You saved my life, you gave me food and water." She waved her hand to indicate her clothing. "You even gave me clothing, and you've asked for nothing." She covered her eyes for a moment. "Is there nothing I can give you in return? Is there nothing I have that you want?"

"What I want is to help you get home," Jeremy replied.

Kasumi's crest fell, and she made a series of distressed chirps. "What?"

"I ... I must tell you something," Kasumi replied. "The spirits spoke to me last night." She paused as Jeremy raised an eyebrow. "The First Teacher would tell stories," she began. "Stories that taught."

"Ah, parables," Jeremy said in understanding. He waved a hand.

"Parables, hmm, yes," agreed Kasumi. "Most stories were about a princess."

"Princess?" After a moment, Jeremy nodded. "Let me guess, the princess was spoiled and selfish." Kasumi nodded. "And the spirits compared you to the princess?"

Kasumi chirped in shock. "I was the princess," she choked out. "But how …?"

Jeremy just raised an eyebrow. Kasumi's crest flattened.

"Yes," she chirped. Kasumi was silent for several long minutes. "The spirits were right," she said finally. "I am spoiled and … and selfish, and my core, my friends, died because of it." She looked at the floor. "And I was too much of a coward to follow them."

"How did they die?" Jeremy asked.

"They challenged Sun-Warmed Boulder's charges by rite of combat," Kasumi replied.

"A duel?" Jeremy exclaimed in disbelief. "Your people travel between the stars, and you duel?" He shook his head. "With what, light sabers?"

"What's a … oh." Kasumi paused as her Torque whispered to her. "I don't think such a thing is possible," she exclaimed. "No, we use something like these 'light sabers,' except they are made of metal."

Jeremy blinked. He was silent for a several minutes before he stood. "Come with me, Kasumi," he said in stern, almost brusque tones.

"Germy?" Kasumi chirped.

"Come with me," Jeremy repeated. Without waiting for a reply Jeremy turned on his heel and walked away. After a moment, Kasumi followed.

Jeremy led her away from the solar panel, but instead of going to the garage, he headed for yet another building. Inside, one wall was covered with large mirrors, while the wall opposite was covered with racks of weapons.

"Spirits, it looks like a training hall," Kasumi chirped.

"That's because it is," Jeremy replied. He stopped in front of a framed section of one long wall. It held a number of pictures, some of which looked hand-drawn.

Kasumi commented that while the individuals in the pictures were obviosly human, their features were different from Jeremy's.

"They're Chinese," Jeremy replied. "Bow," he commanded. He bent the upper part of his body toward the pictures. "Bow," he repeated.

Kasumi repeated the gesture. Jeremy had her do it two more times before he straightened and walk over to a cabinet. "I built this place for Mei Lin," he said. "She ..." He stopped. "Never mind," he said and unlocked the cabinet.

Inside were three long objects. Jeremy bowed to the cabinet and removed one of them. He turned to Kasumi. "Are your blades anything like this?" He unsheathed the one he held.

Kasumi's crest extended to its fullest. "Spirits!" she chirped in a whisper. "It's beautiful." She covered her eyes for a second. "Whoever made it was very skilled," she said in admiration.

"Yes, he was," agreed Jeremy. "Mei Lin's grandfather," he continued. "He made it for her when she was born." Jeremy chuckled. "Mei Lin used to complain that she didn't dare not learn how to use it." He sheathed the sword and returned it to its place in the cabinet and then locked the cabinet.

Jeremy walked over to the weapons wall and removed a sword. He handed it to Kasumi and then took a second one for himself. Jeremy walked to the center of the hall and raised the sword. "Attack me," he ordered.

"Germy?" chirped Kasumi.

"Attack me," repeated Jeremy. "Don't question, don't think, just do it," he growled.

Kasumi's crest fluttered wildly for a second, and then her expression firmed and she attacked. She swung the blade. The next thing she knew, her hand was empty, and the blade clattered against a wall.

"Pick it up," ordered Jeremy. "And try again."

Kasumi picked up the blade and tried a more deliberate attack. She lasted longer, but the result was the same: her hand was empty, and the sword was clattering against a far wall. Kasumi glared angrily at Jeremy. She stalked over to the blade, snatched it up, and then charged. She retained the blade but found herself on her back and staring at the ceiling in shock.

"How?" she chirped through the Torque. "I know I'm faster than you," she growled. "I had the best teacher."

"And yet you refused to fight Rocky?" Jeremy pointed out.

"He's ... he's better than anyone," Kasumi shot back.

"But you had the best teacher," Jeremy pointed out.

"But ... but ..." Kasumi chirped.

"Your father is very wealthy, is he not?" Jeremy said in a quiet voice. "I doubt anyone would want to displease him."

When the implications of what Jeremy was saying registered with Kasumi, she fell to her knees and began to sob. "She lied," she chirped in despair. "They all lied." She hung her head. "Sun-Warmed Boulder was right to mutiny."

"Nonsense," Jeremy replied sharply. "If anyone is at fault, it is your father," he declared. "Or your teacher." Jeremy knelt down and lifted the little alien's chin with a gentle finger. "It was not your fault." He urged Kasumi to her feet. "I'm even somewhat impressed with you."

Kasumi's head crest flared in surprise. "Impressed?" she chirped in astonishment.

"Yes, impressed," Jeremy replied. "At some level, you were aware of your deficiencies."

"I'm a coward, and you're impressed," Kasumi grumbled.

"You're spoiled, insecure, and impatient," returned Jeremy. "But one thing you are not is a coward."

"I didn't challenge Sun-Warmed Boulder," countered Kasumi.

"And you're obviously intelligent," Jeremy added dryly. "Courting certain death when you have the opportunity to live is not bravery."

Jeremy's voice took on a lecturing tone. "It's gross stupidity." He smiled wryly. "Dying is easy; any idiot can do it."

Despite her shock over being defeated so easily, Kasumi couldn't help but chirp a laugh. "That sounds like something the First Teacher would have said," she told him. "She claimed you had to trick some people into thinking."

Jeremy barked a laugh. "True that," he declared. "Except I would have said *most* instead of *some*." He raised an eyebrow. "What else did the First Teacher say?"

Kasumi covered her eyes briefly. "One of her most repeated phrases is, 'Hands cannot lie,'" she said. "Another is, 'Being poor is not a crime; being rich is not a virtue.'" Kasumi's crest fluttered. "She used to say, 'The toughest foe is the one who looks through your eyes.' I was never sure what that meant."

"Mastering others is strength, mastering oneself is true power," Jeremy quoted.

"Why ... what ...?" began Kasumi.

"Lao Tzu said that a couple thousand years ago," Jeremy replied. "I think your teacher was trying to say the same thing." He smiled. "Lao Tzu also said, 'At the center of your being, you have the answer. You know who you are, and you know what you want.'" He looked into Kasumi's eyes. "Who are you? What do you want?"

Kasumi chirped and whistled. "I used to think I knew who I was," came the translation. "I was Small Snow Flower of the Hot Springs Clan. Youngest Rynn to command her own ship." She looked at Jeremy, and he could see tears in her eyes. "If they lied to me about this," she shook the practice blade, "what else did they lie to me about?" She wiped at her eyes. "I want to go home, Germy."

"Can you go home?" Jeremy asked.

Kasumi nodded. "I can contact the ship," she said. "Sun-Warmed Boulder will have no choice but to return and fight me or lose his command of the ship."

"Interesting," Jeremy murmured.

"But ... but if I challenge ..." Kasumi's crest drooped.

"Are you afraid of dying?" asked Jeremy. Kasumi nodded. "Then you will die," he stated bluntly. Kasumi looked up in shock. "Only when you no longer fear death can you even hope to win." He raised a hand to forestall any questions. "That does not mean being suicidal. It means …" Jeremy paused. "Humans have something called a 'fight or flight' instinct," he told her. "Under stress, humans stop being rational and either go berserk or run away."

Kasumi nodded. "We are the same."

"The problem is that we may run when we should fight and fight when we should run," Jeremy pointed out. He tapped the side of his head. "We stop thinking."

"Are you saying that being afraid makes you stop thinking?" guessed Kasumi. "That is what you are saying!" she exclaimed.

"And our greatest fear is death," agreed Jeremy. "Once you stop being afraid, you can … you can do anything." He smiled. "You can even beat Rocky."

"Rocky?" A puzzled expression appeared on the little alien's face. "Rocky?" she repeated. Suddenly, Kasumi chirped a giggle. "Oh, I don't think Sun-Warmed Boulder would appreciate being called Rocky," she said, chirping her giggle again. "Oh, not at all."

"Good," Jeremy replied. "When you see him next, be sure to call him that as often as possible."

Kasumi's expression immediately sobered and her crest lowered. "Do you think …" She paused. "I'm still afraid, Germy."

"On the contrary, my dear Kasumi," Jeremy replied almost cheerfully. "You are not as afraid as you were before." He smiled. "You no longer seem to be afraid of me." He leaned his face closer to the little alien woman. To his approval, Kasumi did not flinch. "Fear can be conquered," he said. "You just need to work at it."

Kasumi looked into the alien face just inches from her own. She realized that Germy was right; she was no longer afraid of the giant being. *When did that happen?* she wondered silently. True, the creature was gigantic and strange-looking, but no longer frightening. In fact, the creature felt almost comforting. She covered her eyes for a moment. "If you are willing to teach me, I am willing to learn," she vowed.

4

TO RIDE A UNICORN

The princess stood in front of the Temple of Light. There was an old monk sweeping the steps. The princess walked over to the monk and covered her eyes. "Excuse me, holy one, may I enter the temple?"

The old monk stopped sweeping and leaned on the broom. "Who asks to enter the temple?" *she intoned.*

"One who has lost all, even her name," *replied the princess.*

"Have you thirsted with a thirst that cracked your lips?" *challenged the monk.*

The princess covered her eyes. "I have thirsted," *she replied.* "Yet no matter how much I drink, I continue to thirst."

"Have you ever been hungry?" *asked the monk.* "With a hunger that twists your guts and bends your spine?"

The princess covered her eyes. "I have hungered," *she replied.* "Yet no matter how much I eat, I continue to hunger."

"Have you ever been naked?" *asked the monk.* "Have you ever had the cold wind blow against your bare body, the sun burn your skin, and the dust of the road cover every inch?"

The princess removed her fine robes and covered her eyes. "I stand before you naked," *she replied.*

"What have you learned?" *asked the monk.*

The princess covered her eyes again. "I am not who I thought I was," *she replied. "Everything I had was unearned." She looked at the ground. "Even my name."*

The princess felt a finger lift her chin, and she found herself looking into the old monk's eyes. "The path home will be hard, and there is no guarantee you will complete the journey." The old monk smiled gently. "Kasumi."

Kasumi woke with a start. "I was the princess again," she whispered. "She called me Kasumi," she added a moment later. Kasumi got out of the strangely shaped kip and padded out of the bedroom and into the kitchen. She poured herself a glass of water and then looked at the glass. "I now know what it means to thirst." She drank the water.

Kasumi filled the glass a second time and, on a whim, decided to sit on the porch. It was still night, and the sky was sprinkled with stars. She looked at the night sky. "Torque, where is home?" A green circle appeared. With her eyes fastened on the green circle, she slowly sipped the water. "The path home will be hard," she mused. "But there is still a path home."

A tone sounded in Kasumi's ear. "Torque?"

"As requested, I have been monitoring the status of the being known as Germy," the Torque reported. "I have detected a blockage in a major coronary artery," the Torque continued. "Unless corrective action is taken immediately, it is unlikely the being will see the sun greet the day."

"Spirits!" gasped Kasumi. "What actions are available?" she demanded.

"There are two doses of Omiset available," the Torque replied. "It is unknown if that will be sufficient to reverse the damage."

Kasumi ran toward the garage. After fumbling with the handle, she was able to swing the garage door up. She ducked inside and reached for a case among the items in the back of the truck. Case in hand, she ran back to the house.

Kasumi paused at the door to Jeremy's bedroom. "Spirits help me." She opened the door and hurried to the creature's bedside. Even to her eyes, the creature looked more dead than alive. "Torque?"

"Pulse is almost nonexistent," the Torque reported. "Recommend using a full dose of Omiset." If the Torque was the greatest technological achievement of the Rynn, Omiset was their greatest biological one.

Kasumi opened the case, extracted a tube-shaped item, and pressed one rounded end against Jeremy's neck. There was a faint hiss. "Torque, continue monitoring."

To Kasumi, it seemed that the Torque was silent too long. "Pulse strengthening," the Torque finally reported. "Blockage is dissolving."

"Thank the spirits," breathed Kasumi. She leaned closer. "Germy?" she said urgently. "Germy, wake up."

Again, time seemed to slow, but Jeremy finally and almost grudgingly opened his eyes. "Wha ... Kasumi?" Jeremy groaned. "What happened?" He rubbed his chest. "Never mind, I think I know." He blew out a breath. "My heart."

"You knew," Kasumi accused. Jeremy nodded. "Why didn't you have it treated?" she demanded.

Jeremy shrugged. "What for?" he asked. "I'm old for a human," he pointed out. "At best, I'd get another two or three years."

"Torque," chirped Kasumi. "Analyze and determine current life expectancy for Germy." she ordered. Kasumi sat on the edge of the bed. "Forgive me, Germy. I gave you something without your permission," she said. "Among my people, that would be considered unethical."

"Mine too," Jeremy replied. Then he chuckled. "I think I can forgive you, though."

"Thank you, Germy," Kasumi replied quietly.

There was a tone. "Analysis complete. Best estimate is a minimum of fifteen sun paths," intoned the Torque.

"I hope you can forgive me again," Kasumi said. "You're going to live somewhat longer than two or three of your years." She smiled slightly. "Our years are slightly shorter than yours, but the Omiset has given you at least another fifteen years."

"Truth?" asked Jeremy.

"Truth," confirmed Kasumi. She took his massive hand in both of hers. "Even if I never go home, I owe you ... I owe you everything."

Jeremy was silent for a long time, and Kasumi was afraid her monstrous benefactor was angry. "Help me up," Jeremy grunted. When he was on his feet, he walked out of the bedroom. Kasumi followed closely. Jeremy walked into the kitchen and picked up a small device.

"It appears to be a microwave communication system," the Torque whispered into Kasumi's ear.

"They're more advanced than I realized," Kasumi whispered in response. She quieted when Jeremy started speaking.

"Mel?" Jeremy said. "It's Gramps." He pulled the device away from his ear. "Don't shout," he growled. "Yes, I'm still alive," he said. "Mel, shut up," he barked. "I found a unicorn." He chuckled. "I thought that would get your attention." He put the device down and turned to Kasumi. "We are going to have a visitor," he rumbled.

A motorcycle growled up the road, turned into a dirt and gravel driveway, and stopped in front of the cabin. The rider dropped the kickstand and dismounted. It was obvious, once off the motorcycle, that the newcomer in the bright red riding leathers was short—barely five feet in height, if that.

The door of the cabin opened, and an even smaller figure stepped out. The figure wore a hooded sweatshirt with the hood pulled forward to hide its face and a long skirt that almost touched the ground. There was a chirping sound. "You must be Mel," the figure said.

The rider removed the red helmet to reveal a slightly freckled face, with short-cut red hair and almond-shaped eyes. "And you must be the unicorn," Mel replied. "Where's my grandfather?"

There was another round of chirping. "Germy is resting," came the reply. "His heart is still weak."

"Still weak?" the redhead replied. "Your statement implies it's getting stronger," she said. "Which is impossible." She tilted her head. "Impossible for our technology, anyway," she added, "Germy?"

"I have some difficulty with some names," the figure replied. "Germy calls me Kasumi for the same reason."

"Kasumi, huh?" the redhead replied. "What is your real name?"

There was a chittering that sounded like laughter. "Actually, it's now Kasumi," the hooded figure replied. "I doubt you'd be able to pronounce my original name any better than Germy did."

"No doubt," the redhead replied in dry tones.

Kasumi waved to the door, and the redhead's eyes narrowed. "Please come in," Kasumi said. "Germy is eager to speak to you."

"You really are a unicorn, aren't you?" Mel breathed. "Your hands, your fingers." She walked closer to Kasumi. "Sometimes your hoodie moves as if something is sitting on top of your head."

"Nothing is sitting on my head," Kasumi returned.

"No, I don't suppose anything is," Mel murmured. "The way you move ... I doubt your feet are anything like mine either."

"Germy claims anyone can do what you just did," Kasumi replied. "I think humans are incredibly perceptive."

"Humans?" Mel chuckled. "Not even going to pretend otherwise, are you?" She stuck out a hand. "Hi, Kasumi. My name is Melanie Blunt." She added, "Call me Mel."

Kasumi looked at the hand for a second and then grasped it. "Kasumi of the Rynn," she replied. "Hello, Mel." She pushed the hood back to reveal her face. Mel raised an eyebrow. Kasumi's crest fluttered. "I love how you humans do that," she chirped. "Tea?"

Melanie smiled wryly. "I'd love some."

Mel watched as Kasumi chirped and twittered. "You don't know how nice it is to not have to constantly look up when someone is talking," came the translation.

"Yes, I do," Mel replied in amusement. "But I take your meaning," she added. "So what you're telling me is that Gramps saved your life, and you've been living with him ever since?" Kasumi nodded in agreement. "And that's how long?"

"About two Earth weeks," Kasumi replied. "What I want to know is why Germy wanted you here."

Mel's eyes widened. "He didn't tell you?"

"No," replied Kasumi. "He just laughs and tells me he wants to tell both of us at the same time." Her crest flattened slightly. "And he's still too weak to teach me anything."

"Which, now that Mel's here, we can do something about," Jeremy said from the kitchen doorway.

"Gramps!" exclaimed Mel. She jumped out of her chair and raced over to give the old man a hug. For a long moment, Mel and Jeremy remained in a tight embrace, and then Mel pushed away and looked at his face closely. "How are you really?"

"Honestly, better than I've been in years," he replied. "Still pee too often and my joints still snap." He laughed. "For a moment, I was afraid Kasumi had rejuvenated me."

"If I take back my ship, we can …" began Kasumi.

"No," Jeremy replied firmly.

"But …" objected Kasumi.

"No," Jeremy repeated. "I don't mind an extra decade. Mei Lin has waited this long, she can wait another ten years or so." He smiled. "But I don't think it would be right for her to wait much longer than that."

Kasumi looked at Jeremy searchingly before she covered her eyes. "Forgive me," she said. "I was being selfish and forgot about Mei Lin."

"Maybe you can sing for her tonight," Jeremy replied in gentler tones. "I think she likes your singing." He looked at Mel. "I think you'll like Kasumi's singing as well." He sat down at the kitchen table. Kasumi got up and returned with a mug of tea that she had to carry with both hands. She placed the mug in front of Jeremy and returned to her own seat.

"Now, as to why I called Mel here." Jeremy took a sip of the tea. He smiled. "Perfect," he said to Kasumi. "While I can train Kasumi, I'm too weak to actually spar with her."

"Spar?" Mel sat up straight. "You're going to teach her Kung Fu?" she said in shock.

"Mostly swordplay, but yes," replied Jeremy. "Short explanation: Kasumi was captain of a trading ship, there was a mutiny, the only way she can get her ship back is to duel for it." He smiled. "I'm going to train her, and you're going to be her partner."

"Wait, what, huh?" Mel sputtered.

"In return, Kasumi is going to take you with her when she goes," Jeremy continued. Both Mel and Kasumi locked gazes on the old man. "Kasumi will bring you back in not less than five nor more than ten years afterward."

Kasumi turned to Mel to find the redhead looking back at her. A thought came to her. "Did Germy train you?" she asked. Mel nodded. "If you are willing, I will agree," she said.

"When I was a little girl," Mel said almost to herself, "I had this dream. In the dream, I was walking through a forest and entered a clearing. In the middle of the clearing was a unicorn."

A ball of light formed in front of Mel, and the shape of a horse-like animal with a spiral horn appeared in the ball of light. "What a beautiful creature!" chirped Kasumi.

"New trick, Kasumi?" Jeremy asked.

"My Torque is now at 20 percent capacity, so I've enabled a few additional functions," Kasumi replied. She turned to Mel. "What happened then?" she asked.

Mel shook herself but continued to look at the three-dimensional image of a unicorn. "The one in my dream was pink," she said. The image changed to pink. Mel giggled. "Thanks," she said. "Anyway, in the dream, I walked up to the unicorn and asked for a ride."

"And then what happened?" Kasumi asked in rapt tones.

"It's amazing how realistic your translated voice is," commented Mel. "What happened was that I woke up."

"She cried for two days," Jeremy put in.

"More like a week, Gramps," Mel replied. "I just stopped crying during the day." Mel sighed. "I told Gramps about my dream, and he said …"

"'One day I'll find you a unicorn, and you will get to ride it.'" Jeremy finished.

"Who's telling the story here, Gramps?" mock-grumbled Mel. "He also promised that if he ever came across a unicorn, he'd tell me right away."

"But I also told her that I wasn't sure what a unicorn really looked like." He smiled. "After all, no one has actually seen one in a very long time, if ever." His smile became a grin. "So if I found something I thought might be a unicorn, she'd come see whatever it was I was talking about and check it out herself."

"In twenty-something years, he's sent me to ride a camel in the Mideast, hike through Nepal, live with the Inuit, and study with his grandmaster in southern China." She looked at her grandfather. "I enjoyed every single one of them." She smiled. The old man smiled back. Mel shrugged. "I never found a unicorn, but what I did find more than made up for it."

"That was the idea," Jeremy replied in dry tones. It was his turn to shrug. "I missed a lot of Brandon's growing up. I didn't want to repeat that with you."

"Dad loves you, Gramps," Mel said in soft tones.

"I never doubted that," Jeremy replied quietly. "But …" He shook his head. "Never mind that," he grumbled. "Let's talk about unicorns."

Mel looked at Kasumi. The little alien had been quietly observing the behavior of the two humans. Kasumi's crest seemed to convey a sense of affectionate approval. "Captain of a ship, huh?"

"Not a very big one," Kasumi replied. "The smallest in my father's fleet."

"Your father has a fleet of spaceships?" Mel asked. She whistled in admiration.

Kasumi nodded. "Twenty-three ships," she said. "Mostly freighters, five armed escorts, and …" She smiled wryly. "One scout explorer that my father acquired when a colleague lost his clan."

Mel nodded uncertainly. "I'm not sure you mean exactly what I think you mean, but I assume your ship is the scout explorer?" Kasumi's crest rose slightly as she nodded. "How big is a scout explorer?

Kasumi's crest fluttered. "It can accommodate up to one hundred people, with twenty being crew," she said. "In total there were seventy-four people on board when it left Nest." Her crest drooped. "Seventy-one now."

"Nest?" Mel asked.

"The Rynn home world is called Nest," Kasumi explained.

"Her father hired a professional duelist to run security on her ship," Jeremy offered.

"The picture is getting clearer." Mel sat back. "I'd go even if I never got back," she said. "But why that particular deal?"

"Think about it and get back to me," Jeremy replied with a satisfied smile. "We start training tomorrow."

Kasumi covered her eyes. "Thank you, Germy," she chirped.

"Hey, you did that without the translator," exclaimed Mel.

"I speak some Earth words," chirped Kasumi. "Learn more all time." She smiled and chirped and twittered. "But this is a more efficient way of speaking," came the translation.

"Can you still drive a truck, Mel?" Jeremy asked.

"Yeah, sure," the redhead replied warily.

"Grocery shopping," Jeremy said. "We have enough for another month or so," he said. "Kasumi eats next to nothing, but she still eats, so …" He shrugged. "I was actually thinking of taking Kasumi with me when I went for supplies." He smiled wide. "But now, she'll go with you."

Mel stared at her grandfather in shock, which slowly became understanding, which gave way to a sour expression. "Let me guess," she said in disgust. "Training?"

"Training," agreed Jeremy. "Kasumi will learn how to pass as a human, and you will learn how to keep her from being discovered."

Without taking her eyes off her grandfather, Mel hissed out of the side of her mouth, "You may love my grandfather now, Kasumi, but you're going to hate him once we start training."

"I will never hate Germy," declared Kasumi.

"You haven't trained with him yet," Mel hissed in dire tones. "And to Gramps, everything is training." She turned to her grandfather. "It's dangerous."

"So is regaining her ship," Jeremy replied. "But more importantly, I fear Kasumi is developing an unrealistic impression of humans."

"Translation, she doesn't hold them in the same contempt you do," Mel replied. "Not that I totally blame you. Humans suck." She turned to the alien. "Well, we do," she said. "We're a violent, selfish, and stupid species."

Kasumi's crest flattened. "I have seen no evidence of any of those traits," she chirped. The translator managed to make the statement sound unsure. "Germy has been nothing but patient and generous, and I think he's extraordinarily intelligent." The translator managed to convey defiance.

"Germy, I mean *Gramps*—damn, you got me doing it," Mel replied. "*Gramps* is as violent as they come," she stated coldly. "Aren't you, Gramps?"

"I've had my moments," agreed Jeremy.

"What Gramps has, that most do not have, is discipline," Mel continued. "He's spent most of his life training in the martial arts. He's learned how to control his worst instincts."

"So have you," Jeremy shot back. "Why, it's been years since you've kicked someone's butt."

Mel grinned lopsidedly. "Year, not years," she returned. "I had to put an idiot in his place last summer." Her grin turned cold. "Broke his leg."

"Got off easy, did he?" Jeremy's grin matched his granddaughter's.

"You know it, Gramps," Mel replied. She waved a hand. "Okay, point made," she conceded.

Kasumi chirped and twittered. "I don't understand you two," she complained. "You both seem to be trying to convince me humans are dangerous." Her crest rose to its highest level. "You don't know how much I wish the Rynn were half as dangerous as you claim humans to be." Kasumi stood and started pacing. "We've been exploring space for over two hundred of your years, and we have found three—" she raised a long fingered hand "—three technological species. You're the fourth." She went over to the stove and poured herself another cup of tea. She stared into the cup. "Two of them think Rynn are ... food."

"And the third?" asked Mel.

Kasumi's crest flicked. "We don't know; we hid from them," she said. "And that's the whole point," she twittered angrily. "We've hidden from the Graz'to, and we avoid the Zaski and the Polig-Grug whenever possible," she said. "And run when we can't." Kasumi looked down. "Yes, we duel, but only against each other." Kasumi looked at Jeremy. "If Sun-Warmed Boulder had known how advanced humans were, he'd never have landed here."

"Interesting," Jeremy murmured.

"Humans may be violent, though I've not seen any proof of that," Kasumi chirped. "You may even be selfish," she added. "But you've treated me as a person, not as a meal." She looked at Mel. "As for being stupid ... ignorant, maybe, but spirits, I wish I was half as stupid as you claim to be."

"You're right, Gramps," Mel said. "We're no saints, Kasumi," she told the little alien. "We really are a violent species, but … never mind, let's just figure out how we can make you pass as a human."

"Rynn really aren't too different," Jeremy commented.

"Sure, if you ignore the crest, the cinnamon skin, and the weird feet," Mel said in amused tones. "Not to mention the Voldemort nose." She smiled. "It shouldn't work, but damn, Rynn are cute." Her smile widened when Kasumi chittered. "Well, you are."

"I think humans are very handsome," Kasumi replied. "Even if you are giants."

"Never thought I'd ever be called that," Mel said in an aside.

"Humans are giants," Kasumi repeated. "Nether the Graz'to, the Zaski, or the Polig-Grug are anywhere near as massive as a human." Her crest flicked. "Well, not as massive as you," she said to Jeremy. A globe appeared in front of Kasumi and an image formed. Both Jeremy and Mel reared back.

"What the hell is that?" Mel asked in horror.

"Polig-Grug," Kasumi said in identification.

"Shit, it looks like a cross between a roach and an alligator." Mel shuddered. "Are those tentacles?" she said in complaint. "Ugh."

The image changed as they looked. Now Jeremy was standing next to the Polig-Grug. "Next to humans, the Polig-Grug are the largest technologically advanced beings we've encountered. As you can see, Jeremy is still much more massive." The image changed. Standing next to Jeremy was what appeared at first to be a four-foot-tall mushroom.

"Mushrooms are not supposed to have teeth," Mel pointed out in a faint voice.

"Zaski," Kasumi said in identification. "They produce appendages at will, but most of the time, this is what they look like." Her crest shivered. "A single Zaski consumed over 10 Rynn before it was destroyed."

"You realize we only have your word about these beings," Jeremy commented quietly.

Kasumi's crest drooped. "I know," she admitted. "I know you

have no reason to trust anything I say," she began, but stopped when Jeremy raised a quelling hand.

"I also have no reason to believe you are lying to me either," Jeremy said. "You could have let me die."

"I could just be selfish and be keeping you alive so I can survive," Kasumi countered.

"True," Jeremy admitted. "But I doubt you're that good an actress." He smiled. "Or that your being marooned is part of some plot."

"Not to mention, you're pretty damn easy to read," Mel put in. "So, what about the third one, what did you call them?"

"Graz'to," Kasumi said in answer. The image changed.

"Hey, they look a lot like Grays," Mel said in recognition. The image showed a bipedal creature with a large hairless head, large black eyes, two slits where a nose would be, and a small slash for a mouth. "Humans have been seeing something like that for years," Mel continued. "There have even been stories about people being abducted by them."

"They are an unknown when it comes to intent," Kasumi replied. "As far as we can tell, they do not know of the Rynn." Her crest flattened slightly. "We only know of them through intercepted messages and some artifacts we've found." Her crest rose. "Regardless, we cannot take the chance."

"No, you can't," agreed Jeremy. "Just as you cannot take a chance with us."

"It might be too late, Gramps," Mel said with a pensive expression on her face. "If the Grays are real, then there is a good chance they know a spaceship landed, and it wasn't one of theirs."

Kasumi started chirping urgently. The chirps and twitters went on for several minutes. "Spirits watch over us," Kasumi whispered. "The Graz'to are definitely here," she reported. "And actively searching."

"They're here," sang Mel. She gave Kasumi an apologetic look. "Sorry, old movie," she shrugged. "Nothing we can do about it."

"Can the Torque alert you if they're close?" Jeremy asked.

"Done," Kasumi replied. "If a Graz'to ship is anywhere within a thousand pedin of here, I will be alerted."

"'Pedin'?" Mel asked.

Kasumi spread her hands apart. "That's about a pedin."

"Huh," grunted Jeremy. "About a foot and a half or so," he mused. "So, about a quarter mile." He rubbed his chin. "So if the Graz'to are our Grays, they're going to be cautious and try not to bring attention to themselves." He continued to rub his chin. "Kasumi has been here a couple weeks and they haven't visited us yet." He gave Kasumi a questioning look. "How are you detecting them?"

"By their ships' energy output," Kasumi replied. "Which may explain why they haven't found me," she continued. "They would need to be well within that thousand-pedin radius in order to pick up my bio-signature." She smiled. "And I can mask that." Her smile became proud. "Which I've done."

"You're assuming your technology is better than theirs," Mel pointed out.

"If they can penetrate my masking field, then they are more advanced than any of the known beings in this galaxy," Kasumi replied. "In which case …"

"In which case, you're as good as captured, and there won't be a damn thing we can do about it," Jeremy finished. Kasumi nodded. "That doesn't mean you're safe," Jeremy added. "They could also have a masking field." He clasped his hands behind his back and looked downward. "We assume they do," he said finally.

"If only my Torque were fully charged," Kasumi said in an annoyed voice. Only the shivering of her crest indicated her nervousness. She sighed. "Maybe it would be best if I left."

"Girl, you are not going anywhere," Mel disagreed. "Gramps has always been a good judge of character," she declared. "He may say not to trust humans, and he's probably right, but he trusts you," she said. "That's good enough for me."

"But ..." protested Kasumi. "You could be in danger."

Mel shrugged. "Wouldn't be the first time." She smiled. "Besides, if you left, I'd have to go with you," she pointed out. "Part of the deal." She turned to her grandfather. "Right, Gramps?"

"Exactly right," Jeremy replied. He made a tossing gesture. "We'll deal with them if and when we have to," he said. "Until then ... we train."

5

CLOSE ENCOUNTERS

Mel walked into the guest room. She carried a rolled-up pad under one arm. "I hope you don't snore," she chided cheerfully.

"Snore?" Kasumi asked and then waited as her Torque provided information. "Oh, no, I don't ... snore."

"Good." She placed the pad she carried on the floor and unrolled it. "Looks like we're gonna be roomies," she said. "Assuming that's okay with you."

"Oh, spirits sing!" exclaimed Kasumi. "You don't know how much it's okay," she said earnestly. "Rynn do not like to sleep alone."

"No?" Mel went to the closet and pulled out a thick blanket and placed it over the pad. "What do you do? Sleep in groups?"

"Well, yes," Kasumi replied. "Sometimes," she amended. "I had a ... we call our basic social unit a *core*." Her crest drooped. "I was part of a core once." Her crest flattened limply against her scalp. "Dancing Water was so graceful—just watching her walk could make me smile. And Gnarled Root ..." She chirped a chuckle. "He was a little clumsy but honest and strong."

"She? He?" Mel asked. "One of each?"

"One of each?" Kasumi queried. "Oh," she said in understanding. "I suppose it depends on who the center is." She sat down on her own futon. "A core is usually made up of Rynn who plan on having children together," she explained. "The most common configurations are two males and a female or two females and a male." Her crest rippled. "Occasionally three females would form a core."

"How about three males?" Mel asked in fascination.

"It's rare, but it happens," Kasumi replied. Her crest flicked. "I was hoping, after this voyage ... It will never happen now." Kasumi's crest drooped again.

Mel quickly sat down next to Kasumi and gathered the little alien in her arms. "I'm sorry. I shouldn't have said anything." Kasumi's crest flared. "Oh crap, I just made it worse, didn't I?"

"No, no, not worse," Kasumi chittered in English. "Surprised." She leaned her forehead against Mel's. She chirped and chittered. "I hate sleeping alone. Spirits weep, I hate it." Kasumi raised her head. "I had hoped Germy ..." Her crest drooped.

"Gramps?" Mel shook her head. "Never happen," she said. "Gramps would consider that cheating on Mei Lin."

Kasumi nodded in understanding. "He speaks to her spirit every night," she said. "Sometimes I think she answers."

"Sometimes I think so too," Mel replied. She began to release Kasumi.

"Please, just a little longer," Kasumi pleaded. "It's been so long." She chirped contentedly when Mel tightened her hold. "Thank you."

Mel smiled. "Anytime." She leaned down and kissed Kasumi on the top of her head.

Kasumi trilled softly. "It's surprising how comfortable it is being held by a human," she murmured. "The first time I saw Germy, I thought he was a monster." Her crest flicked. "Now ..." Kasumi's crest flicked again. Again the conversation ebbed for a while. "Do you have a core, Mel?"

"Humans form pairs, not, um, triples," Mel replied. "In fact, it's illegal in many countries."

Kasumi pulled away and stared at Mel. "Illegal?" she chirped in astonishment. "You make relationships illegal?"

"No one ever said humans are rational," Mel replied. "In much of the world, the only legitimate relationship is one man, one woman."

"Spirits weep," Kasumi chirped in disbelief. "Maybe Germy is right after all."

Mel chuckled in response.

"Or maybe we're not as similar as we thought," Kasumi mused. "Most Rynn have had male and female lovers at some point in their lives." She leaned back into Mel's embrace. "The First Teacher told the story of a young Rynn who wanted, with all her heart, to become a stone artist. In school she excelled working with stone. All who knew her expected her to become a stone artist." Kasumi's crest lowered slightly. "But her parents were farmers and insisted the young Rynn follow their path."

"Poor thing," commented Mel. "She probably ended up sad and lonely. And I bet she was a lousy farmer."

"Not lousy—her loyalty to her family prevented that—but yes, she was sad and lonely." Kasumi covered her eyes at Mel. "It is good to know that the understanding I see in Germy shows in you as well." Her crest lowered as she frowned. "Is such understanding so rare, then, among humans?" she questioned. "Why pass a ruling that makes so many unhappy?"

Mel raised her hands defensively. "Hey, don't look at me to defend that rule," she declared. "It would make me unhappy too." Mel hesitated. "Um, I think you should know … I like girls."

"I like girls too," Kasumi replied.

"Um, yeah, well when humans say something like that, they mean they, um …" Mel hesitated again. "It means they look to girls as, um, sexual partners."

Kasumi leaned back slightly to look into Mel's eyes. "And what did you think Dancing Waters was?" Kasumi asked. "Gnarled Root used to say his third favorite thing was to watch me and Dancing Waters."

Mel giggled. "Third favorite?" she questioned.

"Well, he always said that Dancing Waters and I were his

favorites." She chirped a laugh. "Though he'd never say which one of us he preferred."

"Smart man." Mel giggled again.

Kasumi chirped a sad-sounding giggle. "That would be first time anyone described Gnarled Root that way," she sighed. "He was a simple spirit, but loyal. Too loyal." Her crest fell even further as she sighed again. "They both were." Mel nodded in understanding. "We were a new core, just learning about each other," Kasumi said quietly. "But I still loved them."

Mel gently pushed the little alien away and looked into her eyes. "I think that's partly why Gramps is helping you," she said. "I think Rynn and humans are very similar after all." Mel shrugged. "That's not necessarily a good thing."

"No," agreed Kasumi. "But it's also not necessarily a bad thing."

"Now you're starting to sound like Gramps," laughed Mel.

Kasumi's crest rose, and she covered her eyes for a second. "Spirits know I do not deserve such praise," she said. "But I thank you." Kasumi tilted her head. "Germy's love for Mei Lin prevents him from sleeping with me, but I believe he is attracted to me," she observed. "Despite our being two different species."

"He'd have to be dead to not be attracted," Mel stated in amused tones. "But he's still not going to sleep with you."

Kasumi was silent for a moment and then she looked at Mel with what seemed to be longing. "Do you find me attractive, Mel?"

The princess bowed to the old monk. "Greetings, honored one."

"Ah, it is Kasumi," *the old monk replied.*

"Yes, honored one," *the princess replied. She covered her eyes.* "If it is allowed, I wish to enter the temple."

"Even though the path is uncertain and the way is hard?" *asked the monk.* "Even though death may greet you at the end?"

The princess's crest fluttered in agitation. "Even though," *she said finally.* The princess gave the old monk a weak smile. *"I fear with a fear that freezes one in place, yet I must go on."*

"A fear shared is a fear halved," the old monk replied. She gestured. The princess turned to see a strange being, in shape very much like the princess, except she had no face. Yet somehow the princess knew it was looking at her.

"Who are you?" whispered the princess.

"I could be a friend," the being replied from its mouthless face. *"If you'll let me."*

"I would like a friend," the princess replied.

Mel woke up the following morning to the sound of birdsong. The birdsong originated not from outside the window but from the diminutive—even more so than Mel—form of the birdlike Rynn, Kasumi, lying in bed next to her.

"Someone is in a good mood this morning," Mel commented. She stretched hugely. "Come to think of it, so am I," she giggled. "Amazing how similar our two species are."

Kasumi chirped her own giggle. "Mel, gut-ah, gut-ah bed-uh dancer," she said in broken English.

"Bed dancer, huh?" Mel replied.

Kasumi reached over to a nightstand, picked up her Torque, and put it on. "A very good bed dancer," Kasumi corrected. "If I take back my ship—"

"*When*," corrected Mel firmly.

Kasumi chirped and nodded. "*When* I take back my ship, I don't think I will tell anyone how good a bed dancer you are."

"No?" Mel raised an eyebrow. "Afraid someone might steal me away?" Kasumi's crest fluttered. "Not gonna happen, baby," Mel replied. She gathered the little alien into a hug. "I think I'm already half in love with you."

"There are other, prettier Rynn females on the ship," Kasumi pointed out, though she made no attempt to escape the hug.

"And there are other, prettier human females … well, everywhere," Mel countered. She placed a finger on Kasumi's lips. "We can spend our time worrying that this will end, or we can spend our time enjoying our time together. We can't do both."

Kasumi's crest fluttered, and then it rose almost to its fullest extension. "Humans are so wise," she said in admiration. "I think I prefer enjoying our time together."

"Good girl," Mel said in approval. "Speaking of either/or situations, we either get up or we spend the day … bed dancing."

Kasumi chirped a laugh. "That's an easy decision." She cuddled closer.

"Speak for yourself," Mel replied. "I'm hungry and I gotta pee."

"Okay, we eat, pee, and then come back and do more bed dancing," Kasumi said. Mel laughed.

There was a knock on the door. "Get up, you two," Jeremy's voice came through the closed door. "We have things to do."

"Spoilsport," grumbled Mel. "We're up, Gramps."

"Good," Jeremy replied through the door. "Dao chung, ten minutes."

"Yes, Gramps," Mel replied. She turned to Kasumi. "Time to go to work, baby."

"Work?" Kasumi asked.

"Training," Mel replied.

Kasumi's crest fell. "Why am I suddenly afraid?" Kasumi asked in a quiet chirp.

"Good instincts," Mel replied with a laugh. "We better get up. The less time we give Gramps to consider how to train us, the better."

"Pee first," Kasumi chirped. Mel laughed.

Mel and Kasumi entered the training hall, the *dao chung*. Mel immediately bowed to an altar. Kasumi copied the bow a moment later. Jeremy, wearing a black silk outfit, waited patiently for the two women—one human, one alien—to assemble in front of him.

"Bow to the past masters," he ordered. "Bow to me," he said. "Bow to each other." He clasped his hands behind his back. "Of all the times you bow, the bow you make to each other is the most important." His gaze moved from woman to woman. "Despite your experimentations of last night, you are not yet partners in truth."

Mel and Kasumi looked at each other. "From now on, you will eat together, sleep together, train together," Jeremy continued. "At no time will you not know where the other is." Mel and Kasumi looked at each other again.

"Mel, Kasumi is weaker than you," Jeremy stated. "Kasumi, Mel is slower than you."

"Makes sense," murmured Mel. "Excuse me, tai si fu, may I speak?" Jeremy waved a hand. "Thank you, tai si fu," Mel said. "We only need Kasumi to be able to defeat Rocky," she said. "Why?"

"Defeating Rocky is only part of what is needed," Jeremy answered. He snorted. "The easiest part." He pursed his lips. "Last night, you and Kasumi proved humans and Rynn are compatible." A brief smile crossed his face and was immediately erased. "Now we will find out if we can build on that."

"I don't understand, Germy," Kasumi asked.

"*Tai si fu*," Jeremy said sternly. "In here, you will address me as tai si fu."

"'Supreme master'?" Kasumi asked after the Torque translated.

"Close," Mel said. "'Grand master' is a better translation."

Kasumi nodded and chirped quietly.

"Gramps is a grand master in a number of martial arts," Mel explained.

Kasumi nodded. "I don't understand, tai si fu," Kasumi asked. "What are you trying to do?"

"If you recall, I asked that Mel accompany you when you take back your ship," Jeremy replied. "But she will not be a passenger," he said. "Or just your lover." He raised a quelling hand to stop Kasumi from protesting. "You lost your ship because you were isolated and, forgive me, weak." Kasumi's crest fluttered, but she did not object to Jeremy's words. "I can make you stronger, but what you really need is a friend."

"Friend, tai si fu?" Mel asked. "Sounds to me more like you want me to be a bodyguard."

"How often do bodyguards sleep with their charges?" Jeremy asked in amused tones. "You're not going to be a bodyguard, not exactly." He rubbed the back of his head. "If Kasumi is attacked, you will defend her," he said. "As she will defend you, if you are attacked in turn." His expression became grim. "If she is killed, I expect you to kill her murderer." He made a slashing gesture with his hand. "Enough talk!" he growled. "The training begins … now."

For the next several hours, training is what they did. First Jeremy led Mel and Kasumi through a series of qigong exercises that started off gentle and got progressively more difficult, so that by the time Jeremy allowed a break and a chance for Mel and Kasumi to drink some water, the two women were covered in sweat.

Not that the break lasted all that long; the training quickly resumed. After the qigong, Jeremy had Mel and Kasumi strike a practice dummy with wooden wands. It was only after Kasumi felt her muscles begin to burn that Jeremy began actual sword training.

If she had thought her previous training would offer some advantage, she was quickly disappointed, as it seemed that nothing she had learned before was correct. There were times when Kasumi wanted to quit or at least scream, but every time she considered it, she recalled the old monk from her dream. *The path is uncertain and the way is hard*, she thought. *So be it.*

Finally, after what seemed like an eternity but turned out to be only three Earth hours, Jeremy called a halt. "That's enough for today," Jeremy barked. "Line up." The two women stood side by side in front of Jeremy. "Not bad, Kasumi," he said. "I thought for sure you'd try to quit at least once."

"I did think it, Ger … tai si fu," Kasumi replied.

Jeremy snorted. "I'm sure," he said. "Hot bath for both of you. Breakfast will be ready when you get out." He smiled. "I think we have some carrots left." He raised his hands and cupped his fist with one hand. "Bow," he commanded. The two women bowed. "Dismissed."

Mel grabbed Kasumi's hand. "Come on, let's get out of here before Gramps changes his mind." The two women ran out of the dao chung laughing.

Jeremy watched them go, though it wasn't until they exited the training salon that his stern expression faded and was replaced by an approving one. "Well done, Kasumi," he said quietly.

Mel and Kasumi walked into the bathroom. They had already stripped off their sweat-soaked clothes and were wrapped in towels. Mel immediately started filling the large tub with warm water. "How are you holding up, baby?" she asked Kasumi.

Kasumi was sitting on the toilet seat rubbing her shoulder. She chirped and twittered. "I think my aches have aches," came the translation. Mel laughed in response. "How do you do it?" Kasumi asked. "You were barely breathing hard."

"Training," Mel replied. "Don't sell yourself short. You did very well." Mel turned off the tub's taps. "That should be enough," she said. Mel climbed into the tub. "Get in."

Kasumi walked over to the tub and prodded the water with a toe. "Ow, hot!" she complained, even as she lowered herself into the water. "I think humans like hot water too much," she sighed as she was pulled into an embrace by Mel. "The things I have to do in order to get a hug," she mock-complained.

Mel chuckled. "Think of it as additional training," she teased. "You impressed the hell out of Gramps, you know." She started washing Kasumi's back. "He was trying to get you to quit."

Kasumi twisted around and looked at Mel in shock. "He was? I don't understand. Isn't he trying to help me?"

"Of course he's trying to help you," Mel said soothingly. "But he needed to see if you were truly committed to getting your ship back." She rinsed off some of the suds. "If you had broken, he would still have helped. He just would have changed how he went about it."

"And now?" Kasumi asked.

"Now?" Mel shrugged. "If I'm reading Gramps right, he's just getting started." She tapped Kasumi on the shoulder. "Do my back," she ordered. The two girls switched positions, and Kasumi started soaping Mel's back. "And in case you haven't figured it out, that's a compliment," she said. "He doesn't waste his time on slackers."

Kasumi was silent for a while. "I did almost quit," she chirped quietly.

"Yeah, but you didn't," Mel replied. "Remember that." Mel stood in the tub. "I think we're clean enough," she said. "I'm hungry."

After breakfast—which did feature carrots, much to Kasumi's delight—she and Mel took a walk. Since Jeremy had told them where to walk, it was no surprise that they ended up in the clearing where the shuttle had landed, marooning Kasumi.

"This is the first time I've been here since …" Kasumi said quietly. "It looks so peaceful," she said with a touch of confusion. "I expected … I don't know what I expected," she admitted. "But there should be something …"

"Evil? Forbidding?" Mel laughed. "A dark, swirling cloud hanging over the clearing?"

Kasumi's crest almost flattened in embarrassment. "I swear, humans read minds," she chirped in annoyance. "Yes, something like that." She waved a hand. "Not … this."

"It makes it worse, doesn't it?" Mel commented.

"Yes!" exclaimed Kasumi. Mel chuckled.

The two women walked around the clearing. Suddenly, Kasumi stopped and pointed. The ground in front of her was flattened and depressed by several inches. "It landed right here."

Mel grunted an acknowledgement and examined the ground closely. "Ah, now I know why Gramps wanted us to come here." She reached down and picked up a metal cube that was about an inch on a side. "Looks like he forgot something." She handed the cube to Kasumi.

"That's a message cube," Kasumi exclaimed.

"Probably Rocky getting the last word," Mel suggested.

Kasumi shook her head. "Why bother?" she asked. "He had already taken everything." She held the cube in the palm of her hand. A globe of light appeared above the cube. A figure appeared inside the globe. "That's Morning Mist!" Kasumi exclaimed.

The image chirped and twittered. Then the image froze. Kasumi chirped quietly and then the image started moving again. "I don't have much time, Small Snow Flower," the image spoke.

"Hey, I understand him!" Mel exclaimed. She looked at the image more closely. "Her?"

"Her," Kasumi confirmed. The image paused. "We should play this back at the cabin." Her crest rose. "If Morning Mist left a message, I may still have allies on the ship."

"Morning Mist, huh?" Mel said as the two women started jogging back the way they came. "We may have to change your name," she said. "Just to keep from being confused."

"Not really," Kasumi replied. "I now call myself Kasumi," she explained. "It will just be a sound to other Rynn."

"Ah, got ya," Mel replied.

It wasn't long before they reached the cabin. Jeremy was sitting in his favorite chair on the porch. He stood as they approached. "Problem?" he asked when they arrived, breathless, at the cabin.

"Not sure, Gramps," Mel replied.

Kasumi held up the cube. "A message from my ship," she chirped. "From a potential ally."

"Her name is Morning Mist," added Mel. She smiled as Jeremy raised an eyebrow. "Pretty cool coincidence."

"It's still a coincidence," Jeremy replied. "What did she say?" he asked Kasumi.

"I did not play the whole message." Kasumi looked at the cube in her hand. "Spirits, I did not realize how much I missed my own until I saw her," she chirped quietly. Her crest rose. "We will listen together."

They relocated inside the cabin. Kasumi placed the cube on the low coffee table. Again, a globe of light appeared above the cube and the form of Morning Mist appeared. "I don't have much time, Small Snow Flower," the figure on the image said. "You are not abandoned," Morning Mist said fiercely. "Sun-Warmed Boulder does not know this planet is inhabited."

"Spirits," chirped Kasumi.

"I have analyzed their transmissions," Morning Mist continued. "Despite their monstrous form, they seem to be very much like us."

"Very much," agreed Kasumi with a look first toward Jeremy and then toward Mel.

"Spirits willing, you may be able to find shelter among them," Morning Mist continued. "I was able to retrieve your Torque and hide it among your supplies. Forgive me, but I had to drain much of its charge in order for it to remain undetected." The image appeared to lean closer. "Stay strong, and may the spirits watch over you." The image froze.

"I was not abandoned," Kasumi whispered.

"She gave you a chance," Jeremy said to Kasumi. Kasumi nodded. "You will repay her courage by getting your ship back," he said sternly.

"She deserves more than that," Mel shot back. "What would be an appropriate reward for her actions?" she asked.

"Me," Kasumi replied. "We … we had considered asking her to join us." Kasumi's crest lowered then suddenly raised. She looked at Jeremy. "How long?"

"Several months," Jeremy replied. "I want to make sure you will have a fighting chance."

Kasumi nodded. "Then I had better …" she began.

"You train when and how I tell you," Jeremy said sternly. "You've trained enough for today." He raised a quelling finger. "Do not argue with me."

For a moment, Kasumi looked like she was about to do just that. Her crest flared to its fullest, and she even extended her vestigial claws. Jeremy just folded his arms across his chest and waited.

Finally, with a visible effort, she retracted her claws, though her crest stayed up. "I ... will not argue," she chirped.

"I only have your best interests in mind," Jeremy said in a gentler tone. "For the rest of the week, you will work on the basics while building up your strength and endurance." He smiled. It was not a comforting smile. "Then the training really begins."

"Told you you'd end up hating him," Mel said in an aside.

The princess looked at the temple. For the first time, the doors were open. She walked to the doorway and stopped.

"Why do you hesitate?" a familiar voice asked. "The way is open ... just as you demanded."

Kasumi turned her head to see the old monk. She covered her eyes for a moment. "I cannot leave without ..." She paused. "Without apologizing." She covered her eyes again. "I had no right to demand."

The old monk smiled in approval. "Truly, you have grown." She made a gesture, and the princess felt more than saw two figures flank her, one on her left and one on her right. The one on her left was the faceless figure of before, while the one on her right was barely more than ... a mist. "The doors are open, and the path lies before you," the old monk said. "The way will be hard and success uncertain."

The princess nodded. "That may be true, but I have my core," she said. "Failure cannot take that away."

Kasumi's eyes opened in the darkness. She was in her bed with the comforting weight of Mel's arm across her waist.

"Mel?" she whispered. She reached over, picked up her Torque, and put it on.

Mel snorted. "Hmmm?" she noised sleepily.

"If ... *when* I take my ship back, when we ..." Kasumi paused.

"I have no claim over you, but my life would be incomplete without you next to me."

Mel chuckled sleepily. "Are you asking me to marry you?"

"We do not marry as you do, but … yes," Kasumi chirped.

Mel chuckled. "Well, what do you know? My first marriage proposal, and it comes from an alien princess." She felt Kasumi stiffen. "Did I say something wrong?"

"I still think humans read minds," Kasumi replied after a moment of silence. "I dreamt I was the princess again."

"Was I in the dream?' Mel teased.

Kasumi was silent again. "I think so," she said eventually. "I had two companions in my dream, a mist-like being—"

"Morning Mist?" Mel asked.

"I think so, and a faceless companion." Kasumi reached over and touched Mel's face. "But I think she was you." Her finger traced Mel's nose.

"Hmm," Melanie noised. "Faceless, huh?" she said musingly. "I'm sure there is some deep psychological reason why I'm faceless in your dreams." Mel smiled. "Yes."

"Yes?" Kasumi asked in confused tones.

"Yes, I'll marry you, or whatever it is you do," Mel replied.

6

Outward Bound

The next day was like the first. Kasumi and Mel were awakened before dawn and spent the next three hours training. Jeremy made breakfast, with carrots, while the two women bathed. Afterward, the two women took a long walk and returned in time for lunch.

After lunch, Jeremy led the two women through a series of gentle stretching exercises, followed by another walk. They returned in time for dinner. That night, Kasumi sang for Mei Lin.

The third day was like the second, except instead of a walk, the two women jogged. Again, Kasumi sang.

By the end of the week, they started ending their jogs with a race toward the cabin. That night, while Kasumi sang, Mel hummed and clapped her hands in accompaniment. And every night after the two women went to bed, Jeremy would sit on the porch, smoke his one allowed cigarette, and speak to his dead wife.

"I want to teach her your grandfather's style, Mei," Jeremy said to the night sky. "I know it's not supposed to be taught outside the family, but …" An owl's hoot interrupted him. "Why me, of course." He chuckled. "I'll take that as permission," he said. "Thank you, Mei."

The following morning, when they reached the dao chung, Jeremy made his announcement: "Today we begin training."

"Begin?" Kasumi questioned. "What have we been doing for the last five days?"

"Building up your strength and stamina," Jeremy replied. "Fortunately, you are both in decent shape." He pursed his lips. "However, I feel Kasumi is still lacking … in confidence."

"Uh-oh," Mel murmured.

Kasumi snapped her head around to stare at Mel.

"Kasumi would never survive …" Mel began.

"Not by herself, no," agreed Jeremy.

"What are you two talking about?" Kasumi asked. The translation captured her nervousness.

"How are you with heights, Kasumi?" Mel asked sourly.

Kasumi's crest flared. "I'm fine with heights," she replied in annoyed tones. "I am the captain of a trading ship and an accomplished pilot."

"I'm not talking about those kinds of heights," Mel replied. "Have you ever gone rock climbing?"

"Rock climbing?" questioned Kasumi. "Well … no."

"There's a big difference between looking down at the ground from inside an airplane or spaceship and looking down hanging from the side of a mountain." Mel glared at her grandfather. "Really, Gramps, why is this even necessary?"

"For the same reason it was necessary for you," Jeremy replied. He looked at Kasumi. "Understand, I do not question your courage," he said. "Everything you've done since I brought you here is proof of your bravery." He shook his head. "No, it's not your courage I question; it is your will."

"Much as I hate to admit it," Mel said in grudging tones, "Gramps has a point." She looked at her grandfather. "The same trail?" she asked. Jeremy nodded. Mel blew out a breath. "She's gonna hate both of us," she muttered.

"You seem to have gotten over it," Jeremy said in amused tones.

Mel growled in response. "You will leave in the morning," Jeremy added. "Now ... bow," he ordered. Both Mel and Kasumi bowed to Jeremy.

Mel took Kasumi's hand and pulled her out of the dao chung. "Leave in the morning," she grumbled. "You had to go and rejuvenate him. I have half a mind ..." Mel continued grumbling under her breath.

Kasumi had a confused look on her face as Mel pulled her along. "I don't understand," she complained. "Is Germy mad at me?"

"Hardly," Mel replied. "If anything, he's treating you like family." She added, "Unfortunately."

"I don't understand," Kasumi complained again.

Mel half-dragged Kasumi into the spare bedroom and started going through the closet. "I know I left some of my camping gear ... ah, here it is." Mel dragged a box out of the closet and opened it. "I assume you have shoes or boots."

"Of course," Kasumi replied.

"I hope they're tough," Mel continued. "Here, try this on." She tossed Kasumi a pair of pants. They were of a thick material. "And this." She tossed Kasumi a shirt of an equally thick material.

Kasumi looked at the two items of clothing. "I don't understand," she repeated. "I can't tell if you're angry at Germy or angry at me."

"I'm not angry," Mel replied. "Well, a little angry." She sighed. "Okay, maybe I should explain."

"Please," begged Kasumi.

"Gramps ... Gramps was right when he felt you lacked will, lacked confidence," Mel said. "You do." She raised a hand. "When I was fifteen or so ..." Mel paused. "Puberty was not kind to me," she said. "I sort of developed backward." She smiled sourly. "My hips were too big, and my tits were too small." She raised her hand again. "Just shut up and listen."

Kasumi nodded uncertainly.

"So, there I was feeling like a freak and unsure of my sexuality,"

Mel shrugged. "Tomboy was probably the least offensive insult thrown at me." Mel sat down on the edge of the bed. Kasumi sat down next to her. "I started losing competitions."

"Competitions?" asked Kasumi.

"Oh yeah, right." Mel shook herself. "Gramps had taught me martial arts almost as soon as I could walk." A small smile appeared on her face. "By the time I was ten, I was one of the leading competitors in my age group." Her smile became fixed. "By the time I was fourteen, I was the leading competitor in all age groups." Mel sighed. "Puberty hit me late, and like I said, I started losing competitions."

Kasumi leaned against Mel to offer comfort. "Thanks," said Mel. "Anyways, Gramps came up with a solution." She sighed. "I hated him the whole year afterward." Her expression turned wry. "Funny thing was, it worked."

"And Germy thinks this … solution will work on me?" Kasumi asked.

"That or kill you," Mel replied. "And I'm not exaggerating. Much." She looked at the pants and shirt Kasumi was holding. "Try those on," she ordered. Kasumi removed her Chinese pantsuit and put on the pants. "Not too bad," Mel said. "We can just roll them up."

"They're very thick," Kasumi said in half-complaint.

"The mountains get cold at night," Mel replied. "I figure you can wear my old hiking jacket," she said almost to herself. "Can you eat fish?"

Kasumi nodded.

"Okay, good." Mel ran her hand through her hair. "Here's the deal. You and I are going camping."

"Camping?" asked Kasumi.

"Camping as in sleeping outside—well, in a tent—and foraging for our food." Mel chuckled sourly. "We have to travel to a designated spot and back." She chuckled sourly again. "When Gramps and I did this, it took two days to get to the spot and three days to get back." She gave Kasumi a concerned look. "Okay, I was exaggerating about it killing you, but just barely." She took Kasumi's hand. "It's going to be tough, and you're going to be cold and miserable and your feet will hurt and ... and at the end, you're going to know what your limits truly are."

"The path home will be hard and success uncertain," Kasumi said softly. She looked at Mel curiously. "Was Germy ever a ... I think the closest word would be ... 'monk'?"

"Actually, yeah, he was. Right after Grandma Mei was killed," Mel replied in surprise. "Why?"

Kasumi smiled. "It just makes sense." Kasumi stood and removed the heavy pants and shirt. "I didn't realize until just now that Germy loves me."

The princess walked through the open doors of the temple. On her left was the mist-like being and on her right was the faceless one. "I will not be of much help," the mist-like being said in a faint voice. "I can only observe."

A chuckle came from the faceless being. "Just watch our backs." The mist-like being seemed to nod. "So, where do we go?"

The princess waved a hand to indicate the path. "We follow where it will go," she said.

"Great and difficult tasks await you," said a gravelly voice.

The princess turned to see the old monk. She was leaning on a broom in the doorway. The princess covered her eyes. "That may be true, monk," she replied. "But at least I no longer journey alone."

The old monk smiled in approval. "The journey will be hard and success uncertain," the monk said. "Yet if you do succeed, the rewards will be great."

The princess covered her eyes. "My reward will be seeing my home again," she said. "I do not ask for more."

"Ah, but if you do succeed, more will be asked of you," countered the old monk. "And if you succeed, seeing your home may be all you may do."

Kasumi awoke. "Seeing my home may be all I may do," she said quietly.

A figure stirred next to Kasumi. "What was that?" Mel mumbled sleepily.

"I had ..." Kasumi's crest fluttered. "I had that dream again."

"The temple?" Mel asked. Kasumi made a sound of agreement. Mel sat up. "So what happened this time?"

"The old monk ..." Kasumi chirped a giggle. "The old monk reminds me a lot of one of my teachers and a lot of Germy," she said. "The old monk said that seeing my home may be all I do."

Mel pursed her lips. "Interesting," she said. "Was I still there?" she asked.

"Yes ... well, the faceless companion was there," Kasumi said. "I just think it's supposed to be you."

"It probably is," Mel replied. "Seeing home is all you may do, huh?" Mel leaned against the headboard. "Makes sense," she added after a minute.

"It does?" Kasumi asked in surprise.

"Well, yeah," Mel replied. "You've told me that we're the fourth technological civilization you've discovered. And it's quite possible that Rynn and humans may ..." Mel giggled. "Scratch that, Rynn and humans *do* get along." She smiled when Kasumi leaned against her. "We're certainly not going to be unique, you and I, you know." After a moment, Kasumi nodded. "So what happens when Rynn suddenly find they have an ally in a dangerous universe?" she asked. "An ally that is as mean and as tough as anything the universe could throw at you."

"We're not allies yet," began Kasumi. She paused and her crest rose to its fullest as the realization hit her. "Oh spirits, we'd ... we'd be able to face down ... everyone."

"In one," agreed Mel. "Humans like to fight," she pointed out. "And we're good at it." She laughed. "Plus, we have this instinct to protect children, or basically anything that looks like a child." She reached over and ran her hand through Kasumi's crest. "And baby, you look enough like a human child that we'll be very protective."

"I'm not sure the Rynn will appreciate being compared to children," Kasumi complained. "Okay, even if that's true, why do you think it makes sense that I may only see home?"

"Because, baby, you're going to be very, very busy," Mel replied. "Ooh, so that's why Gramps made that deal with you," Mel said suddenly. "Looks like we're both gonna be very, very busy for some time."

7

LEAP OF FAITH

Mel and Kasumi got out of the truck. Kasumi looked around curiously. "It doesn't look much different than the land around the cabin," Kasumi said.

Mel chuckled. "For now," she said. Mel pointed toward the hills rising up before them. "Wait until we start climbing." So saying, she shrugged on her backpack. She waited until Kasumi did the same. "Okay, let's go."

Mel and Kasumi had left the cabin earlier in the day. It had taken several hours to reach the entrance of the park. Jeremy had already made the reservations for camping, and all Mel had to do was sign in.

Kasumi was initially afraid that she'd be quickly discovered, but except for a few curious looks, no one seemed to pay her much mind. At the beginning of their hike, they'd pass small groups and single hikers, but after a couple hours they encountered fewer and fewer people. By the time they stopped for lunch, they hadn't seen any other hikers for over an hour.

Kasumi leaned against a tree and nibbled on a carrot stick with a blissful smile. Birds were calling from the surrounding trees, and Kasumi amused herself by imitating some of the more interesting sounds. "Sometimes I feel like I can almost understand them," she said. Kasumi made a few chirps and was answered almost immediately. She laughed.

"What did you say?" Mel asked in curious tones.

Kasumi laughed again. "Something Germy says whenever the … oh, he never told me its name." Kasumi made a low hooting sound.

"Owl," supplied Mel.

"Owl," repeated Kasumi.

"'Why me, of course'?" Mel guessed. Kasumi nodded. "You sound like a bird to me," Mel said in tentative tones. "But what, um, what do we sound like to you?"

"A shir-chirr," Kasumi replied. A glowing globe appeared in front of the two girls, and a figure formed.

"That's a shir-chirr?" Mel asked. Kasumi nodded in agreement. Mel examined the image. "Looks sort of like a feathered iguana," she said after a while. "Well, something lizard-like." The image moved, and the creature hooted and barked. Mel shook her head. "It does sorta sound like a person, doesn't it?" she said. "Weird."

Kasumi reached over and touched a lock of Mel's red hair. "From my point of view, this is a human's weirdest feature." She chirped a laugh. "Even weirder than that oversized lump you call a nose."

Mel covered her nose with a hand. "Oversized?" she exclaimed in outrage. "I'll have you know I have a tiny nose."

Kasumi touched the slight bump that represented her own nose. "Not compared to me," she replied. "Though I will admit, your nose is much, much smaller than Germy's."

"He does have a schnoz on him, doesn't he?" giggled Mel. "Funny, but I kind of considered your crest as, um, almost normal," Mel laughed. "I've seen humans with crests that would put yours to shame," she laughed. "And theirs don't even move."

Kasumi chirped in amusement. "Well, if it's not my crest, then what is a Rynn's weirdest feature?" she asked. The translation seemed to make it seem teasing in tone.

Mel looked Kasumi up and down and settled on her face. "The fact that you look like some kind of bird thing from the neck up and the knees down, and in between is ... is a girl," she said in slightly confused tones. "And who the hell would have thought that a bird thing would be cute?" she exclaimed.

"Who would have thought some fuzzy ... fuzzy ... spirits, there's nothing like you on Nest." Kasumi replied. "Nothing on Nest has hair." Her crest flared in annoyance. "And somehow this giant, fuzzy, lumpy creature," Kasumi's almost human mouth curved into a smile, "is cute."

"Never thought *I'd* be considered a giant," Mel said with a laugh.

Kasumi chirped. "Mel, I'm tall for a Rynn. Only Sun-Warm ... *Rocky* is taller," she smiled at the self-correction and then up at Mel. Her smile turned ironic.

"Point made," Mel replied. She shook her head. "I take it back—the fact that I'm considered a giant is the weirdest thing about Rynn."

Kasumi chirped a laugh in response. Kasumi looked at the sky. "The sun will soon seek its rest."

"If that means it's getting late," Mel said, standing, "You're right." She shrugged on her pack and waited for Kasumi to do the same. "We've got a good hour of walking before we make camp," she said.

Later, after the hour of walking, the setting up of the camp, and the cooking of dinner, Kasumi and Mel lay in their bedrolls watching the fire slowly burn down. Mel had already lit one propane lantern for illumination.

Kasumi rolled over and looked at the starlit sky. "I should sleep," she said. "I suspect tomorrow will be ... testing."

The princess walked along the winding path. Walking just behind her were her two companions—one nothing more than a Rynn-shaped mist, the other fully formed but without a face.

"Mist," the princess said in a commanding voice. "Go on ahead and see where this path leads. Let us know if there is danger ahead."

The mist-like figure nodded. "I go," she said and flew into the air and along the path.

To the princess's surprise, the mist soon returned. "Trouble already?" she asked.

"Not exactly," the mist replied. "You will see; it's just around that next bend." Mist said no more until after they reached the bend. Mist gestured and said, "Just to the top of the rise."

A short walk, and the nature of the trouble was revealed. The rise had hidden a rift in the earth. The princess could see the path continue on the far side of the rift. She looked down. The rift seemed bottomless. "How do we get across?"

⁂

"How do we get across?" Kasumi asked.

"Usually people say 'Good morning,'" Mel said with a groan.

"Did I say something?" asked Kasumi.

"Yeah," Mel replied. "You said, 'How do we get across?' … Across what?"

"A chasm," Kasumi replied quietly. "My dream. For a moment … never mind." Kasumi sat up in her bedroll. "Mist, the faceless one, and the princess were faced with a chasm that blocked the path," she said. "And in my dream, the princess asked …"

"'How do we get across?'" Mel finished. She shrugged. "Answer is simple enough," she replied. "You leap." She smiled at the puzzled look on Kasumi's face. "Haven't you ever heard the phrase 'leap of faith'?" Kasumi shook her head. "Well, if I had that dream, that's what I'd think it was."

"But Mel, why would I dream using a metaphor that does not exist in my culture?" Kasumi asked. "What is a 'leap of faith'?"

"It's where you do something—something profound—because someone or something you trust above all else told you to," Mel explained. "Even leaping across an impossible gap."

"Strange," commented Kasumi. "Well, it is a dream, after all." She stretched. "Good morning."

After a quick breakfast, the two women continued their hike further up the mountain path. As strenuous as the hike was, Kasumi was beginning to think that the trip was going to be a lot easier than described and was just starting to feel disappointed when the first true obstacle was reached.

Kasumi stared in dismay at the vine-covered sheer wall that loomed in front of her. "How do we get around that?" She had to tilt her head back to see the top.

"We don't," Mel replied with a grim smile. "We climb."

"Climb? That?" Kasumi's crest flattened. She was just about to declare the feat as impossible when Mel grabbed a vine and started climbing.

"Come on, girlfriend," Mel shouted as she climbed.

Kasumi stared at the retreating form of Mel for several long seconds. Her crest flared, and then she grabbed a vine and started to climb. At first the ascent was difficult but not impossible. The vines were thick enough to support her weight and seemed to reach to the top of the cliff. But when she was a little more than halfway up, she realized that was an illusion. Oh, there were vines covering the cliff's face, but most seemed to end at a narrow ledge, and the ones that reached to the top of the cliff were either out of reach or too flimsy to carry even Kasumi's light weight. It was at that ledge that Mel and Kasumi stopped.

Mel sat down on the edge of the ledge. "Might as well take a short rest," she said to the air. She looked at Kasumi with a wry smile. "Bet you thought it was going to be easy."

Kasumi's crest fluttered along with her sigh. "I was beginning to think that," she admitted. Kasumi looked around and then looked up. "There seem to be a few handholds," she said doubtfully.

"Good girl," Mel said in encouragement. "Keep talking."

Kasumi's crest half closed as she squinted at the rock wall. The dangling roots were thicker off to the left, and she walked toward them. She looked at the cliff wall again. "Someone's been here before," she said and pointed. A metal spike had been jammed into the rock just over her head. "It looks like it was designed to hold something."

"It's called a piton," Mel said. "And we can clip a rope to it."

Kasumi nodded as she took in the information. She walked back to Mel. "I'd like to try going first," she said simply. Mel raised an eyebrow in response. Kasumi chirped a laugh. "I love how you humans can do that," she said. Her expression became serious. "That's the whole point of this, isn't it?" she said and waved a hand toward the rock face. "I either can do it or I can't," she declared. "But I must try."

"Gramps was right about you," Mel said cheerfully. "Not that I didn't think the same thing," she added. She pulled a clip from her belt, walked over to the piton, and attached it. Then she threaded a strong nylon rope through it. "Attach this to your belt," she ordered. She waited until Kasumi had complied, and then she checked it anyway. "Okay, you're set."

Mel started playing out some rope and then handed Kasumi a handful of clips. "There should be a set of these going up the face. Free-climb until you reach one, attach the clip, then run the rope through it," she instructed. "Do not continue on until you are sure it's set." Kasumi nodded. "And don't rush. We have plenty of sunlight left."

Kasumi nodded again. She looked at the rock face, selected her first handhold, and began her ascent. She found the second piton quickly and continued on her way. She reached the third.

"Don't look down," Mel yelled up. "Look up or at the face."

Kasumi nodded and continued up the face. After a while, all Kasumi could see was the rock face, and all she could think about was finding the next handhold and foothold. Time itself seemed to lose all meaning. She found another piton, attached the clip, and threaded the rope. Up and up she went.

Kasumi had both booted feet balanced precariously on thin projections. Her left hand, claws extended, was jammed into a crack, while her right hand searched for another handhold. "There should be another piton," she chirped quietly. She continued to search for several minutes more. "It's not here," she shouted. "I can't find another piton."

"That's because you're almost to the top," came a cheerful voice to her left. Kasumi turned her head. There, just slightly below her, was Mel. "Look up," Mel said.

Kasumi looked up. There, barely a pedin above her right hand, the cliff-face just ended. "How do I get there?" she chirped. "It's too far."

"No, it isn't," Mel said. "Think," she ordered. "Come on, baby, you can do it."

Kasumi looked at Mel and then turned her attention back to the cliff edge that was both so close and yet seemingly out of reach. "I can't …" she gasped.

"Yes, you can," Mel said firmly. "Think," she said again.

Kasumi looked at the cliff edge again. "There's nothing to grab on to," she said. "It's too far to …" Kasumi trailed off. Her crest rose higher as she looked at the cliff edge. *A leap of faith,* she thought giddily.

She didn't hear Mel's "That's it, baby, you got it." She concentrated until all she could see was the cliff edge. She flexed her legs and her left arm and then, with a hawklike scream, she jumped. Her right arm swung to its fullest, her vestigial claws extended. For one brief terrifying moment, she thought she was short, and then her claws bit into the cliff edge.

"That's my girl!" shouted Mel. "Now you just hang there and I'll come up and …"

"No," Kasumi shouted back. "I can do this," she half-screamed. "I will do this." Her left arm joined her right, and then with another scream—this one of triumph—she pulled herself to the top of the cliff. A quick scramble, and she was over.

Kasumi was still on her back, panting with both exertion and exhilaration, when Mel came and sat down next to her. She didn't say anything, just pulled out a canteen and handed it to the little alien. Kasumi took the canteen and sat up. She took a long swallow before handing the canteen back to Mel.

"I thought I was going to die," chirped Kasumi. "And then I thought that I'd rather die than fail." Her crest opened and closed several times. "And then when I thought that ..." She fell silent.

"You stopped being afraid?" Mel said into the silence.

"Yes!" Kasumi exclaimed. She climbed to her feet and stared at the sky. "You can't scare me anymore, Sun-Warmed Boulder. You can't scare me anymore," she screamed. "I want my ship back." Kasumi started to dance around. "What's next?" she demanded. "I don't care what it is," she declared. "I feel like I can do ... anything."

"Yeah?" Mel said. "I hate to tell you, but compared to the next challenge, what you just did is nothing."

"I don't care," repeated Kasumi fiercely. "What's next?" She pointed toward a tall tree. "I'll climb that," she said. She pointed toward a waterfall. "I'll swim up that if I have to." Her crest flared to its fullest. "Tell me," she demanded. "What's next?"

"We go back to the truck and then go visit the nearest town," Mel replied.

Kasumi's crest immediately flattened. "Town?" she chirped. "With other people?"

"Scared?" Mel asked.

Kasumi was silent for a long moment. "Terrified," she admitted. Then her crest slowly rose again. She looked into Mel's eyes. "What did Germy have you do?" she asked.

"Compete in another tournament," Mel said quietly. Her mouth curled up on one side. "Gramps later told me he was afraid I would seriously hurt my opponent."

"Your face is turning red," Kasumi observed. "Are you ill?"

"No," Mel replied. "I'll explain another time," she said quickly. "Gramps was right to worry, but I got control before it got out of hand." She walked over to Kasumi and put her hand on the little alien's shoulder. "Remember to keep your temper under control," she cautioned. "You have a right to be angry, but … not in a fight."

"As Germy said, 'Anger, like fear, makes you stupid,'" agreed Kasumi. She briefly covered her eyes with her hands. "I will try not to be angry."

"Good," Mel replied. "Ready to go?"

Mel and Kasumi climbed back down the cliff face and then started the hike back toward the park entrance. It took the rest of the day and part of the next, but by the following afternoon, they were back in the truck and heading back. When they had headed toward the park, Kasumi had kept her face hidden under the hood of the sweatshirt she wore. Now, on the way back, the hood was pushed back.

"I must admit, this is a very enjoyable way to travel." Kasumi's hand was outside the window feeling the air. "I think my ancestors might have traveled like this once," she said. "It's a shame we stopped."

"Did you stop traveling?" Mel asked in curiosity.

Kasumi laughed. "Spirits, no," she chirped. "We just stopped opening windows." Her crest fluttered. "I'm not really sure why," she continued. "Our air was and still is clean. We even have parklands set aside, and Rynn do enjoy nature …" Her crest flicked in the way Mel had learned to interpret as a shrug. "But …" Again her crest flicked in a shrug. "It's such a simple thing," she nodded toward the window.

"As Gramps would say, simple things are always best," Mel replied.

Kasumi covered her eyes. "So wise," she said quietly. "Sometimes I feel I am speaking with the First Teacher herself."

"For heaven's sake, don't tell Gramps that," Mel admonished with a laugh. "He'll spend the rest of the day trying to convince you he's a fraud." She laughed again. "He'll probably tell you that he's just repeating what others have said before."

Kasumi nodded. "The First Teacher said the same," she chirped. "It's just that she said it better than anyone before her."

"Ah," Mel said in understanding. "Heads up, we're coming into town."

Kasumi made to raise the hood of her sweatshirt and then stopped. She settled it around her neck. "I will not hide what I am," she declared. "If Rynn and humans hope to … walk the path together, we should start now."

"A journey of a thousand miles begins with a single step," quoted Mel. "Some ancient Chinese philosopher," Mel explained. "Gramps would know who."

"Of course he would," agreed Kasumi. "All great teachers study the words of those who came before."

Mel laughed. "Careful, Kasumi," she chided. "You keep talking like that, and someone will start calling you 'Teacher.'"

Kasumi's crest flattened in embarrassment. Before she could respond, the truck rounded a corner, and the town appeared before her. Kasumi peered through the windshield eagerly, her earlier hesitation forgotten in the excitement of actually walking among humans.

To Rynn eyes, the town was absolute proof that she was on a world populated by something other than Rynn—though some things were not so dissimilar from what would be found on Nest.

There were storefronts with goods displayed behind windows, but the storefronts were rectangular, as were the windows, instead of the more rounded constructions favored by Rynn.

One storefront caught Kasumi's eye. "Spirits," she exclaimed. "Is that a food market?" She turned to Mel. "Do you think they have carrots?"

Mel grinned at the hopeful tone in the translated voice and pulled the truck into a convenient parking space. "Let's find out." She turned off the engine. "Okay, hat and sunglasses on," she ordered. She waited until Kasumi had the hat—floppy and broad-brimmed—on and the sunglasses in place. "Ready?" Mel asked. Kasumi nodded. "Okay, let's go," Mel said cheerfully.

Kasumi opened the truck door and exited. For the first time, she was truly among humans. She and Mel started walking toward the grocery. Almost immediately, Kasumi realized just how tall humans in general were. She unconsciously moved closer to Mel. For a moment, she considered running back to the truck, but the fear of disappointing Jeremy and Mel held her in check. "I can do this," she chirped quietly.

"Yes, you can," Mel agreed. "Besides, they have carrots." She pointed to a large bin that was completely filled with the orange root vegetable. She giggled as Kasumi suddenly picked up her pace. "Like a kid in a candy store," she muttered.

Mel grabbed a basket, and she and Kasumi walked slowly around the store. The first item that went into the basket was, of course, carrots, but those weren't the only items. As was typical of many such markets, there were samples available of many of the fruits and vegetables being offered.

"Ooh, what are those?" Kasumi chirped, pointing to another bin of root vegetables.

A store clerk overheard and walked over. "You mean you've never had ginger before?" She cut off a small section and quickly peeled it. "Some people find it a little spicy," she said and offered it to Kasumi.

Kasumi took a cautious nibble. Her eyes widened. "Torque, analyze," she chirped quietly. After a moment, the Torque chirped back, "Class 5 bioactive herb. Low toxicity, safe to consume."

"Is there a bird in here?" The clerk looked around. "I keep hearing chirping."

"I wouldn't be surprised," Mel responded easily. She waved a hand. "All this food and stuff." She turned to Kasumi and gestured at the ginger. "Should I get some?" Kasumi nodded.

The clerk continued to look around, looking for the source of the chirping. She shook herself. "Let me know if you wish to try anything else," she said. "Oh, and raw peanuts are on sale today."

"Peanuds?" Kasumi repeated without the Torque.

"I personally like the roasted and salted ones myself," Mel said to Kasumi. The clerk pointed to a bin. "Thanks."

Kasumi and Mel spent the next half hour walking through the vegetable market and grocery, trying and eventually buying a number of fruits and vegetables. They finally left with two bags apiece and headed back to the truck.

Kasumi noticed she had received several curious looks but no one stared or found her presence disturbing. "That ... that was easier than I expected."

"People tend to see what they expect to see," Mel said in comment. "And trust me, no one is expecting an alien." Kasumi nodded thoughtfully. "I don't know about you," Mel continued, "but I could use a cup of coffee. Let's stash the groceries."

Groceries safely in the truck, the two women went off in search of a coffee shop. "Gotta be a Starbucks or something," Mel stated. They turned a corner and passed a storefront. "Oh my," Mel said softly.

"What is it?" Kasumi chirped. She looked at the storefront. Inside were a number of women sitting at tables with their hands, and sometimes their feet, being worked on by a number of women wearing blue smocks.

"A nail salon," Mel said. "God, I don't remember the last time I had a facial or a mani-pedi."

Mel chirped and chittered for a few seconds. "I think there is something wrong with the Torque's translator function," she said in confusion. "It is defining a facial as some kind of sex act."

Mel started laughing uncontrollably. "Oh lord." She wiped her eyes. "Oh lord," she repeated. She raised a hand. "Give me a second." She took a breath. "Well, it's not exactly wrong," she said between chuckles. "Just not appropriate for this situation."

Kasumi chirped a few times. "Face washing?" she asked after a few more chirps. She looked through the window. "I think that makes more sense." Mel continued to chuckle. Kasumi chittered. "Though the first one sounded more fun."

Mel shrugged, though she continued to smile. "It can be, if you're into that," she said. "Before I decided I liked women better, I had a couple boyfriends who were."

Kasumi looked through the window again. "Face washing," she mused. "Sounds nice."

"Nothing better than being pampered," Mel agreed. She raised a hand. "And my hands are a mess."

Kasumi looked at her own hands. "Spirits weep."

Mel tapped her lips with a finger. "Now that would be a real test," she said in a thoughtful voice.

Kasumi looked at Mel in alarm. "You are not seriously thinking about going in there, are you?" she protested. "It's one thing to walk around like this—" she waved a hand to indicate her sunglasses and hat. "Going in there would be foolish."

Mel sighed. "You're probably right," she admitted. "Still …"

"If you want a face washing, let me do it," Kasumi interrupted.

Mel brightened up. "Now that sounds like a plan." She looked at the shop again. "We're still going in there," she said.

"Mel!" Kasumi chirped in protest.

Mel raised a quelling hand. "Just to buy some stuff," she laughed. "Trust me." Kasumi chirped disconsolately. Mel put a companionable arm across the little alien's shoulders. "Come along, Sister."

Kasumi looked at Mel. "The things I do for you," she grumbled.

There was a bell over the door that tinkled when they entered. Kasumi kept the brim of her wide floppy hat pulled down and kept her hands in her jacket pockets. There wasn't much she could do about her feet, but hopefully the legs of her loose jeans would be enough.

A woman approached. Except for some looks that seemed to be more about their size than anything else, the visit was unremarkable, and it wasn't long before Mel and Kasumi were again—with one additional stop to get coffee—heading back to the car.

Kasumi breathed a huge sigh of relief when she sat down in the passenger seat. "I think I prefer rock climbing," she chirped. "Humans are giants! I kept expecting to be stepped on." Mel laughed.

Despite Kasumi's complaints, it was obvious the alien girl had, at least in part, become comfortable with humans. More importantly, she seemed more confident. *Trust Gramps to figure out the best way to get through to someone*, Mel thought. She started the truck, and soon they were leaving the town behind.

Kasumi rolled down the window and let the cool mountain air caress her face. After a while, Mel became aware of a trilling and chirping and quickly realized the little alien was singing. The song seemed, at least to Mel, to evoke a feeling of something like longing, yet it was, at the same time, hopeful.

They stopped at a small rest stop for lunch and a chance to stretch their legs. There were a half dozen other adults at the rest stop along with a handful of children. Kasumi watched the children run and play. "So like Rynn," she chirped.

One child ran past where Mel and Kasumi were sitting, barely giving the two women a glance. Then the same child ran by again and slowed. Her interest in Kasumi was obvious. "Uh-oh," muttered Mel. "Maybe it's time to go."

The child, at most five years old, approached the two women and stopped in front of Kasumi. "You're tiny," the little girl stated.

Kasumi nodded. "Yes, I know."

"Your feet are funny," the little girl continued.

Kasumi shrugged. "Everyone in my family has feet like mine."

The little girl nodded sagely. "Mommy says I have my daddy's eyes."

"Maybe you should give them back," Kasumi replied. "He might need them."

The little girl giggled. "You're silly." She ran off.

Kasumi and Mel gathered up the remains of their lunch, and soon they were back on the road. Kasumi looked out the window silently. "You okay?" Mel asked after the silence continued.

"I'm fine, Core Sister," Kasumi replied. "Seeing the children, that little girl …" She stopped. "That was a little girl, yes?" Mel made a noise of agreement. "Gnarled Root would have been a good father," she said quietly. "If I take back my ship …" Kasumi began.

"When," Mel corrected firmly.

"Of course, Core Sister," Kasumi replied. "When I take back my ship, I plan on having a child right away."

"Got a man in mind?" Mel asked. "Or will any man do?"

"Gnarled Root has a brother," Kasumi replied. "Sunlit Meadow."

"I love Rynn names," Mel said in an aside. "I hope Sunny won't mind having a human in his core."

"And I love how humans shorten names they find too long," Kasumi replied. "I wasn't planning on inviting Sunny into my core, at least not long-term," she said. "Just long enough to give me a child." Kasumi paused. "I hope you won't mind him sleeping with us until that happens," she said in concern. "I know you don't find men all that attractive."

"Well, it will take a little getting used to, but I've slept with men before," Mel replied. "Besides, it's you he's going to be having sex with." She raised an eyebrow at Kasumi's chirping laugh. "Let me guess, sex is communal too." Kasumi nodded. "Definitely going to take some getting used to," Mel said. "Whatever you need, Core Sister."

Kasumi smiled. She closed her eyes and let the wind caress her face.

They made it back to the cabin in the early afternoon. "I hope you brought groceries," Jeremy said from the doorway of the cabin.

"Got enough for the rest of the month." Mel replied. "The town we stopped at didn't have a big selection."

"They had carrots," Kasumi chirped cheerfully. Both Mel and Jeremy laughed. "It wasn't too bad," she added. She chirped a laugh. "Even if Mel kept on trying to convince me humans are monsters."

"I think that part of your plan failed, Gramps," Mel said woefully. "I tried."

"I didn't say I didn't think humans weren't dangerous," Kasumi replied. "Just that you aren't monsters."

"Well, there is that, at least," Jeremy said. "Well, bring in the groceries," he said. "And I'll make dinner."

8

IMPATIENCE

The following morning, they were awakened at dawn, and Kasumi found herself back in the dao chung. She bowed to the altar and then to Mel and Jeremy.

As before, Jeremy led the two women in qigong exercises to warm up, followed by an hour of drills. It was only when she and Mel started sparring that Kasumi realized just how much fun she seemed to be having. She raised a hand and backed away.

"Problem, Kasumi?" Jeremy asked in concern.

Kasumi seemed to consider before she started chirping. "I'm not sure, tai si fu." The translation sounded as unsure as her words. "I feel fine," she said, and her crest flattened slightly. "I feel better than fine; I feel better than I have in my entire life."

Both Jeremy and Mel raised an eyebrow. "And that's a problem?" Jeremy asked.

"I don't know," she chirped in frustration. "Shouldn't I be worried about my duel with Rocky?" she asked. "He's a trained duelist. He's killed everyone he's ever faced." Her crest rose to its fullest. "And all I can feel is *impatience*." She looked at Jeremy. "Why am I so eager to face him? Why is this fun?"

"Oh, I almost feel sorry for Rocky," Mel said in a quiet aside to her grandfather. "Almost." She walked over to the little alien. "Fun, huh?" She walked over to a wall rack and removed two curved blades. They were metal but not sharpened. She held the blades out. "Choose."

Kasumi crest started to lower and then rose to its fullest once again. She looked at the blades. One was slightly shorter than the other, and that was the one she picked. Mel nodded and walked several paces away. She raised her sword in a salute. "Let's see if you still think it's fun after I beat you," she said.

Kasumi raised the blade and saluted back. "You may beat me, Core Sister, but you may not," she replied.

"Begin!" barked Jeremy.

Kasumi moved forward quickly but deliberately. "Stay light," she mentally recited. "What your opponent does not move, do not move." Her blade flashed forward almost on its own. "When your opponent moves, you have already moved."

Kasumi felt more than saw the low slashing attack and leaped over the blade. Her blade came down in a whistling strike. It was blocked, but Kasumi had already retreated before the expected counter was initiated. She circled the blade behind her neck, and her left hand came out, just as Jeremy had taught her.

Mel's blade sliced the air, neck high. The back of Kasumi's blade blocked it. Kasumi spun on one heel, and her blade slashed low toward Mel's ankles.

Back and forth across the training hall went the two women. Kasumi's speed and agility countered Mel's strength and power. At one point, Kasumi used a wall as a springboard to attack from the left flank. At another, she dived toward the ground and rolled, and then her blade flashed upward … and was blocked. But before Mel could take advantage, Kasumi had already retreated to safety.

Back and forth, high and low, the two women battled. Their blades crossed again and again. Sweat started to pour down Kasumi's face. She backed away to wipe off the sweat and then charged. She was met in the middle of the dao chung, and now they added their bodies to the battle.

Kasumi kicked. To her delight, the blow landed, and Mel backed off. It was a short-lived victory, as Mel came back with her own kicks, one of which almost knocked Kasumi off her feet. She started moving her blade in the flashing figure-eight pattern Jeremy called a flower. She couldn't stop the laugh that bubbled up. "Ready for some more, Core Sister?" she called.

"Any time, Core Sister," Mel called back, and she added her own laughter.

"Halt," barked Jeremy. He started a slow clapping as he walked toward the two combatants. "Well done, Kasumi," he said in rare approval. "Very well done." To Kasumi's surprise, he covered his eyes for a moment. "You have come far."

Kasumi covered her own eyes and then bowed. "If I have come far, it is because you showed me the path, Teacher."

Jeremy smiled in approval. "Mel," he said in a commanding tone. "Teach her the family sword form."

"Yes, tai si fu," Mel responded proudly.

"Learn it well, Kasumi," Jeremy said in serious tones. "For when you have mastered that form, you will challenge."

Kasumi blinked and then bowed low. "Yes, tai si fu."

Jeremy was sitting on the porch of his cabin and slowly smoking the one cigarette he allowed himself when the cabin door opened and Kasumi walked out. "Good evening, Kasumi," Jeremy said in greeting.

"Good evening, Germy," Kasumi replied. She sat down on the porch floor and leaned her head against Jeremy's legs. She sat there silently and apparently contentedly while Jeremy finished his cigarette and carefully stubbed it out. Kasumi smiled when she felt Jeremy's hand rest lightly on her head. "Have you spoken to Mei tonight?" she asked.

"Not yet," Jeremy replied quietly. "Did you want to sing for her?"

Kasumi hesitated for a moment. "I will always sing for her," she replied. "But, with your permission, I'd like to speak to her first."

Jeremy looked down at the little alien leaning against his legs. "I'm never sure if you're humoring me or truly believe I speak to Mei," he said quietly.

Kasumi's crest fluttered, and she chirped a laugh. "In all honesty, I wonder the same," she said. "Yet a part of me truly wants to believe you speak with Mei," she said. "It's surprisingly comforting."

"It is," agreed Jeremy. "You have my permission."

"Thank you." Kasumi straightened and covered her eyes for a moment. "Good evening, Mei Lin Blunt," she began. "I who was once called Small Snow Flower but am now Kasumi greet you." The forest responded to her words silently. "I have been having a dream almost every night. It's a most unusual dream, as it does not repeat, but is instead more like a story."

Kasumi paused. "Among the Rynn there are stories of a princess who loses all because she is spoiled and privileged. In my dreams, I am the princess." Her crest fluttered. "In my dreams, I have two companions, a figure made of mist and one who is faceless. I have learned who they are, and I am most content with my companions."

Kasumi looked over her shoulder at Jeremy before returning her attention to the night. "But I realized tonight that there is a third companion, a wise teacher who, in my dreams, is an old monk." Kasumi made to cover her eyes and then checked her motions and bowed instead. "Thank you for allowing me to learn from your mate, Jeremy, who I call Germy." A gentle breeze sprung up and caressed Kasumi's face. Kasumi smiled.

Kasumi's days took on a new focus. The mornings were still the same qigong exercises followed by strength and endurance training, but now the afternoons had Mel teaching Kasumi what Jeremy kept referring to as the family sword form. Kasumi wasn't too sure what that meant and had asked Mel.

"It's called the family sword form because it's exactly that: a form that only members of the Blunt family are permitted to learn," Mel had replied. "Mei Lin's grandfather taught Gramps. Gramps taught me, and I'm teaching you, Sister." Kasumi spent the rest of that afternoon singing as she trained.

The form turned out to be amazingly complex, but as she learned it, she began to discern a meaning to the moves. It was a sequence that contained an odd series of foot moves that Mel called *chicken-walking* that triggered her growing understanding. "I don't understand this move," Kasumi had complained.

Mel had laughed and led Kasumi outside. It had rained the previous night, and the ground was muddy in spots. Mel pointed to an especially muddy spot of ground. "Do that sequence right there," she commanded. It was the third repetition that brought realization. "It's for fighting in mud!" Kasumi exclaimed in excitement.

"Exactly," Mel replied. "The entire form is designed to teach you how to react and respond to different terrains as well as attacks."

As each day followed, Kasumi learned more of the form and gained insight after insight. She became so entranced with the form and the knowledge it gave her that she'd continue practicing long after the training sessions had ended. An amused Mel would sometimes have to physically remove her from the salon to get her to eat and rest.

In the evenings, she'd sit with Jeremy on the porch and wait for him to finish his evening cigarette before she'd sing for Mei Lin. Every night, she'd sleep wrapped in Mel's arms.

It seemed like a perfect life, but instead of being contented, Kasumi found herself growing more and more impatient to face Sun-Warmed Boulder.

The princess looked at the chasm and smiled. "It's nothing," she declared in contempt. Her companions looked at her.

"It's endless," the mist protested. "And I could never reach the

bottom." The faceless companion said nothing. "You do not agree?" the mist asked.

The faceless one looked at the chasm. "Nothing is endless," she said. "Not even space and time."

"Exactly," agreed the princess. "What do you call something that is, that cannot be?" she asked. "A lie," she said, answering her own question. She looked at the chasm again. She pointed. "That," she declared. "Is a lie."

Without another word, the princess took a running start and … leaped into the void. She barely heard the scream from the mist before her feet touched down. She turned. "See?" she said in triumph. "It was but an illusion." To the princess's eyes, her companions were no more than a few pedin away.

A moment later, the faceless one joined the princess on the other side of the chasm. Mist, however, seemed unable to cross the divide. "Close your eyes," ordered the princess. "Trust me."

The mist trembled and then closed her eyes. She rose slowly into the air.

"Follow my voice," the princess said.

The mist slowly crossed the chasm.

"That's right. You are almost there," the princess said in encouragement. "Almost, almost."

She reached out, and her fingers met the outstretched hand of the mist-like being.

"Take my hand."

Insubstantial fingers wrapped desperately around the solid flesh of the princess. The princess pulled the mist to her side.

"You are there, my friend."

Kasumi opened her eyes to find herself back in the cabin, with Mel a warm and comforting presence beside her. "When is an obstacle an illusion?" she whispered.

Mel stirred. "The dream again?" she asked. Kasumi nodded.

"Did you make it across the chasm?" she asked. Kasumi nodded again. "Then you should already know the answer," she said and smiled. "An obstacle is an illusion when belief overrides reality. In other words, when you believe you can't, you can't."

Kasumi's crest fluttered. "Does the reverse hold true?" she asked.

"To quote one of Gramps' favorite philosophers, 'The best way to move a mountain is one stone at a time,'" Mel said. "The secret, Kasumi, is to break down an impossible task into possible steps."

"You followed me across the chasm," Kasumi said after a moment. "You did not question; you just followed." She chirped a quiet laugh. "It was Mist who required some convincing."

"That's because I know Kasumi," Mel answered, "while Morning Mist has only met Small Snow Flower."

9

Forest Cabin Clan

Kasumi went through the Blunt family form. It had been almost two Earth months since she had begun learning it. She must have gone through the form hundreds of times. She must have questioned each move an equal number of times—questions that both Mel and Jeremy would force her to answer herself. It was a sometimes painful and frustrating method of learning, but she found that the lesson, once learned, stuck.

The form itself was unlike anything she had ever learned before. Controlled chaos was how Jeremy once described it, and Kasumi could only agree. It was wild yet constrained. Ordered and disordered. At times, Kasumi felt as if she were performing some strange and savage dance. It was exhausting and exhilarating at the same time.

With a final salute and bow, she closed the form. She held her pose and waited patiently for Jeremy's critique.

"Tell me why you wish to fight Sun-Warmed Boulder," Jeremy asked.

Kasumi blinked and turned toward her friend and teacher. "Why?" she asked.

"Yes. Why?" Jeremy replied in serious tones. "Think and tell me why."

Kasumi blinked again. The usual reasons surged through her thoughts: to get revenge for the deaths of Gnarled Root and Dancing Water, to reclaim her ship, to avenge her humiliation. All were true, and yet none of them seemed complete. "How odd," she chirped.

"Why?" repeated Jeremy in a demanding bark.

"Why is it odd, or why do I wish to fight Rocky?" Kasumi replied. She bowed. "Forgive me," she said. Jeremy waved a negating hand and waited. "I have no real answer, save, 'I must.' When I think of Rocky in command of my ship, I feel like the floor is tilted," she said in a confused voice.

"Go on," Jeremy ordered.

"My father gave me that ship. It was given, not earned," Kasumi continued. "But Rocky stole it. I may not have earned the ship, but I cared enough to try to earn it, and he stole my chance to …" She paused in thought. " … to become me."

"Do you wish revenge for the deaths of Gnarled Root and Dancing Waters?" Jeremy asked in a soft voice.

"That is what is odd," Kasumi replied. "I loved Gnarled Root and Dancing Waters, but revenge will not bring them back."

"Then why?" Jeremy asked again.

"Because … because unless I do, unless I try, I am incomplete, unfinished," Kasumi replied. "I must try. Whether I live or die, I must try."

"Don't you fear death?" Jeremy asked in the same soft voice.

"I think I fear this feeling of unbalance more than death," Kasumi said. "Isn't that strange?" she asked in a voice of wonder.

"Call your ship, Kasumi Blunt," Jeremy ordered.

Kasumi's crest flattened and then rose to its fullest. "You do me too much honor," Kasumi said and bowed. "Grandfather."

The following evening, Kasumi knelt in front of the Blunt family altar and placed a bowl-shaped object on the floor. She chirped a command, and a glowing orb appeared above the bowl's depression.

A face, a Rynn face, appeared in the glowing orb. The Rynn's crest fluttered in shock. "Small Snow Flower!"

"Tell that offal eater that we have unfinished business," she snapped. "Dawn. Two sun walks from now. Be there or be branded the coward he is." She chirped another command, and the globe vanished.

Kasumi sat back. "It is done," she chirped.

"I liked it," Mel said in approving tones. "Short and sweet." She placed a restraining hand on Kasumi's shoulder when the little alien began to stand. "We're not done here," she said.

"Not done?" Kasumi asked in a confused chirp.

"Not done," Jeremy Blunt said firmly. Kasumi looked over to see her friend and mentor standing in the doorway. Kasumi blinked. The aged Earth being was wearing an outfit the likes of which she had never seen before. It was yellow-red in color and consisted of a hip-length tunic over drawstring pants. To her additional surprise, Jeremy had shaved his head. "Germy?"

Jeremy raised a hand. "Mei Lin Blunt," he said. "Prepare your sister."

"Mei Lin?" Kasumi looked at Mel. "Mei Lin?" she repeated.

"I was named after my grandmother," Mel said quietly. "I called myself Melanie or Mel, but my given name is Mei Lin." She stood. "Come, Sister." She pulled Kasumi to her feet. "You will be the first who Gramps has brought into this family," she said seriously. "Think on that."

Kasumi trembled for a moment and then covered her eyes. "I come."

Mel led Kasumi to a small room, almost a closet, behind a sliding door. The room was empty except for a stack of fabric the same color as what Jeremy was wearing. It was not only the color that was the same. Mel lifted a stack and offered it to Kasumi. It was a tunic and leggings outfit almost identical to what Jeremy was wearing. "Put that on," Mel ordered.

Kasumi put on the clothes in a near daze, and she didn't realize that Mel was changing into a similar outfit until she was nearly dressed. It was a very confused Kasumi who returned to the salon.

Jeremy stood in front of the altar with his arms crossed. He nodded in approval. "Now you look like a proper disciple." He pointed toward a spot. "Stand there." He waited until Kasumi stood in the spot indicated and Mel took up a position next to her. He turned to the altar. He raised his arms and slowly clapped his hands together. Two sharp claps.

"Greetings, honored ancestors," he intoned. "Forgive me for not speaking to you in far too long." He bowed. "I had lost faith," he said. "I present to you she who restored my faith." He clapped his hands together again. "Honored ancestors, I present to you, Kasumi Blunt." He turned to Kasumi.

Kasumi's crest fluttered almost uncontrollably. She hesitantly raised her own hands and clapped them together. Thee sound was deafening in the quiet room. "Greetings, honored ancestors."

Jeremy nodded in approval. He returned his attention to the altar. "She comes from the stars and will one day return to the stars, but before she does, she has one last trial ahead of her," he intoned. "I beg you, watch over her, give her your strength, and give her your courage. She is a true daughter of our clan, honorable and faithful."

Jeremy leaned down and removed something that had been placed in front of the altar. In her confusion, she had not noticed it. Jeremy straightened and turned toward Kasumi. He extended his arms and offered her the object.

"Mei Lin's blade," Kasumi gasped. "I ... I cannot ..."

"I spoke with Mei Lin last night and asked her permission." Jeremy's expression softened. "I got the distinct impression she approved."

Kasumi slowly reached for the blade. "Both hands," Mel whispered. Kasumi nodded and took the blade in both hands.

"May I speak?" Kasumi whispered.

Jeremy smiled and nodded.

Kasumi faced the altar. "Among the Rynn, being made a

member of a clan is not something that can be taken lightly. It is a statement of allegiance. It is a statement of identity. I, who was once Small Snow Flower of the Hot Springs Clan, am now Kasumi Blunt of the …" She paused, and then a smile appeared on her face. "The Forest Cabin Clan." She looked at Jeremy. He paused to consider and then nodded approvingly. "On my honor as a member of this clan, I will not disgrace this blade." She bowed.

Dawn broke and lit the clearing with a soft glow. The sky was still sprinkled with stars, but their lights quickly faded with the rising sun. Three people stood silently at the edge of the clearing. All three were wearing yellow-red outfits: a tunic and drawstring pants. One of the waiting trio, the shortest, had a sheathed sword slung across her shoulders.

"He comes," said Kasumi and pointed.

A bright pinpoint of light moved against the sky and slowly grew larger and larger until it resolved into a teardrop shape. From a distance, it could have almost been mistaken for a military helicopter until one realized that it had no rotors.

"Is that your ship?" Mel asked in awed tones.

"Shuttle," Kasumi replied in a distracted voice. "One of four."

The shuttle landed with a roar, and the watchers were buffeted by a blast of displaced air. The wind died down, and for a long minute all that could be heard was a slowly fading hum. The silence that followed seemed forbidding. There was another humming as a large hatchway opened. Again there was silence, and then a half dozen figures appeared in the hatchway. One figure was significantly larger than the rest.

"Let me guess—that's Rocky," Mel said. "Why, the boy is taller than me."

"By Rynn standards, he's a giant," Kasumi replied. She set her shoulders and started walking toward the ship. Jeremy and Mel followed in flanking positions. When she was at most twenty paces from the ship, she stopped. "So, offal eater, you finally showed," she sneered.

"What are those animals doing here?" Sun-Warmed Boulder said in disgust, indicating Jeremy and Mel with a sweep of a hand. He made a quick hand sign, and two of the flanking Rynn moved forward. "Get rid of them."

The two chosen Rynn quickly moved toward Jeremy and Mel. They had closed half the distance when both Rynn squawked in pain and stumbled to their knees. They each had a circular blade embedded in their thigh, and pink Rynn blood began to stain their clothes and drip onto the green grass of the clearing.

"They're no fun. They fell right over," Mel said in amused tones. "I'd get that looked at," she called out to them. Chirps and twitters sounded as her words were translated by Kasumi's Torque.

"Enough," Kasumi snapped. "These are my witnesses. As is my right." To Sun-Warmed Boulder, she said, "We have unfinished business, you and I."

Sun-Warmed Boulder gave Jeremy and Mel a dismissive look and leaped to the ground. He landed easily. "As you wish," he said. "I am impressed you lived as long as you have, Small Snow Flower."

"Small Snow Flower is dead," Kasumi replied coldly. "You killed her when you took her ship and stranded her here. It is Kasumi Blunt of the Forest Cabin Clan who stands before you."

"A meaningless name," Sun-Warmed Boulder sneered. "Appropriate for a meaningless child." He reached out, and one of the flanking Rynn placed a sheathed blade in his hand. In a slow and deliberately menacing fashion, he unsheathed the blade.

"Duelist's blade," Jeremy commented impassively. "He relies on speed and accuracy." He added, "He has great regard for his own skill and contempt for others." Jeremy slowly smiled. "Teach him respect."

"Yes, tai si fu," Kasumi replied. She reached behind and slowly drew her own blade—Mei Lin's blade. She smiled as Sun-Warmed Boulder's crest twitched.

"A pretty blade," Sun-Warmed Boulder said. "I may keep it as a trophy."

Kasumi nodded. "In truth, it is a beautiful weapon. Created by a master." She started to move the blade in a slow figure eight. "But I am not the owner," she said. "Not yet."

A frown appeared on Sun-Warmed Boulder's face when Kasumi easily blocked his first attack after first ignoring a feint. "Not yet?"

Kasumi nodded. "I must prove myself worthy of the blade." She blocked the next attack with the back of the blade and then returned to moving the blade in a slow figure eight. Slow the movements may have been, yet somehow the blade was always in just the right place to block or deflect Sun-Warmed Boulder's attacks. "I tire of this," Kasumi said.

Sun-Warmed Boulder jumped backward in shock as the blade suddenly came within a finger length of his face. There was a whistle as the blade flashed, and Sun-Warmed Boulder ducked. Blue feathers floated to the ground. Sun-Warmed Boulder reached up and felt at his crest.

"He looks better that way, Sister," Mel called cheerfully. "I always did think men looked better with a buzz cut."

"You ... dare," spat Sun-Warmed Boulder. He charged Kasumi with his blade outstretched and aimed directly at her heart. Kasumi seemed to just fade away from his blade, and then she knelt and slashed with hers. Sun-Warmed Boulder stumbled past and just barely kept from falling. The shock of missing delayed the realization that he had been struck until the stinging in his side overrode the shock. Sun-Warmed Boulder's hand went to his side. His crest flattened as his hand came away covered in pink Rynn blood.

"Yes, I dare," Kasumi said almost conversationally. Again her blade spun in that deceptively lazy figure eight. "I am going to tell you a truth, Rocky." She smiled as some of the Rynn watchers started to chirp in amusement.

"You were right about me," she said. "I was indeed incompetent. I was unsure, untried, and unready for command." Suddenly, she stopped defending and began to attack. She attacked high, forcing Sun-Warmed Boulder to duck, and then low, forcing him to leap over the flashing blade. The attacks slowly began to get through. No one attack caused any true damage, but blood began to stream from what seemed like dozens of shallow cuts.

"But here is another truth," she said. Her blade swung, and she struck the now reeling duelist on the side of his head with the flat side of the sword. "I was not so incompetent that I could not learn."

She lowered the blade and stared coldly at the bleeding and beaten Sun-Warmed Boulder. "Submit and live," she said. "Or continue to resist and die." Her crest rose to its fullest. "The choice—a choice you refused my core—is yours."

"Never," growled Sun-Warmed Boulder. He threw down his sword and pulled something from his pocket. It was a lethal-looking thing.

"So," Kasumi said in contempt. "Your true self finally comes out." Her crest, already high, seemed to get even higher. She stretched her arms to the side. "Go ahead and kill me for all the good it will do." She waved her hands. "All will attest to your cowardice."

"And all will know you di …" Sun-Warmed Boulder's voice suddenly cut off and the handle of a blade seemed to sprout from his right eye. He staggered for a second and then fell, dead before his body hit the ground.

"Forgive me, Granddaughter," Jeremy said in mild tones. "But I seem to have interfered in your fight."

Kasumi stared at Jeremy for a moment and then began to shiver. She found herself being held by Mel. "It's okay, Sister. I have you," Mel said comfortingly.

Jeremy walked over to the dead Sun-Warmed Boulder, knelt down, and jerked the blade free. He wiped the blade clean of gore using the dead Rynn's uniform before returning it to its sheath. He walked over to the still shivering Kasumi. He bowed respectfully. "Do you still feel unbalanced, granddaughter of my heart?"

Kasumi closed her eyes for a second and let Mel hold her,

and then she straightened. Mel let her go to stand on her own. "No, Grandfather. My balance has been restored." She bowed. "Thank you."

Kasumi looked at Sun-Warmed Boulder's body for a moment and then walked toward the silently watching Rynn. "I want statements from all of you," she said in a commanding voice. "I want the truth to be known."

One by one, the surrounding, silent Rynn covered their eyes. Two of the Rynn went over to the cooling body. "What shall be done with the usurper, expedition leader?"

Kasumi appeared to consider. "Sun-Warmed Boulder is dead. He has paid for his crimes. We shall return him to his family." The two Rynn covered their eyes and hoisted the body. They carried it to the shuttle. Kasumi touched her Torque. "Where is Morning Mist?" she demanded.

Another of the silent Rynn covered her eyes. "She was confined and her Torque removed."

"Release her and restore her Torque immediately," Kasumi ordered. "Then ask her—ask her politely—if she will be willing to meet with me." She tapped her Torque. "Hear me. I am Kasumi Blunt, who you knew as Small Snow Flower. Hear me. The ship is mine."

Less than a half hour later, another shuttle landed in the clearing. In the meantime, a camp of sorts had been set up, and Kasumi sat in a pavilion-like structure listening as the events on the ship during her absence were conveyed by one Rynn after another. Jeremy and Mel were looming and intimidating presences who kept the reports short.

A figure stepped into the pavilion. "Small Snow Flower?"

"Morning Mist!" Kasumi stood quickly and almost ran over to the diminutive—even for a Rynn—figure, sweeping her into an embrace. "It's Kasumi now," she said warmly.

"Kasumi?" Morning Mist asked in confusion.

"By some strange chance, it means … mist," Kasumi said.

"Come along, Core Sister, and meet your new family." She leaned over and said, "I know they are somewhat strange-looking, but their hearts are great."

"Are they the reason you look like some barbarian princess?" Morning Mist asked. Kasumi nodded cheerfully. "Then I would be most happy to meet them."

Year 2

10

Baby Steps

"There's that bogey again," Communications Officer Lieutenant William R. Daniels reported. "Whatever it is, it's real." He tapped in a number. "Commander, it's Daniels," he said crisply. "Yeah, it's back." He checked a console. "We can barely get a lock on it, but CompCom has finally come up with a probable flight path." He frowned. "Commander, if it belongs to Russia, we've already lost. It's faster than anything we have—heck, it's faster than anything should be within an atmosphere."

Klaxons began to scream angrily, and within minutes the near empty situation room was filled with the men and women of the California National Guard. Lieutenant Commander David Eisenstadt strode into the room and demanded, "On the board, Lieutenant." Tall, tanned, and trim—with close-cropped steel-colored hair, a strong chin below a determined mouth, a nose that was a little too large, and deep set brown eyes—Eisenstadt looked like what he was: military to the bone.

"The track is an estimate based on …" Daniels began. He stopped when the commander waved his hand in a cutting motion. "Yes sir." He picked up a remote. "The bogey is definitely originating outside our atmosphere and terminating somewhere northeast of Knox Gulch."

"What do we know about Knox Gulch?" the commander asked.

"It's more a halfway point between other places than a destination, commander," Daniels replied. "It's the kind of place people move to, to not be found." He checked a monitor. "People there live mostly off the grid: hunters, fisherman, small farms." He snorted. "It's basically in the middle of nowhere."

"Do we have a satellite available to take a look?" the commander asked.

"It'll take another ten minutes to get one in position," another officer reported.

"Designation?"

"Preliminary AN designation would be AAZ-1," reported a third officer.

The commander raised an eyebrow as he decoded the designation. "Invisible?"

"The only reason we detected it was the new stealth detection units have finally come on line," the third officer explained. "It's invisible to radar. It is not emitting any EM radiation at all. The only reason we know it's there is that it doesn't sound like anything we have on file."

The commander sat down in his command chair. He pursed his lips. "I am not reporting a UFO to the Pentagon or NORAD," he said in sour tones. "Not without proof."

"Satellite coming in range," sang the second officer. "On screen ... now."

The commander turned his attention to the large central view screen. "Sharpen that up," he barked. The screen split into pixels for a second as the computers worked to resolve the image. The image sharpened. There seemed to be a collective intake of breath.

"Oh my god," a voice said.

"Quiet," barked the commander.

The image displayed three vaguely teardrop shapes in the middle of a clearing. Figures could be made out moving between the three teardrops and a smaller rectangle. "Is that a truck?"

"Looks like a Ford F-150," the third officer reported. "Well, there goes the alien theory."

"It just means there's a truck there," Daniels disagreed. "Locals." He looked at the screen. "Spectroscopic analysis is ... inconclusive," he said after a moment. "They're real, but that's about all we can say. Using the truck as a reference, each one of those ... things are about the size of a CH-53E Super Stallion."

"They could almost pass as Super Stallions," the second officer commented.

"Commander, we have the license plate," Daniels reported in triumph. "I'll have Optics see if they can make it out." He spoke into his pickup.

"Don't bother," came a female voice over the base sound system.

"Who said that?" demanded the commander. "Identify yourselves."

"Call me Mel," came the voice. "Who's this?" the voice asked cheerfully. "I know you are military and where you are, just not who you are."

"Do you know how many laws you're breaking?" the commander said angrily.

"No, but I'm sure you'll tell me," the voice replied. "Come on, big boy, try being friendly," the voice chided. "Now give me a smile." There was a giggle. "And your name, of course."

"Lieutenant Commander David Eisenstadt," growled the commander. "California National Guard."

"Now was that so hard?" the voice replied. "Nice command center."

"You ... you can see us?" asked the commander. In response, the large screen scrambled. When it cleared, the room was looking at an attractive Eurasian woman with reddish hair.

"Hi," she sang. "Now, I'm sure you have a lot of questions. Let me introduce you to one of the answers." The image pulled back to reveal an ordinary looking desk. What was not ordinary was the being sitting at the desk. It had cinnamon-colored skin, a pale pink cockatoo's crest on its head, and a faintly birdlike appearance. "Commander Eisenstadt, may I introduce you to Captain Kasumi Blunt, of the ... the best translation would be, 'The Seeker.'"

There was a chirping, and the birdlike being in the chair could be seen moving her mouth. "Good afternoon, Commander." The being smiled. "Mel tells me that 'We come in peace' or 'Take me to your leader' would be considered trite, so how about: 'Times are about to get ...'" She paused. "*Interesting.*"

11

Chain Reaction

The White House was in an uproar. The current president, besides dealing with a lingering recession and double-digit unemployment, was also fighting off an impeachment movement. With his approval rating in the mid-teens, it seemed that at the very best he would escape impeachment but would not be reelected. "My god, if this gets out, I won't be impeached, I'll be shot." He slammed the desk with his hand. "I am not going to be the president who loses to an alien invasion."

The head of the Joint Chiefs of Staff forced himself to not roll his eyes. *Idiot*, he thought. "It's not proven to be an invasion, sir," he said. "They claim to be here for trade."

"Do you expect me to believe that shit?" the president growled. "They're invaders, pure and simple." He stared at the general. "Drop a fucking nuke on them and get rid of them."

"Sir, we can't just detonate a nuclear weapon," the general said in overly patient tones. "And especially not on American soil," he pointed out. "Even in as sparsely populated an area as Knox Gulch, civilian casualties could be in the thousands."

"I'm the president, and I order you to blow those fucking aliens out of existence," the president shouted. He wiped at the edges of his mouth. "Do you hear me?"

"I hear you, sir," the general replied. "You still need Congressional approval."

"What kind of chickenshit job is president if I have to get permission for everything I do?" the president complained. "My predecessor didn't have to go through all this."

"Actually, he did," said the only other person in the room. Vice President Spencer was a distinguished gray-haired presence. Calm and rational, he was the living embodiment of the professional politician. "Despite all the election rhetoric, he was actually quite constrained."

"Well, I don't like it." The president paced the room. "I want action, and I want it now."

"Yes sir," the general replied. "If you will excuse me, I will begin said action." The president waved a hand in dismissal, and the general left the executive office. *God, but he's an asshole*, the general thought in disgust. He pulled out a cell phone. "Ted?" he said when the phone was answered. "Operation Trading Post is a go. I repeat, go." He hung up.

Instead of returning to his office, he headed toward the House building. Minutes later, he was ushered into the office of the House majority leader. "We need the Iron Bitch too," he said brusquely—"the Iron Bitch" being the self-assigned nickname for the House minority leader. He waited until both leaders were in the room before speaking. "He ordered me to drop a nuclear device on the visitors," the general said without preamble.

"The man is mad," the minority leader exclaimed. "Will you testify to that?" she asked. The general nodded. She turned toward the majority leader. "Am I going to have to fight you, George?"

The majority leader blew out a breath. "Call your committee," he said. He walked over to a credenza. "Does anyone beside me want a drink?"

"Make mine a double," the Iron Bitch replied.

"Heads up, we got company" Melanie Blunt barked. Her words were converted to the chirps and trills of standard Rynn by the Torque she wore around her neck. The Rynn security team snapped into action. The Rynn might not have fully accepted her as head of security, but they were professionals. *Of course, it doesn't hurt that they're scared shitless of me*, she thought grimly. Her expression softened when she saw the tiny form of Morning Mist running toward her. *Well, not all of them.*

Morning Mist ran up to Mel and threw herself into the human's arms. "Oh, I'm so excited. More humans!"

"You're just hoping they have carrots," teased Mel. She grinned as most of the security staffs' crests quivered. "Okay, everyone. It's showtime," she said. "Kasumi?"

"Ready," came Kasumi's voice through the Torque. "What do we have?"

"Three military-grade copters," Mel replied. "I think someone wants to talk." She turned. "Okay, boys and girls, look fierce."

"It's hard to look fierce when your opponents are twice as tall as you," one of her security people grumbled. She sighed and raised her crest. "How's that?"

"It would be more intimidating if you didn't have flowers in your crest, Summer Rain," Mel replied. *Well, well, they're starting to joke with me*, she thought in approval. "Next time, wear war paint."

"War paint?" the Rynn guard asked. Mel could hear her chirp to her Torque. "Ooh." Her features blurred, and there were blue stripes suddenly running diagonally across her features.

"Not bad, Summer Rain!" Mel said in approval. "The rest of you, do what Summer Rain did." She grinned, as she was now surrounded by war-painted Rynn. "Nice." She nodded toward where the helicopters were landing. "Now remember, do not point the weapons directly at them, but make it look like you're trying hard not to."

"Yes, Security Chief," came a ragged chorus of replies. "I still think red stripes would be better," she overheard one Rynn say to another. Mel suppressed a sigh. "Honor guard, move!" she ordered.

Mel and her squad jogged to where the three helicopters had landed. She had the squad form into two parallel rows and waited.

The first people out of the helicopters were a team of very tough-looking men and women. They wore full combat fatigues and carried extremely lethal-looking weapons. They quickly formed two matching rows. "Shields, everyone," Mel ordered.

The two double rows of beings stared at each other.

"They're fucking children," one of the marines suddenly sneered.

"I assure you, they are all fully grown," Mel said cheerfully. "Melanie Blunt, chief of security for the Rynn."

"Hey. You're a human," exclaimed the same marine.

"Very good," Mel replied. "Now the big question is, can you count past ten without taking your shoes off?"

The Rynn behind her chittered in amusement.

"Listen, bitch …" began the marine.

"No, you listen, fuckwad," Mel interrupted. "If you don't want to start an interplanetary incident, one you will lose, you will shut up and stay shut until I give you permission to speak."

"Hendriks, shut up," barked a voice. "My apologies, Ms. Blunt."

"Well, well, Commander Eisenstadt," Mel said in surprise. "I didn't expect to see you." She grinned. "Let me guess—you pissed someone off."

"Apparently, I didn't piss them off enough," Eisenstadt replied sourly. "Unfortunately, I was the first person you contacted." He smiled crookedly. "Have you ever considered the military?"

"I tried," Mel replied. "Didn't meet the height requirements."

"Pity," the commander replied. He saluted and then offered Mel a leather-bound folder. "My orders are to a) not start that interplanetary incident you mentioned; b) get you to leave; and c) if I can't do b without doing a, get some kind of agreement out of you."

Mel laughed and took the folder. "Tell you what. If fuckwad over there apologies and promises to keep his mouth shut, I'll introduce you to the captain."

Without turning, the commander barked, "Hendriks, apologize! That is an order."

The big marine gritted his teeth. "I apologize," he ground out. "Sir."

"Wonderful," Mel replied. She walked over to the big marine. "I want to show you something, Hendriks," she said. She pointed to a large tree stump. "Ice Storm in the Mountains," she barked. "Remove that."

The named Rynn looked at the stump and then aimed his weapon. There was a flash and a sizzle, and where the stump had been was now a pile of smoldering dust. "Size isn't everything, Hendriks," Mel said. "It's how you use what you got."

"I dunno," one of the Rynn said in a stage whisper. "I think I kind of like *big*." She gave the big marine an admiring look.

"They're smart. They're well-trained," Mel said in mournful tones. "But discipline is not one of their strengths." She rolled her eyes. "One more thing, Hendriks: don't touch without asking."

"Touch?" the marine said in confusion, and then his eyes widened. "That's a girl?"

Mel nodded. The marine gave the Rynn who spoke a closer look. The Rynn woman smiled back. To Mel's surprise, the marine blushed.

"You don't think ..." the commander began.

"Humans and Rynn are, um, compatible," Mel replied in serious tones. "Word of warning: rape is a capital offense among the Rynn."

The commander spun around. "If I hear of anyone, *anyone*, touching a Rynn man or woman without permission, I will personally shoot the son of a bitch," he growled. "Do you feel me?"

"Sir. Yes sir," chorused the marines.

"Now *that's* how you respond to an order," Mel said in admiration. "Cool Evening Breeze," she said, indicating the Rynn woman who spoke. "You're in charge of keeping the commander's boys and girls out of trouble."

The Rynn woman rubbed her hands together gleefully. "Yes,

Security Chief," she chirped cheerfully. "Summer Rain, Night Clouds, you're with me."

"Come along, Commander," Mel said. "The captain awaits." She turned at a chirp from the tiny Rynn woman at her side. "Oops, sorry," she said to the little Rynn. "Commander, may I present Morning Mist Blunt."

"Blunt?" the commander said. "Wait, you're Melanie Blunt, and the captain calls herself Kasumi Blunt." He looked at the tiny Rynn woman. "That makes her …?"

"My wife," Melanie replied. "Sort of," she amended. "The proper title would be 'core sister.'" Morning Mist nodded in agreement. "Like I said, humans and Rynn are compatible."

"Do you have a core?" Morning Mist asked through the Torque.

"She means, are you married?" Melanie supplied. "Down girl."

"Meanie," Morning Mist replied in teasing tones. "Well? Do you?" she chirped. "Oh look, he's turning pink," she chittered. "That's so cute."

The flustered commander pulled out a handkerchief from his back pocket and wiped his neck and face. "Um, no ma'am."

To the commander's surprise, the little alien skipped over and took his hand. "I hope Kasumi likes you," she said.

Melanie sighed. "You're embarrassing the commander, Morning Mist," she chided. "And we're keeping Kasumi waiting." She sighed again when Morning Mist started pulling the commander along. "Interesting times, indeed," she muttered and followed.

With Morning Mist holding on to his hand, the commander was taken to the tentlike structure that had been erected against one side of the large clearing. Even before they reached it, the commander could see that a steady stream of Rynn were entering and leaving the pavilion. *Reminds me of a field headquarters*, he thought. His eyes narrowed and he pointed. "What the hell is that?"

"Power generator," Mel replied.

"It looks like a mini nuclear reactor," the commander said nervously.

"Fusion reactor," Morning Mist corrected. "We really weren't expecting to have to build a trading base, and fusion reactors are easy to assemble from local material," she informed the commander.

"Easy to assemble," the commander repeated slowly.

"Oh, yes," Morning Mist replied.

"I had the same reaction you did, Commander," Mel put in. "From the Rynn point of view, a fusion reactor is barely above a campfire." She stopped as Morning Mist chittered. "Okay, okay, barely above a water wheel."

"You joke," the commander protested. Mel shook her head. He licked his suddenly dry lips. "What would they consider, um, modern?"

"Well, if we really had the time, we'd build a singularity reactor," Morning Mist replied. "Though I suppose a matter-antimatter reactor could be done using Earth technology," she said thoughtfully. "That's almost as good."

The commander swallowed nervously.

12

In Other News

"This is CNN with late-breaking news." The CNN logo rippled like a flag before it was replaced by the face of one of the network's most popular female newscasters. "This is Crystal Chandler reporting." Behind the reporter, the familiar image of the current president was displayed. "In a surprising joint news conference, both the House majority and minority leaders have announced that the long-simmering impeachment investigation has resulted in a recommendation to impeach, and that a vote is imminent."

The image of the president was replaced by an image of the mentioned House leaders. "This afternoon, the House impeachment committee has returned a recommendation to impeach," the majority leader said in somber tones. "Their investigations have uncovered strong evidence of influence peddling, corruption, and—most worrisome of all—indications that the president and or members of his advisory staff may have provided classified information to Russia."

The image returned to the newscaster. "In other late-breaking news, the California National Guard has announced that it will be conducting readiness drills near the California/Oregon border. The CNG has thrown up a no-fly zone over the area and will be redirecting any air traffic away from it." The reporter turned to face another camera. "More late-breaking news when we come back."

The reporter waited for the all-clear signal from the director before dropping her professional smile. "Readiness drills, my ass," she half-snarled. "My nose is twitching like crazy," she said to the air. She stood and ordered, "Danny, see if we can get someone up there."

The director shrugged. "Most of the senior reporters are going to be heading to Washington," he said. "I kind of think an impeachment trumps military maneuvers."

"Send an intern," the reporter said. "Send someone," she snapped. "If I could, I'd go myself. No one puts up a no-fly over an exercise." She walked over to a computer terminal. "What the fuck is up there?"

"Except for some recent UFO reports, that area is mostly known for being the home for people too crazy even for California," the director laughed. "You know, survivalists and—" the director made air quotes "—militias."

"Gun nuts, you mean," the reporter said sourly. "Get someone up there, Danny."

"Commander," called a voice. Lieutenant Commander Eisenstadt turned. Approaching him was a Rynn woman. She was the tallest Rynn he'd seen so far—though still tiny by human standards—and unlike most Rynn, she wore what appeared to be a Chinese monk's tunic and pants dyed orange-red. In addition to what he had started thinking of as a standard-issue ray gun, she wore a sword strapped to her back. "Captain Kasumi," he said in greeting.

"I'm glad I've run into you," the alien captain said. "Someone took another shot at one of the Rynn," she said in even tones.

"Were they hurt?" the commander asked in concern. He blew out a relieved breath when the alien captain shook her head. "That's a relief."

"That's the third time in the past five days," the alien captain replied. She tapped her Torque. "Fortunately, bullets are easy to deflect," she said. The commander nodded. "But it's only a matter of time before someone does get hurt." She ran her long fingers through her pinkish head crest. "This is your planet, Commander, but I cannot allow this to continue."

Eisenstadt nodded again. In the two weeks since he'd arrived at the alien camp, he had learned to respect the Rynn. More importantly, he liked the alien captain. "I can send out some patrols. Maybe they can find out who's doing the shooting," he said. "Check that: I have a proposal."

The alien captain waved him on to continue.

"What would you think of a joint patrol?" the commander said.

Kasumi smiled. "I would think that I am talking to someone who has come to the conclusion that Rynn and humans have a future together," she said in approval. "Five and five?" she suggested. "With a human in command." The last was a statement. Her crest twitched. "It is your planet, after all."

"To quote a line from one of my favorite movies," the commander replied, "this looks like the beginning of a beautiful friendship."

"Speaking of beautiful friendships …" Kasumi took hold of the commander's arm. "Are you free for dinner?" She smiled up at the commander. "Morning Mist keeps asking about you." She chittered in amusement. "I love how humans change color."

"It's bad enough being stuck in the middle of nowhere, but how did I get stuck in the middle of nowhere with a bunch of alien children?" complained Corporal Hendriks.

There was a stream of chirps and chitters. "How many times do I have to tell you? I'm a fully grown Rynn," complained the tiny alien walking at his side. "It's not our fault humans are giants." She looked up at Hendriks. "And you're more giant than most, fuzz ball."

"Now listen, featherbrain," Hendriks snapped back.

"Hendriks, Cool Evening Breeze, zip it," Sergeant Stilson snapped.

The sergeant was a broadly built and muscular black man in his mid-thirties. With his shaved head and a nose that looked as if it had been broken multiple times, he looked the living embodiment of a soldier. This was one of the few times where looks were not deceiving. The sergeant was the veteran of five tours in Afghanistan and Iraq, and the recipient of two Purple Hearts. The scar that ran along his right temple was the result of an IED and earned him one of those Purple Hearts. He was exactly what he appeared to be.

"I wish those two would just fuck the shit out of each other and get it over with," Stilson grumbled under his breath. There was a chittering at his shoulder.

"Truth," came the translation from Summer Rain's Torque. "Can't you just, I don't know, order them to share a kip?"

"It doesn't work that way, Ms. Rain," Stilson replied. "Unfortunately."

Summer Rain chittered.

"Did I say something funny?" asked the sergeant.

"Obviously not intentionally," Summer Rain replied. "But 'Ms. Rain' sounds very much like another word for these." She cupped her breasts.

"I called you 'tits'?" Stilson said in disbelief. "Oh, great."

Summer Rain chittered again. "I wouldn't worry about it," she said. "Besides, it was oddly flattering."

"Humans fifty pedin to the west," Ice Storm called out. At the same time, there was a crack, and Hendriks stumbled and fell.

"Hendriks!" screamed Cool Evening Breeze. She jumped on top of the fallen soldier just as the forest erupted with gunfire. She activated her portable defense shield and expanded it to cover both her and the human. "You better not be dead, you big, dumb, ugly fuzz ball," she chirped in anger. "I'll never forgive you if you're dead. Do you hear me? Never."

Hendriks groaned. "How's a man gonna get some sleep with you chirping in his ear?" he grumbled. "It's just a fucking scratch. I'll live."

"Do that," Cool Evening Breeze said in relief. She looked toward the source of the bullets. Cool Evening Breeze stood and pulled her weapon. She started chirping angrily. For some reason, the translator didn't change the chirps into English. She started firing. Small explosions started to erupt.

"Ooh, she is really mad," Summer Rain chirped.

"Sounds it," agreed Stilson. "Could have used those screens in Afghanistan," he said in musing tones. "Any chance we can get the specs on them?"

"If it were up to me, I'd give you the specs on anything you wanted," Summer Rain replied. Her crest rippled. "Spirits, she is really, really mad."

"Not that I want to get between that girl and whoever she's mad at, but I'd like at least one of them alive so I can find out who the fuck that is," Stilson grumbled. "I thought you said Rynn were too peaceful for their own good."

"So did I," Summer Rain replied. "Ice Storm, shut down Cool Evening Breeze's weapon." A moment later, the explosions stopped, but they could see that Cool Evening Breeze kept trying to fire before the lack of explosions registered. "Hendriks better live through this, or I'm going to have an angry geologist on my hands."

"She's a geologist?" Stilson said in surprise. "I thought she was, well, a marine." He paused. "She curses like one, at least." He looked at where Cool Evening Breeze was now apparently applying first aid. "Girl is wasted as a geologist."

An hour later, Stilson was interrogating one of the survivors. He wasn't too surprised to find they were part of a survivalist compound. What did surprise him was the stockpile of weaponry retrieved. "Jesus, all that's missing is some DU rounds," he said to Summer Rain. The Rynn's crest fluttered in agitation. He looked at the prisoner currently being interrogated; he had his eyes locked on Summer Rain.

"There's an interrogation technique we call good cop/bad cop," Stilson said in a low voice. He quickly explained the concept. "How would you like to be bad cop?"

"I have a better idea," Summer Rain replied.

Five minutes later, Cool Evening Breeze was in the interrogation room. Twenty seconds after that, they were restraining the Rynn geologist, who had her crest fully extended and her vestigial claws slashing angrily at the now cowering militia man.

"Now that's one fine bad cop," Stilson whispered in admiration.

"Keep it away from me!" screamed the militia man.

"A really fine bad cop," Stilson whispered again. "You start talking, and maybe we'll find someone else for it to eat," the sergeant said coldly. The militia man screamed.

Corporal Hendriks was lying in a cot in the temporary sick bay staring moodily at the ceiling, his head resting on one massive arm. He looked over when he heard a chirping. Cool Evening Breeze was standing in the doorway.

"May I come in?" she asked quietly.

"I was wondering when you'd show up," the corporal said. He raised a hand. "I gotta say something." He paused. "I'm not good at words, kinda why I'm a soldier." He blew out a breath. "You're one hell of a woman, you know that?"

"I think you're one hell of a man," Cool Evening Breeze replied. "So why do we always fight?" she asked plaintively.

"My ex-wife used to ask me the same thing," Hendriks chuckled. "I think I used to pick fights with her on purpose."

"Why would you do that?" Cool Evening Breeze asked. She walked over and sat down on the edge of the cot.

"Honestly?" he asked. The Rynn geologist nodded. "Well, cause the makeup sex was so fucking good. That's why." His smile twisted when Cool Evening Breeze chirped in amusement. "She finally left me for an accountant." He blew out another breath. "I got a bad temper, I drink when I'm not on duty, and those are my good points."

Cool Evening Breeze nodded. "I have one question."

The corporal raised an eyebrow. "Just one?"

Cool Evening Breeze nodded.

"Well, if anyone has earned a question, you have. Ask your question."

Cool Evening Breeze leaned closer. "When do we have the makeup sex?"

13

CORE BROTHERS

Two months after the first soldiers had come to meet the alien Rynn, a town of sorts had sprung up in the clearing. From the original two dozen military personnel, there were now close to fifty soldiers, though a good number of the newest arrivals were highly trained technical specialists.

One of the newest arrivals was Technical Specialist Joseph Franklin. Like all tech specialists, he had gone through basic combat training, but unlike the others, he had not taken the advanced individual training; he had been allowed to skip it due to his degrees in mathematics, engineering, and computer science.

Despite his military training, he was more lean than muscular. He wore horn-rimmed glasses and had a tendency to be somewhat obsessive. While he was not close to anyone, he had a reputation for being friendly and helpful.

"Hey Joe, me and the guys are heading over to the canteen," called out Combat Engineer Marcus Freeman. "You coming?"

"I'll catch up to you later, Marcus," Franklin replied. "I'm in the middle of something."

"You're always in the middle of something," complained Freeman. He waved a finger. "All work and all that," he pointed out. "You gotta make time for fun."

Franklin laughed. "Working on Rynn tech is fun," he said in emphasis. He waved a hand. "Go on. Just don't drink all the beer before I get there."

"Hey, there's no way I'm gonna promise that," Freeman replied with a laugh and headed out.

Franklin sighed and turned back to his terminal. While it was true that he was in the middle of a project, that wasn't the real reason he wasn't going off with Marcus and the rest of the team. *Back to work, Jo-Jo*, he told himself.

He had to admit Rynn tech was fascinating. The Rynn seemed to be falling all over themselves to provide technology that could be easily duplicated, and part of Franklin's job was to evaluate the technology provided. *Easter-egg hunting* was the unofficial term. So far, he hadn't found anything of concern.

A close-by chirping caused Franklin to start, and he looked toward the sound. Two Rynn males had entered the lab and were heading toward him. He recognized them as two of the Rynn who apparently were assigned to help with the technological transfer. He couldn't help smiling in welcome. "Hi, Red Clouds Paint the Sky. Hi, Black Rocks," he called in greeting.

"Greetings, Technician Joseph Franklin," Red Clouds Paint the Sky replied. "You work passed your assigned hours again, we see."

"If you mean I'm working late, then yeah," Franklin replied.

Black Rocks covered his eyes for a second. "The First Teacher said, 'Hard work brings rewards, but take the time to enjoy those rewards.'"

Franklin rubbed his head in embarrassment. "What's with everyone telling me to ease up?" he grumbled. "Marcus just told me pretty much the same thing."

"He must care," Black Rocks replied. "Forgive me if I offend, but is it that he wishes to be your core brother?"

"Core brother?" Franklin asked in confusion. "I just got here, so if that was part of the briefing …"

"I would not call being among us for two of your 'weeks' *just*,"

Red Clouds Paint the Sky replied. "And in those two weeks, I have never seen you do other than work." His crest flattened slightly. "And you do not smile."

"I smile," protested Franklin.

"You smile when people are looking," Red Clouds Paint the Sky said in disagreement. "Black Rocks and I noticed that …" His crest flattened even more. "When you think no one is looking, you appear sad."

"I'm just busy, that's all," Franklin protested.

"You are frustrated and alone," Black Rocks replied. "You need a core brother to remove that frustration."

Franklin's mouth suddenly became dry. "Why do you keep saying 'core brother'? Why not 'core sister'?" He stopped as both Rynn males chittered in amusement. "What?"

"A core sister is not what you desire." Black Rocks's crest fluttered. "That is as obvious as that great lump you call a nose," he added.

Red Clouds Paint the Sky nodded in agreement. The two Rynn men walked closer, and Black Rocks put a hand on Franklin's forearm. "Why do you pretend otherwise?"

"The First Teacher said, 'Denying your true self is to deny happiness,'" Red Clouds Paint the Sky said in concern. "Why do you wish to be unhappy?"

Franklin shook off the Rynn's hand. "You're wrong," he growled. "I – I …" He hung his head. "Why do you care?"

"Because we do," Black Rocks replied. "We see your pain, and it hurts us." He added, "When you smile, it is as if the sun has come to greet the day."

Franklin raised his head, though he did not look at either Rynn male. "I don't know how," he said in a voice full of pain. "I've had to hide … for so long." The two Rynn men leaned against him. "I'm afraid," he whispered.

"There is no need to fear," Red Clouds Paint the Sky said in a quiet voice. "Your core brothers are with you." He and Black Rocks pulled the human to his feet. "Come, Core Brother," he said. "Let us see if we can make the sun greet the day."

"Let us try, Core Brother," Black Rocks pleaded.

The morning mess hall was as packed and as noisy as usual as everyone hurried to get breakfast and find a place to sit. Most groups had a set table, and the techs were no different. "Has anyone seen Franklin?" Freeman asked as he sat down with his tray. "His bunk wasn't used last night."

"You try the lab?" one of the techs replied. "He's fallen asleep there more than once."

"First place I looked," Freeman replied. "It's not like him." He rubbed his chin. "He may be a bit of a flake, but he's pretty reliable." He pursed his lips. "If you see Franklin, tell him …"

"Tell me what?" Franklin said from the edge of the table as he sat down. "Sorry I'm late; overslept," he said cheerfully and dug hungrily into his breakfast.

"Where were you last night?" Freeman asked.

Franklin pointed upward. "Spent the night in the Seeker," he said around a mouthful of food. "That is one amazing ship."

All eyes focused on Franklin. "You … you were on the Seeker?" Freeman asked. "How the fuck did you end up there?"

"The same way anyone else does. I took a shuttle," snickered Franklin. "Red Clouds Paint the Sky and Black Rocks insisted." His smile seemed to get wider. "You have got to try sleeping in a Rynn bed," he said.

"You slept in a Rynn bed?" one of the techs asked in obvious jealous tones.

"Eventually," Franklin replied. He stretched. "Man, do I feel good," he said. "Oh, that reminds me, got to talk to the CO." He stood. "I'll meet you guys in the lab." He picked up his now empty tray and walked away, whistling as he went.

Freeman and the techs watched him leave in open-mouthed

wonder. "What the hell?" he exclaimed. "Do you think he got his hands on some Rynn happy pills?"

"I recognized those names Franklin mentioned—Red Clouds and Black Rocks are Rynn men," one of the techs said in mild tones. "Core brothers."

"Franklin?" Freeman exclaimed in disbelief.

"Looks like," the tech replied.

Franklin walked to the large tent that had been set up as C&C for what was now being referred to as "the colony." The tent was large enough that it could be divided into individual sections, with the outer section acting as a reception and the inner part of the tent contained the CO's office and a conference room. The sergeant currently running the reception looked up. "Is the CO in?" Franklin asked.

"You're Franklin, aren't you?" the sergeant asked. "Well, that saves me a trip," he said cryptically. He tapped a board. "TS Franklin is here to see you, commander," he said into a throat mike. "Nope, just walked in on his own." He looked at Franklin. "Go in. He wants to talk to you."

Franklin frowned as he entered the CO's office. To his surprise, the Rynn captain was already there. The CO looked at him sourly, while the Rynn captain seemed delighted to see him. He saluted.

"At ease," said Lieutenant Commander Eisenstadt. "Your name has been mentioned frequently in the last hour, Specialist," the commander said brusquely. "Do I understand correctly that you spent the ... um, evening aboard the Seeker?"

"Yes, sir," Franklin replied cautiously.

"And were you in the company of ..." He looked at a piece of paper. "Red Clouds Paint the Sky and Black Rocks?"

"Yes, sir." Franklin replied. "Am I in trouble, sir?"

"I should throw you in the brig, if we had a brig, for desertion," the commander replied in irritated tones. "The only thing that's keeping me from doing it is that Captain Kasumi threatened me if I did."

"I didn't threaten you, David," chided Kasumi through her translator. "I just said that if you ever wanted to spend any more time with my core, you'd let the matter proceed without interference."

"Dammit, Kasumi, he—" began the commander.

"Oh please, David," Kasumi chirped. "The suites aboard the Seeker are a lot more spacious—not to mention, the kips are bigger." Kasumi chittered a laugh. "Though there were a few complaints about the noise." She turned in her chair. "One would think it was your first time." Her crest raised at Franklin's blush. "Really?" she said in amused tones. "Spirits sing."

"It's going to ruin discipline, Kasumi," complained the commander.

"Hendriks and Cool Evening Breeze haven't caused any problems that I'm aware of," Kasumi replied. "Though we are going to need some more human women around here, since none of the Rynn women seem interested in joining them." She chittered again. "None of the Rynn men either. Cool Evening Breeze has been a little too descriptive of Hendriks's, um, *assets*, and has scared them off."

"The men or the women?" asked the commander.

"Both." Kasumi chittered again. She gave Franklin an approving look. "Three is a much more stable configuration, and I had despaired of Black Rocks and Red Clouds Paints the Sky — finding their third." She turned back to the commander. "From my point of view, Franklin has improved discipline, at least among my crew." She nodded her head toward Franklin. "Put it this way, David. If you don't want him, I can and will make a place for him among my crew." She turned in her chair again. "Red Clouds Paint the Sky and Black Rocks have both requested that Franklin be permitted to move into their ship quarters." She smiled and her crest fluttered. "If I wish to maintain … discipline," she chittered, "you will say yes."

"Would that be permitted, sir?" Franklin asked the commander.

"It might be better and safer if you did," the commander said in grudging tones. "California is liberal, but soldiers are usually not," he grumbled. "Permission granted."

Franklin saluted. "Thank you, sir." He then looked at the Rynn captain and briefly covered his eyes. "Thank you, ma'am." Kasumi chittered in amusement in response.

"Dismissed," the commander said, and Franklin left the office. He waited for a moment and then returned his attention to Kasumi. "They're pairing up."

"Three-ing," corrected Kasumi with a Rynn smile.

"You know what I mean," the commander replied testily. "And it doesn't help that you're encouraging it."

Kasumi chittered again. "Of course I'm encouraging it," she said. "If everything goes as we hope, the Seeker is going to leave with humans aboard it," she pointed out. "And the ones who are best able to interact with the Rynn are the ones I want on my ship." Her crest stiffened. "Right now, I am willing to take Hendriks and Franklin," she grinned. "And you." She rubbed her chin. "We need more human women," she repeated. "Mel probably won't mind, but I'd rather there be more human women regardless."

14

Press Corp

"This is CNN. Crystal Chandler reporting," the blonde reporter said. "In late-breaking news, the House has voted to impeach President Overbid." The reporter's expression became serious. "With the passage of the articles of impeachment, the Senate will now vote to determine if President Overbid will be removed from office. In previous impeachments, getting the required supermajority has proved difficult, and this current proceeding may be no different," she said. "A vote has been scheduled for this Wednesday, and the Senate will not be broadcasting the proceedings.

"In other late-breaking news, there have been unconfirmed reports of military action in and around Knox Gulch." The reporter turned to another camera, and an image of a forested and mountainous region appeared behind her. "In a press release, the CNG has only acknowledged that there have been reports but has not confirmed those reports."

The reporter turned to another camera. "More when we return." She waited until the director gave the all clear before removing her mic. "Danny!" she yelled. "Anything from Knox Gulch?"

"Nothing related to any shootings, Crystal," Danny replied. "I got a call from some kook who claims there's a secret alien base there, but that's about it." He laughed. "He even sent me a photo of what he claims is an alien." Danny pulled out his cell phone, called up the file, and sent it to Crystal.

Crystal Chandler looked at the picture. It was grainy, as if it was taken by a cell phone at night, and it showed two figures. One was a soldier in military gear, while the other was barely more than half the size of the soldier and had what looked like a cockatoo's crest on its head. Crystal frowned. "Where was this taken?" she asked.

"The caller claims it's a few miles outside of Knox Gulch," Danny replied. "About five miles south of an alt-right colony." Danny pursed his lips in thought. "Come to think of it, if there is an alt-right colony over there, there's a good chance they'd consider any military presence anywhere near them an incursion." He started looking though the papers on his desk. "Hmm, that's interesting. There is a report of a Jeremiah Johnson being treated at a local clinic for burns."

"Burns?" the reporter asked.

"Yeah, like a really bad case of sunburn, except it's been overcast there. Mr. Johnson gave his mailing address as the alt-right colony." He added, "What's interesting is that Mr. Johnson claimed he was shot by a bird."

"Bird?" echoed the reporter, and she looked at the picture again. "Danny, I think I need to go to Knox Gulch." She pulled out her phone and punched in a number. "Deirdre? It's Crystal."

A car stopped on the shoulder of the road. The driver, an attractive black woman with finger-length dreads, got out of the car and looked around. "Well, according to the GPS," she said, waving a hand, "that is Knox Gulch."

"There's nothing here," the female passenger replied as she joined the driver. "Are you sure this is right, Dierdre?"

"I updated the GPS a week ago," Dierdre McIntosh replied. "I'm as sure as I can be." She shrugged. "We're here, Crystal. Wherever the fuck here is."

"But there's nothing here," complained Crystal Chandler. "There isn't even a marker." She looked around. "I'm almost expecting to see some toothless kid with a banjo sitting on a stump."

"If I see a toothless kid with a banjo, we are getting back in the car and hightailing it out of here," Dierdre replied. She tossed her head and made her curls bounce. "As it is, I'm half inclined to leave now anyways. My grandparents may have liked the country, but this little black girl likes her comforts."

"Says the girl who spent two weeks living on MREs in Iraq," Crystal shot back. "Who you trying to kid?"

"That was then," Dierdre replied. "I was young and ... do you hear something?" She turned her head. "Sounds like a truck." Her hand went inside her coat. "Probably just another traveler, but ..." The truck sound got louder, and it wasn't long before a vehicle—a late-model Ford—rounded the bend from the north. The truck slowed and then stopped next to them.

A woman with auburn hair leaned out the window. "Car trouble?" she asked. There was a chirping from the passenger side. "Nah, they definitely look like city people," she said to the unseen passenger. She looked back at Crystal and Dierdre. "Car trouble?" she asked again.

"Actually, we were looking for Knox Gulch." Dierdre replied. The redhead laughed. "Problem?"

"Nah, no problem," the woman replied. "No Knox Gulch either. Not if you're looking for a town. A gulch, yes; town, no." She grinned. "When someone says they're from Knox Gulch, it just means there from somewhere around here." She waved a hand to include all the woodland. "The biggest settlement is a bunch of survivalists about five miles north. That who you looking for?"

"Actually I'm looking for the California National Guard that's supposedly running some field exercises around here." Crystal pulled out a card. "Crystal Chandler, CNN."

There was a chirping from the passenger side. "She's a reporter, honey," the redhead said to the unseen passenger. "That means she butts into other people's business and blabs it on the television." There was a chittering laugh in response.

"The press performs a vital function," Crystal said in affronted tones.

"Yeah, yeah," the redhead replied. "Why are you looking for them?" she asked. "If they're out here, they probably don't want to be found." She laughed. "That's usually the reason for just about anyone around here."

"Does that include you ... Ms ...?" Crystal asked.

"Blunt. Melanie Blunt," the redhead replied. She waggled a hand. "Actually, it's my grandfather who likes his privacy." There was a chirping again. Mel looked at the black woman. "Morning Mist says she likes your hair." She turned back to the passenger. "I don't think that's a good idea, honey," Mel sighed. "I know this is going to be a mistake. Oh, go ahead."

The passenger door opened, and a diminutive figure walked around to the driver side. She wore a pink hooded sweatshirt with the hood pulled over her face and a long skirt. She walked over to Dierdre. There was a chirping. "Your hair is beautiful," said a pleasant soprano voice. "May I touch it?"

"You haven't met too many black girls, have you, girlfriend?" Dierdre replied. "We're not fond of people touching our hair."

There was a chirping. "You would be the first," came the voice. There was a chittering. "I propose a trade," she said. "If you let me touch your hair, I'll let you see my face." There was another chittering. "I don't think you've seen anyone like me before either."

"That's for sure," Mel said under her breath. "If you do that, we're gonna have to take them with us."

Again there was a chirping. "I believe if I showed my face, they'd want to go with us," the little figure said. "I believe they actually came out here to find us."

Crystal looked at the tiny person and then the grainy image flashed through her mind. "If—*if,* mind you—you are what I really, really, really hope you are, you'd have to shoot me to get rid of me."

There was a chittering and then a chirping. Crystal felt as if she could almost make out … not meaning, but separate sounds in the apparent birdsong. "We'd rather not shoot you." The figure reached up and lowered her hood.

"Oh, Lord Jesus," Dierdre breathed. She leaned forward and tilted her head toward the birdlike being. "A deal's a deal," she said. She watched as a long-fingered hand reached up and delicately touched her curls. Dierdre gestured toward the creature's crest. "May I?" Dierdre touched the featherlike crest when the being nodded. "I'm Dierdre."

"I'm Morning Mist," the little alien said. "It's a pleasure to meet you."

Dierdre McIntosh followed the truck into a compound. It was obviously new, as it was still under construction. What was once a natural clearing in the woods had been expanded to twice its original size, and a large stack of downed trees had been placed along one side. A temporary chain-link fence was quickly being replaced by a more permanent one. One end of the compound was dominated by an aircraft hangar, and a series of trailers were lined up nearby. It was toward the trailers that the truck was headed. Dierdre followed.

"Lots of soldiers," Dierdre commented. "Lord Jesus, look at that." She pointed toward the hangar. A large, somewhat teardrop-shaped craft was floating out of the hanger. It rotated and then rose into the air with a loud hum.

"You realize they're not going to just let us leave, don't you?" Crystal said in warning.

"Leave?" Dierdre replied. "Who the hell wants to leave? I want to go up in one of those," she said. "And if the price to do that is never coming back, so be it." She sighed. "When I first saw *Close Encounters*, all I could think was, 'Take me, please take me.'"

"Oh, the places you'll go," Crystal said in a singsong. "I don't think Dr. Seuss had that in mind."

"Maybe, but I bet he'd have been the first in line," Dierdre shot back. "Lord Jesus, there are more of those little people." She pointed.

The truck parked in front of one of the trailers, and Dierdre parked her car next to it. She and Crystal got out.

Mel and Morning Mist walked over. "Without thinking, what is the first thing that comes to mind?" Mel asked.

Both women blinked. "I didn't think there was going to be a test," Crystal said.

Mel laughed and then pointed to Dierdre. "And you?"

"Thank you, Jesus," Dierdre breathed.

"Different," Mel said. "And somewhat surprising," she added. At Dierdre's questioning look, she continued. "Maybe it's my own bias speaking, but thanking god for something that must cause you to question your beliefs is usually not something I would expect from the religious."

Dierdre nodded. "I can't blame you for thinking that," she replied. "And if I am going to be honest, there are many in my church who'd probably be screaming that this is the devil's work." She shrugged. "I'm just not one of them. Ever since I was a child, I looked at the stars and knew there were others ... looking back."

Mel nodded. "I'm sure you both realize that, at least for the time being, we cannot let you leave," she said in serious tones. "The Rynn are ..." She pursed her lips in thought. "Look, I know the Rynn are good people, but how can you know that they aren't influencing me somehow?"

"That in itself tells me they're probably not," Crystal Chandler replied. "Dierdre and I have already figured that out, but we're not unknown," she said. "Someone will start looking for us if we don't check in."

"Then you will check in, but you can't leave," Mel replied.

"Roach or California?" Dierdre asked. She grinned at Mel's blank look. "What kind of hotel is this going to be?"

"Got it." She turned to Morning Mist. "Human joke," she said. "I'll explain later." She turned back to the two women. "Neither, actually," she said in serious tones. "But I'll let the commander and Kasumi explain in detail."

Several minutes later, the two women were standing in the middle of one of the trailers. The trailer had obviously been set up as a meeting area, as it was dominated by a large oval table. The chairs that surrounded the table were an odd mix of standard chairs and circular padded ones. The reason for the mix became obvious when two people joined them. One was human: a man in uniform with a stern demeanor and close-cropped graying hair. The other was a Rynn. She was taller than most of the Rynn seen so far, and unlike the other Rynn, she wore a yellowish-red tunic and pants that would not be out of place in a Buddhist monastery. Also unlike the other Rynn, she wore a blade strapped to her back. The Rynn woman curled up in one of the round chairs, and the military man took a chair next to her.

"Please be seated," the Rynn woman said.

"Hey, you said that in English, and not through a translator," Dierdre said.

"I've learned a few words, yes," the Rynn woman said. She waited until the two women sat before continuing. "In case you haven't figured it out, I am Captain Kasumi." She chittered quietly for a moment. "Neither label is truly correct but will do."

"What the captain means is that *captain* is not a Rynn term and *Kasumi* is not a Rynn name, but it is the name she goes by," the military man said, "I am Lieutenant Commander Eisenstadt." Kasumi nodded in agreement. "Let's get down to it. I know who both of you are, and you present a not-unexpected difficulty." He nodded to Crystal. "You are Crystal Chandler, a relatively well-known newscaster," he said. "And you are Dierdre McIntosh, a Pulitzer award-winning photojournalist."

"And we've met before, haven't we?" Dierdre replied. "Afghanistan, wasn't it?"

"Correct on both counts," Eisenstadt replied. "I know you, and I know I can trust you," he said in honest tones. "I'm not so sure about your boss."

"I'm not her boss," Crystal corrected. "I asked her to come with me, and she said yes, that's it." She leaned forward slightly. "She's who I call when I want someone who might see something I missed."

"Is she your core sister?" Kasumi asked in curious tones.

"Core sister?" Dierdre asked.

"Think a combination of buddy, partner, and lover," Mel interjected from the side of the room. "Kasumi, Morning Mist, and I are core sisters."

Dierdre snorted in amusement. "Partner, yes. Buddy, sometimes. But lover, never." She smiled. "Crystal is hopelessly hetero."

"And you, Ms. McIntosh? Are you … hopelessly hetero?" Kasumi asked.

"I've been known to, shall we say, sleep on the other side of the bed," Dierdre replied. "Why? Is it important?"

Kasumi's crest flicked in the Rynn equivalent of a shrug. "It can be," she said. "At the very least, if you have a problem with certain kinds of relationships, you may have a problem with the Rynn."

Crystal leaned forward with narrowed eyes. "Are you saying that Rynn are inherently gay?"

"That would be absurd and counter-survival," Kasumi chided. "No, what I am saying is that Rynn culture accepts that sexuality is on a spectrum and what works for a core and for their children is all that is important. And when I say *works*, I mean that it promotes the best and healthiest relationships and offspring as possible."

"Child abuse is a capital crime among the Rynn," Mel interjected. "Rape is a capital crime. Abuse is a capital crime." She smiled grimly. "Gross incompetence of any sort is a capital crime."

"Wait a minute: child abuse, rape, and, I assume, spousal abuse is considered incompetence?" Crystal asked in surprise.

"If you cannot properly raise a family, run a business, be in a marriage, or the Rynn equivalent, then you have no business doing those things," Kasumi said sternly. "It isn't just yourself who is getting hurt." She added, "Mel claims that human morality is based on an abhorrence of theft."

This time it was Dierdre who blinked in surprise. "Theft?" She shook her head. "That's not true. We … Western culture, at least, is based on the ten commandments."

"I think you need to have a discussion with my grandfather," Mel said in amusement. "But what is murder but theft of life? What is adultery but theft of commitment? And what is lying but theft of honor and truth?"

Dierdre noticed that with each statement, the Rynn present would quickly cover their eyes with their hands. "But …"

"At the heart, all Western religions guard against theft. Theft of respect, of life, of commitment," Mel said. "Theft of being human." She made a slashing motion. "We can discuss theology in greater detail at another time. Right now, we are discussing how to get along with the Rynn."

"If you promise something to a Rynn, you'd better deliver," the commander said firmly. "Do not make promises you cannot keep."

"For example, can you promise not to contact your superiors, friends, and families and tell them about the Rynn?' Kasumi asked. "Breaking such a promise would be considered incompetent." Her crest flattened. "Or, as Mel would have it, theft."

"Right now, Rynn and humans are coexisting because, so far, neither side has broken this pact," the commander said. "And personally, I would rather shoot you than jeopardize that coexistence," he said. "And by *personally*, I mean I would personally shoot you."

"Whoa," breathed Dierdre. "I think he means it, Crystal." She looked at the commander. "What will you do if we can't make that promise?"

"if you can't make that promise or we believe you are incapable of keeping that promise, we will, at the very least, lock you up." The commander's expression was grim. "I cannot and will not allow anyone to jeopardize this mission."

"Your cell phones will not work in this compound, and you will not be allowed to leave," Kasumi said. "I apologize, but I have no choice."

"There are already rumors of your existence," Crystal pointed out. "Including pictures." She took out her cell phone and brought up an image. "See?"

Kasumi and the commander looked at the image. "A bit grainy," the commander commented. "Thank you for bringing it to our attention," he said. "A few accidentally discarded Halloween masks should be enough."

"Crystal, if you don't promise to be good, I will tell them where every skeleton you have buried is buried, and you know I can do it," Dierdre said. "And if you break your word, I will personally hold you down while the commander blows your brains out."

"I believe the first, but I'm not so sure about the second," Crystal replied. She raised both hands in surrender. "Aw, come on, Dierdre," she complained. "I'm a reporter, and this is news."

"Crystal …" Dierdre growled in warning tones.

"All right, all right," Crystal replied. "But I got one demand of my own," she said. "When you finally do come out, I get the exclusive, and I'm your official press secretary."

"I told you not to bet against Gramps," Mel said in amusement. "That would be acceptable, Ms. Chandler."

"Who's Gramps?" Crystal asked in response.

"I am," said a gruff voice. Crystal and Dierdre turned in their chairs. An old man with thinning white hair was sitting in a chair at the other end of the room. He wore black silk pajamas that seemed more uniform than sleepwear. "Forgive me for not introducing myself earlier."

"Where did you come from?" Dierdre asked in shock.

"He was here when you came in," Kasumi replied. "Germy is very good at not being noticed when he does not want to be." She covered her eyes briefly. "What do you think, Teacher?"

"I think you should take Ms. McIntosh for a tour of the main ship," Jeremy Blunt said. "And introduce Ms. Chandler to Hendriks and Cool Evening Breeze."

Kasumi chittered. "Truly?"

"Think of it as a ... hmm, human interest is not accurate, is it?" Jeremy mused. "How about a sentient-being interest story?"

"Awkward, Gramps," Mel said with a grin.

"Cpt. Hendriks and Cool Evening Breeze are the first, or rather the second, interspecies core pairing, Ms. Chandler," Jeremy explained. "If you are going to be our ... spokesperson, then it follows you should see, firsthand as it were, how they get along."

Commander Eisenstadt had a slightly annoyed look on his face. *If I could bottle whatever that old man has, I could rule the world*, he thought. He had learned early on that unless the old man approved, nothing he proposed would ever be implemented. On the other hand, it was rare that Jeremy Blunt would disagree. He might offer an alternative or variation, but outright disagreement was rare. "I will arrange for the flight for Ms. McIntosh," he said. "That's assuming you wish to go."

"Jesus Lord, yes," Dierdre breathed. "May I take my camera?"

"I think that was Mr. Blunt's intention," Eisenstadt said. Jeremy nodded. "Come along, Ms. McIntosh."

"Be back before dinner," Mel warned. "Or you will have a very annoyed Morning Mist on your hands."

Eisenstadt mock-shuddered. "I wouldn't want that," he said. "Don't worry, Morning Mist. I will contact you if I am delayed."

"Do that," chirped Morning Mist through her translator. "I suppose I am the one to take Ms. Chandler to see Hendriks and Cool Evening Breeze?"

Soon the trailer was empty except for Mel, Kasumi, and Jeremy. "You realize that if they end up forming a core, you will never again be able to claim you're just an old martial artist," Mel said in mock despair.

"It's too late for that, Core Sister," Kasumi chirped cheerfully. "Though even I find this prediction unlikely."

"Oh, I don't know," Jeremy said with a smile. "I think Ms. McIntosh is mostly correct. Hendriks is about as macho a man as possible, and if I read Ms. Chandler correctly, that would be exactly her kind of man." He smiled. "Now Ms. McIntosh, on the other hand, is going to have a hard time resisting temptation."

"He's going to be impossible to live with if either of his predictions is right," Mel complained.

"He was right about Franklin," Kasumi pointed out. She chittered. "And David." She smiled at Jeremy. "Will it be acceptable for me to speak to Mei Lin tonight?"

"I think she misses speaking to you," Jeremy replied. "Only if you promise to sing for her."

15

TIDE

The princess looked at the Temple of Light. "Spirits watch over you, Granddaughter," said a familiar voice. The princess turned to see the old monk. She covered her eyes. "Honored one," she said in greeting. "I had not expected to return."

The old monk leaned her broom against the door of the temple. "You are here because you are worried," the old monk replied. "What worries you, Granddaughter?"

"I do not know that I am worried," the princess protested.

"Maybe worried is not correct," the old monk acknowledged. "Concerned perhaps?"

The princess covered her eyes. "I feel as if I am trying to swim against a strong tide," the princess admitted. "Yet if I stop swimming, I will drown."

The old woman pointed to the stairs. "Sit," she said. "Let us sit together and speak."

Without waiting, the old monk sat on the top step. The princess hesitated for a moment and then sat down on the next step below the monk. "You need not swim against the tide," the old woman chided. "The tide will take you where it will go."

"But is it where I should go?" questioned the princess. To her surprise, the old woman smiled at the princess in great approval. "The tide may take me out to the depths when it goes out," the princess continued.

"And return you when it comes back in," the old woman replied. "The tide will always bring you home, Granddaughter." She smiled gently. "The way forward is frightening, because it is unknown, but you have faced greater dangers than this already." The old woman looked past the princess. "And you still have your companions," the old monk laughed. "And a new one, I see."

The princess followed the gaze of the old monk. Standing at the bottom of the stairs were the faceless one and the mist, and standing behind them was a statue made of stone.

"He seems most formidable," the old woman said in approval. "You may need his strength in the near future. And he seems most willing to lend you his strength." The old monk rose. "Trust them to follow you when the tide goes out," she said. "And trust them to follow you when the tide comes back in again."

The princess stood. "Thank you, honored one," she said. "Will you grant me one last question?"

"Oh, I doubt this will be your last question," the old monk laughed. "What is it that you wish to know."

"You call me granddaughter," the princess said in leading tones.

"Granddaughter of my heart," the old woman replied. "If you will, do grant me one boon in return, Granddaughter."

"Anything," the princess replied.

"Tell the Great Teacher I will wait," the old monk replied. "Tell him that I will be here when he comes, no matter how long that may be."

Kasumi awoke in the dark. She waited until her heart stopped racing before slowly easing herself out of the kip she shared with Mel, Morning Mist, and more recently, David Eisenstadt. She exited the trailer she shared with them. As she expected, there was a soldier standing guard outside. The guard, a human, saluted. "Has Jeremy Blunt returned to his cabin?" she asked quietly.

"No, Captain Kasumi," the guard replied. "He decided it was too late, and he sleeps in the guest trailer."

"Excellent," Kasumi replied and pattered barefooted across the compound. As she half expected, the old man was sitting in a chair outside the trailer. She covered her eyes. "Greetings, Grandfather." She sat down on the ground at the old man's feet and rested her head against his knees. "I had the dream again."

"Was the old monk in the dream?" the old man asked quietly.

Kasumi nodded against the old man's legs. "She … she gave me a message for you," Kasumi said, and her crest trembled. "She said …

she will wait no matter how long that may be." She looked up at the old man. "Grandfather?" she said in a voice that cracked nervously. "I am a member of an advanced species. While we believe in dreams, I have never heard of anyone dreaming as I do."

"Has she been wrong?" Jeremy asked. "Has she given you poor advice?"

"No, Grandfather," Kasumi replied.

"Then don't worry about what you dream." Jeremy placed a hand on the little alien's head. "Instead, be thankful," he said. "And the next time you dream, tell her ... tell her I miss her."

16

Haunted by the Past

"Daniels!" Lieutenant Commander Eisenstadt said heartily to the screen image of his former subordinate. "To what do I owe the pleasure, Lieutenant?"

"OPS has just completed the background checks on all the civilians on the trade base," the lieutenant replied. "Sir, command has requested that you remove the Blunts immediately."

Eisenstadt laughed. "I thought command wanted the trade negotiations to succeed," he said ironically. "Doing that would guarantee failure." His voice took on a growling quality. "I don't know who is making that decision, but they obviously are not reading my weekly briefs."

"Sir?"

"Daniels," the commander said in patient tones. "If they were reading the briefs, they would know that the Rynn captain is very close to Ms. Melanie Blunt."

"I'm sure the Rynn captain would understand, sir." Daniels replied.

"She might," conceded the commander. "But what she would not understand is the removal of Mr. Jeremy Blunt."

"He's a murderer, sir," the lieutenant blurted out. "He spent ten years in prison for manslaughter, and there is evidence that those two were not his only victims." He frowned when the commander laughed. "Sir," he said in affronted tones. "I am looking at the report right now. He, and I quote, 'damaged the eyes of both victims before crushing their throats,' end quote. I looked at the photographs. He crushed their eyes, sir." Daniels shuddered. "Even if they had lived, they would have been blind."

"And yet, he was only convicted of manslaughter," the commander replied. "Doesn't that tell you something?" The commander sighed. "Then I will spell it out for you: Mr. Blunt's wife was assaulted, raped, and then stabbed through the throat," the commander replied. "She lived long enough to identify her killers to her husband." His voice was a snarl. "In my opinion, he killed them way too quickly."

"Sir?" Daniels replied uncertainly.

"I personally would have ripped their balls off and made them eat them," the commander replied. "And even if Mr. Blunt was in actuality a cold-blooded killer as that report is suggesting, you and everyone else are missing one really important fact." The commander leaned toward the screen. "The Rynn think of Jeremy Blunt as something akin to a messiah," he said. "Or at the very least, some kind of holy man."

"Sir, it's an order," Daniels replied firmly.

"Then whoever is issuing that order needs to come here and deliver it in person, in front of the Rynn," the commander snapped. He cut the connection and sat back. "Did you get all that, Kasumi?"

"You were magnificent." Kasumi stood up from the round padded chair she had been reclining on and padded over to the commander. "Why now?"

The commander rubbed his chin thoughtfully. "I know I've expressed Mr. Blunt's importance in nearly every report," he mused. "So someone either doesn't know or doesn't …" He paused. "Or doesn't care," he said finally. "Revenge?" He leaned forward and tapped a command into the laptop. He waited until an image formed. "Network issue," he said to the person on the screen to explain his abrupt departure from the conversation earlier.

"Yes, sir," Daniels said impassively.

"Who issued that command, Lieutenant?" the commander asked.

Daniels looked at the order. "Colonel Bridgestone, sir."

"And the names of Mr. Blunt's alleged victims?" the commander asked.

"Trey and Obediah Coolidge," the lieutenant replied. "Brothers," he answered the unasked question. The lieutenant frowned. "Excuse me, sir. I want to check something." He tapped a few keys and looked at the result. His eyes widened. "They were cousins to Senator Malcolm Coolidge," he reported. "Sir, Malcolm Coolidge was Colonel Bridgestone's roommate at VSU."

"And how do you happen to know that, Lieutenant?" the commander replied. "An odd piece of data to know offhand," he said in obvious curiosity.

"Because I went to VSU, sir," the lieutenant replied. "It's hard to not know that. There are pictures of the two of them all over the place. 'The Wonder Twins,' they were called." He said. "Football," he added. "Sir, I apologize."

"For what?" Eisenstadt replied. "For doing your job?" He smiled. It was a grim smile. "I think we should invite the good senator for a visit."

Kasumi leaned into the camera pickup. Daniels leaned back in surprise. "No, tell him I'm demanding his presence," Kasumi instructed. "Tell him I am ordering him here to apologize, and if he does not come within the week, I will remove every Rynn and Rynn associate from here and relocate to a more … agreeable location," she snarled through her Torque. "And tell him that my first public statement will be to explain why the Rynn will not provide any technological transfers to the United States."

Daniels swallowed visibly. "Yes, ma'am," he said shakily. This time it was Kasumi who broke the connection.

President Spencer stared at his commander of the Joint Chiefs of Staff in disbelief. "They are demanding what?" he exclaimed in outrage. "Who are they to demand anything?"

"They are a visiting starfaring race," General Oswalt replied. "We have two choices: try to destroy them or try to negotiate," the general replied. "Based on the reports I have been receiving, our chances of being able to destroy them is not quite zero, but not by much."

The general placed the attaché he was holding on the president's desk and opened it. He took out a vial and showed it to the president. "This is Omiset," he said in explanation. "It is nontoxic and easily tolerated by humans." The general looked at the vial almost reverently. "And, if the medical geeks are to be believed, it will cure just about anything." He barked a sardonic laugh. "Supposedly, it can even revive someone who's been declared dead if administered within an hour after brain activity has ceased."

He looked at the president. "They gave us the method for producing it, for free." He shook his head. "No, not for free—out of gratitude for the services provided by one Jeremy Blunt." He almost glared at the president. "The same Jeremy Blunt that your buddy Senator Coolidge wants them to disassociate themselves from."

The general put the vial back in the attaché. "Now, Mr. President, you can ignore Commander Eisenstadt's advice. You can ignore Captain Kasumi's demands," he said. "The choice is yours." He snapped the attaché closed. "But if that is your decision, you will have my resignation on your desk five seconds afterward." He reached into his coat and pulled out a sealed envelope. He held it just above the desk. "What is your decision, sir?"

"Are you threatening me?" the president asked in disbelief.

"I have a niece who faced a year of chemotherapy, and her prognosis was not hopeful. She was able to leave the hospital, in full remission, one day after receiving a single dose of Omiset," the general replied. "Your decision?"

The military helicopter touched down inside the Rynn enclave. The fence was completed, and only a few people knew that the fence was mostly for show and completely unnecessary for the defense of the Rynn compound. The trailers that housed the military personnel, Rynn when they were downside, and the occasional—such as now—visiting dignitaries were rapidly being replaced with more permanent dwellings.

Corporal Hendriks and Cool Evening Breeze led their picked squads and formed them into two lines. A blonde white woman and a black woman with short curls took up position off to one side. The black woman held a video recorder.

"Think you can keep your flock from chirping, featherhead?" taunted the big marine.

"Easier than you can keep your troop from scratching themselves, fuzzy butt," the diminutive Rynn geologist returned. They grinned at each other.

"Cut the chatter," growled Sergeant Stilson. He gave the two squad leaders a twisted smile. "You're definitely wasted as a geologist," he said to Cool Evening Breeze. Stilson schooled his features into the "attentive but dumb" look he used when he expected fireworks. *And there are definitely going to be fireworks*, he thought.

The first out of the helicopter was Colonel Bridgestone. Tall and graying, he'd retained the athletic build he had in college. He'd had a single tour in Afghanistan before rotating back stateside to take command of appropriations. He was on the short list for promotion to general.

Stilson shot a warning glance at Cool Evening Breeze. "Say nothing," he mouthed. Cool Evening Breeze waggled her crest in amusement before nodding. "Atten-hut!" barked Stilson. The soldiers, human and Rynn, snapped to attention.

The colonel absentmindedly saluted and turned to wait for the next person to disembark. Surprisingly, it was not the senator. Rather, it was a young woman, at most nineteen years of age. Her eyes widened when she saw her first Rynn, and she seemed to physically refrain from saying anything. She turned to the helicopter as the third person descended the short steps.

Colonel Bridgestone may have kept in shape as military men tended to do, but not so Senator Coolidge. The senator was tall, balding, and paunchy. His expression soured when he saw the Rynn. "Come along, Denise," he said. "The sooner this is done, the sooner I can get out of here." He turned to the colonel. "Alton."

The colonel nodded and led the senator and the young woman through the double row. The young woman kept looking at the Rynn with an almost gleeful look. She took out a cell phone.

"Sorry, ma'am." Stilson interposed himself between the phone and the Rynn. "No pictures, no communication." He held out his hand. "The phone, please."

"Put the phone away, Denise," the senator grumbled.

"But Daddy," whined the girl. She wilted under the glare of her father. "Oh, all right." She put the phone back in her purse.

Stilson debated whether to make an issue of it and then decided to do as all good noncoms did and buck the issue upwards. *Fireworks*, he thought in almost gleeful anticipation.

The visitors were led to one of the more recent installations. It was a single-story building. Built round instead of rectangular, it had round windows and an arched door. The sergeant opened the door and waved the visitors in. Stilson winked at the two human women who followed just behind. "Promise me you'll let me see the reaming," he whispered to Dierdre McIntosh.

"If it goes as Crystal and I expect, I'll broadcast it to the entire compound," Dierdre whispered back. She followed Crystal into the building.

The senator, his daughter, and the colonel found themselves in a mostly empty vestibule. A single Rynn was curled up in a round cushioned chair just to the side of a low archway. The Rynn raised his head and blinked sleepily at the visitors. "What are you bringing me this time, Sergeant?"

"They're expected, Raindrops in a Tide Pool," Stilson replied.

A globe appeared in front of the Rynn. "They're late," he said in complaint after looking at the globe. "The captain's time is finite," he scolded. He waved his hands in dismissal. "Take them to the guesthouse and I will see if I can shift some appointments."

"Now see here," the senator barked.

"No, you see here," Raindrops in a Tide Pool snapped back. "The captain is a very busy woman. She made time available. Are you so incompetent that you cannot even be on time?" he chirped angrily.

The door behind Raindrops in a Tide Pool opened. There was a string of chirps and chitters. The Rynn standing in the doorway saw the visitors. "Oh, you finally made it," she said through the translator. "You might as well come in."

"Such incompetence," muttered Raindrops in a Tide Pool as the visitors walked by. He looked up at Crystal and Dierdre and waggled his crest. The two women covered their mouths to stifle the laughter. Dierdre leaned over. "Good boy," she cooed. "I'll expect you and Night Storm for dinner." She grinned as the Rynn's crest flared fully open. She wiggled her fingers at the Rynn and followed Crystal.

"Getting lucky, huh, boy?" Stilson said to the Rynn when the door closed.

The Rynn chittered. "It isn't luck," he said smugly.

Stilson laughed. He looked at the door. "Fireworks," he said.

The Rynn woman led the visitors into another room. This one was much larger and had several low desks off to one side and a number of chairs of various types forming a conversation nook. The Rynn woman led them to the conversation nook and sat in one of the odd round Rynn chairs. "Well, I'm waiting."

"Excuse me," Senator Coolidge said. "Who in blazes are you?"

"Raindrops in a Tide Pool was right. You are incompetent,"

the Rynn woman chirped. "We do not all look the same," she said through the translator.

"Oh, give him a break, Granddaughter," a gravelly baritone voice said. A man rose from a seat near the back of the room. "People are not elected to public office because they are the smartest or the most competent."

"It's amazing you've advanced as far as you have then," the Rynn woman replied. "Oh, very well. If you haven't guessed yet …"

"And he probably hasn't," the old man said in an aside to Crystal and Dierdre.

"I am Kasumi Blunt," the Rynn woman said. "Expedition leader and, for lack of a better term, captain of the trading ship the *Seeker*," she said. "You are, unsurprisingly, Senator Coolidge," she chirped. "You are here to apologize."

The senator's expression darkened, but it wasn't Kasumi he was looking at. It was the old man. "You!" he growled. "You dare show your face." Before anyone could react, he pulled a pistol from his pocket and fired several rounds at the old man. He smiled triumphantly as the room erupted in screams and shouts. His triumphant smile faded immediately, however, when the old man refused to fall.

"I would drop that gun right now, senator," said another voice. A tall gray-haired man in military greens was aiming his own pistol in the senator's direction. "If you do not, I will shoot you."

"Commander, put down that gun now," Colonel Bridgestone barked. "That is an order."

"You may wish to rethink that order, Colonel," Lieutenant Commander Eisenstadt replied, "or I will be forced to arrest you as well as an accessory to attempted murder."

Another door opened, and Cool Evening Breeze and Corporal Hendriks marched in. "Sir?" the big corporal asked.

"Confine the senator to the brig," the commander ordered. "And have someone escort the colonel and Ms. Coolidge to the guest house." He walked over to the senator. "And if you open your mouth to complain, I will execute you for treason right here and right now," he snarled. "If you had succeeded in killing Mr. Blunt, I don't know if any human on this base would survive an hour afterward."

"They would have lived, David," Kasumi replied. "But most would have been exiled from the compound. *Most*," she repeated. "And those who remained would have had a very difficult decision to make."

The commander jerked his head. The big corporal handcuffed the senator, and then he and Cool Evening Breeze forced the man from the room.

"Daddy!" the young girl screamed in panic.

"I would not attempt to follow, Miss Coolidge," Kasumi said coolly. "It would do you no good, and you could be hurt."

"What are you going to do to my father?" demanded the young woman.

"Whatever I wish," Kasumi snapped. "If he were Rynn, he would have been executed immediately," she added. "He is fortunate that he is not."

"He has diplomatic immunity," the young woman returned.

Kasumi shook her head. "No, he does not," she replied. "There is no treaty. There is not even an acknowledgement that we exist." Her crest flared, and the young woman took a fearful step backward. "He, and you, could disappear, and there is not one thing you could do about it." She waved a hand. "Now leave," she ordered. "I will decide what to do about the two of you ... later."

The young woman looked at the Rynn captain in disbelief. "You ... you can't dismiss me like some ... some ... common trash," she snarled. "My father is powerful. He knows people."

"Your father is incompetent," Kasumi snapped back. "There is no greater crime among the Rynn." Her crest remained at its fullest. She tapped herself on the chest. "I was accused of incompetence and almost lost my life." She glared at Denise Coolidge. "It was only by the favor of the spirits that I met the one human who could help me regain my honor."

"She fought a duel—a duel to the death, I might add—to regain her honor," Mel added. "I doubt your father has the balls to do the same."

"It is for the sake of Jeremy Blunt that I would even consider establishing trade with Earth," Kasumi chirped angrily. "His sake and no other, not even the human I call core sister."

"That's me," Mel said with a cold grin. "Right now, my grandfather is the most important human being on Earth." She walked over to the young woman. "And your father just tried to murder him." The door to the office opened again, and this time, Sergeant Stilson walked in. "Take the colonel and Ms. Coolidge to the guest house," Mel said. "Confiscate any communication devices and keep them confined until we figure out what to do with them."

"Yes ma'am," Sergeant Stilson replied. "Colonel, Miss Coolidge," he said. "Please follow me." He added, "And sir, miss, please don't force me to order you strip-searched."

Kasumi waited until the colonel and the senator's daughter left the office before letting her crest lower. "Spirits, but this is a mess," she chirped despondently.

"Not as big a mess as it would have been if Coolidge had succeeded," Eisenstadt replied. "The first thing you will do is file a protest with the state department." He smiled slightly. "Along with Ms. McIntosh's video record, of course."

"Of course," Dierdre smiled back. "And I have an idea for what should be done next."

17

California Dreaming

"This is unacceptable," President Spencer snapped. "Tell them to release Malcolm immediately," he growled. "Or else."

"No sir," the current head of the Joint Chiefs of Staff replied. Even though he had forced the senator to travel to the Rynn enclave, General Oswalt had resigned anyway. Admiral Pharos was his replacement. "I've read Oswalt's briefing. He was correct in his original assessment."

The door opened, and the president's executive secretary walked in. "Excuse me, Mr. President, but Governor Newgate is on the phone. He says it's urgent."

"Newgate?" President Spencer said in surprise. His eyes widened. "They wouldn't."

"It's his state," Admiral Pharos said. "Looks like they're calling your bluff, Mr. President," the admiral said in almost cheerful tones.

The president glared at the admiral and then went over to his desk and pressed a button. "Darren, what's the problem this time?" he growled.

"Stow it, Spencer," the governor of California snapped. "I just learned I have some honest-to-god aliens opening up a trading post in the northern part of my state," he growled. "Two things: One is that they gave me a sample of one of their items for sale—a desalinization process that will convert sea water to potable fresh water for pennies an acre foot," he said. "And two, they say that you've insulted them and they're now planning to leave in a huff."

"Now, now, Darren, it's just a misunderstanding," the president said reassuringly.

"That idiot Coolidge trying to assassinate a human they revere—a California native, I might add—is just a misunderstanding?" the voice boomed. "Now I am going to send a delegation to the aliens, and hopefully, hopefully, I will be able to mend some fences."

"Now wait a minute, Newgate," the president said angrily.

"Shut up, Spencer," the governor replied. "I also had a chat with Lieutenant Commander Eisenstadt." The president could almost hear the governor grinding his teeth together. "Not only did that shithead of yours try to assassinate Blunt, but the idiot brought his daughter along. Since when are the children of senators allowed to go on sensitive and confidential diplomatic missions?" There was a click as the call was disconnected.

The president looked at the phone.

"Heads up, Fuzzy Butt, we got company," Cool Evening Breeze called out.

"That is not how you report, Lickin' Chicken," Corporal Hendriks replied with a grin. "And that's Corporal Fuzzy Butt to you." His grin got wider when Cool Evening Breeze chittered. "What you got?"

"Six of those SUV things," Cool Evening Breeze replied. "One's got flags." She put the image on the larger screen.

"Well, well, it looks like the governor himself is paying a visit," the corporal said in interested tones. "Let's get a welcoming committee over there. I'll let the captain know."

"How about an all-Rynn committee?" Cool Evening Breeze suggested. "Humans can't be trusted, after all."

"Did anyone ever tell you, you have a nasty streak?" Hendriks replied. He nodded. "Do it."

Cool Evening Breeze chittered to herself for a few moments. "Done," she reported. She grinned a Rynn grin. "And I have Raindrops in a Tide Pool heading the reception committee."

Hendriks whistled. "A really wide nasty streak," he said in admiration.

The convoy of six SUVs stopped at the gate. The governor stepped out. He was young—one of the youngest men ever to be elected governor of California—with wavy black hair and Hollywood looks. Unlike others with those looks, he also had a first-class brain. "I don't want to see anything that looks like a weapon anywhere in sight," he ordered. "I want friendly and accommodating. I don't care what they do, you will be friendly and accommodating."

The bodyguards who half-surrounded him nodded glumly. One pointed toward the gate. "Welcoming committee."

"Let's see if our intelligence is correct," he mumbled and took possession of a crate that one of his aides was holding—one of a dozen similar crates. The governor walked over to the gate. "Governor Newgate to see Captain Kasumi," he said to the Rynn who appeared to be in command.

"Do you have an appointment?" the Rynn asked.

"Unfortunately, no," the governor replied. "I tried, but you were, understandably I will add, refusing all contact." He shifted the crate to one arm and covered his eyes with his free hand. "Please accept my apologies for my rudeness."

"The captain is a busy Rynn," the Rynn stated.

"I'm sure she is," the governor replied. "I don't expect her to see me right away, but hopefully she can make some time. If not today, then tomorrow."

The Rynn chittered. "That was almost Rynn in form," the Rynn said in approval. He nodded toward the crate. "That will have to be inspected."

The governor nodded. "I have a dozen more just like it," he said. "A peace offering, if you will." He opened the crate and displayed the contents to the Rynn.

The Rynn chittered again. "Someone did his homework," the Rynn said in English. "Maybe humans are not so incompetent after all," he added in approval. "I am Raindrops in a Tide Pool. I will escort you to see the captain."

"So Governor, what should we do with the senator?" Captain Kasumi asked. She munched on one of the carrots the governor had brought in obvious delight. She and the governor had spent the last hour together. They had gone over a wide range of topics, and it was obvious the governor was doing his best to get some kind of technology transfer out of the Rynn.

While Kasumi didn't express it, she was impressed with the governor. *Knowledgeable, concerned about his state and people, and above all, competent* was her assessment.

"He can rot in hell for all I care," the governor spat. "Unfortunately, that won't serve either of our interests," he added seriously. "I think the only thing you can do is send him back, but make it known that he will be unwelcome in any setting that the Rynn are involved in." He chuckled nastily. "For someone like Senator Coolidge, that would be a true slap in the face."

"He brought his daughter to a top-secret facility," Lieutenant Commander Eisenstadt commented.

"A top-secret facility that does not exist," the governor corrected. "Regardless, it is not a federal facility," he pointed out. "Much as I'd love to see him impeached, it isn't going to happen." The governor pursed his lips. "Still, he's going to be trouble." He waved a dismissive hand. "Nothing we can do about it now," he said. "Let's talk about how we are going to introduce you to the public."

18

A Good Core Is Three

"Hey, Crystal," Cool Evening Breeze called in greeting.

"Hey, Breeze," the reporter replied. "Where's your boyfriend?"

Cool Evening Breeze chittered. "Why?" she asked. "Getting lonely?" she said teasingly. She chittered again when the blonde reporter blushed. "I really don't understand your attitude," she complained lightly. "You like him; that's obvious. And he likes you." She chittered again. "And I like you. So what's the problem?"

"It's the 'he's your boyfriend'—that's the problem," Crystal replied. "Don't waggle your crest at me," she complained. "Don't Rynn get jealous?"

"Yes, we do, but not over that," Cool Evening Breeze replied. "How many times do I have to tell you? A good core is at least three."

"Okay, then the fact that you're a girl is also a problem," Crystal replied.

"Dierdre is right. You're hopeless," Cool Evening Breeze said in disgust. "Even Hendriks is not as uptight as you."

"Of course he isn't. He's bucking to have two women," Crystal said. "Every adolescent male's fantasy."

"And I'm bucking to have two men," Cool Evening Breeze replied. She grinned at the look of surprise on the reporter's face. "Hendriks is a hell of a lot of fun, but he's still human." She waggled her crest. "I do plan on having children, after all," she pointed out. "And even though humans and Rynn are physically compatible, we aren't biologically."

"Does Hendriks know this?" Crystal asked.

"Yes, he does," Cool Evening Breeze replied. "Actually, that's where he is right now." She pointed upwards. "He's talking to a couple candidates," she said. "To see if they can get along," she chittered. "And by *get along*, I mean he's going to see which of them is willing to ... well, you get the idea."

"Hendriks? Mr. Macho himself, *Hendriks*, is going to sleep with a Rynn man? Hendriks?" Crystal said in shock.

"Well, unless he's going to spend the night, I doubt he's going to *sleep*," Cool Evening Breeze chittered.

"Hendriks," Crystal replied.

"Hendriks," Cool Evening Breeze smiled. She took the stunned reporter's hand. "Now, I think we've gone around this circle enough times," she chirped cheerfully. "Oh, one thing. While Rynn men are not as endowed as some human men, most are more than enough to satisfy a human woman," she chittered. "Just ask Dierdre."

Crystal did call Dierdre, but not for that reason.

"Governor," Crystal Chandler said in greeting. "Any comments you'd like to make?"

"Crystal Chandler?" the governor said in surprise. "What are you doing here?"

"Writing the biggest story of my life," the reporter replied. She indicated the black woman standing next to her. "This is Dierdre ..."

"McIntosh," finished the governor. "Aren't two Pulitzers enough, Ms. McIntosh?"

"I have a couple empty spots on my bookshelf," the photojournalist replied.

"Of course," Governor Newgate replied. "I'm afraid to ask, but how long have either of you been here?"

"We came together," Crystal replied. "About three weeks ago now." She grinned. "It's been hell," she said. "The biggest story of my life and anyone else's life, and I can't say a thing." Her smile widened. "Not yet."

"I don't know which impresses me more," the governor replied. "The fact that you've been here that long, or that you haven't leaked this story in that time." The governor became serious. "Can you answer one question for me?" he asked. "Why does an alien wear a Chinese sword strapped to her back?" He smiled wryly. "I'm the governor of California—I know Chinese characters when I see them."

"Captain Kasumi was marooned on Earth. The person who found and sheltered her is, among other things, a grand master in kung fu," Crystal replied. "She wears it as a reminder ... and a warning."

The governor nodded. "I suspected it was something like that," he replied. "Actually, I have another question."

"They're for real, Governor," Dierdre said firmly.

"That I understood," the governor replied. "My question is, why?" He ran his hand through his hair. "About all we can offer them is carrots." He looked back at the hangar. "And they're offering us ... the universe."

"You want to know what the catch is, right?" Crystal replied with a grim smile. "Oh, there is definitely a catch." The governor raised an eyebrow. "The question is, do you really want to know?" Crystal asked. "Dierdre and I know what the catch is—mainly because when the Rynn leave, we're going with them."

"They're leaving?" the governor exclaimed. "But I thought they were going to open a trade post."

"Maybe we should have said, when *these* Rynn leave," Crystal replied. "If—and it's still an if—the Rynn decide to open a trade relationship with Earth, there will be more Rynn here. But the *Seeker* will resume its explorations."

"I'm confused," the governor said almost petulantly. "They've already provided some technological transfer—the desalinization process, the fusion technology, Omiset."

"The equivalent of trade beads, Governor," Dierdre said in amused tones. "Obsolete technology, at least for the Rynn." She smiled. "Well, not the Omiset, but I think you get the idea." She shrugged. "Everything they've given us are things that are maintainable by our current technology."

"The catch, Crystal. What's the catch?" the governor demanded.

"The catch, governor, is that it's a dangerous universe," she said in serious tones. "If we join with the Rynn, then we will be subject to those dangers. There are alien races that think of the Rynn as food," she said. "And if we are with them, we will most likely be considered food as well."

"And you're willing to go with them knowing that?" the governor said in shock.

"They do," Crystal replied. "Of course, they run like the blazes when they encounter anyone out there, but they keep exploring." She smiled wryly. "Funny thing is, the Rynn think of themselves as cowards." She shook her head. "And yet they keep going."

"Lord Jesus, but you have to admire them," Dierdre said.

"They're willing to give us the universe, and all we have to do is be their friends." Crystal wiped at her eyes for a second. "All we have to do is love them."

"Amen, Sister," Dierdre said.

The governor was silent for a long time. He found he had to clear his throat several times before he trusted his voice. "I think … I think I have some calls to make," he said.

19

Interesting Times

"This is CNN with a late-breaking exclusive report," blared the station. The grizzled anchor looked at the camera. "For those who've wondered where Crystal Chandler has been for the past couple of months, the answer is astounding." He walked over to where several people were sitting. One was a famous astronomer, one a popular science educator, and the third a special effects expert. "I apologize for not briefing any of you about what is contained in the video, but I wanted your honest and unfiltered opinions."

A large video screen lit up, and the familiar face of Crystal Chandler appeared. "Good evening," Crystal said. "I am Crystal Chandler." She smiled. "When I was a child, I'd look at the night sky and wonder if there was anyone up there looking at their night sky and wondering the same thing. What you are about to see will answer that question, once and for all."

She made a gesture, and the image changed to show a compound. "This is the colony. It's a trading post," Crystal said in voice-over. A figure exited a building and walked toward the camera. "And this," she paused, "is an alien." The being had cinnamon-brown skin, with a faintly birdlike appearance accentuated by the pink cockatoo crest on its head. The image froze.

"My god," the astronomer exclaimed.

The special effects wizard looked at the image open-mouthed, while the science educator started to laugh. "Fantastic," the educator exclaimed. "Wonderful," he said between laughs.

"Professor, you're laughing?" the host said. "Do you think this is fake?"

"Hell no," the educator said. "I'm laughing because every so-called expert who dismissed the idea of there being aliens or such beings coming to Earth is probably having one large collective heart attack." He giggled. "Excuse me, but this is just too wonderful."

The astronomer looked at the image intently. "They must come from a very similar star system to ours," he said, almost under his breath. "Notice she is not wearing anything to cover her eyes and does not appear distressed by our environment."

"She?" the anchor said.

"Well, I may be making an unfounded assumption," the astronomer admitted. "But it does look like a woman to me."

"You are correct, Dr. Simon," came a voice over the sound system. "I am indeed a woman." The image on the screen shifted, and the alien who had been in the image was replaced by the same alien now sitting at a desk. "Good evening, Dr. Simon, Mr. Wise, Mr. Sparks, Mr. Wilter," she said, naming the guests and the host. "I am Kasumi Blunt," she smiled. "The name was given to me by an Earth man who had trouble saying my Rynn name." Her crest waggled. "To be more accurate, I am a Rynn woman."

"Mr. Sparks, is this a CGI image?" the anchor asked.

"If it is, it's the best one ever done." He shook his head. "Look at that skin tone. Heck, look at the shadows." He looked at the alien. "Madame, will it be possible to meet with you?"

"Captain," corrected Kasumi. "It's Captain Kasumi. The title, like my name, is an accommodation to Earth beings." She smiled. "I'm sure that can be arranged."

The science educator continued to laugh. The astronomer rolled his eyes. "I assume your sun is a yellow dwarf?"

"More orange than yellow, but yes," Kasumi replied. "Slightly cooler," she said. "Three moons, longer days, shorter years." Her crest flicked. "It works out to about the same."

"You're a therapsid," the educator suddenly exclaimed. "A mammal-like reptile."

Kasumi's crest waggled. "Something similar, most likely," the alien replied. "Nest did not have the same level of extinction events Earth had." She raised a long-fingered hand. "I am here to answer whatever questions you may have," she said. "But I want to make something clear; we are not here to invade, threaten, or predate on humans. Under normal circumstances, we would not have even contacted humans, but circumstances were not normal." She ran her fingers through her crest. "Serendipity is a two-way street."

"You're here by accident?" the educator asked.

"We're here by accident," agreed Kasumi. "Humans have a belief in something called *fate*," she said. "Rynn do not. And yet, there are times when I have no other explanation."

She looked out at the camera, and it seemed she was no longer talking to the people in the studio. "I have been on Earth for slightly more than an Earth year. I should have died my first day here, and instead I met a human—no, I met a *man*—who from the very first moment treated me as a friend. But more than that, he was the key to my very survival."

She briefly covered her eyes with her hands. "We do not believe in fate, and yet ..." She reached out with a long-fingered hand. "People of Earth, my people do not believe in fate, yet I must believe we are fated to be together," she said. "My people have roamed the galaxy for more than two hundred of your years, and we have seen wonders, but in our two centuries of roaming we have not found another race who did not automatically think of us as food or as an enemy. And by accident, we found you." She again briefly covered her eyes with her hands.

The studio was quiet. It seemed that no one wanted to break the silence. It took a quiet cough to break the spell that seemed to have been cast. The anchor shook himself. "We'll be right back," he said quietly.

The uproar that followed was as loud as it was predictable. There were those in nearly every country who denounced the whole interview as a fraud, with calls for investigations and demands for firings. There were many more in nearly every country who believed what they saw, and they too were split into several predictable camps: those who believed and wanted to work with the Rynn, those who believed and wanted the Rynn to leave, and those who believed and thought the Rynn were the harbingers of Armageddon.

Also predictably, the members of the second and third groups united. What was not predictable and most surprising was that the members of the group that wanted to welcome the Rynn far outnumbered all the other groups combined. However, there was one more predictable outcome: the number of violent crimes soared as various groups took the Rynn's existence as a license to settle scores and eliminate rivals. Governments collapsed overnight, and civil liberties were suspended by many of those that did not.

Year 3

20

Discord

The union that was the United States split asunder. It started when President Spencer ordered the immediate confiscation of all Rynn technology and the Rynn themselves to be rounded up and transferred to a holding facility. California refused to cooperate. In response, President Spencer ordered the military to arrest Governor Darren Newgate, his staff, and his family, and authorized lethal force if there was resistance. The head of the Joint Chiefs of Staff refused the order as illegal. Within days, states started taking various positions in regard to the aliens and the federal response.

Governor Newgate suddenly found himself the head of a newly christened Republic of California—a republic that, within days, was rechristened the Western States of America when Oregon, Washington, and Nevada requested to form an alliance. It was a loose confederacy at the moment, but President Newgate was working feverishly to create something more structured. Unlike many governors of other states, he had an ace in the hole, and she was sitting in his office.

"I figure we can convince Nevada to get in line by providing a reliable source of fresh water," Newgate said. "And once we get the new fusion reactors on line, we can start exporting energy to some of the other states, like Montana and Idaho." He chewed his lower lip. "It's Texas that's going to be the problem."

"I'm sorry, Darren. I did not expect this," Kasumi began.

"The country was fragile and had been for years," Newgate cut her off. "If anything, we should be grateful." His mouth twisted. "You tore the scab off, and maybe now we can heal." He made a patting motion with one hand. "Now stop apologizing and help me figure out how to prevent a war with Texas."

"Why do you think Texas is going to start a war?" Kasumi asked.

Newgate snorted. "Because they need something to distract their populace from how bad things are going," he explained. "President Prescott has run his state into the ground, and he needs a new source of revenue, resources, and anything else he can grab. He's already invaded New Mexico and Oklahoma, but that won't fill his coffers. No, he needs to take over something big," he said. "Besides, if he takes California, he becomes basically King of America." He pointed to a map. "According to our satellites and the transmissions your people have intercepted, he's moving munitions, people, and machinery west."

Kasumi looked at the map of the former USA. "Arizona?" asked Kasumi.

"Arizona," Newgate agreed. "He takes Arizona, and he can attack either California or Nevada." He pursed his lips. "We're in talks with Utah," he said musingly.

Kasumi chittered. "I like the Mormons, but they are a bit strange. I keep telling the ambassador that in Rynn, *Kolob* is the name of a type of mudfish and not my planet's name, but I don't think he believes me."

"They may be strange, but they are your most devoted followers," Newgate shared a laugh with the alien captain. "I was wondering if you'd be willing to put a trading post in Salt Lake City."

"A small one, and only open once a month. Anything they need urgently, they can contact me directly," Kasumi agreed. "We can also construct a small power plant and deliver it to them." Her crest rose slightly. "If they stop hesitating and sign the articles."

"Next item on the agenda," Newgate said. "Any word?"

Kasumi nodded. "My father will come," she said. "It will take time to assemble the fleet, but he will come."

"Fuck!" exclaimed Lieutenant Daniels. "North Korea just launched." He keyed a mic. "High Flyer, this is CalCom. We got launch. Repeat, we got launch." He recited a string of coordinates.

"We see it, CalCom," came a chirping voice. "High Flyer taking action now." There was silence, and all those in the room seemed to be holding their breaths. "Target neutralized," came a chirping response. The room collectively blew out a breath.

"Thank you, High Flyer," Daniels replied. "Busy morning, huh?"

"Busy morning," agreed the Rynn pilot. "It was fun the first few times, but it's starting to get irritating."

"I hear you, High Flyer," Daniels replied. "Thanks again."

"As you Earth people say, 'No worries,'" the Rynn pilot chittered and then broke the connection.

Daniels stared at the situation board. Over the past three months since the United States broke apart, there had been over a dozen nuclear launches by almost as many countries. Most of the big powers—China, Russia, and the slowly reuniting United States—had kept their fingers off their respective launch buttons, but some of the more unstable nations were taking turns launching nuclear missiles. Daniels was not sure they even cared who they were shooting at. "They've got to be running out of nuclear devices by now," he muttered.

"Missiles, probably. Nukes, probably not," one of mission specialists responded. "You know someone is going to carry a nuke somewhere on their back."

Daniels nodded grimly. "Just as long as it isn't here," he grumbled. He reached out, tapped a table, and grimaced. "Knocking wood, at my age."

"I don't care what you knock," the specialist replied. "As long as it works."

21

Civil Actions

"Prescott is on the move," David Eisenstadt reported. The former lieutenant commander was now the head of the colony's combined Rynn and human military forces in alliance with the slowly expanding Western States of America. Despite no longer having a rank, he was more often than not referred to as "the commander." Those humans who had joined the colony's military force retained what ranks they had but were now subject to promotions approved by Eisenstadt and Kasumi.

The WSA had originally formed as a coalition of California, Oregon, and Washington after the USA itself had fractured. Within months, Nevada and Utah had joined the new coalition, followed in turn by Arizona and Colorado. Montana, Wyoming, and North and South Dakota had tried to form their own coalition, but it appeared that they too were going to consider joining the WSA.

President Zebediah Prescott's Greater Texas Republic had absorbed New Mexico, Oklahoma, Arkansas, Missouri, and Alabama. The rest of the states of the former USA were either part of the Eastern Coalition, the newly created Christian States of America under President Spencer, or desperately trying to make it on their own. For all intents and purposes, though, the USA was now composed of four independent countries. If Zebediah Prescott had his way, there would be one United States again, but this time under the control of Texas.

The Rynn might not have cared which group came out ahead, except that President Prescott was calling for the confiscation of Rynn technology, and President Spencer was calling for the extermination of any and all Rynn presence on Earth. While the mysterious oligarch of the Eastern Coalition was in favor of any and all trade regardless of origin, she seemed content to take a watch-and-see stance with regard to President Prescott.

"Put it on the board," President Newgate said. A satellite image of North America appeared. The new borders were highlighted in red. Lights of different colors dotted the map.

An arrow appeared on the map. "At 0600 this morning, Prescott started moving his troops to the New Mexico/Arizona border," Eisenstadt reported. "He hasn't yet scrambled his fighters, but we think it will happen within the next two hours." He looked at the map. "If it was just Prescott, we'd be able to shove 'em back," he said. The arrow shifted east. "Unfortunately, the CSA started mobilizing at almost the same time." He blew out a breath. "I think we need to assume it's a joint maneuver."

"Agreed," Newgate replied after a moment of thought. "Damn," he exclaimed under his breath. "Options?"

"It's going to take a while before the CSA ground troops are in play, but they've got air superiority," the commander pointed out. "And that includes High Flyer 1 and 2." He looked at Captain Kasumi. "Hell of a time to pull out the other two shuttles."

"Even Rynn technology requires maintenance," Kasumi replied. "The maintenance team is working through the cycle in order to get them back in rotation." She shook her head. "They still think it's going to take another two cycles before they're complete. On the other hand, we've been able to produce close to one thousand personal shields." She smiled grimly. "Earth people can be extremely competent when then want to be," she said. "Elvin Moss thinks he can get production up to one hundred a day."

"That will help some," agreed the commander. "I still wish we had the other two shuttles."

Technical Specialist Joseph Franklin was waist-deep inside an access port that was itself inside a partially completed torpedo-shaped structure. He reached out a hand. Red Clouds Paint the Sky handed him a wrench-like tool. Black Rocks sat at a station, a glowing globe hovering before his eyes. "The oscillation is decreasing," Black Rocks reported. "Just a speck more," he urged. "I think you've done it, Core Brother."

Franklin exited the access port and stood to survey his handiwork. It was snub-nosed and torpedo-shaped, barely twenty feet in length and no more than a yard in diameter. Half of the little vessel was engine. "She's gonna be cramped."

Black Rocks chittered. "Maybe for a human," he replied. "Plenty of room for a Rynn."

"Assuming we can find a Rynn brave enough to try flying it," Franklin replied.

Black Rocks chittered again. "Getting someone to fly it will be the easy part," he said. "There isn't a shuttle pilot who doesn't want to be the first." His crest waggled. "It's picking someone without starting a riot that will be the hard part." Black Rocks chittered. "Rynn may not be as brave as humans, but we do like to fly. The faster the better."

"She could fall apart the moment she hits the atmosphere," Franklin cautioned.

"Unlikely, Core Brother," Red Clouds Paint the Sky replied. "Your calculations are sound. The construction is solid." He gave his human core brother a proud smile. "If she does fall apart, it will be because the pilot decided to exceed the tolerances." He looked at the craft. "It will be the fastest atmosphere ship ever built," he said. "And you built it."

"We got launch, we got launch," sang Night Storm "High Flyer 1," she called.

"We got it," came a pilot's voice. "Launch neutralized," the pilot said a moment later. "This is ridiculous," the pilot complained. "One warhead would be enough to devastate a city, and they've launched fifty in the last hour."

"Cut the chatter, High Flyer 1," the commander barked. "Prescott does not care how much damage he causes. He just wants to win," he said. "Remember that."

"It's hard to forget," replied the pilot from High Flyer 1, "when that offal-eating idiot keeps reminding me." The pilot growled. "High Flyer 1, out."

Night Storm turned in her seat. "Gentle Snowfall is correct," she said. "This is ridiculous. A Rynn would not be so … sloppy." Her crest curled. "So *incompetent*," she said under her breath.

The commander vented a grim chuckle. "Probably not," he agreed. "Still, if my intel is correct, he can't have too many more left." He went back to his command chair and sat down to ponder. "Since they can't blow us up, at least not while we have High Flyer …"

"Can they attack High Flyer?" the familiar and raspy voice of Jeremy Blunt asked. "They must know by now that we are using Rynn shuttles to strike at the missiles."

"Unlikely," the commander replied. "Not unless they have stealth aircraft." The commander frowned. "Still, we probably should consider the possibility." He pursed his lips. "For all that they're led by an idiot, Texas does have a powerful technological research arm."

"What are you thinking, Grandfather?" Kasumi asked respectfully.

"I'm thinking that sooner or later, someone is going to start shooting at High Flyer and launching a strike simultaneously," Jeremy replied. "I'm somewhat surprised they haven't tried that yet."

"Which may be evidence they don't have stealth aircraft," the commander returned.

"I'll remind you that you yourself noted they have the skill power to accomplish it," Jeremy replied.

"Someone get in touch with Daniels," the commander ordered.

"She's beautiful," the Rynn test pilot gushed. "How fast did you say she's expected to go?"

"At least twenty-five times the speed of sound," Franklin replied. "Not that I expect you to get anywhere near that, Frozen River," he said as he made a number of adjustments to a panel. "This is just the first flight," he cautioned. "Take her out, enter the atmosphere, fly around a bit, and then return."

"Is your core brother always this cautious?" Frozen River asked Black Rocks.

"When it comes to the safety of others, yes, he is," Black Rocks replied. "If he could, he'd fly it himself." He chittered in amusement. "Too bad for him, the pilot module is designed for a Rynn."

"If I had known that before I started ..." growled Franklin. He sighed. "Just keep it below Mach 20."

"Multiple contacts," Night Storm sang out. "Spirits protect us—it looks like hundreds of aircraft." The Rynn started chirping into her Torque. "Spirits," she chittered nervously. "Analysis indicates nearly six hundred fighter jets."

"That can't be right," the commander replied. "The U.S. had at most 2,500 fighter jets." He looked at his view screen. "There were three hundred in California. Texas couldn't have much more than that," he said. "The CSA must have transferred its entire air fleet," he exclaimed. "Order Scramble."

"Scramble. Scramble," Night Storm sang out in calmly

professional tones. "All fighters and interceptors prepare for immediate takeoff."

"This is Commander Eisenstadt," the commander broke in. "ROE is as follows: all aircraft must be destroyed. If a pilot ejects, leave him alone, but the aircraft must be destroyed. That is all."

"Silver Streak entering Earth atmosphere," Red Clouds Paint the Sky reported. "Telemetry looks good," he recited calmly. "Engines … on."

"Look at her go!" Black Rocks said from another station. "Frozen River, report. Frozen River, report," he repeated when there was no response.

"Spirits sing!" came the breathless and excited voice of the test pilot. "I swear I broke the light barrier for a moment," laughed the Rynn pilot. "Instrumentation is nominal," he started reporting in more controlled tones. "Everything is within expected parameters. Air speed … spirits … air speed is Mach 17 already," he reported. "Permission to take it to Mach 20."

"Granted," Franklin replied.

"Thank you, control," Frozen River replied. "Mach 18, 19 … 20," he reported. "I am holding at 20." The Rynn test pilot chittered. "Not even a … Spirits!"

"Frozen River?" called Black Rocks. "Frozen River, report."

"I just passed ten stealth-enabled craft," the test pilot reported. "Sending imagery."

"Put it on screen," Franklin ordered. "Oh shit," he exclaimed. "Get Knox Gulch on the horn now!" he barked. "Captain Kasumi, come in please."

"We're kind of busy down here, Franklin," Kasumi chirped.

"You're gonna be dead if you're not careful." He tapped a control. "You got some high-flying bombers heading your way."

"What?" exclaimed Kasumi. "There's nothing on sensors."

"Nothing on ours either," said Franklin. "This was seen by a Mark I eyeball."

"You have a bird up there?" came Commander Eisenstadt's voice.

"Yes, sir," Franklin replied.

"Launch, we have launch," sang Night Storm. "High Flyer 1, we have launch," she reported. "High Flyer 2, we have launch."

"High Flyer 1 intercepting," reported a Rynn voice.

"High Flyer 2 intercepting," reported the pilot of the second shuttle a moment later.

"Do we have anything to go after the bombers?" Eisenstadt demanded. "Anything at all?" Night Storm turned in her chair and shook her head. "Fuck!"

Franklin listened in growing horror as the severity of the situation became clearer and clearer. "They'll be slaughtered," he all but screamed. "There's nothing that can …" Franklin broke off. "Franklin to Frozen River."

"I hear you, Franklin," the test pilot replied.

"Frozen River …" Franklin licked dry lips. "Streak can hit Mach 30," he said. "She'll kick up one hell of a bow wave."

The pilot was quiet for a long time. "How close do I have to get?" the pilot asked finally.

"Black Rocks?" Franklin asked quietly.

"There's no guarantee the ship will hold together," the Rynn tech said quietly.

"How close?" the test pilot repeated.

Black Rocks' crest flattened to his skull. "You need to be within thirty pedin," he said in a bleak voice.

"Thank you, control," the test pilot replied. "Remember me," Frozen River said.

"Your name will never die," Black Rocks replied. He, Red Clouds Paint the Sky, and Franklin all covered their eyes.

"Silver Streak is turning," came the pilot's voice. "Mach 23, 25 … 27." The pilot's voice started to vibrate. "She's starting to shake," the pilot said. "Mach 29. Vibration holding steady. Mach 30," the pilot sang in triumph. "She's holding." The pilot was quiet, then, "Enemy squadron in sight. They are maintaining formation," he chirped. "Mach 32. Contact in 10 … 9 … 8 … 7 … 6 … 5 … 4 … 3 … 2 … Contac …"

"Fireball at 50,000 feet altitude, ten miles south," sang Night Storm. She chirped to her Torque. "It was the bombers," she said. "Something … something just ripped them apart."

Up in the Rynn mother craft, Franklin, Black Rocks, and Red Clouds Paint the Sky huddled together trying to give each other some comfort. After a while, Black Rocks raised his head and started to sing. It was a traditional Rynn funeral song. Like humans, Rynn found comfort in song. The song evoked the melancholy of loss and yet somehow seemed to convey a sense of pride—pride that somehow they themselves were worthy because they could count the deceased as a friend.

Franklin cried as the song swept over him, and then his expression firmed. "We have to find him," he said quietly. "We have to bring him home."

Black Rocks and Red Clouds Paint the Sky looked at each other, and their crests rose. "You are right, Core Brother," Black Rocks said. He chirped, and a glowing orb appeared in front of him. A moment later, a similar orb appeared in front of both Red Clouds Paint the Sky and Franklin. Minute after long minute passed, and then suddenly Black Rocks' crest rose fully. "Found him!"

"Spirits, he's in orbit!" Red Clouds Paint the Sky said a moment later. "Barely."

Even though the two remaining shuttles were down for maintenance, that didn't mean they could not function. They wouldn't be able to fight, and their speed was going to be limited, but they could fly. When the trio explained why they needed the shuttle, two maintenance techs volunteered to go along to make sure the shuttle stayed operational. Soon—though to the trio, it seemed an interminable wait—the shuttle was heading out toward the tumbling speedster.

"There she is," Franklin said. "Damn, tractor is offline."

"Give me a moment," one tech said. He crawled into an access hatch. "Try now," he said after a minute or so.

"Targeting," Franklin said. "Got it," he added triumphantly.

"Slowly," said the other tech. "That ship looks beat up." He looked curiously at the trio, but they were too intent on getting the little craft to safety to respond. Slowly, they used the tractor to bring the speedster closer and closer to the shuttle.

"Opening access port," one tech said. "Switching to docking tractor," he chirped to his Torque, and the little ship was pulled into the docking bay. Franklin, Red Clouds Paint the Sky, and Black Rocks watched anxiously as it was gently lowered onto the docking bay floor.

The ship was dented and blackened, and parts of the rear assembly seemed to have melted, but it was mostly intact. The access port to the pilot was so deformed that it could not be opened, but one tech ran over with a molecular torch—a device that could break the molecular bonds—and sliced through the hatchway. They pulled away the hatch to reveal the still and bruised body of Frozen River. A tech leaned over, and there was a faint hiss as he administered a dose of Omiset.

Franklin leaned in and lifted the pilot's body out of the craft. Without letting go, he carried the limp body from the shuttle bay into the small sick bay. He placed the pilot's body on a round medical kip. "You were too fucking brave for your own good," he said to the still body. He turned away. There was a moan, and Franklin turned back.

"Spirits," Frozen River said in a weak voice. He chittered tiredly. "You need to work on the inertial compensators," the Rynn pilot croaked.

"I'll do that," Franklin replied. "Core Brother."

The commander clenched his fist as the two air forces met. The forces were virtually even, as the larger Texas fleet was offset by Rynn technology. Around him, he could hear the chirps and mutters of the Rynn and humans coordinating the defense. He forced himself to sit back in his command chair and appear calm.

"Commander, ground forces are coming over the New Mexico border," one voice rang out.

Kasumi Blunt, captain of the *Seeker* and leader of the Rynn's Earth colony, looked closely at the glowing orb that floated just in front of her. "When your opponent moves, you have already moved," she chirped. "Morning Mist?"

"As the humans say, the board is green," replied the voice of Kasumi's core sister. "All personnel are in place."

Kasumi nodded. "Mel?"

"The board is green," Mel Blunt replied over the Torque. "Looks like approximately fifty M1s, a dozen towed Howitzers, and a couple dozen troop transports."

"There should be half dozen or so Apaches," Kasumi said in a concerned voice.

"Nothing ... oh, there they are," Morning Mist said triumphantly. "They're hugging the ground," she said. "Sending coordinates."

"Operation Feather Duster is go," ordered Kasumi. "Go. Go. Go."

Cool Evening Breeze chittered in anticipation. "Wakey, wakey, Fuzzy Butt," the little Rynn geologist said to her muscular human companion.

"That's Sergeant Fuzzy Butt to you, Corporal Feather Head," said Hendriks. He and the Rynn exchanged grins. "Ready to go to work, partner?"

"Ready when you are, partner," Cool Evening Breeze replied. "Crystal, you ready?"

"You know this is a stupid idea, don't you?" Crystal Chandler said over the Torque. "Don't worry, Dierdre and I will get the whole thing on tape," she said. "But if either of you gets yourself killed, I will never forgive you."

"We love you too," Cool Evening Breeze replied.

The First Texas Heavy Infantry "Alamo" forces traveled along Highway 40. They had crossed over the Texas-Arizona border an hour earlier and had not yet run into any resistance. Leading the forces in his restructured Humvee was Colonel Travis Prescott, grandson to the current president of the Greater Texas Republic and designated heir to the presidency once the country was reunited—under his grandfather's rule, of course.

Right now, his immediate goal was to get to the California border. Once the Texas Air Force destroyed California's military, he would race up 5 with Sacramento as his target. "Once Sacramento falls, the WSA falls," his grandfather had predicted.

His secondary goal was to capture as much alien technology as he could and destroy what he could not.

"Sir, there is someone standing in the road," his driver said, breaking into the colonel's thoughts. Colonel Prescott looked. Sure enough, there were two figures standing in the road: one large, one tiny.

"Signal the convoy to halt," the colonel ordered. "And bring the Apaches forward."

The Humvee stopped just yards from the two figures. "Sir," his driver said in a hushed voice. "I think that's one of those bird people."

The colonel nodded in agreement and got out of the Humvee. He unholstered his sidearm and walked toward the two figures. "You are prisoners of war," he said. "Any resistance will be met with lethal force."

The alien chittered in amusement. "Am I supposed to be impressed, Fuzzy Butt?" she asked the big man standing next to her.

"I think you're supposed to be frightened," the big man replied. "Big bad Texan, you know."

"Don't worry, I'll protect you," the little alien chittered. She looked up when a number of helicopters flew over the stopped convoy and hovered overhead. "Isn't that a bit much?" she complained to the colonel.

"You don't seem to understand the gravity of the situation," the colonel said in annoyed tones. "You are my prisoner." He grimaced angrily when both the human and the Rynn laughed. "Oh, fuck it." He raised the gun and aimed it at the big human. He pulled the trigger. There was the usual explosive crack. What was not usual was that the big man did not fall.

"Is that how Texans usually say hello?" the little alien chirped in annoyance. "It seems terribly unfriendly."

"Well, they are invaders," the big man said with a grin. "By definition, that makes them the bad guys."

"You Earth people," complained the little alien.

"Oh, you know you love us," the big man said.

"Just some of you," countered the little alien. She chittered. "Do you think we've wasted enough time?" There was a flash and the hovering helicopters suddenly started to wobble and then veered off. "That seems like a yes."

"Seems like," agreed the big man. He looked at the colonel and then unholstered his own weapon and pointed it. "What was that you said? Oh yeah. You are prisoners of war. Any resistance will be met with lethal force." He smiled. It was not a friendly smile. "To be perfectly honest, I kind of hope you resist."

"This is absurd," the colonel retorted. "Do you honestly believe I am going to surrender my entire regiment to two maniacs?"

"Why yes. Yes we do," chirped Cool Evening Breeze. She chirped again, but there was no translation. Instead, the ground seemed to erupt as a hundred camouflaged soldiers stood up on both sides of the road—soldiers who did not fall when the Texans opened fire. The Texans fired until they ran out of ammunition, and not a single defender fell. Some of the Texas military even tried to use their now empty rifles as clubs, but they only bounced off an unseen barrier surrounding the defenders.

Sergeant Hendriks walked over to the open-mouthed Colonel

Prescott and placed his gun against the colonel's temple. "Surrender or die," he said conversationally. "I really don't care one way or the other. But make no mistake: I will pull the trigger if you do not."

Colonel Prescott looked on as soldier after soldier was subdued by a seemingly invulnerable defender. He slowly raised his hands in surrender.

The air battle over Sacramento was entering its second hour. The missile barrage had ended, and all that remained was the dogfighting fighter jets. Even with Rynn technology, damage was heavy on the WSA forces. Rynn defensive shields could protect against smaller-caliber ordnance but could and did collapse under the continuous impact of the high-caliber, high-velocity rounds used by fighter aircraft.

"If this keeps up much longer, we're going to lose," Eisenstadt grumbled.

"David?" Kasumi chirped.

"We've lost almost half of our fighter squadron," the commander explained. "Even if we win this battle, we won't have enough assets to stave off another incursion." He rubbed his temples wearily. "Intel suggests Prescott has at least another hundred fighters in reserve. If only we had some surface-to-air support." He shook himself. "Any word from Feather Duster?"

"Nothing yet," replied a communication specialist—a human—from his station. "That EMP pulse they shot off to disable the Apaches still hasn't cleared up."

"Too bad we couldn't use it against the fighters," Kasumi said regretfully. "But it would have knocked out our own jets as well." She flicked her crest. "Keep trying to reach them."

"Yes ma'am," the tech replied and returned his attention to his station.

"Crystal to Feather Duster. Crystal to Feather Duster." Crystal Chandler slammed her fist on the console. "Dammit, if you two have snuck off for a little after-battle nookie, I swear I'm gonna skin the both of you." She glared at the snickering Dierdre McIntosh. "It isn't funny."

"Them sneaking off, no," agreed Dierdre. "You sounding like a pissed-off housewife, yeah." She raised her hands in surrender. "Look, the satellite images show that the fighting is over," she said soothingly. "And apparently we won."

"It'll take another minute or so before the ionization blocking communication fades enough to get through," a Rynn tech said. "Maybe less," he said hurriedly at the glare from Crystal.

Crystal drummed impatiently on the workstation as she waited. "Still mad at Breeze?" Dierdre asked in amused tones.

"She lied to me," grumbled Crystal. "She made me think … grrr."

Dierdre laughed. "She didn't exactly lie. She just stretched the truth a little." She placed a hand on her friend's shoulder. "She did tell you that most Rynn men found Hendriks' … um … *assets* intimidating." She giggled at Crystal's blush. "Is he really as big as she claims?" she asked in honest curiosity.

"Bigger," grumbled Crystal. "Oh, who am I kidding?" she complained to the air. "What I really hate is that I'm always worrying about them."

"They do not fight as much since you joined their core," the Rynn technician said in approving tones. "You give them a strong center." He turned around. "Forgive me if I intrude, but without you, they are not a true core." He turned back to his station. "I think the ionization levels should have dropped sufficiently."

Crystal looked at the technician for a moment, then moistened her lips. "Breeze? Hendriks?"

"Hey, Crystal," Cool Evening Breeze replied. "Fuzzy Butt sends his love."

"Yeah, well, you tell Fuzzy Butt …" She paused. "I never asked, but if he's Fuzzy Butt, and you're Feather Head …"

"Or Lickin' Chicken," Cool Evening Breeze retorted with a chittering laugh. "Don't laugh, but we sort of think of you as … Momma."

"Oh," Crystal said quietly. She shook herself. "Come home."

"Right away, Momma," Cool Evening Breeze replied.

"We got more incoming," Morning Mist chirped.

"Now what?" Eisenstadt demanded.

"It looks like another fighter squadron," Morning Mist replied. "I count sixty—repeat, six zero—fighters."

"Oh fuck," Eisenstadt snarled. "Prescott sent his reserves." He shook his head. "ETA?"

"Ten minutes," Morning Mist replied. "Something funny about this squadron, though," she continued.

"Funny?"

"The track is wrong," Morning Mist replied. "Unless they went north a couple hundred miles before heading west," she said. "I mean, it's possible, but it doesn't make sense." She paused. "Wait, I'm getting a transmission."

"On speaker," commanded Eisenstadt.

"… peat, this is Gotham Squadron to WSA AirCom. Please reply," came the voice.

"Gotham Squadron?" the commander said in confusion. "This is Commander Eisenstadt, WSA Defense Force."

"Fan-fucking-tastic," replied the voice. "This is Captain Bloom of Empire. The oligarch sends her love." The voice chuckled. "Now, I bet your people are real tired right now, so how about letting us clean up the rest of this mess for you?" The voice chuckled again. "It's gonna take another ten minutes or so to get there, so why don't you give the oligarch a call? Just to confirm."

"Morning Mist, see if you can get the oligarch," Kasumi shouted. Morning Mist chirped quietly to her Torque.

"Well hello, darlings!" boomed a new voice over the communication system. "I just can't wait to meet our guests from outer space." The woman's voice laughed heartily. "I'm sure Captain Bloom already made his offer, but the cavalry has arrived!"

"Trap?" asked Kasumi.

"Doubtful," Jeremy replied from his seat in the corner of the command post. "I recognize her voice."

"Morning Mist, send the recall order," Eisenstadt said. "And Madame Oligarch, you have our thanks."

"Call me Ophelia, darling," the woman replied. "All my friends do."

22

The Oligarch

The Rynn shuttle landed gently next to the shuttle hangar in the colony. A Rynn/human honor guard marched smartly toward the shuttle and formed two rows. For once, both Cool Evening Breeze and Sergeant Hendriks maintained a professional demeanor. Crystal Chandler and Dierdre McIntosh took up their station in order to record and comment on the event.

David Eisenstadt, Kasumi Blunt, Mel Blunt, Morning Mist, and Jeremy Blunt waited at the end of the double column.

The shuttle door opened, and a gangway lowered quietly. After a minute, two men strode down the gangway. They looked at the honor guard and the surroundings. One turned and nodded. A woman strolled down the gangway.

She was big. She was the color of milk chocolate, and her round face was framed by a mass of black curls. Each finger had at least one ring. Her ears held hoops and studs. Her gold necklace had an emerald the size of a chicken egg. She was obviously wealthy and powerful, but mostly she was *big*.

"Darlings!" she exclaimed in a voice that was as big as the woman. "Don't you dare salute," she admonished. She giggled, and it was a surprisingly delicate sound. "But you can give me a hug." She knelt in front of Morning Mist. "Especially you, darling." She spread her arms. "Give Big Momma a hug." Morning Mist chittered in delight as the big woman hugged her. She repeated the embrace with all the assembled greeters.

"Well, well, if it isn't Jeremy Blunt," the oligarch cooed.

"Hello, Ophelia," Jeremy replied. "I'm surprised you remember me."

"Of course I remember you." She linked her arm through Jeremy's. "You were my first big interview."

Dierdre turned to Crystal. "Lord Jesus, the oligarch is Ophelia Winslow?" Crystal nodded slowly.

"Gramps, you did not tell me you knew Ms. Winslow," Mel said accusingly.

"Call me Ophelia," the oligarch said. "Gramps?" She leaned closer. "I think I see a little bit of Jeremy in you," she said. "I interviewed Jeremy after he was released from prison," she said. "It was, after all, the crime of the century." She fanned herself. "Oh my, the screaming. The recriminations. The tears. And that was just from the chief of police." She laughed. "Jeremy was, understandably, a little reticent to discuss the matter."

"I did the interview after she, um, convinced the police chief—another Coolidge, by the way—to resign," Jeremy replied. "Ophelia, let me formally introduce everyone." He waved a hand. "My granddaughter, Melanie."

"Call me Mel," Mel said.

"My granddaughter, Kasumi." Jeremy smiled.

"Germy honors me greatly," Kasumi said to the oligarch's questioning look. "He calls me his granddaughter of his heart, and Mel is his granddaughter of his soul." She covered her eyes briefly. "I call him Teacher." The oligarch nodded.

"And Mel and Kasumi's core sister, Morning Mist," continued Jeremy.

"Core sister?" the oligarch asked.

"Wife and partner," Jeremy explained.

"Oh poo, and here I was hoping you were single," the oligarch pouted. "Any more at home like you?" she asked. Morning Mist chittered in delight.

"Our military commander, David Eisenstadt, and core brother to Mel, Kasumi, and Morning Mist," Jeremy said. "Don't pretend, David. Everyone knows."

"My, how wonderful!" the oligarch gushed. "I am so glad I decided to send my people to help you."

"So are we, Oligarch," Commander Eisenstadt replied. "President Newgate sends his thanks as well. He is currently visiting some of the hospitalized. He hopes you'll understand."

"People over politics?" the oligarch asked. "How refreshing."

"Germy lectured him about responsibility." Kasumi gave her adoptive grandfather a proud Rynn smile. She walked over to the oligarch and took her free hand. She looked up at the big woman. "Why did you send aid?"

"It was the right thing to do," the oligarch replied quietly.

"The First Teacher spoke of three blessings: to give water to the thirsty, to feed the hungry, and to give shelter to the naked—and to do so because it is right thing to do and for no other reason." Kasumi released the oligarch's hand and covered her eyes. "Germy says doing the right thing, no matter how hard, is the true definition of honor," she said. "May the spirits bless you for all eternity."

Darren Newgate, president of the WSA, hurried from his helicopter toward the now completed command building. The building was circular, as was typical of Rynn structures, and was referred to as the "birds' nest" until someone remembered that the Chinese already had a structure by that name. After some debate, the command building became simply referred to as the center.

"I might as well just move the capital here," he grumbled as he jogged toward the entrance. "I'm here almost as much as Sacramento." It was a half-hearted complaint, as the president actually enjoyed his time among the Rynn. Over the past year, the population of the colony had soared to over five hundred. While the majority of the residents were human, at any time there could be as many as fifty Rynn inside the compound. Considering there were only seventy Rynn altogether on the *Seeker*, it was remarkable that so many Rynn were allowed to travel downside.

He entered the center and was immediately flanked by two familiar faces. "Well, if it isn't everyone's favorite marines," he said cheerfully. "Hello, Cool Evening Breeze, Hendriks," he said in greeting. "Where's your third?"

Cool Evening Breeze pointed upwards with a long finger. "Crystal is getting a checkup," she chirped.

"Is something wrong?" President Newgate asked in concern.

"Only if you consider being pregnant as something wrong," chittered Cool Evening Breeze. "Our med techs are almost as excited as Crystal," she explained. "This is the first human pregnancy they've seen, and they're curious as hell."

"Wouldn't it be better if she had some Earth doctors examining her?" President Newgate asked.

"Oh, she has those too," Hendriks replied. "Three of them."

"Sounds like she's going to be in the best of hands," President Newgate replied. "How's it going with the oligarch?"

Hendriks snickered as Cool Evening Breeze chittered. "She's got about a dozen Rynn waiting on her hand and foot," Hendriks replied.

"And another dozen humans competing with the Rynn for her attention," Cool Evening Breeze added. "She's almost as popular as Teacher Jeremy," she said. "She is one of the most competent people, Rynn or human, that we've ever met."

President Newgate chuckled. "I doubt anyone will argue with that," he said. They stopped in front of a door, and Cool Evening Breeze stepped forward to open it. "As always, a pleasure," he said.

"By the way, Mr. President," Cool Evening Breeze said. President Newgate paused. "We support you because you are also very competent." President Newgate smiled slightly and then briefly covered his eyes. He walked through the door.

"Darren, darling!" boomed the oligarch. "We were just talking about you."

"Good afternoon, Ophelia," President Newgate replied. "Good afternoon, Kasumi, Mel, Morning Mist," he said. He bowed to the older man sitting on a couch near a window. "Mr. Blunt." And then he shook hands with the graying military man. "David."

The oligarch looked at one of the hovering Rynn stationed around the room. "Get President Newgate his afternoon coffee," she directed. "And someone make sure we have some snacks," she added. "I fear it's going to be a long afternoon."

"Problems?" President Newgate asked. "Or rather, new problems?"

"Depends on your point of view, I suppose," Kasumi chirped. "Our location has gotten out," she said. "We're starting to see more and more people at the boundary. So far, most seem willing to just get a look at a Rynn." Her crest flicked. "Most."

"Ah," President Newgate grunted. "Since no one seems concerned, I gather it hasn't progressed much beyond name-calling?"

"Not as yet," Kasumi confirmed. "Ophelia has agreed to take on doing our public relations."

"Crystal and Dierdre have been doing a good job," the oligarch said firmly. "But I do have a few additional resources at my disposal." She looked down at her tablet. "Next on the agenda: Prescott."

"We can't let his attack go unanswered," Kasumi said firmly. "David wants to launch a counterattack, but that feels wrong."

"Has anyone spoken to or even contacted what remains of the federal forces?" President Newgate asked.

"I have," David Eistenstadt replied. "They are maintaining a 'wait and see' approach. Basically, they are devoting their efforts to keeping external concerns at bay, while …" He grimaced. "While we settle our domestic issues."

"Domestic issues," snorted President Newgate.

"You can't blame them, Darren," Mel responded. "They're going to have to work with whomever wins."

"Which is why I keep pushing for a counterattack," the commander growled. "The sooner we break the Greater Texas Republic, the sooner we can focus on putting the country back together."

"No one is disagreeing, David," Jeremy commented. "In fact, I agree with you that some retaliation in force would be recommended." He raised his hand to forestall any comments. "But not against Texas," he said. "Not yet, anyway."

He walked over to the wall map of the United States—a map that had been modified to show the current alliances. "We, meaning the WSA and Empire, are now in control of 50 percent of the country. Texas has about 25 percent, and the loose alliance of the Great Lakes Unity has 10 percent." He took a marker and circled a section that encompassed what once was called the Old South and was now referred to under a different name. "The rest is under the control of the CSA"

"As bad as Greater Texas is, the CSA is worse," Mel said.

"If we break the CSA, then Texas is isolated," Jeremy said. "And if that's not incentive enough, we are getting reports that they're starting to reintroduce slavery."

"You're joking," President Newgate exclaimed in shock.

"One guess who they've decided would make good slaves," growled the oligarch. "Darren, regardless of what you will do, I will not stand for this."

"The CSA has money, weapons, and a well-trained military," President Newgate said in serious tones.

"I have more money," the oligarch replied.

"Germy?" Kasumi said. "Do humans truly think they can own other humans?"

Mel chuckled sourly. "We keep trying to tell you, Core Sister. Humans are scum." She looked at her grandfather. "Right, Gramps?"

Jeremy sighed. "Unfortunately, humans have often considered other humans as nothing more than property." He walked over to a bookshelf and pulled out a thick volume. "The Bible," he said and handed it to Kasumi. "The source of most of the comfort and most of the pain for Western civilization." He barked a laugh. "They once asked Mahatma Ghandi, a great teacher, what he thought of Western civilization." He sighed again. "Do you know what he said?"

"How would I know that, Germy?" Kasumi asked.

"Yeah, but his answer will give you some insight into humans," Jeremy replied. "He said, when asked what he thought of Western civilization, that it would be a good idea."

Kasumi tilted her head and her crest flicked and folded several times before it fully flattened. "That ... that's horrible."

"You should have heard what he said about the followers of that book you're holding," Mel added. "The same people who are running the CSA."

"The *C* stands for Christian," Jeremy supplied in an aside to Kasumi.

"I'm a Christian too, Jeremy," the oligarch said tartly.

"Don't get Gramps started, Ophelia." Mel looked hard at the big woman. "And don't even try to apologize for them," she said. "They are not misguided. They are not misinformed, mistaken, they are not 'mis' anything." She growled. "They are what they are."

"Oligarch," Kasumi said sharply. She lifted the heavy book she had been handed. "We have come to admire and respect you, but if this contains what I fear it contains, then we may have to reconsider what help we may give you."

"You can't seriously expect me to accept that millions of people will be treated as animals because of how someone interprets the word of God?" the oligarch said in shock.

"No one said that we will allow this ... slavery to continue," Kasumi disagreed. "Rynn do not and never have had Rynn owning Rynn. Even Sun-Warmed Boulder, may the spirits shun him, would have been appalled." Her crest rose fully. "But any philosophy that would even consider it, is ..." Kasumi's crest, already fully extended, seemed to rise even more. "I do not have the words to express my disgust." She looked at the oligarch coldly and then walked out of the room.

"Lord Jesus," the oligarch whispered.

The oligarch sat in the room provided for her and nursed a drink. It was her third drink, and it did not seem to be helping. She sighed. In the time since Captain Kasumi had left their meeting, every single alien had suddenly found an excuse not to interact with her in any way. Oh, they were polite and would respond to requests, but even finding a Rynn to respond to requests was getting more and more difficult.

The oligarch replayed the event in her head for what seemed liked the hundredth time, and she still wasn't sure how she had offended the alien. She looked up at a knock. "Yes?"

"It's Dierdre McIntosh," came the voice through the door. "I need to speak to you."

"Please," the oligarch said anxiously. She downed the remains of her drink and walked over and opened the door. "Jesus, I'm glad to see you," she began.

"Don't be," Dierdre interrupted. "Right now, I am not your friend."

"Dierdre?" the oligarch replied in shock.

"Why couldn't you have just pissed on the floor?" growled Dierdre. "They might have forgiven you for that." She shook her head. "But no, you had to shove your big fat foot into your mouth all the way to the knee." She looked at the big woman angrily. "I just spent the last three hours trying to explain away your stupidity, and the best I can say is that the technological transfer will go through."

"What did I do?" pleaded the oligarch. "I still don't understand what I did."

"'I'm a Christian too,'" snapped Dierdre. "That's what you said, wasn't it?" The oligarch nodded. "Too? Too?" She jabbed the big woman with a finger in punctuation. "Too?"

"But," protested the oligarch. "You're a Christian."

"I. Am. Not. A. Christian," Dierdre bit out. "I follow the teachings of Jesus Christ. But I will not call myself a Christian. That name has been defiled. Forever."

The princess approached the Temple of Light. Somehow the temple seemed subdued, and there was a feeling of emptiness. She looked around for the old monk, but she was nowhere to be found. The princess sat down on the steps and wept.

"Tears?" came a familiar voice.

The princess looked up to see the old monk looking down at her. "Oh, Grandmother, I don't know what to do," she cried. The old monk sat down next to the princess. "My friend has wronged another," she said. "And I was ..." She swallowed in a dry throat. "I was silent."

"And why were you silent?" asked the monk.

"Because she was my friend," whispered the princess in response. "And now, she is not." She turned to the old monk. "I want my friend back, but I can't until she undoes what she has done—but even if she does, will she ever be my friend again?"

"A true quandary," agreed the old monk. "Trust once lost can only be regained through great effort," she smiled sadly. "And with great pain," she said. "And only you can decide if the effort and the pain is worth it." The old monk stood. "And only she can decide if she will make the effort."

The princess nodded. "Yes, Grandmother," she replied.

Kasumi opened her eyes. "Spirits," she whispered. She carefully untangled herself from the mass of bodies that shared her kip. She got up and quietly started to dress.

"You had another dream, didn't you?" came Mel's sleepy voice.

"Yes, Core Sister," Kasumi replied quietly.

"And now you are going to try to patch things up with Ophelia," Mel continued.

"Yes, Core Sister," Kasumi replied.

"Trust is hard to restore once it is lost," Mel said. "But it is worth the effort."

Kasumi's crest flattened at Mel's words. "Yes, Core Sister," she said in a shaky voice.

Kasumi opened the door of her quarters and headed toward the room the oligarch had been given, only to see the oligarch walking slowly toward her. *Spirits, first my core sister and now this,* she thought. "Oligarch?" she said in cautious greeting.

The oligarch was silent for a long moment, and then she reached into her blouse and pulled out a necklace. It was a gold crucifix on a gold chain. She removed the necklace and held it in her hand. "There were times, many times, in my life when the only thing that kept me going was my faith," she said quietly. "My life has turned out so well that I truly believed I was singled out by God." She shook her head. "When what I was, was arrogant."

Kasumi's crest lowered until it was almost flat against her scalp. "I was raised in privilege," Kasumi said. "I thought that my being named the youngest captain in my father's fleet was due to my being better than anyone. That I truly earned my position." Her crest rose slightly as she shook her head. "When what I was, was arrogant."

"You shame me, Kasumi," the oligarch replied.

"You shame me, Ophelia," Kasumi responded. "I was given the opportunity to earn what I was given. I was given a chance to prove myself. A chance I denied you. I am ashamed."

The oligarch extended the hand holding the crucifix. "No, you were right," she said. "The shame is mine." She took one of Kasumi's hands and dropped the crucifix into it, then closed Kasumi's hand over it. "If it is at all possible, I would like the opportunity to start over," she said. "I beg of you—let me prove myself."

Kasumi nodded silently.

23

Brothers in Arms

"What have you built this time, Core Brother?" Red Clouds Paint the Sky asked Joseph Franklin. He looked at the triangular craft sitting in a docking cradle in the *Seeker*'s hold. The craft was slightly more than thirty feet in length and slightly more than half that at the tips of its forward-slung stubby wings. A semitransparent dome that rose just above the plane of the craft's upper body dominated the central part of the craft. There were two ominous-looking cylinders, one on each side, nestled under the wings.

"It looks fast," Frozen River commented. "Like a metal Swift Strike. A flying predator on Nest known for its speed." He ran a hand over one wing. "And just as deadly." He looked at Franklin. "How fast?"

Franklin shrugged. "Mach 30, Mach 35. Somewhere in there." He grinned. "Who wants to find out for sure?" He laughed when his three core brothers all raised their hands. He walked over to the low dome and tapped it. It irised open. "Frozen River, you take the pilot's seat. Black Rocks, you have sensors and communications. Red Clouds, you have diagnostics." He patted the rearmost seat. "And I have weapons."

"Weapons, Core Brother?" Black Rocks asked.

"EMP, RGG, and my personal favorite, the quantum disrupter."

Franklin patted the console. "Brothers, I believe Rynn and humans are destined to cross the cosmos together, and the only thing that stands in the way of that destiny is hatred and ignorance. The CSA is the home of hatred and ignorance." He took a breath. "I intend to fly this ship, the *Silver Shrike*, into the heart of the CSA and destroy their ability to wage war. Are you with me?"

His three core brothers briefly covered their eyes. "Spirits," whispered Black Rocks. "When our core brother speaks, I can believe the spirits listen." His crest rose fully. "Lead on, Core Brother."

Colonel Thaddeus Hooker gazed contentedly out across the airfield at Langley. Row after row of shining F-22s filled the field. "Greatest fighting wing on the planet," he thought smugly. Colonel Hooker turned to his situation board. All green and clean. The smile was wiped off his face, however, when the windows of the observation tower exploded. He instinctively covered his face with his arms, and then cautiously lowered them when the expected hailstorm of shattered glass did not come.

"What the …?" the colonel exclaimed. A quick glance showed that the tower room was almost completely devoid of glass but was littered with papers and other lightweight objects.

"Some kind of low-pressure phenomenon, colonel," shouted one of the air controllers. "I think."

"What do you mean, 'you think'?" demanded the colonel.

"Sir, the only thing I know of that could do something like this would be a cyclone," the controller replied. He pointed out the window. "And if it were a cyclone or something like one, it should be raining."

"Sir!" shouted another controller. "We have a bogey! It just appeared." He swallowed. "Sir, it's … it's right overhead."

Colonel Hooker ran to the window and looked out. There, hovering no more than one hundred feet above the field, was a silver arrowhead-shaped object. It was tilted slightly forward and seemed to be looking balefully at the control tower. "Sound scramble!" the colonel ordered. In moments, Klaxons filled the air, and pilots and crew rushed toward the jets. The hovering arrowhead seemed to ignore the commotion below.

"What is it waiting for?" the colonel growled under his breath. The apparent answer came when the first of the jets moved into position. There was a sudden flash of reddish light, and the tail section of the F-22 simply vanished.

High above the airfield, two other craft waited. In one craft, two figures, one human and one Rynn, stared into a glowing ball that hovered in front of them. The human barked a laugh. "Looks like the Fantastic Four have everything under control."

"Fantastic Four?" chirped the Rynn. "What is it with humans and nicknames, Fuzzy Butt?" asked Corporal Cool Evening Breeze.

"I wouldn't talk, Feather Head," Sergeant Hendriks replied. He stood. "Okay, ladies, Operation Moses is a go," he barked. "Let me repeat our objectives: one, we will land in and secure every plantation and workhouse we have identified as a potential slave center; two, we will ascertain if people are indeed being illegally detained; and three, if there is cause to believe that the Thirteenth Amendment has been violated, we will detain all personnel involved."

Cool Evening Breeze stood. "Rules of engagement are as follows: you are not authorized to respond with lethal force except if it appears that civilians' lives are in jeopardy and action is required to save them," she chirped. "Is that understood?" Her crest rose as the mixed group of humans and Rynn crisply responded in the affirmative.

Floor lights started flashing. "Ape Squad, stand by," barked Hendriks.

"Bird Squad, stand by," barked Cool Evening Breeze. She turned to Hendriks. "And you keep your head down, Fuzz Ball. You got a baby coming."

"You do the same, Feather Head," Hendriks replied. "Crystal will kill me if something happens to you."

"Shields up!" barked Cool Evening Breeze.

Lord Thomas Wincroft sat under the shade of a tall oak. "Another drink, boy," he ordered his house servant, a young black child barely into his teens. Wincroft's title was a recent acquisition and reflected both his wealth and the power he wielded as one of the CSA's leading political figures.

It was Wincroft who had declared that the Thirteenth Amendment did not apply to the CSA. It was Wincroft who had led the domestic forces that had "recovered the escaped slaves," and it was Wincroft who had executed those who resisted. Some personally.

He frowned when his butler walked over with his cell phone on a silver platter. The gray-haired white butler had a concerned look on his face. "What is it, Jeffries?"

"It's President Spencer, sir," the butler replied. "He seems … upset."

Lord Wincroft rolled his eyes and picked up the cell phone. "Wincroft here," he said in identification. His brows shot up. "What?" he exclaimed. "Impossible," he snapped. "Why isn't the air force …?" He trailed off. "The army?" He sat up. "Gotham is doing what?"

"Okay, darlings." The oligarch's image was broadcast to her entire force. "You all know how I feel about excessive violence, and despite my own anger over the evil that has transpired in the CSA, I will not tolerate any of you sinking to the level of the Beast." She briefly covered her eyes. "May the spirits watch over you."

"You heard the oligarch," barked Brigadier General Devon Li, a tall, fit Asian man in his fifties. His steel gray hair was cut close to his scalp. "ROE is as follows: lethal force is allowed for defensive purposes only. If you are fired upon, first response will be suppression fire. If resistance continues, then and only then will lethal response be considered."

He walked over to a map. "Our objective is simple. The CSA is to be broken. Operations will continue until all CSA military is neutralized and all military, political, and religious leaders that are on the target list are in custody." He turned to his audience, both present and virtual. "Questions?" He waited. "If there are no questions, you are dismissed to your assignments."

Colonel Thaddeus Hooker stared disbelievingly at the wreckage that littered the airfield. The silver arrowhead continued to hover above and seemed to only react if an F-22 attempted to take off, and then it acted immediately. A dozen jets had attempted to launch. "Where are my damned SAMs?" he growled. "We're sitting ducks down here."

"Working on it, sir," responded one tech.

"Well, work faster," growled the colonel.

24

Armageddon

"Ape Squad, forward," barked Sergeant Hendriks.

"Bird Squad, forward," echoed Corporal Cool Evening Breeze a second later.

The two squads jogged out of the landing bay of High Flyer 1. Bird Squad went toward the row of shacks that lined the fields, while Ape Squad headed for the main house. A dog barked, but otherwise the night was silent.

Bird Squad reached the first shack. "Spirits, the offal eaters bolted the doors from the outside," Cool Evening Breeze chirped angrily. "Williams, open that door."

"Yes, ma'am," the soldier replied and bent over the lock. He pulled what appeared to be a knife from his belt. The knife began to hum, and the blade cut through the lock like it was butter. He opened the door. "My god," he exclaimed in horror when he looked into the darkened shack.

There were bunk beds from floor to almost ceiling, five cots high. A quick count showed that there were eight bunks. Each narrow cot held a single occupant. Not one had a sheet or pillow or any comfort whatsoever. It became quickly apparent that each occupant, male and female, had two things in common. The first was that they were all chained to their cots. The second …

"They're fucking children," a trooper in Bird Squad exclaimed.

"Fuck, fuck, fuck, fuck," another trooper cursed. "Where are the adults?"

"Dead," a depressed voice said from the darkness. "All dead," the voice continued. "You'll be dead too if'n they catch you here." The voice paused. "I hear a bird singing."

"That's me," chirped a voice. Cool Evening Breeze walked toward the child. "Hi," she chirped. "Don't be afraid."

"Are you gonna eat us?" the voice asked. "That's what they told us, that the Bird Devils will eat us." The figure sat up. "That's why they lock us up, so the Bird Devils won't eat us." The figure leaned forward and, in the dimness, was revealed to be a young girl of maybe twelve years of age. She was skinny, her curly hair was matted, and she seemed covered in dirt.

"Spirits weep," Cool Evening Breeze replied. "No, I'm not going to eat you." She forced herself to keep her voice steady. "We're here to help you."

The girl reached out and touched Cool Evening Breeze's face. "You don't look like a devil," she said. "You're pretty."

"So are you," Cool Evening Breeze replied. "Now, we're going to cut off the chains, and I want you to go with the soldiers." She kept her voice light, even though she wanted to weep. "And they'll take you someplace safe." She stood. "That goes for all of you."

"Corporal." One of the soldiers walked over. "Some of them were whipped. They might not be able to walk."

"Then we carry them," Cool Evening Breeze chirped angrily. "Bird Squad, get these children out of here. Hup."

"You heard the corporal," barked another voice. "Move it."

There were ten shacks in all. Each shack had been bolted from the outside, and each shack, like the first, contained forty children. By the time they had cleared the tenth shack, Cool Evening Breeze didn't know whether to cry or take down the main house with her bare hands.

"Hendriks," she chirped into her Torque. "We're done here."

"You okay, Breeze?" Hendriks replied over his own Torque.

"No," Cool Evening Breeze replied. "Children, Hendriks, they are all children." Her voice quavered. "If what they're telling us is true, they killed their parents." She looked back toward the shacks. "Tell me you got the bastards."

"We got'em, Breeze," Hendriks replied. "And another dozen girls and boys." He growled. "I don't think he killed the parents just because they resisted," he said. "It seems he likes them young." His voice seemed to smile. "I was wondering if you'd like to meet the ... massa?"

"Oh, spirits weep, yes, I would," Cool Evening Breeze replied. "I can't promise I won't rip his eyes out, though."

"Did you hear me ask you to promise anything?" Hendriks replied. "You know, I think the shuttle is going to be too full, and we're going to have to reduce the number of people we can carry." Now Cool Evening Breeze was sure Hendriks was smiling. "By one."

"And when are we going to discover the ship is overloaded?" Cool Evening Breeze asked.

"I was thinking about ten miles up," Hendriks replied.

"Let's not tell Crystal," Cool Evening Breeze said. "Okay, Fuzzy Butt?"

"Wouldn't dream of it, Feather Head," Hendriks replied.

Mark Spencer, president of the CSA, former president of the USA, listened glumly as the reports came in. "Mississippi has fallen. Alabama has fallen. Tennessee has fallen." The reports kept coming. "Kentucky's military has been routed."

"Where is Virginia?" demanded the president. "Where is Hooker?"

"Last reports state that they are being prevented from launching their F-22s," his chief of staff replied. "SAM units are moving in to assist."

"That makes no sense," one of his advisors complained. "It

would take the entire WSA or Gotham air forces to stop Langley, and they're out hitting other targets. Where did they get the additional squadron?"

"According to the reports, it isn't a squadron, it's one fucking airship," the chief of staff replied. "Supposedly, it's just sitting over the base and taking out any ship that attempts to take off."

"Mr. President, enemy forces are approaching Atlanta," another aide said. "Our forces are moving to engage."

"SAM units have reached Langley," another aide exclaimed. He pressed his finger against his headset. "They are firing."

"Well I was getting bored anyway," Joseph Franklin said conversationally. He smiled as his core brothers chittered in amusement. "Let's see if the RGG lives up to its advertising." He smiled. "Torque: RGG targeting activate," he said. Immediately, his vision was overlaid with pin lights indicating launched missiles, along with their speed and trajectory. His hands closed over a joystick.

"You do know that the computer can do the fighting, don't you, Core Brother?" asked Black Rocks.

"Why should the computer have all the fun?" Franklin replied. His finger tightened on the firing trigger.

"Spirits, I think our core brother is a better marksman than the computer," Red Clouds Paint the Sky said in admiration. "Spirits, but I love humans."

Corporal Cool Evening Breeze and Sergeant Hendriks slumped in their seats as the shuttle, loaded with another fifty rescued slaves, headed back to the *Seeker*. All the rescued were taken first to the *Seeker* for medical treatment before being taken to one of a dozen safe zones in either the Empire or the WSA.

"Spirits, I've never been so tired in my life," chirped Cool

Evening Breeze. She sat up tiredly as one of the rescues made his way toward them. He was, as most of the rescues were, young—at most fifteen—yet he seemed far, far older.

In some ways, the young man reminded her of the girl who was among the first rescued. It was the eyes, Cool Evening Breeze decided. Eyes that had seen a lifetime of horror in just a few years. "Is everything okay?" she asked. "Do you need anything? Food? Water?"

"What happens now?" the young man croaked in a voice that was raspy from lack of use.

"We're taking you to the ship," began Cool Evening Breeze.

"I think he means now that he's free," Hendriks interrupted. "That's up to you, kid," he said. "What do you want to do?"

The young man swallowed. "I want to go home," he whispered. "I want to play on the swings. I want to eat a burger with fries. I want … I want my mom. My dad." Tears began to fall. "I want what they took from me."

"You want revenge," Hendriks said.

"Yes," the young man rasped.

"The Teacher said, before seeking revenge, first dig two graves," Cool Evening Breeze replied. She briefly covered her eyes. "We cannot help you with revenge." She raised her hand to stop the young man. She had heard the sentiment from dozens of those she had helped rescue. "But we won't stop you, either," she said. "I cannot in truth say I understand what you've been through. I cannot." She briefly covered her eyes.

"What does that mean?" he demanded and briefly covered his own eyes. "What does it mean?"

"It is a gesture of respect," Cool Evening Breeze replied. "It means, literally, 'Your truth is like the sun; it blinds as well as illuminates,'" she told the boy. "So I cover my eyes to not be blinded, but not completely, so I am illuminated."

Mark Spencer listened glumly as the reports came in. "Why has God forsaken us?" he said after the last report. He sank to his knees. "Oh Lord, have we not kept the law?" He clasped his hands together. "Did we not banish the ungodly from your land? Did we not save the unborn? Did we not cleanse the land of all who refused to follow your will?" he cried. "And did we not provide honest labor befitting everyone's proper station?" he asked. "Is this land gone so far astray that not even our works can save it?"

Silence answered his prayers.

Spencer rose to his feet. "Bring everyone to Atlanta," he ordered his chief of staff. "This will be the final battle. This will be our Armageddon."

"Looks like you called it, Mr. Blunt," David Eisenstadt said. "All CSA forces are pulling back to Atlanta."

"This is when they will be the most dangerous," Jeremy cautioned. "Spencer is a religious fanatic. He most likely believes that the devil is loose, and it is his calling to save God's creation." His mouth twisted. "By destroying mankind."

"Eisenstadt to *Silver Shrike*. Eisenstadt to *Silver Shrike*."

"This is the *Silver Shrike*," Black Rocks replied. "Go ahead, Commander."

"We have reason to believe that the CSA is going to …" David Eisenstadt paused. "There are about a hundred nuclear devices that cannot be accounted for," he said. "One hundred devices that were stored in Georgia."

"Spirits," exclaimed Black Rocks. "Please wait," he said. "We're all listening, Commander," he said. "Your thoughts."

"Boys," Eisenstadt said, "we think the CSA is going to commit suicide and take 35 million people with them." He paused. "At least

35 million. Worst case scenario is closer to 100 million." They could hear the sigh. "We're doing what we can, but ..."

"Brothers?" Joseph Franklin said.

"Where you lead, we follow, Core Brother," Red Clouds Paint the Sky said.

"We'll do our best, Commander," Franklin said. "*Silver Shrike* out." He spoke to his Torque quietly for a moment. The Torque responded after a minute, and Franklin said, "Frozen River, take us to Atlanta." The silver arrowhead rotated, and then with a boom that caused several of the remaining grounded F-22s to be tossed into the air, the ship streaked away.

It took only minutes for the *Silver Shrike* to reach Atlanta, and then the ship slowed. Black Rocks concentrated on the information his Torque kept feeding him. "Found them," he said after their third circuit of the city. "Spirits weep!" He chirped a command, and his three core brothers could now see what he was seeing.

"Oh, shit!" Franklin exclaimed. "They're under the entire city."

"Worse than that, Core Brother," Red Clouds said. "My calculations suggest that the commander's upper estimate is off by at least a factor of two." His crest dropped tight against his skull. "How could any rational being even contemplate this?"

"Who said he was rational?" Franklin replied. He spoke quietly to his Torque and waited for a response. He blew out a breath. "Frozen River, I'm providing a flight plan," he said. "You're going to have to stay below Mach 1. I've put defense in the hands of the ship's computer. Black Rocks, broadcast to anyone who will listen that there are live nuclear devices under the city, and they need to evacuate."

"What should I do, Core Brother?" Red Clouds Paint the Sky asked.

"Pray," replied Joseph Franklin.

The *Silver Shrike* started its run. As it traveled along its flight path, an angry red beam would periodically flick out like a demon's tongue. And what the tongue touched would dissolve into its component elements. Ground, trees, plants, cars ... and people would all turn into ... nothing. Joseph Franklin tried not to think about the last every time the beam shot out. He started to count. "Twenty, Twenty-one, Twenty-two."

In the capitol building, President Spencer walked over to a panel and inserted a key. He opened the panel and removed a shoebox-sized device. Another key was produced, and the device lit. President Spencer consulted a manual and started to enter numbers. When the last number was entered, he pressed a button, and a countdown started.

Red Clouds Paint the Sky spoke to Frozen River on a private frequency. "Our human core brother is taking the pain onto himself," he said.

"He still has difficulty sharing his feelings," agreed Frozen River.

"He is not the only one, is he, Core Brother?" Red Clouds chided. "Why have you not told Joseph that you desire female companionship?"

"I was waiting until he felt more secure," admitted Frozen River.

As the *Silver Shrike*'s flight path spiraled inward, the ship came under attack from more and more antiaircraft missiles. The ship's computer spat out bullets, chaff, and its own missiles in response.

"Forty-three, forty-four," counted Franklin.

"I understand Light of Three Moons has expressed interest," Red Clouds said. "Though she would prefer if Joseph wasn't so ... fixated."

"Fifty-one."

"She can be persuasive when she wants to be," Frozen River said. "I think she would make an excellent core sister."

"Seventy-eight!" Joseph said. "Come on, come on. Only twenty-two more to go."

"We're not going to make it, are we?" Frozen River asked calmly.

"No," agreed Red Clouds. "But we've already saved more than half of those who would have died."

"Eighty-three!" Franklin exclaimed.

"I am content then, core brothers," Black Rocks said into the private line. "But do not count us out yet," he said. "The *Silver Shrike* has a few extra tricks."

"God will not be denied," intoned President Spencer as the countdown reached zero.

There was a flash and then another, and then it seemed as if the ground below had turned into the sun. David Eisenstadt and the rest of the observers in California and New York watched as Atlanta vanished and was replaced by a dozen mushroom clouds.

It was not until the explosions began to subside that the observers seemed to collectively shake themselves and return their attention to their monitors and Torques.

"Atlanta is gone, Commander," Lieutenant Daniels reported quietly.

Eisenstadt nodded. "Please broadcast the events to all world governments and advise them to be aware of potential fallout issues," he said. "And then see if we can get an estimate of casualties." He looked at the monitor and shuddered. "They're going to need ... everything," he muttered. "Ophelia, are you still there?"

"I'm still here, David," the oligarch replied in a hushed voice.

"You're closer," the commander replied. "Can you provide assistance?"

"Of course, David," the oligarch replied. "Kasumi, how effective is Omiset against radiation sickness?"

"Honestly, we don't know," Kasumi replied. "We ... we never

had …." She broke off. "Start with a double dose," she said. "We can produce as much as you need."

"Thank you, Kasumi," the oligarch replied.

"Commander!" Lieutenant Daniels shouted. "I'm getting a mayday." He turned to face the room. "It's the Shrike!"

"They're alive?" Eisenstadt asked in disbelief. "How?" He shook his head. "Never mind that, get High Flyer 1 to retrieve them."

"On it, sir," Lieutenant Daniels replied and returned to his console.

"Thank god," Eisenstadt said. "We could use some good news about now."

"Commander!" Lieutenant Daniels shouted again. "Bogies on the monitors."

"Now what?" Eisenstadt replied. "On screen," he ordered. The image shifted. Three disc-shaped objects were displayed. "Flying saucers?" he asked. "Kasumi, are those yours?"

"No, David," Kasumi replied. Her crest flattened. "But I know who they are," she said in tones of worry. "Graz'to."

25

Graz'to

The three disc-shaped objects approached the colony. They were so much the classic "flying saucer" that it was almost a caricature—disc-shaped overall with a dome on top and a smaller ring underneath. Kasumi forced herself to observe the oncoming craft dispassionately. She felt more than saw Jeremy Blunt walk up beside her.

"I know I'm only a primitive from a non-spacefaring race, but I would think an interstellar craft would be larger," he commented. "Those are barely larger than a fighter jet."

Kasumi blinked as she thought about what her friend and mentor said. Her crest lifted. "I never thought about it," she admitted. "But you are right." Her crest rose higher. "At best, those would be interplanetary."

"Which means … what?" Jeremy asked.

"I'm not sure," Kasumi replied. "But unless their technology is vastly superior to ours, those are not starships." She shook her head. "We've intercepted Graz'to transmissions, so what we know is mostly inferred, but based on what we do know, they're no more advanced than the Rynn—and most likely not nearly as advanced." She chirped to her Torque. "I've put the *Seeker*'s sensors on full spectrum," she said.

"You're thinking that these are no more than shuttles or fighter craft and that the real starship is somewhere else," Jeremy stated.

"You're thinking the same," Kasumi replied. She looked at Jeremy. The older man was smiling down at her approvingly. "Friend or foe?' she asked.

Jeremy shrugged. "Either, neither, or both," he returned. "What we do know is that they are secretive." He smiled. "Not unlike a certain spacefaring species I've come to know."

"Secretive and apparently watching Earth for some time," Kasumi said. "Since they haven't overtly interfered with human development," she said musingly.

"Keep going, Granddaughter," Jeremy said into the silence. "Why now?"

"Always teaching, aren't you, Grandfather?" Kasumi replied affectionately. "Obviously, the recent conflict has something to do with it, but whether it's because the Rynn were involved is not proven." She smiled at the chuckle from Jeremy. "For all we know, they are attracted to nuclear explosions."

"A definite possibility," agreed Jeremy.

"But unlikely," Kasumi countered. "Especially since they are headed here and not Atlanta." She ran her long-fingered hand through her crest. "No, I'm going to assume that it's because the Rynn were involved in an Earth conflict."

"They're not responding to our hails," Eisenstadt said. "If these Graz'to are our Grays, you'd think they'd know Earth languages."

"Or have a translation program like the Rynn do," Kasumi replied. "What would the normal protocol be for aliens?"

"If it wasn't for the fact that you are an alien, I'd laugh at the comment," Eisenstadt replied. "We discussed it in officer training," he added. "General consensus was that any beings capable of interstellar travel would probably be too advanced to combat with conventional weapons."

"Well, that would be true for the Rynn," agreed Kasumi.

"Even so, we could not allow them to have free rein," Eisenstadt replied. "Most of my colleagues would probably consider trying to shoot them down about now."

"But ...?" asked Jeremy.

"You're enjoying this, aren't you, Grandfather?" Kasumi accused. "This would be a test, wouldn't it, Grandfather?"

"It has that feel," agreed Jeremy.

"Eisenstadt to all personnel," the commander said, and his voice reverberated throughout the colony. "Stand down and let our newest visitors land unhindered," he ordered. "Ape and Bird squads, honor guard." He stood. "Are you still there, Ophelia?"

"Still here, David," the oligarch replied.

"If worse comes to worse, Newgate is going to need all the allies he can get," the commander said.

"I understand, David," the oligarch said. "Spirits watch over you."

The commander, Kasumi, and Jeremy, along with Mel and Morning Mist, left the command room and headed out toward the field. The three saucer-shaped craft were now overhead. One started to descend as they headed toward a clear area. The other two craft remained hovering.

"Waited for us to appear," Eisenstadt murmured. "Looks like we passed the first test."

The group arrived where the two squads had set up facing rows. The Rynn members of the squad were wearing war paint, their faces entirely painted red with black slashes running diagonally. For the first time, the commander thought of the Rynn as being menacing. He nodded in approval. "The squads are looking good, Sergeant Major."

"Thank you, Commander," Sergeant Major Stilson replied. When Stilson resigned from the CNG to join the combined Rynn-human defense force Kasumi had originally intended to promote him to Captain. Stilson refused the title saying he was 'a working marine' and requested the title of Sergeant Major. "Those are not Rynn craft," he said offhandedly.

"Graz'to," the commander replied. "Keep your boys and girls on their leashes."

"They're marines, sir," the sergeant major said almost reprovingly. "They are always on leash." He added, "Until they're not."

The commander smiled at the sergeant major's inclusion of the Rynn in his comment. "Of course."

"They're using a magnetic propulsion system," Morning Mist said. "Definitely not interstellar." She chirped to her Torque. "Hull is a reinforced aluminum alloy. Fusion reactor power source." Her crest lifted. "Judging by the isotope levels in the hull, I'd guess the ship is approximately one thousand Earth years old."

"Rynn are long-lived," Kasumi said quietly. "But not that long-lived."

"I suspect neither are our guests," Jeremy replied. He watched as the ship landed gently. "I would suggest that David be the one to approach the craft," he said in a louder voice.

"I agree with Germy," Kasumi added. "This is your world."

The commander pursed his lips in thought. "Normally I would defer to Mr. Blunt, but in this case, I think Kasumi should accompany me—though it might be better if she walks just behind."

"I see where you're going, David," Jeremy replied. "But ..." He stopped. "Let's compromise: you approach first and then call Kasumi forward once the initial greetings are over. That way, Kasumi is not mistaken as having either a subordinate or superior role. You'd be introducing an ally instead of an advisor."

"Point taken, Mr. Blunt," Eisenstadt replied. He watched as an access hatch slid open and then a ramp extended. "Showtime," he said. He squared his shoulders and walked deliberately toward the ship. He stopped a couple of yards from the base of the ramp and waited.

For several long minutes, nothing happened, and then three figures appeared at the entranceway. They were short and slim like the Rynn, but there was no possibility of confusing the two species. The newcomers each had a large, dome-like bald head with oversized dark, pupil-less eyes, two vertical slits instead of a nose, and a thin slit for a mouth. Their skin—what could be seen that was not covered by a silvery one-piece suit—was wrinkled and gray.

"Stay frosty," murmured Stilson as his squads shifted uneasily. The Rynn and humans stopped fidgeting, but the tension was palpable.

The three figures walked slowly down the ramp in an odd, shuffling manner, as if they either did not have knees or what knees they had did not bend in the same way those of the humans or Rynn did. They reached the bottom of the ramp and stopped.

"This is your world, David," Jeremy half-whispered. "Let them speak first."

Apparently the commander had the same thought, and he waited patiently. Finally, the center member of the visiting trio took a shuffling step forward.

"Xan Do Holt am I," the being said in oddly accented English. "Graz'to am I." The being looked past the commander. "Rynn here, why?"

"Welcome, Xan Do Holt," the commander replied. "I could ask you the same question. Why are the Graz'to here?"

"Observers, am I," the Graz'to replied.

"Interesting," murmured Jeremy. "Everything is in first person." He turned to Kasumi. "Notice how similar they look."

"Virtually identical," agreed Kasumi. Her crest flared. "Clones?"

"Rynn here, why?" the gray alien repeated.

"I will let the Rynn explain that themselves," the commander replied. "But understand, we consider them allies." The commander's mouth turned up slightly. "Even friends." He raised a hand.

Kasumi walked forward until she was standing next to the commander. "I am Kasumi Blunt of the Rynn."

"Earth name, that is," Xan Do Holt said. "Explain."

"I am the adopted granddaughter of a human," Kasumi replied. "I bear the name he gave me," she said. "A name I wear proudly."

"Violent, humans are," Xan Do Holt said. "Dangerous are."

"I cannot deny that," Kasumi replied. "It's a dangerous galaxy, and the Rynn need allies." She smiled. "Humans may be the most dangerous intelligent species of them all." Her smile widened and her crest rose fully. "In a dangerous galaxy, it makes sense to have allies that would make a Zaski or a Polig-Grug look for easier prey."

The gray being stared at Kasumi for a long time. "Rynn foolish are," it stated finally. "Humans foolish are," it said. "Graz'to foolish not. Grazto'to leave will." It then turned and shuffled back up the ramp. The saucer rose into the air to join the two that were still hovering. Then all three shot off.

"Morning Mist, track them," Kasumi ordered.

"Tracking, Kasumi," Morning Mist replied. Then she noted, "Kasumi, a dozen more Graz'to ships have joined the three that were here. All traveling on the same heading." She chirped to her Torque. "Wherever they're going, they're not in a hurry."

"Probably not," Jeremy commented. "Nor do I think we've seen the last of them." He rubbed his chin. "One thing I do know. They're afraid of a human-Rynn alliance."

"Afraid?" asked the commander. "They're hundreds of years ahead of us, and they're afraid?"

"They're flying around in a thousand-year-old spacecraft," Kasumi pointed out. "And while their propulsion system is powerful, it too is probably ancient." She looked at her adopted grandfather. "An old race that is no longer advancing?"

"A definite possibility," agreed Jeremy. "What else is possible?" he asked.

Kasumi's crest lowered partially as she thought. "Prior to now, our knowledge of the Graz'to was limited to a handful of sightings and intercepted transmissions." She chirped a chuckle. "Our short meeting today has provided more information than anything we've learned in the past one hundred Rynn years."

"I was able to get a full bio scan," Morning Mist reported. "I haven't analyzed it yet, but I would not be surprised if I found evidence of genetic senescence."

"Neither would I," agreed Kasumi. "I said this to Germy earlier, but I think they might have been clones."

"I will check for that as well," Morning Mist asserted.

"Well, this was interesting, but we have more important things to deal with," the commander said. "Sergeant Major, dismiss your squads," he ordered. "We have work to do."

Bright Sunlight of the Hot Springs Clan sat in his command chair as his navigator brought the starship *Safe Haven* out of hyperspace. Bright Sunlight forced himself to wait calmly as his crew ran through all the post-jump safety checks. Finally, his crew chief turned in his chair.

"All checks complete, Trade Master," the crew chief reported. "The fleet has arrived in good condition."

Bright Sunlight grunted in acknowledgement. "Open a channel to the *Seeker*."

"Trade Master, we are being hailed," the communication officer said. His crest rose in surprise. "They're asking for you."

"Let's hear it," Bright Sunlight barked. The communication officer nodded. "Bright Sunlight of the Hot Spring Clan speaking."

"Hello, darling," boomed a voice. "Kasumi sends her love, but she is a little busy right now."

"Who in all the spirits' names is Kasumi?" Bright Sunlight growled.

"Oh, that's right, you wouldn't know," the voice replied. "Your daughter has taken a new name." There was a chirping. "Yes, maybe that would be best," said the voice.

"Spirits bless you," came another voice. "This is Morning Mist speaking. The one once known as Small Snow Flower has changed her name. She is now Kasumi Blunt of the Forest Cabin Clan."

"What nonsense is this?" Bright Sunlight growled. "Does my daughter disown her family?"

"Kasumi, who once was Small Snow Flower, does not feel

comfortable being part of a clan that does not properly train its successors," Morning Mist replied. "She does not wish to claim incompetence, but that is only out of love for her parents."

"Incompetence?" sputtered Bright Sunlight. "How dare ..."

"Not properly training a successor is incompetence. Placing a successor in the hands of an unstable individual is incompetence. Not recognizing a successor's weaknesses and not taking action to correct the weaknesses is incompetence," Morning Mist chirped angrily. "Your actions led to a mutiny, placed the ship's personnel in the hands of a madman, and nearly cost Kasumi her life," she snapped. "It was only by the spirits' blessings that she and we survived."

"What?" Bright Sunlight bolted half out of his command chair. "I know nothing of this," he protested. "All that I know is that Small Snow Flower ..."

"Kasumi," corrected Morning Mist.

"As you will," grumbled Bright Sunlight. "All I know is that after a worrisome silence, my daughter advises me that all is well and that I should come to these coordinates to discuss a trading opportunity," he said. "Was that a lie?"

Morning Mist chittered in amusement. "No, that was no lie," she confirmed. "If anything, it was an understatement."

"Trade Leader, an unknown craft is approaching," reported a bridge officer. "Spirits!" the officer chirped to its Torque. "Sensors indicate that the ship has a combined crew of Rynn and ... something else."

"They're called *humans*," Morning Mist chittered in amusement again. "As the humans say, you are now living in interesting times." She added, "Whether that is a blessing or a curse has yet to be determined."

Year 5

26

Time Is an Illusion That Only the Dead Do Not Share

Bright Sunlight, patriarch of the Hot Springs Clan, chief trader, and up until recently the most powerful Rynn on the planet known as Nest, stared nervously at the figure seated opposite him. She was tall for a Rynn and extremely muscular, and she carried a sword strapped to her back. That would be enough to convince any Rynn to deal cautiously with her.

He had recently watched as this Rynn woman went through an exercise session using that same sword. What he had seen caused two conflicting emotions to fight for dominance within his soul.

The first emotion was a fear that bordered on terror. The skill demonstrated was beyond anything he had imagined possible. *It's no wonder she was able to defeat Sun-Warmed Boulder so easily*, he had thought. *Spirits, but she looks like some barbarian warrior out of legend*. Bright Sunlight, who was himself an accomplished swordsman, had no doubt that he'd fare no better than the dead duelist.

The second emotion was pride. This same barbarian warrior who so terrified him was his daughter, Small Snow Flower.

And now she calls herself Kasumi Blunt of the Forest Cabin Clan, he thought almost mournfully. His once loving and respectful daughter was now a stern and menacing presence. "That was an impressive demonstration, Daughter," he said in falsely calm tones.

Kasumi chittered in cold amusement. "It was passable," she corrected. "Teacher Germy pointed out a few areas that needed attention." She indicated one of the other beings present.

Bright Sunlight forced himself to look at the strange being sitting on the edge of the strangely shaped desk and not show his fear. The creature was tall—taller than any sentient being had any right to be—and his shoulders were absurdly wide. He was mostly Rynn-like in form, though his skin was strangely leathery, and what bare skin Bright Sunlight could see seemed to be lightly covered in a white filament. *Hair*, the Rynn reminded himself.

"You still have a habit of lifting your shoulders when you are about to attack," the creature said. "An observant opponent will notice and exploit it."

"Oh quit it, Gramps," said another being in the room. Obviously of the same species as the white-haired being, this one's hair was reddish. While tall, this creature was of a more reasonable height. "She's only been training for a little over four years. I think she's doing fantastic."

"Thank you, Mel," the Rynn woman now known as Kasumi replied. "But if Germy says I have a weakness, then it must be so." She smiled at the white-haired being and briefly covered her eyes.

"I have trained for most of my life," Bright Sunlight said. "And I don't doubt that Small … I mean, Kasumi could easily defeat me."

The tall white-haired being leaned over and bared his teeth. Bright Sunlight flinched. "Remember that," he said in soft tones that somehow conveyed menace. Bright Sunlight nodded. The white-haired being stood. "If you will excuse me, granddaughters, I have some errands to attend to."

"Will you be at dinner tonight, Grandfather?" Kasumi asked. "Morning Mist is cooking, and she'd be very disappointed if you were not there."

The white-haired being laughed. "Well, we can't have that," he agreed cheerfully. "Tell Morning Mist to set a place for me." He walked over and hugged Kasumi and the other female known as Mel, gave Bright Sunlight a cold look, and left.

Bright Sunlight took out a square of cloth and wiped his crest. "I do not think Teacher Jeremy likes me very much," he said quietly.

"Well, Gramps is very protective," Mel replied. She bared her teeth at Bright Sunlight in much the same way the older man had. "Personally, I've always found Gramps a little too forgiving." She leaned over much as the white-haired being had. "Fortunately for you, Kasumi still thinks you are worth forgiving," she said.

Kasumi nodded. "Germy does not hate you, Father," she said. "But he is still angry at you." She raised a long-fingered hand to stop any comments. "This is not the time or place to discuss your failings," she said. "We have more important matters."

"Trade," Bright Sunlight said. "They are very primitive, Daughter," he said in serious tones. "Some of what you wish to provide them may be beyond their current level of development."

"You have not lived among humans, Father," Kasumi said in wry tones. "They have a habit of surprising you." She chirped and a globe of light appeared in front of her. "Remember that ship that greeted you?" she asked. Bright Sunlight nodded. "It was created by a human, by hand, a few weeks after he discovered the *theory* behind the propulsion system."

"Impossible," exclaimed Bright Sunlight.

"Not for a human," Kasumi replied. "They're as smart, as intelligent as we are and twice as creative." She smiled slightly. "If they somehow managed not to destroy themselves, we probably would have met in space in less than a hundred years."

"I wouldn't bet against us destroying ourselves," Mel said under her breath.

"Maybe not, Core Sister," Kasumi agreed. "But betting against humans does not seem wise." She looked at the globe. "Germy has suggested a two-tier approach," she said. "Humans on Earth will be provided the technology to construct fusion reactors, inertial compensators, and any other instrumentality that can be maintained by humans with little or no supervision," she said. "Humans who travel with Rynn will be allowed access to any technology they wish."

"But Daughter …" protested Bright Sunlight.

"In return, humans will fight alongside the Rynn," Kasumi replied. "I want you to watch something." She chirped and the globe expanded. Images began to form.

"You are looking at a recording from one recent battle," Kasumi said. "Notice the Rynn involved."

Bright Sunlight watched as the recording unfolded. "What is wrong with their faces?" he shuddered. "They look like monsters."

"That was the general idea," Mel said. "It's called war paint."

"War paint," echoed Bright Sunlight. He continued to watch the recording. His crest flattened as he watched one Rynn slash at a human with his claws and then follow the slash with a kick to the human's knee. The human crashed face first to the ground. "Humans don't seem so …" He stopped as the downed human suddenly grabbed the attacking Rynn and flung it away one-handed. "Spirits."

"Two things, Father," Kasumi said. "Notice that the Rynn is running back toward the fight," she said. "And now notice what his human partner does."

Bright Sunlight watched as, just as Kasumi said, the Rynn fighter did run back into the fray—and then he saw that a human had joined in the fight. "They're protecting each other."

"Very good, Father," agreed Kasumi. "What else?"

Bright Sunlight watched some more. His crest suddenly snapped open. "Are they laughing?" He leaned closer to the globe. "By the Spirits, they appear to be enjoying themselves," he said in awe. "Rynn don't …"

"Don't what, Father?" Kasumi almost purred. "Enjoy fighting? Face an enemy when they can run away?" She smiled. "That Rynn is, or *was*, a maintenance tech."

"If you think he's impressive, you should see Cool Evening Breeze," Mel said cheerfully. She whistled. "Now that is one mean Rynn."

"Only when Hendriks is threatened," Kasumi corrected with a Rynn grin. "Or if Crystal is mad at both of them." She looked at her father, who was listening with his crest half lowered and his mouth open. "Rynn have always believed that we were small and weak," she said. "And because we believed that, we were." She nodded toward the images playing in the globe. "Humans fear just like Rynn, but they have learned how to face their fears." She briefly covered her eyes. "As Germy says, when you are no longer afraid, you can do anything."

Bright Sunlight's crest trembled. "For what end?" he asked plaintively. "Even if some Rynn learn to ... face their fears, then what?" His crest flattened, and he began to visibly shake when a different image appeared. It had an elongated reptilian long-toothed jaw, a blue-black exoskeleton, six segmented legs, and two pairs of tentacles that ended in stubby fingerlike projections.

"How many Rynn ships have been captured by the Polig-Grug?" Kasumi demanded angrily. "How many Rynn have been eaten by these monsters?" She cut her father off with a slicing motion of her hand. "Too many," she answered her own question. "We have been lucky that they have not as yet attacked our home planet," she said. "But it's only a matter of time before they do."

Kasumi stood and stared into her father's eyes. "You asked to what end, Father," she said. "This is my answer. Too long have we cowered in fear. Too long have we ceded planets and resources to the Polig-Grug," she snapped. "With humans by our sides, we will teach the Polig-Grug, the Zaski, and anyone else who thinks we are nothing but prey the true meaning of fear."

"You're mad," gasped Bright Sunlight.

"No, my core sister is not mad," Mel said in almost cheerful tones. "She is acting like a human." She smiled. "My grandfather would probably comment that there is little difference between being mad and being human." Her smile became a grin when Kasumi covered her eyes.

"There are seventy-one Rynn on the *Seeker*. Do you know how many volunteered to fight alongside the humans?" Kasumi asked. "Do you know how many want to go with the *Seeker* when she leaves to hunt our enemies?" Bright Sunlight shook his head and his crest flattened even further. "More than half," Kasumi said, and her crest flared to its fullest. "And of the ones who did not volunteer, all of them were willing to give up their trade shares," she said proudly. "I refused that offer, but asked instead that they donate some portion to refitting *Seeker*." She smiled. "I had to give some of it back."

"Rynn are angry. I almost pity the Polig-Grug," Mel said. "Well, not really, but if I were the Polig-Grug or the Zaski, I'd be getting very, very frightened right about now."

"Do the humans understand what you are proposing?" demanded Bright Sunlight. "Do they even know what a Polig-Grug or a Zaski is capable of?"

"Did you see the Rynn with the war paint?" Kasumi shot back. Bright Sunlight shuddered, then nodded. "Every one of them has at least one human partner willing to go with them."

"Kasumi has two," Mel said. "The only reason Gramps is not going ... well, the reason is complex, but he would if he could." She shrugged. "But when the *Seeker* leaves, me and David will be on it."

The princess walked to the Temple of Light. Like the last time, it seemed empty and deserted. A wry smile came to the princess's face. "Another test," she told herself. She clapped her hands together twice. "Spirits of my ancestors, I am the Princess Kasumi," she said. "I have learned what thirst is. I have learned what hunger is." She removed her fine robes. "I stand before you naked."

"To what end, Granddaughter?" came a familiar voice.

The princess turned and bowed to the old monk. "Greetings,

Grandmother," she said. "To what end?" she asked, repeating the question. "No end other than to speak with you."

"What? No plea for advice?" the old woman asked. "No demands to enter the temple?"

"I have no need to enter the temple," the princess replied. "I am already home." She smiled slightly. "As for pleading for advice, I would hope you would offer me counsel if I needed it." The old monk snorted in amusement. "No, my only reason for being here is to do what I have not yet done." She bowed again. "I have never properly thanked you."

"What I did does not require thanks," the old monk replied, "but it is a measure of your growth that you offer it." She returned a bow. "Still, I see there is a question in your heart," she said after a moment.

"Yes, Grandmother," the princess replied. She waved a hand. "This ... is a dream," she said. "And yet ... it is not."

"Tell me of the Teacher," the old monk said.

The princess blinked and then bowed. "As you wish, Grandmother," she said. "The Teacher is well, though I believe he thinks he's lived overlong."

The old monk snorted. "He always was a fool," she said. "An honorable and true fool, but still a fool." She raised a hand palm outward. "Tell me what you see," she commanded.

The princess narrowed her eyes and looked at the hand. "There is a scar," she said in realization.

"Tell the Teacher what you have seen," she said. "And then tell him I will be angry if he leaves you before his work is done." She smiled. "Now. Say my name."

The princess bowed. "Mei Lin."

Kasumi bolted awake. "Spirits," she gasped.

"She had the dream again," a voice chirped.

"Normal people have dreams," another voice said. "Kasumi has visions."

"I have to speak to Germy," Kasumi said. She threw off the

blanket and scrambled into her clothes. She reached over to the nightstand, picked up her Torque, and put it on. "Torque: status on Germy," she commanded. The Torque was silent and then: "There are unusual fluctuations in brain activity."

David Eisenstadt sat up and spoke to his own Torque. "Get a medic over to Jeremy Blunt's cabin stat," he ordered.

"There is no evidence that anything is wrong, David," Kasumi protested.

"You woke up worried about Jeremy," Eisenstadt replied. "I have no idea what it is that's happening when you have those dreams, but something is definitely happening. I'd rather be wrong and have to apologize for waking him than be sorry I did not."

It seemed mere minutes before Kasumi, Eisenstadt, Morning Mist, and Mel were in a transport vehicle and heading toward Jeremy Blunt's cabin. A medic had already left in another transport.

"She said … she said that she'd be angry if he left before his work was done," Kasumi said. "She didn't say anything was wrong, but …" She turned to Mel. "The old monk in my dreams, she was, she is, Mei Lin."

"Grandma Mei?" Mel said in shock. Kasumi nodded. "Okay, now it's officially freaky," Mel said.

The vehicle turned up the graveled driveway of the Blunt cabin. They could see the medic's vehicle parked right in front of the door, and they pulled up next to it. Kasumi barely waited for the truck to stop before she leaped from the truck and ran into the cabin.

She ran into Jeremy's bedroom, where the medic was applying chest compressions. "Dammit, breathe!" the medic was shouting. "Breathe!"

Kasumi ran over to the side of the bed. "Germy!" she screamed. "Your work is not done. If you die now, Mei Lin will not be waiting for you," she babbled. "She said … she said to tell you she'd be angry." She swallowed. "She had a scar on her right hand," she said urgently. "The monk showed me her hand. She had a scar." She leaned closer. "It looked like something had bitten her," she said. "Mei Lin had the same scar, didn't she?"

There was silence, and the medic had stopped trying to resuscitate the old man. "Time of ..." Suddenly Jeremy convulsed and took a huge breath. "My god!" exclaimed the medic. He grabbed the old man's wrist and checked for a pulse. "Weak, but there," he muttered. He checked the old man's pupils. "Welcome back, Mr. Blunt," he said finally.

Kasumi quietly clapped her hands together twice. "Thank you," she whispered. "Grandfather, can you hear me?"

Jeremy slowly turned his head toward Kasumi and opened his eyes. "When ... we were ... dog attacked ... Brandon. Mei ... Mei put hand ... in dog ... mouth ... bit her." He said laboriously. He struggled to sit up.

"Don't even think it, Mr. Blunt," said the medic. "You just lie there quietly." He stood and nodded to Kasumi. "I'll be back later today," he said. He walked out of the bedroom. Mel followed.

"What happened?" Mel asked.

"I really can't say without running some tests," the medic replied. "When I got here, he was still alive, but his heart was beating slower and slower." He shook his head. "I swear he was willing himself to die." He looked at Mel curiously. "If you hadn't called when you did, he'd be dead by now."

Mel shrugged. "Don't look at me. It was Kasumi who insisted something was wrong."

"Maybe her Torque," suggested the medic.

Mel shook her head. "She wasn't wearing it," she said. "She never wears it when she sleeps." She shrugged again. The medic raised an eyebrow but said nothing. He finally took his leave, and Mel walked back into the bedroom.

Kasumi had climbed into the bed and lay next to the old man. From the way Kasumi's crest trembled, Mel was sure the Rynn woman was trying not to cry. Mel glared at her grandfather. "You fucking selfish bastard," she growled.

"Mel," croaked Jeremy.

"Don't Mel me," she snapped. "If I were Grandma Mei, I'd dump your sorry ass," she said. "The only thing that pisses me off more than you trying to die is that Grandma Mei is talking to Kasumi instead of me."

"You … didn't … need her … help," Jeremy forced out.

"I know that," Mel snapped back. "Grandma Mei said your work is not done. So you better fucking get better," she said angrily. "No more bullshit, you hear me, Gramps?"

"Yes … Granddaughter." Jeremy replied. He closed his eyes. "Tired."

"Kasumi, you stay here with Gramps," Mel said. "And if he gives you any crap, you have my permission to belt him one." She stood up and stalked angrily out of the bedroom.

Kasumi looked at the old man. Jeremy had his eyes closed and seemed to be sleeping. "Another thing you humans can teach the Rynn," she whispered. "We love, but I've never heard of a Rynn willing himself to die for love." She closed her eyes.

Jeremy found himself standing in the middle of nothing. It was neither dark nor light. If he raised his hands in front of his face, he could see them, but that was all he could see. "Where am I?"

"Foolish old man," snapped a voice.

"Mei?" *Jeremy said in shock.* "Where are you?"

"I'm dead, idiot," the voice replied. "Where has no meaning for the dead," said the voice. "Neither does when." The voice softened. "Time is an illusion that only the dead do not share."

"Three times and timeless time?" Jeremy replied.

"Three times and timeless time," agreed the voice. "I can forgive you for missing me, but I will not forgive you for shirking your responsibilities," the voice said. "You accepted responsibility for our granddaughter when you rescued her."

"Yes, Mei," Jeremy replied. "Forgive me for being selfish." He added, "Both our granddaughters do well, do they not?"

"They do indeed," agreed the voice. "Do not shirk your responsibilities to them again. Teach them what they must know."

"Yes, Mei," Jeremy replied.

Jeremy opened his eyes. He felt a weight at his side, and he looked down to see Kasumi. He could see that her cheeks were wet with tears. "Forgive me for doubting, Granddaughter," he whispered. The little alien stirred and looked up at Jeremy. "Your visions were true."

27

Revolution

Bright Sunlight walked slowly through the compound. Everywhere he looked, he saw Rynn and humans working together side by side. Despite his initial misgivings, he had given permission for the staff and crew of the *Safe Haven* to come down to the compound.

Unlike the *Seeker*, the *Safe Haven* carried families. The *Safe Haven* was heavily armored and carried the strongest shields possible. It also had the strongest detection system possible. Carrying families, including children, was risky, but the benefits—in Bright Sunlight's opinion—outweighed the risks. He turned as a chorus of high-pitched shrieks came to his ears.

A dozen or so human children ran by, one with an excitedly chittering Rynn child on its shoulders.

"Magnificent, isn't it, darling?" boomed a voice. Bright Sunlight turned to see the biggest human he had yet seen. Not the tallest—humans in general were tall—but certainly this human outmassed most. He covered his eyes respectfully. "Greetings, Oligarch."

The big woman shook a ringed finger. "Now, now, I thought I told you to call me Ophelia," she chided. "I do love listening to sounds of children playing." She sighed. "I would have loved a child of my own."

"Sometimes they're more trouble than they are worth," Bright Sunlight grumbled.

"You don't really mean that," scolded the oligarch. "If I had a daughter half as talented as Kasumi, I'd be proud as blazes."

Bright Sunlight chirped a sigh. "Among the Rynn, a clan association is more than a family relationship. It is an economic and political statement," he said. "She changed her name. She changed her clan. She called me incompetent," Bright Sunlight said in a voice that seemed to hold tears. "My own daughter." He glared at the oligarch when she laughed. "It's not funny."

"Oh, darling, yes it is," the oligarch replied. "If I had any remaining doubts about Rynn, you just wiped them away." She smiled widely. "You sounded like every human parent since there were humans." She watched the children race by again. "Your daughter is starting a revolution, and if you had any sense, you'd not just join her but throw every resource you have in support."

28

Disciples

Jeremy Blunt sat on the cabin porch and wished he had a cigarette. It wasn't so much that he needed the cigarette, but he was irritated, and a cigarette usually reduced the irritation. And since the reason he was irritated wasn't likely to go away anytime soon, he wished he had a cigarette.

The cause of the irritation was the two people—one human, one Rynn—who hovered nearby. Doctors both, they watched Jeremy closely. The human doctor was bad enough, but the Rynn medical specialist seemed to consider Jeremy both a patient and an ongoing biology experiment. "Enough," barked Jeremy. "Go find someone else to poke and prod."

"Captain Kasumi has ..." began the Rynn medical specialist.

"My granddaughter is overly concerned," Jeremy replied. "I need space, dammit."

"Of course, Mr. Blunt," the human doctor replied. "Too much attention can be detrimental to humans, Sudden Winter Storm," he said. He leaned closer to his Rynn colleague and whispered something.

"Ah," noised the Rynn. "Dr. Williams and I will take a walk."

"Do that," Jeremy grunted. "A long walk." He forced himself to not roll his eyes when both doctors covered theirs briefly. "I promised my granddaughter I won't die just yet," he said in softer tones. The two doctors smiled and walked away.

"Probably have me on a monitor," Jeremy grumbled. He made to get up, and a Rynn ran over and silently offered assistance. Jeremy didn't refuse the help. "Help me into the kitchen," he said kindly. "I need some tea." The Rynn, a young male, nodded. "You're new," Jeremy noted.

"Yes, Teacher," the young Rynn said. "I came on the *Safe Haven*," he said in identification. "I am called Morning Stars Fade." The young Rynn opened the cabin door and let Jeremy lean slightly on him as they made their way to the kitchen. "May I help?" Morning Stars Fade asked. "Just to make the tea," he amended.

"Smart boy," Jeremy said in approval. "Kasumi spoke to you, did she?"

"Yes, Teacher." The Rynn's crest rose. "I hope I do not offend, but that woman is intimidating."

"Scary, you mean," Jeremy said in amusement.

"I meant no disrespect, Teacher," the Rynn replied.

"I intended her to be scary," Jeremy replied. He pointed to a cabinet. "Green box." The young Rynn walked quickly to the cabinet as Jeremy lowered himself into a chair. Jeremy watched the young Rynn look around helplessly. "Look in that drawer," Jeremy pointed. "There's a tea ball." He raised a hand and indicated a size. "About this big." The young Rynn fumbled in the drawer. After a few mistakes, he found the tea ball. "Fill it half full," Jeremy ordered. "Then find two cups."

"Two, Teacher?" the young Rynn asked.

"One for me and one for you," Jeremy replied. "No arguments."

"Yes, Teacher," Morning Stars Fade replied. He went to the cupboard and found two cups—one large and one small—and brought them to the table. Under Jeremy's direction, he finished making the tea. The young Rynn sat opposite Jeremy and sipped his tea.

Jeremy smiled in approval. The young Rynn was nervous

but keeping it under control. "So, what are your future plans, young man?"

The young Rynn was silent for a while. "I studied to be an electronics technician," he said finally.

"But?" Jeremy prompted.

The young Rynn slowly placed the cup down on the table. "Is it true you read minds?" he asked.

Jeremy snorted. "No, young man, I do not read minds."

"Yet you knew I questioned my career choice," the young man pointed out. "And you were correct," he added a moment later. "My parents approved of my career but did not approve of my going into space," he said. "Not even on the *Safe Haven*."

"You are their only child?" Jeremy asked.

"And still you claim you do not read minds," the young Rynn said quietly. "Yes, Teacher."

"Kasumi once told me of a story told by the First Teacher," Jeremy said. "About a young Rynn who wished to be a stone artist." He pursed his lips for a moment. "What may make the parent happy may make the child unhappy."

The young Rynn covered his eyes briefly. "I know why my parents fear," he said. "And sometimes I fear too," he admitted. "But ..." He chirped a Rynn sigh. "I get so tired of being afraid."

"Very good, young man," Jeremy said in approval.

Morning Stars Fade looked up in surprise.

"A life lived in fear is not a life; it is an existence," Jeremy told him. "And a sad existence at best."

The young Rynn covered his eyes briefly.

"It may be cold comfort to realize that you are not unusual in your fear," Jeremy said. "But Rynn are resilient and can learn to control their fear. Just look at Kasumi—or, even better, look at Cool Evening Breeze." He smiled. "Now that is one tough Rynn."

"If I had a giant as a friend, I'd be unafraid as well," Morning Stars Fade chirped quietly.

"That may have been true in the beginning," Jeremy admonished.

"But she has become a force in her own right." He smiled. "Though I have to admit, Hendriks had much to do with it." He leaned forward in his chair. "And while it's true that Rynn need humans to learn how to be brave, it is equally true that humans need Rynn."

"Humans are big and strong and brave," protested Morning Stars Fade. "Why would they need Rynn?"

"To learn how to be humble," Jeremy replied. "We just fought a war because some humans were afraid of that very lesson." He pushed the now empty cup away. "Would you mind cleaning up in here?" he asked. "I'm feeling a little tired."

"Oh, forgive me, Teacher," Morning Stars Fade said. "I should not …"

Jeremy interrupted the young Rynn. "I enjoyed our conversation," he said. "And I hope you will return so we may speak some more." He stood, and the young Rynn scrambled out of his chair to assist. "When I am feeling better, I plan on teaching self-defense," he said. "You would be most welcome."

Morning Stars Fade sat on the steps of the cabin. He looked up as the two doctors approached. "The Teacher sleeps," Morning Stars Fade said. He stood. "I must return to the colony," he said. "But I will return tomorrow." The young Rynn smiled proudly. "By his request." He walked toward a waiting car.

The two doctors watched the young man get into the car and then watched it drive away. "It is said that when the First Teacher spoke, those who heard her shone from within," the Rynn doctor chirped quietly. "I always thought it was a metaphor."

29

THE TRUTH IS LIKE THE SUN

Bright Sunlight entered the shuttle bay of the *Seeker*. His destination was not an accident, as he was looking for very specific core, and he had been told this was the most likely place to find them. *An all-male core*, he thought in disapproval. Like most traditional Rynn, he considered the primary purpose of a core to have and raise children—something not possible in an all-male core. To Bright Sunlight, an all-male core was incomplete.

He found the people he was seeking, and there were indeed four males—three Rynn, one human—but there was a female Rynn among them. He walked closer.

"It's not that I don't like you, Light of Three Moons," the human was saying. "But I've never … you know." To Bright Sunlight's surprise, the human's face was starting to turn red.

"I've never 'you knowed' either," Light of Three Moons shot back. "I have, however, had sex." The female's crest waggled in amusement. "I am offering to join your core because Frozen River asked and because you need someone like me," she said. "And the only one who is having a problem with it is you."

"I don't know how to … with a woman. Jeez, I can't believe this," grumbled the human. "Look, I think you're very pretty, but

I've never been comfortable with women. Not just the sex part—the talking part too."

"You seem to be doing just fine, Joseph," Light of Three Moons replied in amused tones. "I don't bite, you know."

"Well, there was that time," one of the Rynn males said.

"You're not helping, Frozen River," Light of Three Moons said in tart tones. "Look, Joseph, I'm not expecting you to do anything except accept me into the core," she said reasonably. "It's not going to hurt having sex with a female." Her crest waggled. "I promise."

"The things I do for my core," grumbled the human.

"Is that a 'yes'?" asked Light of Three Moons.

The human sighed and nodded.

"Good." She leaned over and kissed the human on the cheek. "See? It didn't hurt." She repeated the cheek kiss with the other three males. "Come by after dinner and help move my things into your suite."

Bright Sunlight waited until the female Rynn left the shuttle bay. He smiled to himself. *That's exactly the kind of woman that core needs*, he thought in approval. He looked at the men. The human had crawled halfway into an access port on the craft.

It was a strange craft, triangular in shape, with a central transparent blister. It looked both fast and deadly. *Like a silver Swift Strike*, he thought. Bright Sunlight had been a pilot in his youth, and part of him yearned to fly the strange ship. He raised his crest into a friendly position and walked over to the craft. "Greetings of the day," he said.

One of the Rynn men covered his eyes respectfully. "And to you, Bright Sunlight," he said. "I don't know if you remember me. I am Red Clouds Paint the Sky. We met just before the *Seeker* embarked." He indicated the others. "May I introduce my core: Black Rocks, Frozen River …" He smiled, and his crest waggled. "And those long legs belong to Joseph Franklin." He kicked the side of the ship. "Come out, Joseph."

The human dragged itself out of the access port. "What's going ... oh, hello."

"Joseph Franklin, this is Bright Sunlight, Kasumi's father," Red Clouds Paint the Sky said.

"Oh." The human stood up. He looked down at Bright Sunlight. "Nice to meet you." He appeared to look longingly at the ship.

"You can get back to making the Shrike deadlier later, Joseph," Red Clouds Paint the Sky chided. He turned to Bright Sunlight. "You'll have to forgive our core brother, but once he gets an idea into his head, he becomes ... fixated."

"I do not," protested the human.

"Tell that to someone who does not live with you," Black Rocks retorted. "Sometimes we have to drag him from here." The other members of the core nodded in agreement.

Bright Sunlight could not help but laugh. "I have met driven people before," he said. "It's a good thing you have a ..." He trailed off. "You truly are a core group, aren't you?" he said in wonder.

"A strong one," Black Rocks said in pride. "And no, Light of Three Moons will not change that," he said to the human in scolding tones. "She will just make it stronger."

"Listen to your core brother," Bright Sunlight found himself saying. "Spirits." He shook his head. "I am a fool." He covered his eyes. "The truth of what you are is like the sun," he said formally. "If I am wrong about this, what else am I wrong about?" His crest lowered. "Is it true that you built this ship by yourself?" he asked instead.

"Well, me and the fabricator," the human replied. "God, do I love the fabricator."

"He taught himself to use it in less than a day," Black Rocks said proudly. "Without a Torque."

"We're building more of them," Red Clouds Paint the Sky added. "But the Shrike is the first, the prototype," he said. "And the one he tests everything out on."

"I see," Bright Sunlight said. "And is it true you plan to go and fight the Polig-Grug?" He asked. "Or the Zaski?" He pointed to the ship. "In that?" The entire core nodded. "Aren't you afraid? You could die. You could be eaten."

"Anything that tries eating me or my core better have an industrial-size bottle of antacids," Franklin vowed. "Cause we ain't gonna go down easy." He bared his teeth, and Bright Sunlight took a step backward. "And I bite back."

Bright Sunlight glanced at the Rynn members of this core. *Spirits, but they're amused!* he thought. *They actually believe they can defeat* ... His thought broke off. He again covered his eyes briefly. "Thank you for speaking to me," he said. "I have much to think about."

Bright Sunlight walked slowly away.

30

Zenpathy

"Good afternoon, Mr. Blunt," greeted the visitor. He was a tall, thin, and slightly stooped man. He was pale, bald, and bearded. Jeremy liked him immediately.

"Good morning ... doctor?" Jeremy asked.

"Monhasses, Edwin Monhasses," the man replied. "Call me Ed."

"Well, Ed. Since I already have two physicians watching my every move, I must assume you are a ... psychologist?" Jeremy asked.

"As perceptive as advertised," Dr. Monhasses replied. "Though to be more exact, I am a neurobiologist. Simply put, I study how the brain functions. May I come in?"

Jeremy waved a hand in welcome. "Please," he said. He turned. "Morning Stars Fade," he called. "Tea for our guest."

A young Rynn male stuck his head out of the kitchen and nodded.

"Quite an intelligent young man," Jeremy said to Dr. Monhasses. "But then, most Rynn are intelligent." He led the doctor to the main room. "Sit anywhere." Jeremy sat on the couch.

Dr. Monhasses raised an eyebrow and sat down in a chair opposite the couch, separated from it by a low wooden table. "Why do I feel as if you are amused by me?" he said.

"That's because the Teacher probably is," said the Rynn male. He carried a tray and placed it on the table. "Teacher?"

"He studies the brain, Morning Stars Fade," Jeremy informed the young man. "Both biologically and cognitively."

The young Rynn male pursed his lips. "Would that mean that he is here to discuss your dreams, Teacher?"

"Probably not just mine, Morning Stars Fade," Jeremy replied. "What else can you determine?"

Morning Stars Fade looked at Dr. Monhasses for a long time before responding. "He makes himself look … harmless."

"Patients usually feel more comfortable when their counselor is unthreatening," Dr. Monhasses said. "I gather this young man is a student of yours."

"I see that the Teacher is not the only perceptive human," Morning Stars Fade replied. "I would have expected a more surprised response." He covered his eyes briefly. "I would consider it an honor to observe your conversation."

"Morning Stars Fade has my confidence," Jeremy said and gave the young man a fond look. "You may speak freely in front of him."

"I suspect disagreeing would cause you to be less than forthcoming," Dr. Monhasses replied. "As you wish." He reached into his jacket and pulled out a pocket recording device. He looked inquiringly at Jeremy. Jeremy nodded. "Thank you." He picked up a teacup and sipped. "According to my sources, your other student, Kasumi, is having recurring dreams," he said. "And a recent dream alerted her to your health issues."

"I was trying to die," Jeremy corrected. "Apparently, it wasn't yet my time." He smiled. "I'm sure it was just a coincidence."

"That would be the most probable explanation," Dr. Monhasses replied. "But you don't really think that, do you?" Jeremy just smiled in response. Dr. Monhasses snorted. "The most likely explanation is, as you said, coincidence. The next most likely explanation is that her Torque alerted her. It does monitor your health, after all," he pointed out. Again Jeremy just smiled. "But also according to my sources, she was not wearing her Torque at the time."

"Kasumi does not wear her Torque while she sleeps," Jeremy confirmed. He looked at Morning Stars Fade.

"Some Rynn wear Torques at all times, some do not," Morning Stars Fade said.

"So we are down to coincidence or something else," said Dr. Monhasses. "This is the first time either humans or Rynn have spent any time with another sapient species," he stated. "At the very least, the brain is going to have to … rewire to accommodate the new paradigm."

"But you don't believe that either," Jeremy replied. "What would be your wildest speculation?" he asked.

Dr. Monhasses leaned over and turned off the recorder. "Off the record, Mr. Blunt, I think it's possible that humans and Rynn are in … call it resonance," he said. "Kasumi was thrown into an extreme situation, and you yourself were near death. Both of you were highly stressed; both of your brains were probably flooded with hormones, forcing the latent resonance to cross the threshold into active communication."

"You most likely would be laughed at if you published such a speculation," Jeremy said in mild tones. "But since we are off the record, Kasumi has had dreams that featured my deceased wife. And I myself had a dream where she spoke to me."

"Spirits," whispered Morning Stars Fade. He covered his eyes with his hands.

"This is confidential," warned Dr. Monhasses.

"Morning Stars Fade will not speak of this to anyone unless I give him permission," Jeremy replied. Morning Stars Fade nodded wide-eyed. "So you believe that humans and Rynn are potentially telepathic with each other?"

"I wouldn't call it telepathy," Dr. Monhasses said. "What we may have is something subtler and more basic." He smiled. "I call it Zenpathy."

"Teacher, my Torque cannot decipher Zenpathy," Morning Stars Fade said.

"I believe Dr. Monhasses described it as a resonance," Jeremy said. He looked at the ceiling. "If I understand the name correctly, you are suggesting that we have an awareness of each other's effect on the local zeitgeist." He shrugged. "And somehow Kasumi pulled memories of Mei Lin not directly from me but from how my thinking about her affects those around me through both thoughts and actions." He looked at the doctor. "Of course, the other possibility is that Mei Lin is indeed speaking to me and Kasumi."

A slightly sour expression appeared on Dr. Monhasses's face. "Of course," he agreed. Then he shrugged. "Either way, it would be worth knowing, wouldn't it?" he said.

"It would indeed, Ed," replied Jeremy. "It would indeed."

31

Pact

Bright Sunlight walked out of the shuttle and started to walk slowly across the colony compound. Everywhere he looked, he saw humans and Rynn together. A mixed squad of human and Rynn warriors—the Rynn wearing their war paint—jogged by. A possible core of two humans and a Rynn walked close together. Another mixed group of what were probably technicians walked together, with both humans and Rynn gesticulating and speaking animatedly.

Bright Sunlight's crest snapped to its fullest, and he changed direction and headed toward the colony's administrative center—a complex of three buildings, two in the blocky style humans favored and the one in the center in the rounded style common to Rynn. It was the center building that was his destination.

He walked through the arch-shaped entranceway and toward a reception area. He stopped at the front desk. "Bright Sunlight of the Hot Springs Clan wishes to speak to Captain Kasumi of the Forest Cabin Clan," he said. "Forgive me for not making an appointment, but I only just decided that I should speak with her."

The Rynn behind the desk gave Bright Sunlight a dispassionate look. "I am Raindrops in a Tide Pool," he said in introduction. "I decide if your petition merits speaking to Kasumi."

Bright Sunlight nodded. "I had come to this planet with the

original intention of retrieving my daughter and bringing her home." His crest lowered but did not flatten. "I learned then that my daughter did not need retrieving."

Raindrops in a Tide Pool nodded in agreement.

"I also learned that my daughter had been given a new name and had created a new clan." Bright Sunlight continued.

Again, Raindrops in a Tide Pool nodded.

"She has made it known that it is her goal to seek out the Polig-Grug and the Zaski."

"She wishes to teach them to respect us," Raindrops in a Tide Pool said. "She wishes to teach them fear." The last was said with a fierceness that seemed out of place on a Rynn.

Bright Sunlight nodded. "Rynn and humans may die," he said.

"Death comes to all," the Rynn secretary said. "The Teacher says, 'Dying is easy; any fool can do it.'" Raindrops in a Tide Pool chittered. "The Teacher also says, 'It is not the dying but the death that counts.'" He smiled. "I mean to have a good death."

"You will go with the *Seeker* when it hunts?" Bright Sunlight asked in surprise.

The Rynn secretary nodded.

Bright Sunlight covered his eyes briefly. "I fear for my daughter, but I fear her scorn more," he said quietly. "I will sign the pact."

"Captain Kasumi is free at the moment," Raindrops in a Tide Pool said. "I will escort you."

"This is Crystal Chandler reporting from the colony," said the visibly pregnant reporter. "President Newgate's copter landed just moments ago." The camera panned to where a large number of people gathered. "The Pacific Alliance, the Eastern Bloc, and the reconstituted EU have all sent representatives to sign probably the most important treaty in human history." The camera returned to the reporter. "As signing the Magna Carta began the march toward democracy, today's signing will begin humanity's march to the stars."

The camera panned to a dais that had been erected in the middle of the colony. A number of Rynn were already on the dais, either seated or conversing with each other. Gone were the utilitarian blue or gray ship suits that most people associated with the Rynn; they were replaced by brightly colored robes or tunics over brightly colored trousers. They wore necklaces and bracelets, and earrings hung from their cup-like ears. Most of the female Rynn had flowers woven into their crests. More than ever did they look like birds.

The camera panned over to where a mixed group of human and Rynn adolescent and preteen children were clustered together. Music could be heard playing, and the teens and preteens formed into parallel lines. The music changed to a bouncy, bass-thumping beat, and the entire group started dancing in unison.

"I haven't heard that song in ages," said Crystal. "They're doing the wobble dance," she said in a laugh-filled voice. "And they look like they're having a blast."

The camera continued to watch the adolescents perform the group dance. Occasionally, Crystal would make a comment, but mostly she let the piece of street theatre play out on its own. The camera seemed to reluctantly pull away when the song ended and the youngsters ran off giggling.

The camera returned to focus on Crystal. "If that doesn't go viral, nothing will," she said. A serious expression replaced the cheerful one. "While most of the modern world is hailing this treaty as a great step forward, there are still some parts of the world that continue to react with fear," she said. "I will quote the Teacher Jeremy Blunt: 'A life lived in fear is not a life; it is an existence, and a poor one at that." She covered her eyes briefly. "The Rynn say, 'Truth is like the sun; it can both blind and illuminate. I cover my eyes to keep from being blinded, but not so much as to prevent illumination.'"

At her signal, the camera panned the mixed crowd of humans and Rynn. "This is the truth: Rynn and humans will travel the stars together, as friends and allies. We beg you to choose life over existence and choose illumination over blindness." She smiled. "We'll be right back."

The camera panned to a large gathering of men. While each man was dressed uniquely, the way they dressed was uniformly somber and conservative. There was a Roman Catholic bishop in black sitting next to a Russian Orthodox priest in black sitting next to a rabbi also in black. About the only persons not in black were a Shinto priest from Japan in white and an old Buddhist monk from Tibet in saffron robes. They were also the only two who seemed to laugh more than not.

Each man had been asked to give a benediction and/or prayer, and one by one they had taken their turn asking for some god's blessing. Incense was burned, chants were sung, salt was thrown, and drums were beaten.

Finally, one man, dressed in black silk pajamas, approached the lectern. "Good afternoon," he began. "I'm not really sure why I am speaking, other than because my granddaughter requested it." He clapped his hands together twice. "I am Jeremy Blunt, and I ask that our common ancestors attend and listen."

The Shinto priest looked at Jeremy in surprise for a moment and then smiled. The Tibetan monk also seemed pleasantly surprised and started to listen more intently.

Jeremy clapped his hands together again, twice. "Ancestors of humanity, look upon us and give your blessings," he said in a quiet yet carrying voice. He then clapped his hands together twice again. "Ancestors of the Rynn, look upon us and give your blessings." The Rynn in the crowd briefly covered their eyes.

"I call upon the ancestors of both," he continued, "because what we do today does not affect just humanity or just the Rynn. What we do today does not just affect America or Europe or Asia. What we do today does not just affect black or white or Asian. It does not just affect the Hot Springs Clan or the Smoking Mountain Clan. It does not just affect Christian or Jew or Muslim or Buddhist or Shinto or even atheist or agnostic. What we do today is unique in both our histories—and, in all honestly, we can use the help."

There was a smattering of chuckles and Rynn chitters.

"Ancestors and spirits," Jeremy concluded, "we are Rynn and humans, and today, history … changes."

The Shinto priest bowed. The other clergy did as they were wont—some genuflected, some bowed, some raised their hands. Nearly all of them had tears in their eyes.

The princess approached the Temple of Light. She felt more than saw her three companions. Even so, she looked to her left, her right, and over her shoulder. There was the faceless one, her first companion; the nearly insubstantial mist, her second; and behind them all, the stone giant. The princess wiped at her eyes.

"Is something wrong, princess?" asked the mist.

"No, not wrong," the princess replied. "I am blessed beyond my worth, and the truth of that is overwhelming." She stopped at the steps. "Holy one," she called. "It is I, Kasumi." She knelt on the first step. "I humbly ask permission to speak with you."

The sound of a broom sweeping came to her ears, and there at the top of the stairs was the old monk. "So, Granddaughter, does the great task begin?"

"Yes, Grandmother," the princess replied. "The journey will be long and success is not guaranteed, but to do nothing will only bring pain."

"More than pain, Granddaughter. Extinction," cautioned the old monk. "And even if you fight, extinction may still be all you reap."

"That may be true, Grandmother, but in my heart, I know this to be the right thing to do." The princess clapped her hands together twice. "Hear me, ancestors. Too long have we cowered in the shadows. I, who have thirsted beyond quenching, hungered beyond satiating, and let the elements tear at my very skin, pledge all that I am to bring us all into the light."

The sky over the temple darkened, and thunder crashed. The princess stood and turned her face to the gathering storm. "Do your worst," she cried. "Kill me ... if you can," she taunted. "But I will fight you."

"We will fight you," corrected the faceless one.

"I will seek you out where you hide," said the mist.

There was a sound like stone rubbing on stone. "Slow to move and slow to anger am I," the stone giant rumbled in a voice that shook the very ground. "When I move, all are ground to dust. When I anger, the heavens tremble."

The clouds retreated to the horizon, and the sun shone down on the temple. The old monk smiled in approval. "And the Teacher will hold it all in trust for you until you return," she said. "Good hunting, Granddaughter."

Kasumi opened her eyes in the darkness. "Good hunting." She smiled. "Good hunting, indeed." Kasumi closed her eyes and quickly fell back to sleep.

Year 8

32

First Blood

"It is astonishing what humans can do once they decide to do something," Bright Sunlight said. He was staring out of a view port on the *Safe Haven*. The reason for his admiration hung motionless in a recently created maintenance cradle. The cradle was a technological marvel in its own right. A thousand meters in length and slightly more than half that in width, it was capable of holding even the *Safe Haven*. Yet as impressive as the cradle was, it paled in comparison to what it currently held.

The vessel was, at three hundred meters in length, significantly smaller than the *Safe Haven* and no more than fifty meters at its widest point, tapering to ten meters at its prow. It looked more like a dagger than a spaceship. Roughly two thirds back from the narrow prow, two wing-like nacelles rose high and swept back.

"I thought the ships designed by Joseph Franklin looked deadly, but this one looks like a hungry *Sky Hunter*," he remarked. "And humans built it in less than a year." His crest fluttered.

"Humans and Rynn," corrected the white-haired old man standing next to Bright Sunlight. He waved a hand to indicate the ship and the construction cradle. "Both species working together to create something beyond the capability of either working alone."

"Alone, we would never have conceived of such a thing," Bright Sunlight admitted. "And that worries me."

"You fear that one day humans will surpass the Rynn and ... leave them behind," Jeremy Blunt said gently.

Bright Sunlight's crest fluttered.

"An understandable fear," Jeremy agreed. "I won't lie to you and tell you that you fear for nothing. Humans can be fickle," he said. "And it may be that we will disagree and possibly even fight each other."

He paused as a mixed group of humans and Rynn walked by. Laughter, both human and Rynn, came to their ears. Jeremy smiled. "But even if we do, I suspect we will get past our disagreements and remain friends."

"I hope you are right, Teacher Jeremy," Bright Sunlight replied. "Just as I hope my ... daughter is right." He sighed.

"She still remains your daughter," Jeremy said. "But she forges her own destiny." He put his hand on the alien's shoulder. "She is most competent."

Bright Sunlight's crest rose. He chittered quietly. "That she is." He straightened and returned his attention to the craft hanging outside the view port. "It does look like a hungry *Sky Hunter*."

When Kasumi had proposed going hunting for the Zaski and Polig-Grug, she had, in her mind, imagined doing so commanding her ship, the *Seeker*. However, it quickly became obvious that trying to retrofit the ship would not only be difficult but also potentially introduce some structural weaknesses. So instead, she had commissioned the creation of a brand-new class of ship. The yet-unnamed ship was to be the first of the Talon class destroyers.

It was hyperspace capable but, more importantly it carried the Franklin-designed thrusters, making it faster than anything its size should be. It had Rynn inertial compensators, though these had been improved by Joseph Franklin as well. The entire ship was protected by both the best force screens possible and the thickest armor practical.

Finally, it was armed with the most lethal weapons that humans and Rynn could conceive of. The list of offensive weaponry was incredible, but the deadliest was the quantum disruptor: the true incarnation of that science-fiction staple, the disintegrator beam. The same weapon had destroyed 90 percent of the nuclear weapons in the now lost city of Atlanta.

As if that wasn't enough, the ship carried a score of Shrike-class fighter craft—Franklin's original fighter design. Sleek and deadly, the arrowhead-shaped craft waited in their docking cradles. One fighter in particular had a pair of human legs sticking out of an access port.

A door slid open, and four Rynn walked into the hold. "I told you we'd find him here," said Red Clouds Paint the Sky, amused. He walked over to the fighter and kicked the legs. "Come out, Core Brother," he said.

"Come out or I'll crawl in there and pull you out," said Light of Three Moons.

"She'll do it too," Red Clouds Paint the Sky said in dire tones.

Franklin exited the access port. "I was just making a few adjustments," he complained.

"You have been making 'a few adjustments' for the past three work segments," Light of Three Moons said tartly. "That's nearly five human hours."

"It hasn't been that long," retorted Franklin. He looked at stern visage of the single female in his core. "Has it?" he amended uncertainly.

"Yes, it has," Light of Three Moons replied. "And I'm certain you have not eaten," she scolded. "I will not have you collapsing from hunger like you did three ten-days ago." Her crest rose. "And the two ten-days before that."

"But …" protested Franklin.

"No buts ... you are going to eat, and then you are taking a nap," Light of Three Moons declared. "Now move."

"I'd move if I were you, Core Brother," Black Rocks said. Frozen River chittered in amusement.

Franklin sighed. "Okay, okay ... I'm moving," he grumbled. He shuffled toward the elevator. Light of Three Moons followed to make sure he didn't get ... distracted.

"She's an excellent core sister, is she not?" Frozen River said. "And exactly what Franklin needs."

"He still gets too fixated," Black Rocks said. "But she is a most excellent core sister," he chittered. "And just as fixated." Frozen River and Red Clouds Paint the Sky joined Black Rocks in laughing.

Kasumi entered the bridge of her yet-unnamed ship. She sat down in her command chair and chirped to her Torque. Instantly, her vision was augmented by the Torque, and she was able to ascertain the status of every system. Another command, and she felt her mind integrate with the ship's weapons system. "The quantum disrupter is offline," she stated.

"That is intentional, captain," the human tech replied. "She's a massive drain on even this ship's power generator." The tech patted the station in front of him in an affectionate matter. "No reason to stress the girl more than she has to be."

"Why do humans always refer to ships as 'she'?" Kasumi asked.

The tech shrugged. "I guess because they act like women," he said. "They're temperamental, fickle, and need lots of attention." He rubbed his hands along the console. "And they're beautiful."

"A beautiful hunter," Kasumi mused. "Torque, search Earth mythology for a female hunter deity." She smiled. "She should also be beautiful." The Torque accepted the command, and Kasumi returned to reviewing the systems.

The Torque chirped. "Possible choices would be Diana, goddess of the hunt, also referred to as Artemis; Flidas, goddess of hunting and fishing; Mielikki, goddess of forests and the hunt; Nieth, goddess of war and the hunt, also known as the 'Opener of Ways' …"

"Hold," commanded Kasumi. "Tell me more of Nieth."

"Nieth or Net, a major and ancient Egyptian deity, goddess of war and hunting, creator of the universe, goddess of life and death …" the Torque intoned.

"Nieth," Kasumi mused. "Would you be willing to crew in a ship called the Nieth, technician?"

"Is Nieth the name of a hunting goddess?" the technician asked. Kasumi nodded. "Sounds mighty fine to me," he said. "Captain."

Kasumi and Mel sparred under the stern and watchful eye of Jeremy Blunt. To those who only saw Jeremy in social settings, this Jeremy would be a shocking stranger. Gone was the amiable philosopher, replaced by a stern and critical taskmaster. He seemed to be able to find flaws in the most perfect of skill exhibition.

"Kasumi! The blade should be higher; you're cutting your opponents throat, not his shoulders," he barked. "Mel! Are you trying to get killed?" he snapped. "You left your stomach completely open."

The two women barely nodded at each correction. They just made the correction and continued sparring.

Bright Sunlight watched wide-eyed. He leaned over to the tall human male sitting next to him. "I've watched tens of times now, and each time I think there is no possibility of her being more skilled, and each time she somehow improves." His crest fluttered. "She's already better than any Rynn sword artist I have ever seen," he said. "And what is even more amazing is that Mel is even better."

"From what Mel tells me, she's studied since she was five." David Eisenstadt pursed his lips. "Humans are barely coordinated at five."

"Remarkable," said Bright Sunlight. "Small …" Bright Sunlight paused. "My daughter began training at eleven sun paths … years." He chirped to his Torque. "Our years are shorter, but physically she had not yet begun …" Bright Sunlight chirped to his Torque.

"Apparently, our species have one more thing in common," he said in amusement. "We also go through a period similar to what humans call *puberty*." He watched the match for a while.

While Mel and Kasumi were wearing pads and using blunted swords—sabers to be exact—they were not holding back. Even with the padding, both combatants would wince when a particularly telling blow would land. They'd usually wince again when Jeremy invariably had a critical analysis of exactly why the blow landed.

Usually, whenever Mel and Kasumi sparred, there would be few if any observers. Eisenstadt would be there primarily because he too was studying swordplay with Jeremy. He'd already finished his training and remained to watch Mel and Kasumi. Bright Sunlight was a frequent observer.

"As impressive as they both are, I'm not sure I understand why they train as hard as they do," Bright Sunlight commented.

Eisenstadt looked at Bright Sunlight and then spoke quietly to his own Torque. A globe sprung up, and an image appeared. "This is a recording of the last Polig-Grug attack," he said. "The Polig-Grug are pretty consistent in their strategy. They overwhelm their prey's defenses and then butcher them."

"Our personal shields were developed to prevent that," Bright Sunlight replied. "As long as the shields have power, they are protected."

"And when they run out of power, they still end up being butchered." David nodded at the playing recording. "Which is exactly what happened." He spoke a command, and the image vanished. "I've seen that recording a dozen times," he said quietly. "It does not get any easier to watch."

"No," agreed Bright Sunlight in his own hushed voice. He swallowed. "You were going to explain why they train so hard."

"It's not just them. Mel and Kasumi are given additional training, but all the marines—human and Rynn—are being trained in using hand weapons." He smiled grimly. "One thing about the Polig-Grug, they do not use personal shields."

"They don't need shields. They are naturally armored," Bright Sunlight pointed out. "And they wear additional armor over their vulnerable points."

"Yes, but according to all the data the Rynn have on the Polig-Grug, that armor has weaknesses—weaknesses that can only be exploited by certain types of weapons." Eisenstadt nodded toward where Mel and Kasumi were sparring. "Weapons like sabers." Suddenly, Eisenstadt laughed. "And you really should see what the Ape and Bird squads are using."

33

War Paint

A recently promoted Lieutenant Hendriks held up a tubular construction. It was actually two tubes, each about three inches in diameter, connected by a sphere over twice that in diameter. "Listen up, ladies," he growled. "This ..." he shook the construct " ... is a Polig-Grug leg. There are six of these on a Polig-Grug." He pointed to the sphere. "That is its knee." He looked at the double squad. "Each leg has two knees." He grinned. "Can anyone, other than Franklin, tell me how many knees you're going to have to break to stop a Polig-Grug?"

"Trick question," Franklin replied. "You don't strike the knees, you strike the leg segments themselves."

"Ooh, we got a smart-ass on our hands," Hendriks sneered.

"I have not heard the humans have two brains," a Rynn trainee muttered. "And why would they have one in ...?"

"It's just a saying," Hendriks said in annoyed tones, to accompanying chuckles and chitters. "TS Franklin is correct. Those knees are virtually indestructible. The legs, however ..." He raised a steel alloy mace over his head and brought it down hard on the analog Polig-Grug leg. There was a loud snap, and green ichor splashed everywhere. "Now Lieutenant Breeze is gonna show you that you don't have to be a human to break a bug's legs."

"Bug?" muttered another Rynn. "They're only superficially insectoid."

"Maybe," chirped Cool Evening Breeze. Like Hendriks she had been recently promoted. As they has similar authority, Kasumi had decided to follow Hendriks recommendation to make their ranks the same. "But it's easier to say and expresses how I feel about them." She went over to the analog leg and raised her own mace. She brought it down hard on the unshattered leg segment. More green ichor splashed. "They're bugs," she said with a hawklike screech. "Dirty. Stinking. Bugs." She raised and lowered the mace another several more times before she stopped. She was panting.

Hendriks gave his friend, lover, and second in command a concerned look. "You okay, Breeze?"

Cool Evening Breeze shook herself. "Weirdly enough, yeah," she said. "Strangely cathartic." She looked at Hendriks. "Don't tell Crystal, okay, Fuzz Ball?"

Lieutenant Hendriks snorted. "Wouldn't dream of it, Feather Head."

"It was bad enough when Rynn started painting their faces," Bright Sunlight complained. "But why the ship?"

"Does she frighten you?" asked Technical Specialist Joseph Franklin. He grinned when Bright Sunlight nodded. "Good," he declared. "That was the general idea."

He and Bright Sunlight looked out the maintenance window at the recently christened *Nieth*. She was indeed painted in red and black slashes similar to those worn by the Rynn. The prow was painted to resemble a face, with two black-rimmed eyes stylized to resemble the Egyptian Eyes of Horus and a fanged mouth. "Hard to believe she's complete," he said almost to himself.

Turning to Franklin, he asked, "Do you and your core still intend to be on board when she leaves?"

Franklin smiled and nodded.

"I can't say I understand, but may the spirits protect you."

"Thank you," Franklin replied. A tone sounded over the station communication system. "Speaking of which, that's my signal to report." He briefly covered his eyes at Bright Sunlight and then hurried away.

Bright Sunlight watched as Rynn and humans rushed by him. Some of the Rynn's faces shimmered as the Torque applied their war paint. While humans normally did not use war paint, a number passed that had black swirls and lines on their faces.

Bright Sunlight followed. By the time he reached the access port to the *Nieth*, there were over two hundred humans and Rynn assembled. He could see Franklin, whose face was now adorned with black swirls and lines, standing with his core, all of whom wore the red and black war paint adopted by the Rynn.

Standing just in front of the access way and on a raised dais stood his daughter, her face painted half red and half black, and her core of Morning Mist, wearing red and black war paint; Mel Blunt, wearing red and black war paint; and David Eisenstadt, who wore black swirls and lines.

Kasumi raised her hands and the crowd quieted. "Warriors!" she cried, and the crowd went silent. "The great Earth Teacher K'ung Fu Tzu once said, 'Before going on a journey of revenge, first dig two graves.'" She briefly covered her eyes, as did the assembled humans and Rynn. "But we are not going on a journey of revenge," she said. "We are going on a journey to reclaim our pride."

"Oo-rah," grunted the assembled Rynn and humans.

"We are going on a journey to claim our place, not just for Rynn, but for Rynn and human."

"Oo-rah," growled the assembled Rynn and humans.

"We are going on a journey to show the Polig-Grug, the Zaski, and anyone else we run into that we are not food. Not prey," she said in a snarl. "And the spirits curse any species who dares to disagree."

"Oo-rah!" screamed the assembled Rynn and humans.

Eisenstadt stepped forward. "Atten-hut!" he barked, and the

two hundred Rynn and humans came to attention. "Ape Company, board ship," he commanded, and half the assembled formed a line. Faster than Bright Sunlight could imagine, the last of the first group passed through the gate. "Bird Company, board ship," barked Eisenstadt. The remainder of the assembled immediately lined up and quickly boarded.

Bright Sunlight noted that while both companies boarded, his daughter, now called Kasumi, stood at attention, her eyes covered. Bright Sunlight covered his own eyes. "The truth of what you are is like the sun," he said quietly. "It can blind and illuminate. I cover my eyes so I am not blinded, but not completely so I can be illuminated."

Kasumi and her core waited until the last of the assembled had entered the ship, and then they briskly followed. Within minutes, Klaxons began to sound. Rear thrusters glowed with energy, and the ship slowly moved out of its maintenance cradle. It rotated slightly and then started to move. Faster and faster it moved, and then the nacelles came to life and with a soundless roar, the ship vanished.

34

Bugs

They had been traveling for a little over a month. Most of that month had been spent making sure the ship and its crew could do what was necessary. David Eisenstadt had conducted battle exercise after battle exercise. He was still not satisfied, but at least he was sure that all systems were operational and that every member of the crew knew where to be at any given time.

Another thing he was sure about: the Rynn on board were nervous, keyed up, and eager to prove to their human partners that they were ready. The humans, most of whom were veterans, did their best to keep the Rynn focused. Still, the Rynn, like humans, needed to release some steam or explode. So far, the explosions were confined to occasional fights in the company canteen. "Never thought I'd say this," he said to Kasumi, "but I hope we find some Polig-Grug soon."

Kasumi chuckled. "I think my father would be surprised that Rynn are getting into fights because they … um …"

"… want to get into a fight?" Mel offered with a twisted smile. "What's that line?" she asked Eisenstadt. "Cry havoc …"

"… and unleash the dogs of war." Eisenstadt nodded. "The Rynn are off their leashes, but there's no prey in sight." He shrugged. "I'll schedule another all-hands drill." He smiled. "With live ammo."

"Captain," called Morning Mist. "Sensors are picking up a

distress call. It's in Rynn." She chirped to her Torque. "It's from the *Moon Shadow*," she reported. "She says she is being fired upon by an unknown ... check that ... Polig-Grug."

"Battle stations, battle stations, this is not a drill. Repeat, this is not a drill," the commander said crisply. Klaxons howled, and the lighting shifted to battle mode. "Helm, plot intercept course, full battle speed."

"Full battle speed, yes sir," reported the human helmsman.

"*Nieth* to *Moon Shadow*. *Nieth* to *Moon Shadow*," Morning Mist said crisply. "Hold on. Help is coming."

"*Nieth?*" replied a voice that thrummed with fear. "What in the spirits ... Spirits weep, we are losing power."

"ETA three minutes," called out the helmsman.

"*Moon Shadow*. Put all remaining power into the shields, including life support," Morning Mist said urgently. "Everything."

"That will only delay our death a few bits," came the voice.

"A few bits are all we need," Morning Mist said. "If the shields drop, retreat into the strongest room and barricade the doors," she urged. "Do not give up. Help is coming."

"They're cutting through the hull!" came the voice.

"Shrike squadron. Status?" barked Eisenstadt.

"Hot and ready to go," Joseph Franklin reported. "Just give the word."

"Retreat into the center of the ship," urged Morning Mist. "Help is on the way."

"Shrike squadron, launch!" ordered the Commander.

"Shrike 1 launching," Franklin replied.

"Shrike 2 launching. Shrike 3 launching. Shrike 4 launching," each fighter reported in turn. Soon twenty ships were flying at top speed.

"Okay, boys and girls, let's get their attention," Franklin shouted. "Give me weapon control," he ordered.

"*Moon Shadow, Moon Shadow*," Morning Mist called urgently. "Hold on. Help is on the way."

"Spirits, spirits, they're in the ship!" sobbed the voice. "They got Desert Wind. Spirits weep. They're … they're eating him." Screams could be heard over the communications channel.

"*Moon Shadow*," yelled Morning Mist.

"Polig-Grug ship turning to meet us, Commander," another bridge officer reported.

"Shields up," ordered the commander. "Weapons."

"Locked and ready, Commander," came the reply.

"Kasumi?" Eisenstadt asked. "Your orders."

"Tear them apart, David," Kasumi said in cold tones.

"Fire at will," Eisenstadt ordered.

"Attack ships, Joseph," Red Clouds Paint the Sky reported.

"I see them," Franklin said in tense tones. "Okay, Frozen River. Time to do some fancy flying."

"What was that line? Oh yes. Once more into the breach," Frozen River shouted.

Shrike 1 seemed to rear like a wild stallion and then plunged headfirst into the mass of incoming Polig-Grug fighters. Polig-Grug may have disdained personal shields, but they didn't seem to have a problem shielding their fighters. Bullets and missiles were deflected or exploded against those shields. In terms of shields and firepower, it seemed that the two forces were even.

"Hey, Frozen River, remember how you took out the Texas squadron?" asked Joseph.

"Spirits weep, you're not suggesting what I think you're suggesting," Frozen River replied. "Besides, we can't generate a shock wave in a vacuum."

"True, but what happens when two shields intersect at high speed?" he asked.

"We'll both be ripped apart," Frozen River protested.

"Maybe not," Franklin replied. "Not if we're spinning."

"Black Rocks, this is more your specialty," Frozen River said.

"It's never been done, but theoretically …" Black Rocks broke off and started chirping quietly to his Torque. "You'll need to get us spinning about twenty or twenty-five times per second on the longitudinal axis," he finally reported.

"Can you be more precise?" Frozen River complained. He swung the ship around and started it spinning. "I just hope the inertial compensators hold out."

"Twenty-two should do it," Black Rocks replied.

"Battle program set," Frozen River chirped tersely. "And … now!"

"Commander, an enemy fighter just … exploded," a technician aboard the *Nieth* reported. "Damn, there goes another."

"All Shrike fighters, I am sending a battle program," Black Rocks voice went out. "Initiate immediately."

"Damn, there goes another one," the technician reported. "Holy shit!" he exclaimed as fighters started exploding.

"*Moon Shadow*, please reply," Morning Mist continued to shout into the communications system.

"This … this is *Moon Shadow*," came the same voice that was speaking earlier. "They've left …" The voice broke off and sobbed. "Ten … ten dead," the voice choked out. "Who are you? What are you?" *Moon Shadow* asked in a shaky voice.

"We're Rynn," Morning Mist replied. "We will sing for your dead, *Moon Shadow*," she promised. "And if you see a giant fuzzy creature, don't panic … they're friends." Morning Mist smiled. "Stay with me, *Moon Shadow*."

Meanwhile, the two mother ships pounded each other with everything they had. Again, it appeared to be a stalemate. "Marines, I have a job for you," Eisenstadt said.

"It's about fucking time," Sergeant Major Stilson complained. "I was getting bored." He grinned. "What's the plan?" he asked. "Oh, please tell me it's Viking."

"You read my mind, Sergeant Major," Eisenstadt replied.

"Yeehaw!" crowed Stilson. "Okay, ladies, it's Viking."

35

Alsoo

"Don't make me have to explain to Crystal how you got lost, Fuzzy Butt," Lieutenant Cool Evening Breeze said seriously.

"You do the same, Feather Head," replied Lieutenant Hendriks.

"Cut the chatter," Sergeant Major Stilson barked. "For those too busy sleeping or whatever, we have been given the green light for Operation Viking." He raised his hands. "Settle down, ladies," he said. "The commander is going to get us as close as possible, and then we are all going for a short walk." He smiled. "Ape Squad One, you got first dibs."

Hendriks stood. "You heard the sergeant major," he barked. "Ape Squad, masks down." He lowered his own face mask. A moment later, he heard Cool Evening Breeze give the same command to Bird Squad One.

"Torque communications online." He walked over to a wall and hit a lever. The wall slid open to reveal the blackness of space. The only thing keeping the air inside the ship was an invisible force field. Lieutenant Hendriks reached down and pulled out his mace. "ROE is as follows: No prisoners, no quarter, no exceptions."

"Oo-rah," responded Ape Squad.

"Leave us a few," Cool Evening Breeze pleaded.

"Sorry, Breeze, no promises," Hendriks replied. "Oh, all right, maybe one," he mock-relented. "On your orders, Sergeant Major."

"Heads up," Stilson barked. "Hull shield going down. Now!"

"Move, move, move," ordered Hendriks. One after another, the members of Ape Squad—which despite the name each had Rynn and humans—leaped into space. Thrusters pushed them quickly toward the Polig-Grug mother ship. Hendriks leaped out after his company.

"Bird Squad, get ready," Stilson ordered.

"Bird Squad ready," replied Cool Evening Breeze.

"Launch!" ordered the sergeant major.

"Move, move, move!" ordered Cool Evening Breeze. Another hundred Rynn and humans launched themselves into the blackness. And even though, like Hendriks, Cool Evening Breeze did not leap into space until after the last of her company had already jumped, she somehow ended up being one of the first to make it to the Polig-Grug ship. She entered through a breech in the ship wall.

No sooner had she entered the ship than she was immediately set upon by a Polig-Grug. The guttural grunts of the quasi-insectoid were picked up by her Torque.

"Meat," came the translation. "Rynn meat." Two of the tentacle-like members reached for Cool Evening Breeze. "Hungry."

"You're gonna have trouble eating anything once I finish with you, bug," screeched Cool Evening Breeze. As she had expected, the Polig-Grug started to batter at her shield. She had studied every recorded instance of a Polig-Grug attack. David Eisenstadt had been correct in his assessment. Once they decided on their prey, the Polig-Grug would single-mindedly attack.

Relying on her shield, Cool Evening Breeze charged the insect-like being. She swung her mace and, to her pleasure, she made a solid connection to one leading segmented leg. The alien stumbled as the leg gave way, and Cool Evening Breeze brought the mace down on the creature's head. She hit the creature several more times before she moved on to the next Polig-Grug.

"Fuzzy Butt, where are you?" Cool Evening Breeze said into her Torque.

"Kinda busy right now, Breeze," Hendriks replied. "These bozos are more like bugs than we thought," he grunted. "It's like a fucking hive."

"And me without a can of bug spray," returned Cool Evening Breeze. Another Polig-Grug charged her.

"Hey, Breeze, did I ever tell you that fighting makes me horny?" Hendriks said through the Torque.

"Everything makes you horny," Cool Evening Breeze replied. "You asking for a date?"

"Yeah," replied Hendriks.

"Whoever squashes the most bugs gets to be on top, deal?" chirped Cool Evening Breeze.

"Deal," agreed Hendriks. "Later, Feather Head."

"There better be a later, Fuzzy Butt," Cool Evening Breeze replied. She turned her attention to the charging Polig-Grug. "This is definitely not your day," she chittered and charged.

The shuttle carrying Kasumi, Mel, and Morning Mist docked with the Polig-Grug ship. They exited, with Morning Mist between Mel and Kasumi. "Are you sure you're up for this, Mist?" Mel asked. "Kasumi and I can protect you, but it's gonna be rough."

Morning Mist's crest was completely flat against her skull. "I'm the best computer tech you have," she said in a faint voice. "You need me."

"We need you alive, baby," Mel replied. "You keep us together."

"I can do this, Mel," Morning Mist replied. "I need to do this."

"And Rynn keep saying they're cowards," Mel said in approving and amused tones. "No worries, baby, they'll have to go through us to get to you."

They made it to the control room with minor impediment. A single Polig-Grug charged but was immediately decapitated by a grim and silent Kasumi. They forced open the control room door and were immediately met by over a dozen Polig-Grug. "Stay behind us, Mist," Kasumi ordered.

"Meat," grunted a Polig-Grug.

"Can't you bugs say anything other than 'meat'?" complained Cool Evening Breeze. Her mace flashed out to impact against another bug's leg.

"Possibly not, Lieutenant," a human soldier commented. "I think we're dealing with a hive mentality." He pursed his lips. "There may be a queen somewhere."

Cool Evening Breeze looked at the human soldier in surprise. "Spirits, I hope you're wrong," she said. She chirped to her Torque. "Everyone, keep your eyes open for a queen Polig-Grug, or the equivalent."

"Your warning would have been more welcome a minute ago, Breeze," Mel replied over the Torque. "There is a queen, and she's right in front of us." She and Kasumi had formed into a defensive shield for Morning Mist. The communication tech was trying to break into the Polig-Grug system, much to the displeasure of the creature in front of them.

It was easily twice the size of a regular Polig-Grug, with a much larger skull and thicker leg segments—legs that kept battering at Kasumi and Mel's shields. It took all of Mel's and Kasumi's skill to keep the giant creature at bay.

"Where's an oversized human when you need one?" Kasumi grumbled. Her saber slashed and scored on one massive leg segment. Green ichor splashed. The Polig-Grug queen backed away.

"Oh, I don't know, Sister," Mel said. "You seem to be doing okay." She looked over her shoulder. "How's it coming, Mist?"

"Slowly," Mist replied. "There is nothing logical about their software." She chirped to her Torque. "Half of it is just random nonsense," she grumbled. "In," she reported triumphantly.

"Vacuum out everything," Kasumi ordered. "Prioritize finding their home system."

"Fuck, we just lost Shrike 11," Black Rocks reported.

"Survivors?" asked Red Clouds Paint the Sky.

"If there are, there's nothing we can do to help," Black Rocks replied. "How many of these ships do they have?" he complained.

"A lot fewer than they had at the beginning," Frozen River replied. "How are you holding up, Joseph?" He frowned when there was no reply. "Joseph?" he repeated. "Black Rocks, you're closest. Check on Joseph."

Black Rocks scrambled from his seat and climbed into the weapons blister. Joseph Franklin was limp in his weapons chair. Blood was streaming from a wound in his neck. "Joseph is hit! Joseph is hit!" Black Rocks said frantically. "Get us out of here, Frozen River," he said, even as he started administering first aid.

"This is Shrike Leader, we are retreating," Frozen River broadcast. "Shrike Leader is retreating."

"Copy, Shrike Leader," came a voice. "Shrike 2 is now Shrike Leader," the voice continued. "All Shrikes acknowledge."

Frozen River piloted the Shrike back to the *Nieth*. The moment he docked, an emergency medical team converged on the fighter and quickly extracted Franklin. They raced away.

Black Rocks, Red Clouds Paint the Sky, and Frozen River sat down on the floor of the hangar and leaned against the Shrike. "He didn't look good," Black Rocks said quietly.

A few minutes later, Light of Three Moons entered the hangar. She walked over to the three members of her core and sat down. She didn't say anything, just sat there. First Frozen River, then Black Rocks, and finally Red Clouds Paint the Sky pressed against her. Light of Three Moons began to sing.

"Done," announced Morning Mist.

"Kasumi to all hands, we have what we came for," she announced via her Torque. "Set scuttling charges and retreat," she ordered. "Repeat, set scuttling charges and retreat." She charged the Polig-Grug queen and sliced through one forelimb. The queen retreated to the other end of the room. With Kasumi walking backward, she, Mel, and Morning Mist made their escape.

"Detail," shouted Cool Evening Breeze. "Dead and wounded evac first," she ordered. "You have thirty minutes." Cool Evening Breeze reached into a side pocket and pulled out a star-shaped object. She twisted a dial. "Thirty minutes from … mark." She pressed a button.

"You better be retreating, Fuzzy Butt," Cool Evening Breeze said over her Torque.

"Got a bit of a situation here, Breeze," Hendriks replied. "Home in on me and see for yourself."

"Squad 1 on me," called Cool Evening Breeze. "The rest of Bird Squad set charges and retreat." Cool Evening Breeze grumbled to herself as the Torque guided her toward Hendriks. He actually wasn't that far away, and she got there in under five minutes. The tall marine was staring into a room. "What the … spirits save us!" she exclaimed.

The room was crowded with cages, and nearly every cage was populated with one or more creatures. All the creatures were the same: a meter in length with a snakelike body; a triangular head with two large forward facing eyes; no visible ears or nose; a mouth like an inverted triangle; and two short forelimbs that ended in a stubby three-fingered hand. The entire creature was covered in brown and gray feathers.

Cool Evening Breeze looked at the creatures and was about to turn away when one of them reached out with a stubby hand and warbled.

"Sound analysis suggests meaning," her Torque chimed. The creature warbled again. "Best translation: 'Help.'"

"Oh crap," Hendriks spat. He went over to the nearest cage and ripped the door open. The creature cowered against the back. Hendriks reached in and pulled the creature out. "Don't bite—I'm trying to save you."

"How many are there?" Cool Evening Breeze asked. She started making a quick count. "Everybody grab four or five."

"But Lieutenant, they're animals," a Rynn protested.

"Animals don't say 'Help,'" Cool Evening Breeze shot back. She pulled open the cage of the one that warbled. She waggled a hand, and the creature grabbed with its own hand. "Cool Evening Breeze to *Nieth*."

"This is *Nieth*. Why aren't you retreating?" came a voice. "You're running out of time."

"No time to explain. Just send over two shuttles. Stat," she ordered.

There was a pause. "Shuttles on their way."

"Good," said Cool Evening Breeze. "Set up a quarantine zone in the hangar." By this time, she was loaded down with a half dozen of the feathered creatures. Hendriks had twice as many. Between her, Hendriks, and the rest of the squad, they accounted for all of the creatures. "If any bolt, do not chase," she ordered. "Let's get as many of these to the shuttles as we can."

Amazingly, by the time they reached the shuttles, not a single one of the strange creatures had bolted. More amazingly, once they were placed in the shuttle, they all clustered against the back. "I don't know if you're sentient," Cool Evening Breeze said half to herself, "but you're damn close." She and the rest of the squad took seats. "Let's get out of here," she said.

The shuttle retreated from the Polig-Grug ship. "Cool Evening Breeze to Bird Squad, do we have a casualty count yet?"

"Not complete yet," replied one of the company members. "Latest report is three dead, eight injured, eight missing."

"Spirits, that's almost 20 percent," Cool Evening Breeze said in horror.

"Considering none of us ever fought a space battle, let alone against the Polig-Grug, I think we did pretty damn good," Hendriks replied. He looked at his watch. "Any moment now." He smiled sadly. "I got similar numbers from Ape Squad." He looked at his watch again. "There should have been …" A flash of light through a port window interrupted him. "Right on time."

One of the feathered snakelike creatures crept over to the window and looked out. It hooted and warbled. Soon the rest were warbling. The same creature crawled over to Cool Evening Breeze and warbled. "Torque?"

"Insufficient data. Possible translations: food, we, question. hungry, we, question," replied the Torque.

"I think they're either saying they're hungry or wondering if we're going to eat them," Hendriks offered. "Considering that they probably were meals, I'd guess the first."

Cool Evening Breeze nodded. "You may be right." She looked down at the strange creature. She slowly reached into a pocket and pulled out a ration bar. She peeled it out of its wrapper and offered it to the creature. The creature looked at it and then slowly took the ration bar. It retreated to the cowering group and offered it to one of them. The second creature also looked at it and then bit off a small piece. It made a grimace but kept chewing.

A couple members of the squad pulled out their own ration bars and offered them to the feathered creatures. These were accepted in the same cautious manner. None of the rations were eaten until the one that had sampled it warbled, and then the rations were carefully broken into roughly identical pieces.

"I wonder if they'd make good troopers," Hendriks mused half to himself.

"Not smart enough," Cool Evening Breeze replied.

"Officers, then?" Hendriks asked.

"Not dumb enough," Cool Evening Breeze replied. She and Hendriks laughed. "Thanks, Fuzzy Butt," she said. "I needed that."

"Any time, Feather Head," Hendriks replied.

One of the feathered snakelike creatures slithered over. It held the upper part of its body erect, and its motion was more like a sidewinder rattler than a typical snake's. It stopped just out of arm's reach—Hendriks' arm's reach. It warbled at Hendriks and Cool Evening Breeze.

"Best translation: event/action question," whispered Hendriks' and Cool Evening Breeze's Torques.

"Now what?" asked Hendriks.

"Within parameters," replied the Torque.

"Torque—try to translate the following: We will not eat you."

The Torque warbled.

The creature warbled back.

"Best translation: Death/dead/us you question," replied the Torque.

"Torque translate: We will not kill you," Cool Evening Breeze replied. "But we are not sure what to do with you."

The Torque warbled to the creature.

The creature warbled for a long time.

"Best translation: Eaters home have/take. People Eaters hide. Eaters People find. People hide/hide. People hungry/scared. Little time/duration no people." The creature warbled some more. "Big split-tail say/talk/speech not Eaters, kill Eaters. Not know/sure/understand. People scared."

"Crap," Hendriks exclaimed. "Torque translate: There are two kinds of split-tails—human …" he pressed a hand against his chest and then pointed to Cool Evening Breeze " … and Rynn." He continued, "We are enemies of the Eaters. We call Eaters Polig-Grug."

The Torque warbled.

"That's a lot to translate, Fuzzy Butt," Cool Evening Breeze cautioned.

"I think they're smarter than we think," Hendriks replied. "Hey, I think he just said Polig-Grug."

"Best translation: Polig-Grug Eaters are, statement."

The creature warbled some more.

"Human split-tail Polig-Grug enemy, Rynn split-tail Polig-Grug enemy. Split-tail People enemy not know/sure, People friend not know/sure," the Torque translated.

"You're right, Fuzz Ball, they are smarter than we thought," Cool Evening Breeze said. "Torque translate: We understand why the People say they don't know. Understand we also don't know about the People." She paused. "We ask that you stay here until we are sure."

The Torque warbled.

The creature warbled back. "People stay here/this place." It raised its hands and then slithered back to the rest of them.

"We'd better go talk to the captain," Hendriks said. "You realize we're gonna get reamed, don't you?"

"At least my conscience will be clear," Cool Evening Breeze replied. "Let's go see the captain."

36

What Was Intended

"Let me see if I understand this," Captain Kasumi chirped angrily. "You found a bunch of … things in cages in the Polig-Grug ship and brought them here, on this ship?" she snapped. "How many of these … animals are there?"

"They call themselves the People," Cool Evening Breeze replied. "In their language, that sounds something like *Alsoo*." Her crest rose. "Which sort of proves that they are not animals." She locked gazes with Kasumi. "Yes, they are primitive. But they have a language. They appear to have a culture. And they're scared and lonely, and spirits weep, if I left them you might forgive me, but I couldn't." She forced her crest to lower to something less combative. "And there is one thing you are not considering," she said.

"And that is?" Kasumi questioned angrily.

"They are exactly what the Polig-Grug had intended for us," Cool Evening Breeze replied. She matched Kasumi glare for glare. It was Kasumi who looked away first.

"Are you willing to take responsibility for our … guests?" Mel asked.

"We both will," Hendriks replied. "With your permission, we'd like to start on that immediately."

"Let it go, Core Sister," Mel said to Kasumi. "They're right, and you know it."

Kasumi kept her face averted but nodded. "Go ahead," she said to Cool Evening Breeze and Hendriks. "We'll expect reports, and any damages come out of your pay."

"You can have my entire paycheck," Hendriks replied. "Come on, Feather Head," he said. "We got some new recruits to train." He and Cool Evening Breeze covered their eyes briefly and then left the bridge.

"Ten to one he wasn't kidding about the recruits comment," Mel said after they left. "You okay, Core Sister?"

"No," Kasumi said quietly. "She was right, and I … I let my hatred of the Polig-Grug blind me." Her crest flattened. "Spirits forgive me. I am ashamed." She looked at her hands. "I keep expecting to see blood."

"That's a very human metaphor," Mel said. "Hold on to that shame, Core Sister," she said. Kasumi looked at Mel in surprise. "That's your conscience speaking. As long as you can hear it, you are not lost."

Kasumi nodded. "Any word on Franklin?" she asked. "Forgive me; I just did it again." She returned her attention to her hands. "There were ten others who were as seriously injured and almost twice that many dead or missing, and all I can think of is the loss of one person."

"Well, he is our most lethal weapons designer," Mel began. "Ah, I see," she said in realization. "We're in a war, Core Sister," she said. "But what's the good of winning a war if you lose your soul?"

Kasumi nodded. "Yeah, that's a hard one."

Mel put an arm across Kasumi's shoulders. "You may think this is strange, but I think you should try to talk to Grandma Mei."

Kasumi turned her head to look into Mel's eyes. "Do you really believe I am talking to your grandmother?" she asked.

Mel smiled. "I'm not the person who needs to answer that, now am I?" she said. "I am going to go talk to Morning Mist, and you are going to take a nap." She pressed her forehead against Kasumi's. "Even if Grandma Mei does not speak to you, a nap will do you good." She stood and pulled Kasumi to her feet. "Now scat."

"Yes, Mel." Kasumi gave Mel a weak smile. "Thanks."

"That's what a good core sister does, right?" Mel said. "Go on." She turned Kasumi around and gave her a gentle push.

Mel watched Kasumi walk away before saying, "Torque: status on Joseph Franklin." She waited close to a full five minutes before there was a response. "Joseph Franklin will live," the Torque reported. Mel gave out a relieved breath. "While Omiset will eventually repair the damage, the medical technicians are foreseeing an extended convalescence."

"How extended?" Mel asked.

"According to the report that has been filed, the technicians will be keeping Joseph Franklin in an induced coma until the Omiset finishes reducing cerebral swelling. After which they will determine to what extent his higher cortical functions were damaged." The Torque replied dispassionately. "The consensus is that he will achieve something close to a full recovery."

"Something close," Mel repeated.

The core of Red Clouds Paint the Sky, Black Rocks, Frozen River, and Light of Three Moons sat huddled together in their quarters. They had returned there after first seeing for themselves that Joseph Franklin still lived and listening to the chief medical technician. To a Rynn who was raised believing that Omiset could cure just about anything short of death, the medical technician's somberly delivered report was almost a physical blow.

The small piece of shrapnel that had felled Franklin had entered through his neck and become lodged in the upper part of the medulla oblongata. Between the massive blood loss and the nerve damage, his injuries were at the very limit of Omiset's ability to repair. He'd live, but at the moment that was about all the medical technician was sure of.

After a while, Light of Three Moons excused herself and made some tea. Rynn had become big fans of Earth tea, and nearly all Rynn had added tea to their daily diets. She was in the middle of her preparations when her Torque chimed, indicating a message. She accepted the message, and an image of Franklin appeared before her.

"Hi, Light," the image said. "I programmed my Torque to send you this if I was separated from the Torque for more than twenty-four hours. So if you are receiving this, I am either dead or close to it."

Light of Three Moons hurriedly paused the recording and ran into the main room. "Everyone, Joseph left us a message." She restarted the message.

"If the rest of you are wondering why I sent this to Light, well, it's because she's the most level-headed of all of you," Franklin's image continued. "Yeah, yeah, I know Frozen River has no nerves, and it takes a lot to rattle Red Clouds, but honestly you guys get all crazy whenever you think I'm fixated."

"What about me?" complained Black Rocks.

"And I know Blackie is complaining that I forgot about him." The image smiled sadly. "I kind of hope I'm not dead, but I knew the risks when I signed on," he said. "Anyway, I just wanted you to know that ever since I met all of you, well, I'm not the same man I was. I hardly laughed before I met you, and now I laugh almost all the time. I was afraid to love, and now I worry I don't love you all enough. I was afraid to live. I'm not afraid of living anymore. What's funny is that I'm not afraid of dying anymore either." The image briefly covered his eyes. "Remember me."

Light of Three Moons, Black Rocks, Red Clouds Paint the Sky, and Frozen River all briefly covered their eyes. "You are not dead yet, Joseph Franklin," Light of Three Moons declared. "But if that is to be, we will always remember you."

The princess approached the Temple of Light. She reached the bottom of the steps and hesitated. The temple was unchanged, yet she felt unwelcome. She sank to her knees at the base of the steps. She started to cry, but abruptly and angrily wiped at her eyes. "No, I will not cry," she said to herself. "I have chosen my path, and I must follow it to the end."

The princess raised her head and looked up at the temple doors. "I am the princess. My thirst for water has turned into a thirst for blood. My hunger for food has become a hunger for the flesh of my enemies. There is no shelter for me."

"My, my, such self-hate," came a familiar voice. "Are you truly fallen so low?" The old monk walked down the steps as she spoke.

The princess nodded. "Yes, Grandmother," she said. "In my search for vengeance, I forgot what I was truly fighting for." She bowed her head. "I nearly became what I hated most in my enemies."

The old monk raised a hand. Nestled in her palm was a tiny red and green snake. It seemed to be made of thousands of individual crystals. "Beautiful, is it not?" She extended her hand to the princess. "Beautiful and fragile and in need of protection."

The princess nodded. "And that is what I forgot," she said. "Forgive me." She reached out, and the snake crawled from the old monk's hand into hers. "Forgive me," she said to the snake. The snake crawled up the princess's arm and then to her shoulder. Finally, it nestled against her neck.

The princess stood. "I am the princess. I, who have thirsted beyond thirst, forgot that others thirst as well. I who have hungered beyond satiation forgot that others hunger as well. And I who stand before you naked forgot that while I discarded my fine clothing, others have always been naked."

"Remember always what you forgot, Granddaughter," said the old monk. "And remember one more thing," she said. "If you were truly lost, you would not have cared that you forgot." The old monk smiled. "When next you see the Teacher, remind him of that as well."

Kasumi walked into the main cargo bay of the *Nieth*. She hadn't been in the bay since before the battle with the Polig-Grug, but she knew that the large stack of packing crates was not there originally. She examined the stack and quickly realized that it wasn't a haphazard pile. First of all, it was symmetrical: two vertical towers of three crates flanked a central section in the shape of a stepped pyramid. Secondly, she could see a number of the Alsoo moving in and around the structure. It seemed that every one of the snakelike creatures was doing something.

She walked toward the structure. A number of the Alsoo surged out, each one carrying a sharpened wooden stick. They formed a defensive wall in front of the structure. The Alsoo were, as she had been told, snakelike from the waist down, and they moved in a manner that had been described as sidewinding. They held their lemur-like upper body perpendicular to the ground. They were feathered everywhere but the underside of their bodies and their owl-like faces. The feathers were thickest on top of their triangular heads.

Kasumi raised her hands to show they were empty. "I came to talk," she said, and her Torque translated her words into the warbles of the Alsoo.

One Alsoo warbled back, "Too close/near home/burrow you."

Kasumi nodded and took a couple steps back. "I came to talk," she repeated.

The Alsoo who spoke before moved forward. "First-Son-First-Born speaker me," he warbled. "Speaker home/burrow me."

Kasumi briefly covered her eyes. "I am Kasumi," she said in introduction. "Speaker for Rynn and humans."

The Alsoo warbled. "Big split-tail Hen'riks and mate Coo'Evn'Brees speak Kasumi/you name." The creature slithered closer and grounded his stick. "Speak/say speaker you. Speak/say great warrior you. Speak/say Eaters enemy you."

Kasumi nodded. "Eaters are my enemy," she agreed. "They ate many Rynn. I have sworn to fight them," she said. "The humans, the big split-tails, will fight them. They are our allies, our friends."

"Truth question," warbled the Alsoo leader.

"Truth," confirmed Kasumi.

"Want/desire/need fight/struggle we," the Alsoo leader warbled. "Small we truth. Warriors we truth." He waved a stubby hand at the structure. "Females protect pledge/oath you. Warrior kill Eaters we." He slapped himself on his chest. "Pledge/oath."

And so my vision is true again, Kasumi thought. She covered her eyes briefly. "I will protect the females. Pledge/oath," she said. "We—Rynn, human, and Alsoo—will fight the Eaters together," she said. "Pledge/oath." She slapped her chest.

"Pledge/oath," replied the Alsoo leader and slapped his chest.

Joseph Franklin opened his eyes and saw nothing. "What?" He croaked. "Dark."

"Your vision will return in time," said a calm voice. "Welcome back, Mr. Franklin."

Franklin felt someone take his hand and, based on the feeling, take his pulse. "Human?"

"Dr. Edwards," the voice said. "Now I want you to try to stay calm. There are some things you need to know."

Franklin nodded.

"Good," the doctor said. "The good news is that you should make an almost complete recovery."

"Almost?" Franklin asked in a quiet voice.

"Omiset is an amazing drug, but it has its limitations," Dr. Edwards said. "One limitation is that it cannot restore anything that is ... no longer there." Franklin could hear the doctor sigh. "The piece of shrapnel that struck you damaged part of the medulla oblongata. That's ..."

"The brain stem," Franklin supplied.

"Exactly," Dr. Edwards said. "Fortunately, the part of the medulla that controls autonomic functions—your breathing, swallowing, etc.—was undamaged," he said. "The damage was confined to the sensory and motor functions. That is why you are currently unable to see."

Franklin was silent for a while as he digested the information. "Walk?" he asked finally.

"Unlikely, Mr. Franklin," Dr. Edwards replied. "Not on your own, anyway." He cleared his throat. "You also might have some difficulty with fine motor control in your hands," he said. "To put it simply, your hands will shake."

"Shake," Franklin repeated. "A lot?"

"We don't know," Dr. Edwards replied.

Franklin licked dry lips. "Thank you for being honest," he forced out through a dry throat. "My core? Do they know?"

"Yes, Mr. Franklin," Dr. Edwards replied.

Franklin nodded. "I'd like to ... I guess *see* is not accurate, is it?" He chuckled. "My vision will return?"

"Probably within the next day or two," Dr. Edwards replied confidently.

Franklin nodded again. "Can my core visit?" he asked.

"Your core is waiting outside," Dr. Edwards said. "They can stay as long as they want."

37

Maker

Captain Kasumi sat at the head of the conference table. This was her senior staff meeting, and in attendance were Mel, Morning Mist, David Eisenstadt, and Sergeant Major Stilson. "Morning Mist, any new information on the Polig-Grug?"

"Yes." Morning Mist's crest flared. "How those … monsters became space farers, I don't think we'll ever know," she said. "By all that I've learned, they shouldn't have been able to build a wall, let alone a starship." She chirped to her Torque, and an image formed. "This is just a segment of the code I vacuumed out of their computers," she chirped in annoyed tones. "Ninety percent of the code is junk. I swear, it only works because there is so much of it."

"An infinite number of monkeys typing into an infinite number of computers," Mel mused. "Just by chance alone, they'd create something usable."

"Something like that," Morning Mist agreed. "And I think that's basically what might have happened." She chirped and the image changed. "Based on what I have been able to interpret, the Polig-Grug are ancient and attained their present form something close to fifty million years ago." She chirped again. This time the image was of the queen surrounded by a number of drones. "There is an orifice at the base of the cranium of every drone." A circle appeared to mark the location. "The queen does not have the orifice, but she does have these." A circle appeared at the base of the queen's skull outlining a ropy mass. "This appears to be a nerve bundle."

"You're going to tell me that the queen plugs into the drones?" Eisenstadt opined.

"Oh, more than that," said Morning Mist. "Two queen tentacles can fit into a drone port." She frowned. "At least two."

"Multiple queens can create a serial connection to ... what?" Mel pursed her lips. "Hundreds, thousands of drones?"

"Each one adding a slight increment to the Polig-Grugs' processing, or rather intellectual, capability," Morning Mist nodded. "Get enough linked, and you'll have ... something insanely intelligent."

"On the other hand, any individual Polig-Grug is not going to be all that bright," Kasumi decided.

"Actually, pretty damn stupid," Mel commented. "But how would they ... oh, I get it." Mel leaned forward. "When the queen connects with the drones, they form basically a single entity that can pilot their spacecraft, devise strategy, etc ... but when they disconnect, they retain their latest ... programming?"

"That seems to be the case," Morning Mist agreed. "If we can disrupt that connection ..." She smiled as everyone at the table started nodding. "I've already formed a research team."

"Excellent work, Morning Mist," Kasumi said in unfeigned approval. She briefly covered her eyes.

"Next on the agenda: the Alsoo," Mel said. "I know you have a lot on your plate, Morning Mist, but have you found their home world?"

Morning Mist shook her head. "Polig-Grug star maps are even more obscure than their software," she said. "I think we'd be better off just following one of their ships and see where it goes."

"I hate to state the obvious, but has anyone asked the Alsoo?" Eisenstadt asked. "At the very least, they can tell us the color of their sun, describe constellations. Something is better than nothing."

"I'll have Hendriks and Breeze do that," Stilson said.

"Have them see if the Alsoo can be trained to use modern weapons," Kasumi stated firmly. "I promised them that they could join the fight against the Polig-Grug, and I mean to deliver on that promise."

Joseph Franklin grunted in suppressed pain as he pulled himself off his bed and onto his mobility unit. It was superficially a wheelchair, except it had no wheels, and his position was more upright than seated. Instead of wheels, it floated in midair. It was less antigravity than a modification of the Rynn force shield.

"Unbelievable," Black Rocks said in admiration. "We've had the force shield for nearly fifty years, and never had anyone considered using it this way."

"It just needed some fresh eyes to look at it," Franklin retorted. He rubbed his own eyes. While his vision had returned, he would get frequent headaches and pains from eyestrain. He reached for the controls and stopped when his hands began to shake. He frowned in annoyance. "This is not going to work," he muttered. "At least not like this," he added. "Hmmm."

Black Rocks smiled to himself. "I have a few things I need to do," he said. "I'll be back in a couple ticks." Franklin nodded absentmindedly.

Black Rocks left the suite he and his core lived in and headed toward the main bay. This was his destination for two reasons. One was that Frozen River and Light of Three Moons were there and he wanted to give them an update on Joseph's progress. The other was one shared by nearly the entire crew: the Alsoo.

There wasn't a single Rynn or human who was not fascinated by the Alsoo. So far, they were the smallest sapient creature discovered and the very first Naga-form. This was a term coined by a human that described a being with a human torso and a snake's body.

The Alsoo were sapient, but just barely. As far as anyone could determine, their language consisted of approximately six hundred words, with a syntax that was understandable if fractured. They had mastered fire, stone-carving and chipping, wood-shaping, and the rudiments of weaving—things that humans and Rynn had also mastered even before they had evolved into their modern versions.

Black Rocks entered the bay and immediately headed toward where the Shrikes were docked. He could see Frozen River inside the blister. He looked for Light of Three Moons, and it wasn't until he was nearly at the ship that he saw her. She was half inside an access port. A bittersweet smile appeared on his face. *That should be Joseph in there*, he thought. "Greetings, Core Brother and Sister," he called out.

"Greetings, Core Brother," Frozen River returned. "What news?"

Black Rocks laughed. "I fear Core Brother Joseph is becoming fixated again."

"Spirits be praised," Frozen River replied. He shared a chittering laugh with Black Rocks.

"Has anyone seen Red Clouds Paint the Sky?" Black Rocks asked.

"He's where everyone who isn't doing something else is," Frozen River replied with a chitter. "Making friends with the Alsoo." His crest fluttered. "I'd go myself, but Light of Three Moons insisted we finish repairing the Shrike." He chittered. "She also insisted that Red Clouds Paint the Sky not help."

Black Rocks chittered and walked over to the access port. He knelt down and stuck his head inside. "Core Brother Joseph is much better this morning," he said quietly. "But he gets frustrated easily."

Light of Three Moons looked at Black Rocks. "Headaches?" she asked. Black Rocks nodded. "I can …" A warbling interrupted her. "What?" Before she or Black Rocks could react, a snakelike figure crawled into the access port. "An Alsoo!" she exclaimed.

The Naga-form crawled over to Light of Three Moons. It warbled, "Chore/work you question," came the translation. The creature picked up a tool with a stubby hand. "Chore/work help me you question."

"I don't ..." Light of Three Moons broke off. She looked at the creature's hands. "I wonder ..." she said in musing tones. "Hello, my name is Light of Three Moons," she said. "What is your name?"

"Greeting 'Li-three-Moo'/you. Second-Daughter-Fifth-Born me," warbled the Alsoo. "Chore/work help me you question," she repeated. She lifted the tool. "Strong me."

"Yes, you are," agreed Light of Three Moons. "Come with me." She crawled out of the access port. The Alsoo followed. Light of Three Moons leaned down and extended a hand. The Alsoo clasped the hand and then crawled up the arm to end up on Light of Three Moons' shoulder. The creature's tail wrapped loosely around her neck, and one hand took a light hold of her crest. Light of Three Moons was surprised at how light the Alsoo was. She started walking.

"Where are you going?" asked Black Rocks.

"I think the spirits are trying to tell me something," Light of Three Moons replied quietly. "I'll see if I'm right when I speak to Joseph." With the Alsoo on her shoulder, she started walking to the suite she shared with her core. "I'm surprised to see you. I thought females were kept safe."

"Truth," replied Second-Daughter-Fifth-Born. "Neuter me," she warbled. "Daughter born yes, many eggs, no eggs, neuter be."

Light of Three Moons blinked as she tried to decipher what the Alsoo was saying. "Alsoo females lay eggs," she said slowly. "And when they can no longer lay eggs, they become ... neuter?"

"Truth," replied Second-Daughter-Fifth-Born. "Many eggs me, three daughters live/they, two sons live/they. Proud me." She leaned around to look into Light of Three Moons' eyes. "Daughters hide me, daughters/they. Safe know not daughters/they, hope me," she said.

"I hope they're safe too," Light of Three Moons replied. She thought about the conversation as she headed toward the suite. It wasn't long before she entered and called out, "Joseph?"

"Hang on," came Joseph Franklin's voice. A moment later, he

floated in. "Hey Light, what's … oh my god," he exclaimed. "Is that an Alsoo?"

"Alsoo me truth," said Second-Daughter-Fifth-Born. "Split-tail fly."

"Only Joseph," Light of Three Moons said to the Alsoo. "Joseph is very smart, very creative," she said. "He makes things. Useful things."

"Hands shake/he," observed the Alsoo. "How Joseph/he split-tail maker/he be/he, hands shake/he question."

"That is indeed the question," agreed Franklin.

"Maker/he need hands," the Alsoo asked. "Second-Daughter-Fifth-Born hands strong."

Light of Three Moons had to force herself to not shake in an almost atavistic fear. *The spirits truly are speaking to me*, she thought in awe. "I …" She swallowed. "I had hoped that Second-Daughter-Fifth-Born could help," she said nervously. She walked over and extended her arm. The Alsoo left its perch and crawled down her arm and onto Franklin's extended arm. Soon the Alsoo was wrapped around Franklin's neck.

"I need to … do something," Light of Three Moons said. "Why don't you see if Second-Daughter-Fifth-Born can …" She trailed off. "You know."

Franklin turned to Light of Three Moons with an expression she hadn't seen on the human's face for some time. He was smiling. "And maybe Second-Daughter-Fifth-Born can stay … for dinner," she said.

"What are we having?" asked Franklin. His hand stroked the Alsoo's feathered back. "Light makes this wonderful dish with fruit and grains," he said to the Naga-form.

Light of Three Moons chittered. "I guess I'm making fellel-chrr," she said. "Be back soon," she promised and left the suite. She hurried down the passageway and entered another room. It was small and bare of any furnishings. It was basically a closet that had once contained spare parts but was now used when Rynn needed some privacy.

Light of Three Moons knelt on the floor and clapped her hands together twice. "Spirits and ancestors," she said. "I don't know which of you sent the Alsoo to me, but thank you," she said. "Joseph smiled, and it was as if the sun greeted the day."

Light of Three Moons sang quietly as she cooked. She had learned that the Alsoo were omnivores but that too much meat could cause digestive problems. She had decided to make fellel-chrr as Joseph had requested, plus an Earth dish that the Rynn had come to love: mac and cheese. "I wonder if Alsoo like salads," Light of Three Moons said to herself.

A noise caught her attention, and she turned. "Speaking of Alsoo," she said. "Greetings, Second-Daughter-Fifth-Born."

The Alsoo warbled, "Greeting 'Li-three-Moo'/you." She sidewinded to the cooking section. "Help/assist/work me you question."

"Not really," replied Light of Three Moons. "But I wouldn't mind the company." Her crest fluttered as the Alsoo climbed the side of the cooking bench and curled up on the counter. "I could have picked you up," she said.

"Split-tail strong truth, Alsoo want/need split-tail see/know Alsoo strong truth," Second-Daughter-Fifth-Born declared. "Truth weak split-tail strong much/much Alsoo." She slithered over to the cutting board and sampled a cut vegetable. "Good."

Light of Three Moons tried to decipher what the Alsoo had just said. "Do you mean that the weakest Rynn is stronger than an Alsoo?"

"Truth," agreed Second-Daughter-Fifth-Born. "Big truth Alsoo weak/prey," she said. "Split-tail not Alsoo prey/food make. Truth question." Her thin shoulders rolled. "Alsoo dizzy/think. Alsoo like/good but dizzy/think Alsoo we/me be."

"Dizzy think?" Light of Three Moons repeated. "Dizzy think.

Hmmm. Oh, confused." Her crest waggled. "Yeah, I suppose when everything keeps trying to eat you, running across something that could eat you and chooses not to would be confusing," she said.

"Big truth," agreed Second-Daughter-Fifth-Born.

"Once, Rynn thought like the Alsoo," Light of Three Moons said. "We ran. We hid." She looked down for a moment. "Then we met the humans." She smiled. "Big truth," she said. "Humans made the Rynn brave."

"Dizzy/think big truth," the Alsoo replied.

Light of Three Moons chittered. "Big dizzy/think big truth."

"Second-Daughter-Fifth-Born want/need stay here/this place," the Alsoo said. "Think/want human Alsoo brave make." She looked at Light of Three Moons. "Room/space make me you question," she said. "Work/chore hard do me," she slapped her chest. "Pledge/oath."

"You made Joseph smile," Light of Three Moons said softly. "For that alone you can stay."

"Pledge/oath question," replied Second-Daughter-Fifth-Born. She slapped her chest.

"Pledge/oath," agreed Light of Three Moons. She slapped her chest.

Joseph Franklin eased his floater, as he dubbed it, over to the table to eat. As he did not trust his hands, he had created an interface with his Torque. It was much slower than using his hands, but at least he ended up where he wanted. "Everything smells great," he said cheerfully.

"Truth," agreed the diminutive Naga-form curled up on the table next to Franklin. Being too small to use any chair, even a Rynn one, Second-Daughter-Fifth-Born had no choice but to sit on the table. It was Second-Daughter-Fifth-Born who had decided that she should sit next to Franklin. Light of Three Moons had used the smallest dishes she could find, but even the smallest utensils were too large for the stubby hands of the snakelike Alsoo.

Second-Daughter-Fifth-Born had solved the problem by quickly creating a spoonlike utensil out of a spare piece of wood.

Light of Three Moons placed a serving of fellel-chrr and mac and cheese on Franklin's plate and a much smaller one on the plate for the Alsoo. Franklin's smile fell when the interface failed. "Damn," he muttered. His shaking hand hovered uncertainly over a fork.

The Alsoo looked at Franklin and then at Franklin's hands. She slithered over and wrapped her tail around Franklin's right wrist and used her stubby hands to stop the shaking. "Maker need/must eat," she declared. "Help maker will/can me."

"Spirits be praised," Light of Three Moons said quietly. She briefly covered her eyes, and then she clapped her hands together twice. "Thank you, spirits and ancestors, for bringing us the Alsoo." She covered her eyes, as did the other Rynn at the table. "Well? What are you waiting for? Let's eat."

38

Snake Squad

Lieutenant Hendriks and Lieutenant Cool Evening Breeze watched as the Alsoo "recruits" went through the hastily constructed obstacle course. The tiny Naga-forms slithered, slid, and side-winded through the course. The main objective of the current exercise was for the Alsoo to navigate through a series of tubes, reach a specific location, attach a box to the floor, and slither back through the maze—and do it all before the allotted time ran out.

"Gotta give 'em credit for stamina," Hendriks grunted. "This is their third pass through the course today."

"They're driving themselves," agreed Cool Evening Breeze. She stood. "Okay, that's enough for today," she chirped. "Snake Squad, line up." The score of Alsoo quickly formed two lines. "Good job, squad," she said in approval. "Get cleaned up, get something to eat, and get some rest," she ordered. "We're going to do this again tomorrow." She slapped her chest. "Pledge/oath."

The assembled Alsoo slapped their chests in response. "Pledge/oath," they chorused. After a moment, they slithered away.

Hendriks and Cool Evening Breeze waited until the last Alsoo was out of sight before they both sighed. "They're going to get slaughtered," Cool Evening Breeze chirped moodily.

"And that's different from what they've gone through how?"

returned Hendriks. "You may be right, Breeze, but I wouldn't count them out," he said. "They've got guts, and they've got heart."

"Why do so many human sayings invoke organs?" Cool Evening Breeze said in mock complaint. She sighed. "I miss Crystal."

"You and me both, Breeze," Hendriks replied.

39

WOBBLE

Crystal Chandler held her lower back as she sat. "Goddamn, I'll be glad when you are born," she said to her swollen belly. She turned to the snickering black woman sitting opposite her. "Laugh away, Dierdre," she sneered. "You're next."

"Gotta find a man who won't mind sharing me with a couple of Rynn first," Dierdre McIntosh replied.

"I did," Crystal replied.

"Only one Rynn," corrected Dierdre. "And you still need to find a Rynn male who won't find Hendriks intimidating. Speaking of Hendriks, there's something I've always wondered." She raised an eyebrow.

"I think I already told you how big he is," Crystal replied with a laugh.

"I'm still not sure I believe you," Dierdre replied. "But that wasn't what I wanted to know." She gave Crystal a pleading look. "Finding out how hung he is was a hell of a lot easier than finding out what his name is," she complained.

Crystal laughed. "He doesn't like his name much," she said. "Not that I blame him," she added with a giggle. "It's Aloysius," she said. "Aloysius Wolfgang Hendriks."

Dierdre laughed. "That's not too bad," she replied. "Besides, he can just call himself Al." She looked up to see a familiar and oversized figure hurrying toward them. "Uh-oh, Ophelia is heading this way."

"And hurrying," Crystal added in a concerned voice. "Since she's heading here, it has to have something to do with our diplomacy efforts."

"You stay seated," Dierdre said firmly. She stood. "Problem, Ophelia?"

"Problems," corrected Ophelia. "With emphasis on the plural." She sat down next to Crystal. "The Vatican is expressing 'concern' over 'foreign spirituality.'" Her fingers made air quotes as she spoke. "The ayatollah of Iran is outraged that 'Shinto cultists' were given equal representation at the pact signing." She sighed. "A sentiment echoed by the UAE and the Saudis." She rolled her eyes. "On the other hand, Japan is ecstatic—or rather, the emperor is."

"Same thing," Crystal commented.

"Probably," agreed Ophelia. "Unfortunately, he followed up his statement of approval with a declaration that Shinto would, once again, be the official religion of Japan."

"Which of course compelled the Chinese to accuse Japan of returning to their expansionist days," Dierdre suggested. "I gather they are mobilizing in the South China Sea?"

"'Patrolling against rising pirate activity,'" Ophelia said sourly. "Which upset the Australians." Ophelia sighed again. "I swear, they are just looking for an excuse to start a war."

"Which, of course, they are," Crystal said in acid tones. "Humans," she said in disgust. "When Hendriks and Breeze get back, I'm going to demand we emigrate."

"Speaking of which, when are they coming back?" Ophelia asked. "I thought they'd be back by now." She covered her mouth in horror. "Oh my dear," she said to Crystal. "I shouldn't …"

Crystal gave Ophelia a fierce smile. "They'll be back," she declared. "Or they'll answer to me."

"Your core or the Bugs?" Dierdre asked in grim amusement.

"Whichever one is responsible," Crystal replied. She wrapped her arms around her swollen abdomen protectively. "This is not getting us anywhere," she said. "We have a planet to calm." She smiled suddenly. "And I think I have an idea on just how to do that."

"This is CNN," said the pretty and very pregnant reporter. "Crystal Chandler-Hendriks reporting." She turned to another camera. "With tensions building in the Pacific and an upsurge of religious fervor in the Mideast, the world is holding its collective breath and waiting for the other shoe to drop." She smiled wryly. "Well, the other shoe has dropped," she said. "The Rynn are leaving." An image of Bright Sunlight appeared on the screen. "This is from an interview with the leader of the Rynn trade delegation yesterday."

"We have been following the developments on Earth with growing concern," Bright Sunlight said in the video. "While we truly admire humans, it appears that the reverse is not as universal as we had believed." Bright Sunlight's crest flattened. "It's obviously too late to undo the technological transfer that has already been done, but we are immediately suspending any additional transfer," he said. "In addition, we will be removing all Rynn from Earth and will close all trade outposts." The Rynn leader smiled sadly. "Perhaps with the Rynn gone, humans will be able to better resolve their internal issues."

The camera returned to Crystal. "What was not said but has been confirmed is that once the *Nieth* returns, it will be scuttled," she said. "And since hyperspace technology has not been transferred to humanity, it appears we're going to be stuck in this solar system until we figure it out ourselves."

"Why was I blindsided?" demanded President Newgate. "Dammit, Bright Sunlight, I thought we had an understanding."

"I'm sorry, Darren Newgate," Bright Sunlight replied in regretful tones and lowered crest. "But unless and until humanity gets ... control over its baser instincts ..." The Rynn leader ran a long-fingered hand through his crest. "Teacher Jeremy warned us of this," he said. "There is much to admire about humans, but even more to fear."

"But leaving?" President Newgate complained. "Surely there is some middle ground, some compromise?"

"If there is, it's going to have to come from humanity," Bright Sunlight replied. He stood. "I must go," he said. Bright Sunlight left the president's office.

President Newgate stared at the door the alien had exited through for several minutes and then shook himself. He picked up a phone receiver. "Clear all my meetings for the day, Doris," he growled. "Then get me Premier Xi."

For the next week, President Newgate had conference call after conference call. He alternately threatened, cajoled, begged, and bargained with government leader after government leader.

Premier Xi and Prime Minister Giacovelli of the EU had both been shaken by the Rynn's announcement. Premier Xi had immediately recalled all his warships, while Prime Minister Giacovelli did something that most considered unthinkable and severed diplomatic relations with the Vatican. He followed that up by declaring a full embargo on the entire Middle East regardless of their position in the Rynn declaration.

"I thought you were trying to calm things down." Ophelia Winslow wrung her ringed hands together. "I'm surprised a shooting war hasn't already started."

"Which I think validates Crystal's approach," Jeremy Blunt said cheerfully. "It's not how I would have approached the issue, but it does seem to be having the desired effect." He gave the reporter an approving smile. "Well done, Crystal."

"Well done?" exclaimed the oligarch in disbelief. "Well done?"

"Well yes, Ophelia," Jeremy replied. "If you're going to get a mule to move, you first have to get its attention." He chuckled. "That was a pretty big stick she used." He raised an eyebrow. "Now what were you planning to use as a carrot?"

In response, Crystal spoke to her Torque and an image appeared. It showed a group of about twenty adolescents and preteens, male and female, human and Rynn. It was the scene from the treaty signing ceremony when apparently the same group had performed the wobble dance together. The scene ended, and another scene appeared. It now showed an older group of even more Rynn and humans huddled together. It was apparent that most of them were crying.

The camera zoomed in on one couple: a human young man and a Rynn young woman. The woman sobbed against his shoulder. The screen split, and a young couple from the earlier video was shown. They were smiling and laughing, and it was obvious that they were smiling and laughing because they were together. After a moment, a second thing became obvious: it was the same people who were now crying in each other's arms.

"Not exactly a carrot," Crystal said. "In fact, it's an even bigger stick. That scene has been broadcast on every major station over the past twenty-four hours." She smiled. "The parents of those children have all requested sanctuary with the Rynn." Her smile got cold. "Bright Sunlight is going to honor their request and offer the same thing to any family that requests it."

"I don't understand how this ..." The oligarch broke off. "Any family?" she asked. Crystal nodded. "That could take ... that could take years," the oligarch said in sudden understanding.

"Decades," corrected Crystal. "Thousands upon thousands of families from around the world clamoring to emigrate. Thousands of families who will be given full access to Rynn technology—especially medical technology." Her cold smile got even colder. "Omiset is only part of their medical arsenal, and not even the largest part," she said. "Rynn live, on average, twice as long as humans." She rubbed her belly. "Apparently, humans can anticipate a similar increase in longevity."

"Interesting," commented Jeremy. "And I suppose that somehow that heretofore unknown fact is going to get leaked out."

"You know how children are," Crystal said airily. "They just can't keep a secret."

"Carrot and stick in one," Jeremy said in approval.

There was a knock on the door to the conference room, and Raindrops in a Tide Pool stuck his head in. "The *Nieth* just came in-system."

Jeremy stared hungrily at the large monitor in the command center. It was currently showing nothing more than random static. A group of Rynn techs were chirping into Torques as they worked on locating the signal from the *Nieth*. "What's taking so long?" Jeremy grumbled.

"Apparently, the *Nieth* suffered some damage, Teacher," Morning Stars Fade said soothingly. "The fact that the ship is approaching at deliberate speed indicates that nothing is seriously wrong." There was a chime. "See, Teacher, all is well."

Jeremy nodded as the main screen slowly began to resolve. In less than a minute, an image appeared. "Granddaughter!"

The Rynn woman on the screen smiled widely. "Greetings, Grandfather," she said. "It is good to see you again. Mel is busy at the moment, but she told me to send her love." Her crest dropped. "It was more difficult than we had expected." Her crest rose. "But what we have learned exceeds our wildest dreams." She made a motion, and a feathered snakelike creature appeared on the back of her command chair. "Grandfather, may I present Speaker First-Son-First-Born." She smiled. "Of the Alsoo."

The Alsoo warbled. "Greet Speaker/Spirit Talker/you me," came the translation. "Eaters fight we/you." The Alsoo clasped his hands together. "Small we truth. Fighters we truth."

"We rescued about three hundred Alsoo so far," Kasumi said. "The only reason we returned home is because we're running out of room to hold them," she said.

"This is Crystal Chandler-Hendriks reporting," the pregnant blond said crisply. "The *Nieth* is back," she said. "And due to some surprising developments, the Rynn's plan to scuttle the ship is being deferred." She turned to face another camera. An image of the *Nieth* appeared behind her. "I met with Captain Kasumi yesterday, and in an interview that will be aired tomorrow, she spoke about the first voyage of the *Nieth*." Crystal turned to face another camera. "I remember a class I took many years ago about project management. The instructor assigned us a project and at the end asked us three things: what went right, what went wrong, and what surprised us."

"First: what went right," Crystal said. "The *Nieth* faced five Polig-Grug pirates in the last six months and were, obviously, victorious in each engagement."

"Second: what went wrong." Crystal frowned. "Captain Kasumi did the best she could with the information she had—information that was sadly lacking in a number of important details. The end result was twenty-five humans and Rynn dead, and an almost equal number severely wounded. The families are still being notified."

"Finally: what was surprising." Crystal smiled lopsidedly. "It was less than a decade ago that humanity was wondering if there was life—" she waved a hand "—out there." An image of a feathered and snakelike being with an owl's face appeared behind her. "Sentient, sapient, and nearing extinction, the Alsoo are exactly what the Rynn feared they might one day be: food for an alien species."

Her expression was grim. "The *Nieth* rescued approximately three hundred of these tiny—they are barely a meter in length, counting their tail—sensitive beings."

She continued, "Captain Kasumi has requested permission to refurbish and repair the *Nieth*." An image of the Rynn captain appeared. "She has a new goal, or rather an additional goal." She winced. "Ooh, excuse me, but …" She winced again. "Danny, I think you'd better call an ambulance," she said. "Before I go, Kasumi has a new goal, and one that I hope humanity shares: save the Alsoo." She ripped off her earpiece. "Oh god."

President Newgate snorted in amusement as he read a report. He handed it to the white-haired man seated across from him. "India *demands*—not requests, not suggests, *demands* that we immediately build a second Talon," he said. "They're apparently willing to absorb the entire cost in order to quote 'save the Naga' unquote."

"Allow them to pay for a quarter of the construction costs and request they provide a full company of soldiers," Jeremy Blunt said. "Then tell Premier Xi and Emperor Hirohito what they asked for and what they got."

"Why not just have them pay for the whole thing?" President Newgate asked. From his tone, it appeared he knew why but wanted to hear it anyway.

"Half a trillion dollars?" Jeremy asked in amused tones. "Let's not bankrupt our allies, Darren," he chided. "You want the goose to keep laying." He put down the briefing report. "How goes the negotiations with the Mideast?"

"Well, it was stalled," he grinned. "Until Commander Eisenstadt and your two—" his smile twisted "—granddaughters paid them a visit." He shook his head. "Did anyone ever tell you that the Blunt family is damn well intimidating?"

"Well, my son is a lawyer, after all," Jeremy agreed cheerfully.

"And they can be vicious." He paused. "I'm surprised Morning Mist wasn't with them."

"Morning Mist is helping Crystal with the baby; it turns out Cool Evening Breeze is as hopeless with babies as Hendriks is," President Newgate said.

Jeremy turned to the silent third person in the room. "Morning Stars Fade, see if you can find a Rynn male who likes children and can also put up with Breeze and Hendriks."

Morning Stars Fade chirped. "I have already begun inquiries, Teacher," he said with the satisfied tones of someone who successfully anticipated a task. "I have found two candidates," he reported. A thoughtful look appeared on the young Rynn's face. "Teacher, from what I understand, the Alsoo are very protective of children."

Jeremy smiled at his protégé. "An interesting thought," he said in approval. "Follow that thought and see where it leads." Jeremy stood. "As always, a pleasure speaking to you, Mr. President."

"The Rynn consider you most competent," Morning Stars Fade added. He briefly covered his eyes. "Until the next time."

Morning Stars Fade followed Jeremy at a respectful distance, his eyes constantly scanning the surroundings; buildings, cars, and people. Jeremy Blunt had what he called "an allergy to excessive protection" and resisted all efforts to provide him with full-time bodyguards. He, however, had no objection to Morning Stars Fade accompanying him on those rare occasions he left his cabin in the woods.

Morning Stars Fade also would have preferred that Teacher Jeremy had more protection, but he considered Jeremy's rejection of that protection consistent with who and what Jeremy was. "The Spirits will protect Teacher Jeremy or they won't," he had once told a friend. "But he will not and cannot hide behind others and still be himself."

Morning Stars Fade continued to scan the surroundings as they headed back to the car park where they had left their transport. Teacher Jeremy had acceded to one demand at least: he no longer drove himself. His driver, a veteran of the California National Guard, had remained with the SUV.

"Teacher," Morning Stars Fade said in low tones.

"I see them, Disciple," Jeremy replied mildly. "How many have you spotted?"

"Three, Teacher," Morning Stars Fade replied. "One across the street: the light-skinned man with the blue garment with the head covering hiding his face."

"It's called a hoodie, Disciple," Jeremy corrected in amused tones. "Agreed. And the others?"

"The two light-skinned men in front of us, the ones wearing the orange ... caps?" Morning Stars Fade replied. "I have not been able to find anyone following us from behind," he said. "But there should be at least one."

"At least," agreed Jeremy. "They are much better than the three you spotted, but there are two more." He smiled. "Let's do a little window-shopping," he said and stopped in front of a store. Jeremy chuckled. "Look at that—Rynn plush toys."

Morning Stars Fade nodded and looked at the display, or at least pretended to. After a minute, his crest fell slightly. "They are much better," he said. "The two very pale men with matching green jackets," Morning Stars Fade frowned. "That paleness does not seem natural."

"'Prison pallor,' it's called," Jeremy replied. "Both men have probably spent at least the past five years in a high-security prison with limited access to the outdoors."

"If they were in prison, that would indicate they are not anyone we could trust," Morning Stars Fade mused. "Kidnapping or assassination?"

"Now, now, Morning Stars Fade," Jeremy chided. "They could just be waiting to beat the crap out of us."

"Oh, of course, Teacher," Morning Stars Fade chittered. "I had overlooked that option." He frowned. "They must know you wear a force shield." His crest lowered some more. "Teacher, is it possible they just wish to cause damage?"

Jeremy smiled. "Let's find out," he said. "I feel like getting a cup of coffee."

"Coffee, Teacher?" Morning Stars Fade questioned. "You don't drink coffee."

"Tea then," Jeremy said cheerfully. "Ah, this looks like a promising establishment." He walked into the store. Morning Stars Fade followed.

It was a typical coffeehouse: slightly dim, with wooden tables and stools in the center and lining the periphery. Customers, mostly young men and women, sat singly or in small groups around the shop. Most were too engrossed in their laptops to immediately notice Jeremy and Morning Stars Fade.

The teacher and his disciple approached the service counter. The woman behind the counter barely looked up. She was young, at most twenty, with reddish hair and a dusting of freckles across her cheeks. "What can I get you?" she said. There was a chirping. "A pot of Jasmine Green for two, please."

The woman turned toward the chirping and saw Morning Stars Fade. Her mouth dropped open. "You ... you're ..." she stammered.

"A pot of Jasmine Green for two," Morning Stars Fade repeated.

"You ... you ..." The woman stopped and swallowed. "Jasmine Green?"

Morning Stars Fade chirped. "If you would," came the translation.

The woman swallowed again. "You guys drink tea?" She shook herself. "Stupid question, you ordered it." A slow smile appeared on the woman's face. "You guys really do look a bit like birds." She waved a hand to indicate her face. "Especially around there."

"Our ancestors had much in common with the ancestors of Earth birds," agreed Morning Stars Fade. "The tea?"

"Oh, sorry," the woman replied and bustled around behind the counter. It wasn't long before she placed a medium-sized teapot in front of Morning Stars Fade. Morning Stars Fade produced a credit card. The woman looked at the card and giggled. "If you'd let me take a picture with you, it'd be on the house," she giggled again. "Hell, even if you didn't let me take the picture, it'd be on the house."

"I think you can accommodate the young lady, Disciple." Jeremy said. "How about ... there?" He pointed to an empty table. Morning Stars Fade looked at the table and then at the front door of the coffeehouse. He smiled and nodded. Morning Stars Fade and the woman posed, and Jeremy took the picture.

"You seem quite comfortable with a Rynn," Jeremy remarked.

"God, I've been wanting to meet an alien since I was five," the young woman replied. "I never expected that an alien would be cute."

"Neither did I," agreed Morning Stars Fade. He chittered.

"But you're the ... oh yeah, right," the woman stammered. She looked up as five men approached the counter. "Never fails," she complained. "I have work to do."

"Come back when you're free," Morning Stars Fade said. "If you want," he added.

The woman smiled widely, nodded, and headed over to the counter. "Sorry. I was talking to our guests," she said. "Isn't it wonderful?"

"Disgusting, I think," one man growled.

"How can you allow animals in a place where people eat?" said another. "Go home, Birdy, before I pluck you," he sneered. "I bet you'll taste just like chicken."

"Teacher, it seems I was wrong about their target," Morning Stars Fade said calmly.

"Listen, shitheads," the woman said angrily. "We decide who comes in here, not you. If you don't like it, you can leave. In fact—leave."

"You need to know where your loyalty should be," snapped one of the men. His arm swept the serving counter, and snacks, souvenirs, and samples went flying.

Morning Stars Fade stood. He walked over to the counter and handed the stunned woman his credit card. "Whatever the damages are, I will pay for them," he said.

"Run away, idiot," the woman exclaimed in desperate tones. "They're crazy." She added, "And they haven't caused much damage."

Morning Stars Fade smiled. "I wasn't talking about their damage," he said. He spun around, and his leg impacted against the apparent leader of the group. The man crashed to the floor. "If you have a problem with me, then you should be dealing with me, not this young lady."

"Hands off our women, birdbrain," snapped the man as he rose back to his feet. "And get the fuck off our planet." His fist shot out, only to be deflected by an almost negligent swipe of the Rynn's hand.

"While I think the young lady is quite attractive, we are not, as yet, intimate," Morning Stars Fade replied. His own hand lashed out in what is usually called a tiger fist. Because of the height difference, Morning Stars Fade's punch hit the man's gut. The man doubled over with a pained grunt. The follow-up kick to the chin sent the big man crashing to the ground.

Jeremy walked over to the counter. "Please do not call the police as of yet," he said to the stunned woman. "My disciple needs the practice."

"Huh? Disciple?" The woman focused on Jeremy for the first time. "Oh my god, you're the one they call the Teacher."

Jeremy nodded. "Morning Stars Fade is one of my better students," he sighed. "But five humans may be slightly more than he can handle. Excuse me." Jeremy turned around, grabbed one of the attackers by the shoulder, spun him around, and grabbed the man by the throat. The man's eyes rolled up, and he crashed to the ground unconscious.

Jeremy turned back to the stunned woman. "Morning Stars Fade is usually a bit shy around women … well, Earth women," he amended. "But he seemed quite comfortable with you." He spun around again, and his foot impacted against another man's crotch. That man also ended up on the ground. "Sorry," he said to the woman.

The woman looked to where the little alien man was battling the remaining three attackers. The alien seemed to almost blur as he blocked, evaded, and deflected blow after blow. "Stop fooling around, Fade, and kick their butts," she shouted.

Morning Stars Fade chirped gleefully and then appeared to climb up one attacker. His fist impacted against the bridge of his opponent's nose. He then used the man as a springboard and landed on the shoulders of another assailant. This time it was an elbow that did the damage.

Jeremy noticed that the fifth and final opponent was reaching into his jacket. "Excuse me," he said to the young woman. Before the man had extracted his gun—and it was a gun, as Jeremy had suspected—Jeremy was in front of the man, and his hand had grabbed the assailant's throat. The man fell to the floor unconscious. "Morning Stars Fade, end this," he barked.

"Yes, Teacher," Morning Stars Fade replied, and he suddenly unleashed a flurry of kicks, punches, and elbow strikes. The humans may have been bigger and more robust than Rynn, but Jeremy had taught his student well. The last two thugs hit the ground.

There was silence, and then the woman ran from behind the counter and over to Morning Stars Fade. She swept him into a hug. "Are you all right?" she asked in concern. "Did they hurt you?"

"I'm fine. Exhilarated, in fact," Morning Stars Fade replied. "Are you all right, Miss …?"

"Emily. Emily Fields." The young woman gave Morning Stars Fade an admiring look. "You were magnificent," she gushed. "I never saw anything like that." She shook her head. "Weren't you afraid?"

"Of course I was," Morning Stars Fade replied. "But Teacher Jeremy has trained me to be afraid … later." Morning Stars Fade shivered. "Like now." Emily tightened her hold on Morning Stars Fade as his shivers increased.

"If you would watch my disciple for a moment, Ms. Fields, I would appreciate it," Jeremy said. "Don't worry, he will be fine. He just needs to know that not everyone wants to hurt him." Emily tightened her hold even more. "Thank you." He turned away as Emily started cooing comfortingly to Morning Stars Fade.

Jeremy walked over to one of the downed men and knelt. "The five of you have been following us for some time," he said. "I don't know if you know my history," he said in conversational tones, "but the last two men who bothered me did not live to bother me further." He leaned closer and smiled. "I may be old, but I still know how to kill," he said in a near whisper.

It was a little over an hour later when Jeremy and Morning Stars Fade entered the back seat of their SUV. "If you would take us straight home, Private," he said to the driver. The woman nodded and started the car. Jeremy turned to Morning Stars Fade. "I do hope you got the young lady's number," he said. Morning Stars Fade nodded. "You did well, Disciple." He tapped his Torque. "Mel? It's Gramps," he said. "Please alert the colony that someone has put a bounty on Rynn. All Rynn."

40

303B and Burl

Cool Evening Breeze awkwardly held the wriggling baby. "Are you sure this is okay?" she said in worried tones. "Babies ... squirm."

"You're doing fine, Breeze," Crystal said in amusement. "Honestly, you're almost as bad as Hendriks." She looked at the big marine standing near the bed. He had a similarly worried look on his face. "And that's saying something," she scolded. "Jesse is as much your son as Hendriks's, and you both better get used to taking care of him."

At that moment, the doorbell chimed. "Thank god," muttered Hendriks and nearly ran to the door. "Yes?" he said when he opened it.

A Rynn male stood there. He looked up at Hendriks and chirped. "You're even bigger up close," he said. "Unlike most Rynn, my name doesn't translate well to human," he chittered. "Call me Burl."

"Burl?" Hendriks blinked.

"As I said, my name does not translate well. *Burl* is the closest analog." The Rynn's crest waggled in amusement. "Strangely enough, most humans seem almost relieved when I introduce myself."

A wry smile appeared on Hendriks's face. "I bet," he said. "What can I do for you, Burl?"

"The question should be: what can we do for you?" Burl replied.

"We?" asked Hendriks. His eyes widened when what he had first taken to be some kind of scarf or cloak raised itself up. "An Alsoo?"

"Third-Daughter-Third-Born/me," warbled the Alsoo. "Neuter/me."

"Her telling you she's neuter is supposed to be reassuring," Burl said. "She is no longer breeding, so she is not taking up resources for children."

"Neuter/me," agreed the Alsoo. "3D3B/call/me easy/you," the Alsoo warbled in amusement.

"Did she just say to call her 3D3B cause it's easier?" Hendriks said in wonder. Burl and the Alsoo both nodded. "You gotta point," he said to the Alsoo.

"So Hendriks," Burl said. "I hear you're uncomfortable around babies."

"You got that right," Hendriks said in exasperated tones. "I'd rather go against a Polig-Grug hive than change a diaper."

"Stupid big split-tail/you be think 3D3B/me," warbled the Alsoo. "Split-tail hatchling/is Eater/not." The Alsoo peered around Hendriks. "Diaper change/now/we." The Alsoo slithered down Burl's body and around Hendriks to enter the apartment.

"Hey, wait, what?" Hendriks said in confusion.

"If 3D3B thinks the baby needs to have its diaper changed, it needs to have its diaper changed," Burl said. He walked around Hendriks and followed in the Alsoo's path.

"Hey, wait," Hendriks tried again and hurried after. By the time he reached the bedroom, the Alsoo was holding the baby and crooning softly while Burl was nearly finished changing the diaper. He looked worriedly at Crystal.

The blonde reporter was looking at the Alsoo with an expression that seemed to keep shifting between bemusement, amusement, and relief. She looked at Hendriks.

"Her name is 3D3B, and his name, believe it or not, is Burl," Hendriks supplied. He looked around and saw Breeze staring at the Alsoo with a set of shifting expressions that matched Crystal's.

"Thank the spirits you two are here," Crystal said in heartfelt tones. "Those two are hopeless." Burl chittered and 3D3B warbled in response. "I hope you can stay for a while."

"We will stay as long as you wish," Burl assured Crystal. He bent down and lifted the baby into his arms. "I bet you want to take a nap," he said. "3D3B, do you want to stay here or with the baby?"

"Here/place/stay 3D3B/me," the Alsoo replied. "Mother/she big split-tail/she 3D3B/me know/not trust/not." She side-winded up the bed. "Truth, 3D3B/me know." She ended up near the pillow that Crystal leaned against. "Mother big split-tail/you learn/gain/you short time 3D3B trust/oath." The Alsoo slapped her own chest. "Truth neuter/me truth/oath."

Crystal's eyes widened as the little Naga-form warbled. "You were a mother too, weren't you?" she said.

"Truth," replied the Alsoo. She ruffled her feathers for a moment.

Crystal looked at the little alien and then her eyes suddenly teared up. "They're dead, aren't they?' she said in a tear-filled whisper.

"Truth," replied the Alsoo in a soft warble, and she repeated the feather ruffle.

Crystal took a deep breath and let it out slowly. "I'm so sorry," she said. The little alien slithered up the pillow and leaned against Crystal. Her tail wrapped loosely around Crystal's wrist. Crystal gathered the little alien against her. "I'm so sorry," she repeated softly. The little alien warbled.

"You know something, Feather Head?" Hendriks said.

"What's that, Fuzzy Butt?" Cool Evening Breeze replied.

"I've killed a lot of people and figured I was destined to burn in hell," Hendriks said. "I thought it was a fair trade." He smiled. "I still think I'm gonna end up in hell," he said, "but seeing that—" he indicated Crystal and 3D3B "—makes it all worthwhile."

"Rynn don't believe in hell, Fuzzy Butt," Cool Evening Breeze replied. "But I think one would have been created just for me if I had left those first Alsoo behind."

"All good marines go to hell, you know." Hendriks smiled wider.

"If Rynn don't have a hell, you'd be more than welcome to share mine."

"Why thanks, Hendriks," Cool Evening Breeze replied. "I may take you up on that offer."

"Do that, Breeze," Hendriks said.

It turned out that not only was Burl able to change a diaper, he was also able to make the formula for baby Jesse. Watching 3D3B feed Jesse was an event in itself, with the baby being nestled in the loops of the Alsoo's tail.

It also turned out that Burl was a good cook. Maybe not professional-grade, but considering that neither Hendriks, Crystal, nor Cool Evening Breeze could even be considered adequate cooks made that evening's dinner something to linger over.

Cool Evening Breeze watched the interplay between all the members of her core and the two newcomers. More often than not, somebody was laughing, and most of the time everybody was smiling. She especially watched the interplay between Hendriks and Burl. Hendriks was laughing at something Burl had said, and Burl was grinning in triumph. *Fuzzy Butt isn't as guarded as he usually is when he's around other men*, she thought.

"Hey Burl," Cool Even Breeze called. "What were you before you decided to become a babysitter?"

"Don't laugh," he cautioned with a sheepish grin. "But I was a …" He chirped something that did not translate.

"What's a 'ker'tik'kik chirrup'?" Hendriks asked in confusion.

"Close, Fuzzy Butt," Cool Evening Breeze grinned. "It means he worked as a stage entertainer: chanting, singing, dancing, that sort of thing."

"Whatever was needed to tell the story," Burl said.

"You were an actor!" exclaimed Crystal. "Were you famous?"

Burl chittered. "Only to my parents," he replied. "Bright Sunlight saw one of my performances and asked me if I would join his crew. I guess you'd say I was the morale officer."

"Well, you've certainly improved the morale around here," Hendriks said in approval.

"Burl/he fine little split-tail/he. Big soul/he," 3D3B chimed in. "Truth/oath." She slapped her chest.

"Truth/oath," agreed Cool Evening Breeze, and she slapped her chest. She grinned when Hendriks echoed her. "Morale officer, huh?" she said. "And now a babysitter."

"Same thing, actually," grinned Burl.

"I do admire a competent male," Cool Evening Breeze said. "You are a very competent babysitter," she said.

"Amen," Hendriks muttered.

Cool Evening Breeze smiled. "And certainly competent preparing a delicious and probably nutritious meal."

"Amen," muttered Crystal.

"We should not forget 3D3B," Burl insisted.

"No, we should not," Cool Evening Breeze agreed. "Yes, I do admire competence," she repeated. "Would the two of you be willing to join our core?" she asked. "As associates at first, of course."

"I would be honored," Burl replied.

"Of course, that's assuming Hendriks and Crystal agreed," cautioned Cool Evening Breeze. She looked at Crystal and then at Hendriks. "He's competent, caring, and not bad to look at," she said with a smile. "I wish I had a crèche nurse like 3D3B."

"3D3B young Alsoo/me/long time/was," the Alsoo warbled. She wiggled. "Many male/they want/me they."

Hendriks laughed. "I just bet you were a hottie when you were younger," he said. He frowned slightly. "But I don't think humans or Rynn are compatible with Alsoo," he said. "Shit, I wonder what the hell the Torque is saying to translate that?" he muttered as his words were converted to the Alsoo warble.

Whatever it was, 3D3B warbled a laugh. 'Big split-tail Hendriks/

he ugly/he, dizzy/not me," she warbled. "Split-tail/you ugly/you yes, safe/feel/me, warm/feel/me. 3D3B split-tail burrow join/me."

"Aloysius Wolfgang Hendriks, if you don't say yes after that, it may be you that will need to find a new core," Crystal said feelingly.

"Ooh, she used all three of your names, Fuzzy Butt," Cool Evening Breeze chittered. "Be very careful with your next words."

"This is going to be very strange," muttered Hendriks.

"Stranger than having an alien for a lover?" Cool Evening Breeze replied. "Stranger than having another alien as a nursemaid?" she asked. "Stranger than fighting bug-lizards?"

"But they're not giant bug-lizards," Hendriks shot back. "They're short bug-lizards, so they're not really that strange." He smiled. "Giant bug-lizards, now that would be strange," he said with a laugh.

Cool Evening Breeze chittered. "Maybe I'm talking to the wrong person here," she said. She pointed at Hendriks. "Are you sure either of you want to be around someone who thinks that was funny?" she said to Burl and the Alsoo.

"She does have a point, 3D3B," Burl said to the Alsoo. The Alsoo warbled in amusement.

"I'm still not sure about the guy/guy thing," Hendriks said.

"Is he really as big as people say?" Burl asked Cool Evening Breeze. She nodded. "It's not just you that is not sure about the … guy/guy thing," he said to Hendriks.

"Have you?" asked Hendriks.

"Of course. I am a Rynn," Burl replied impatiently. "That does not mean I require it." His crest fluttered. "Spirits weep, but if you are as big as it is rumored, I don't think I will ever require it."

"Oh, it grows on you, so to speak," Cool Evening Breeze chittered. "And Crystal can …"

"That will be enough, Breeze," Crystal said quickly. "I mean, we don't need to divulge everything in one night."

Cool Evening Breeze chittered. "Okay, Momma."

"I guess that makes it official," Hendriks said. "Welcome to our core, you two." He looked at the Alsoo. "You're family now."

"Truth/oath," warbled the Alsoo. She slapped her chest.

"Truth/oath," chorused Hendriks, Cool Evening Breeze, and, just a beat behind, Crystal and Burl. They slapped their chests.

Year 10

41

Trojan Horse

"We've got incoming," sang the detection specialist, a human. He spoke to his Torque and an image appeared. "It's faint, but it appears to be Rynn."

"Hail them," said the bridge commander, a Rynn.

"Hailing, ma'am," the detection specialist replied. "Unknown Rynn vessel, this is Earth Command Satellite Three. Identify yourselves." He repeated the message several times. "I'm getting a response." He spoke another command.

"This … Rynn … damage … Poli … support sys … failing," came the faint reply over the bridge team's Torques. "Assis … assis …"

"Scramble, scramble," barked the bridge commander. "We have a damaged Rynn vessel incoming," she snapped. "Denise, get the coordinates to the rescue team, stat."

"Yes ma'am," responded the female, also human, tech. She started relaying information.

"It's the *Silent Shadow*, ma'am," the first tech reported. "Central Sea Clan registry." He checked the information scrolling past his eyes. "She's got a crew of fifty."

"Passengers?" asked the Rynn commander.

"None reported," the tech replied. "She's a mining ship." The tech frowned. "She was reported lost two Earth months ago."

"What?" The commander looked at the faint image. "Rescue team, approach with caution, repeat, approach with caution," she chirped to her Torque. "Captain Kasumi, we have an incoming Rynn mining vessel. The *Silent Shadow*," she reported briskly. "The ship was reported lost almost a season ago."

Captain Kasumi frowned. *Where could she have been for most of a season?* she thought in concern. "Commander, send out Blue Squadron in support," she ordered via her Torque. Also via her Torque, she had the image of the ship displayed.

"She looks beat up," Mel said. She peered at the image. "I don't like this."

"Neither do I," Kasumi agreed. "David?"

"I don't like it either," Eisenstadt grumbled. "Something smells." He rubbed his chin. "Commander Sun Peeks Through the Clouds, hail them again," he ordered.

"Same response, Commander," the bridge commander replied. She paused. "It was exactly the same response," she said. "Sound recall, sound recall," she ordered.

"Battle stations, battle stations," Kasumi said at almost the same moment from the bridge of the *Nieth*. "*Bastet*, power up," she said.

"DefSat One online," came a report over the Torque, followed in quick order by the remaining four defense satellites that ringed Earth.

The two Talon-class destroyers came to full battle readiness. The second Talon, the *Bastet*, was newly commissioned and had not completed its shakedown trials. Despite that, or possibly because of it, she had already acquired a nickname.

"The Bastard is online, powered up and ready to go," reported the ship's human captain. "What do we have, Captain?"

"I'm not sure, Captain," Kasumi replied. "But as Commander Eisenstadt said, something stinks."

"You thinking we got a Trojan horse coming in, Captain?" asked the *Bastet*'s captain.

"Trojan …?" Kasumi began.

"That means it's hiding something deadly," Mel explained quickly. "Morning Mist, sensors?"

"Something is distorting my sensor readings," Morning Mist replied. She started chirping to her Torque. "I've seen that interference pattern before," she mumbled. Suddenly, her crest snapped up. "It's a singularity wave."

"Singularity?" Mel asked. Her eyes widened. "Are you telling me there's a black hole in that ship?" she asked. Morning Mist nodded frantically. "Shit! The damn thing is a bomb."

"Stop that ship!" ordered Kasumi.

"Captain, this is Franklin," interrupted a voice. "I've been monitoring. I agree with Morning Mist: you may have an unstable singularity in that ship," he said. "If you destroy the ship, you chance unleashing a singularity in-system."

"Shit!" exclaimed Mel.

"We can't let that ship get any closer, Franklin," Kasumi replied in grim tones.

"No, we can't," agreed Franklin. "So we have to move her," he said. "Captain Delaney, you have three Shrikes with remote capability, right?"

"If you mean I got three Shrike drones, yeah," replied the *Bastet* captain.

"Get your techs to disable the safety interlocks on the magnetic grapples," Franklin said urgently. "But do not activate them until they are halfway to the *Silent Shadow*."

"Do it, Captain," ordered Eisenstadt. "Report when the drones are on their way."

"The next part's gonna be tricky," Franklin said as they waited for the modifications to be made and the drones to be launched. "Someone is going to have to guide those drones and get them to attach just in front of the main thrusters." An image appeared in front of everyone in conference. Three points blinked. "That's the target area."

"Tricky is right," agreed Delaney. "But I've got a first-class, iron-nerved drone pilot who should be up to the task." He laughed. "Friend of yours, Captain," he said. "Goes by the too-long-to-say name of Raindrops in a Tide Pool." He laughed grimly. "We just call him Tide Pool."

"Sprits be praised," Kasumi replied. "Franklin, coordinate with Raindrops in a Tide Pool."

"Will do, Captain," Franklin replied. "Franklin out."

"Granddaughter," came Jeremy's voice. "An attack such as this is meaningless," he said. "A distraction."

"Gramps is right," Mel added. "Detection Satellite One. Come in."

"This is DefSat One," came a cool voice. "We've been monitoring. Boards are clean and green."

"Keep looking," Mel replied. "We think that the mining ship is a decoy."

"Understood, Command," returned the cool voice. "We got our eyes and ears at max."

"This is Eisenstadt," the commander broadcast. "On my authority, I am raising Earth readiness to Defcon 2. Repeat, Defcon 2."

"This is DefSat One," came the cool voice. "We have multiple bogeys." A three-dimensional map of the solar system appeared. Red circled lights indicated the bogeys. "They were coming in under the plane of the ecliptic," continued the voice. "Very low power, almost none in fact."

"This is Eisenstadt," barked the commander. "On my authority, we are now at Defcon 1. Repeat, Defcon 1."

"This is DefSat One," the cool voice broke back in. "Bogeys have powered up. Repeat, bogeys have powered up." The voice stopped and then broke back in. "Blow those suckers out of our space," the voice growled.

"This is DefSat Three," came another voice. "We are engaging hostile craft."

"*Bastet!*" barked Kasumi. "Get your ass out there."

"Hauling ass now," replied Delaney. "Time for the Bastard to earn its stripes," he said almost jubilantly. "*Bastet*, out."

"Oh shit," Mel exclaimed. "If those are Polig-Grug," she said in horror, "they've probably got Alsoo on their ships."

"I know," Kasumi said in a hushed voice. "Spirits and ancestors forgive me, I know." Kasumi slumped in her command chair and thought.

"This is DefSat Two," came a new voice.

"Now what?" complained Mel. "Report, DefSat Two."

"We picking up a second stream of bogeys," came the voice. "They're already inside Mars orbit."

"How the fuck did they get in so close without being seen?" Mel snapped.

"They're all about twenty meters in length," came the reply. "We only detected them when they started braking."

"Assault craft," Eisenstadt said instantly. "ETA Earth orbit?"

"Twenty-six hours," replied the voice. "But unless they modify their flight path, they will not be going into orbit," he said. "They're on an intercept course."

"This is Eisenstadt," the commander broadcast. "I want air defenses mobilized," he ordered. "Prepare all urban centers for evacuation," he continued. "Prepare all urban centers for invasion," he barked. "And someone find out how many we're dealing with."

"How many?" Joseph Franklin asked in disbelief.

"Three hundred, give or take a dozen or so," Black Rocks replied.

"This makes no sense," Franklin replied. He spoke to his Torque, and an image of a spacecraft appeared. "Assuming that these ships are similar to what we saw on the Polig-Grug raider ships," he said in musing tones, "then each ship is going to contain five or six Polig-Grug." He frowned. "They'll cause damage, but we can clean them out."

"Polig-Grug/Eaters/they come home/ours, not know/we, long

time/short time/not know/we, Eaters/see/not, Eaters/see/many/many," warbled Second-Daughter-Fifth-Born.

Franklin frowned as he worked on deciphering the Alsoo's speech. "Did they come in ships?" he asked finally.

"Eater ships long time show/they," replied Second-Daughter-Fifth-Born.

Franklin looked at the image again. "Franklin to Cool Evening Breeze."

"Cool Evening Breeze here," replied the Rynn marine.

"How many queens did you see on the ship?" he asked.

"Hmmm. Not sure how many there were," she replied. "I personally saw two. Why?"

"I think I saw a couple as well," Hendriks broke in.

"Franklin to Command," Franklin said sharply. "It's not an attack force," he said quickly. "It's an occupation force. The number and type of ships does not make sense if this was an attack, but it makes perfect sense if all they care about is one or two landing."

"Explain," Eisenstadt ordered.

"There really isn't enough data to be certain, but here goes," Franklin said. "We were assuming that those fighter craft were piloted by a temporary group of workers and a queen," he said. "But what if there are no workers, just males and females?"

"Or what if the big one wasn't a queen, but a male?" Jeremy broke in. "A king."

"Of course!" exclaimed Joseph. "We keep letting our thinking be influenced by how it is here on Earth."

"Or Nest," Morning Mist added.

"If Mr. Blunt is correct, and I'm afraid he may be, then each ship contains a breeding group," Joseph said in an excited voice. "Considering how voracious Polig-Grug are …" Franklin trailed off. "Bottom line, we can't allow any of those ships to land."

"Wasn't planning on it," Eisenstadt replied dryly.

"*Bastet* to Command," Delaney broke in.

"Come in, *Bastet*," the commander replied.

"We have the Trojan under control," the *Bastet*'s captain said. "Tide Pool was able to attach the drones, and the ship is braking now," he said. "Command, I'm not getting any reaction from the Polig-Grug, but sensors are saying there are definitely life-forms on the Trojan."

"David, we have to board that ship," Kasumi said urgently. "There may be Alsoo."

"Dammit, Kasumi, I can't ask people to enter a death trap," Eisenstadt replied.

"No need to ask, commander," the captain of the *Bastet* broke in. "The entire marine platoon just volunteered." There was a dry chuckle. "Captain Kasumi is not the only one who wants to sleep well at night."

"There's a rogue singularity in that ship, captain," Eisenstadt snapped.

'Is there really, commander?" Delaney replied. "Or are we just supposed to think so?" he drawled. "Regardless, I have half a hundred marines waiting for me to give them the green light," he said. "If there really was an unshielded and rogue singularity in that ship, then how come we have life signs?"

Eisenstadt looked around the bridge. He knew what Kasumi wanted to do. He knew what he wanted to do. *But is it the smart thing?* he asked himself. "Captain, you have permission, but with one caveat," he said. "Once your marines are launched, you will pull back at least a thousand kilometers."

There was a long silence from the *Bastet*. It lasted so long that Eisenstadt was beginning to wonder if something had happened. "Marines are on their way. *Bastet* is pulling back."

"Spirits watch over you," whispered Kasumi. She sat up straight. "This is *Nieth*. Prepare for launch."

Joseph Franklin floated through the *Nieth*'s passageways. His eyes were half-closed, and he was deep in thought. The only thing keeping his floater from crashing into walls or people was the meter-long snakelike being that guided it.

"Maker/you question have/me," warbled the Alsoo.

"Hmm? Question?" Franklin shook himself. "What's up, Second-Daughter-Fifth-Born?"

"Dizzy/think/me help/we you question," the Alsoo warbled.

"Why are we helping you?" guessed Franklin. The Alsoo responded with the hand wave he associated with a yes. "That's a hard one," he admitted.

"Pain/you dead many split-tails/you," warbled the Alsoo. "Alsoo same/not do," she declared.

"Why are you flying my floater?" Franklin asked.

"Maker/you help need/you," replied the Alsoo.

"Yeah, but why are you doing it?" Franklin asked. "Why didn't any of the Alsoo leave the ship when they had the chance?"

"Know/not we," the Alsoo said in a quiet voice. "Safe safe/not this place/we." The Alsoo ruffled its feathers. "Dizzy/think/we," she warbled in the manner Franklin had come to associate with laughter.

"Dizzy/think all/we." replied Franklin. "Once I was afraid to live and afraid to die," he said. "Then I found my core, my friends, and I stopped being afraid to live." He reached out and ruffled the Alsoo's feathers. "I still don't want to die, but I'm not afraid of it." He smiled. "You want to hear some real dizzy/think?" he said. "We're going into a fight, one I could have sat out, but I decided to go because it's here that I could do the most good. And even if I knew I was going to die, I'd still go."

"Dizzy/think truth/oath," agreed Second-Daughter-Fifth-Born.

"*Nieth*, this is *Bastet*," came Captain Delaney's voice over the comm. "Got a situation."

"What kind of situation?" Kasumi replied.

"A couple thousand Alsoo situation," the *Bastet*'s captain replied. "They're scared shitless and are running from my people," he said.

"On the positive side, my techs have got the singularity bottled up," he said. "We still need to get rid of it, but it's under control."

"Nothing we can do about the Alsoo at the moment, captain," Kasumi replied. "Good job on the singularity, though." She rubbed her crest. "Hang on," she said. "Kasumi to Cool Evening Breeze."

"Yes, captain?" Cool Evening Breeze replied via her Torque.

"I have a job for Snake Squad," Kasumi replied.

Lieutenant Hendriks placed his hands behind his back as he surveyed his troops. Twenty-one feathered, snakelike owl-faced beings returned his stare. "Okay, let's go over this one more time," he said. "There are a lot of Alsoo trapped on a ship. There are more Alsoo on that ship than there are in the citadel."

The Alsoo warbled in excitement. Hendriks had long ago given up trying to explain how many there were; the Alsoo had no number above one hundred—and even one hundred was a difficult number for them to comprehend—but they could understand comparisons. The idea that they could rescue more Alsoo than existed in their citadel was, to the Alsoo, the equivalent of saving their entire species. *They might be right at that*, Hendriks thought. The biologists had explained that even if they rescued the entire two thousand Alsoo, there was no guarantee that the species would not go extinct. But there was hope.

"Your job is simple," Hendriks said. "Convince the Alsoo on that ship to leave the ship and get in the shuttle, and do it orderly," he said. "The shuttle can take up to one hundred Alsoo at a time, so it will take at least twenty trips before the ship is emptied."

"That means you will have to keep your fellow Alsoo from swarming in the ship and be patient waiting their turn to be ferried to the *Nieth*," added Lieutenant Cool Evening Breeze. "Do you understand?"

"Long time/short time question," warbled Speaker First-Son-First-Born.

"It will take a full day before all the Alsoo are ferried to the *Nieth*," Cool Evening Breeze replied to what she thought was the question.

"One more thing. There will be a double squad of split-tails with you," Hendriks said. "Just in case."

"Eaters question," warbled First-Son-First-Born.

"Eaters," agreed Hendriks. The Alsoo ruffled their feathers but remained in place. "Let us split-tails deal with the Eaters," he said firmly. "Your job is to keep your people from panicking."

The Alsoo slapped their chests. "Pledge/oath," they warbled in unison.

For the most part, the Alsoo entered the shuttle in something resembling order. From the constant ruffling of their feathers, it was obvious that the majority of the Alsoo were scared. Yet despite their fear, all the Alsoo got on board and curled up silently in their specially modified seats.

The trip from Earth orbit to the *Silent Shadow* had taken several hours, even with the *Nieth*'s Franklin-modified thrusters, but the *Nieth* had finally reached the derelict ship. Like the *Bastet*, the *Nieth* stayed a thousand kilometers from the *Silent Shadow*. Captain Kasumi maintained contact with Earth command the entire time.

"*Nieth* to *Bastet*," Kasumi hailed the sister ship. "Snake Squad, Ape Squad, and Bird Squad are heading for the *Silent Shadow*," she sent out. "We'll take over Alsoo recovery." She smiled slightly. "The Bastard is free to take over pest control."

"Yee-haw," replied Captain Delaney. "About time we got some real action," he said. "Bastard is on her way."

"Good hunting, Captain," Kasumi replied. "Spirits, ancestors, and your deity of choice watch over you."

"Same to you, Captain," Delaney said. A minute later, the *Bastet*'s engines lit and the ship pivoted and headed back in-system.

Kasumi watched via the Torque as the shuttle headed toward the derelict *Silent Shadow*. "And may the spirits and ancestors watch over the Alsoo," she said quietly.

The shuttle crossed the distance in a matter of minutes. In fact, it took almost as long to dock as it did to cross. "Bird Squad, get ready," barked Cool Evening Breeze. "Snake Squad, stand by."

Cool Evening Breeze held her breath as the airlock opened. She tensed. However, instead of Polig-Grug or Alsoo, she was greeted by a very human trooper. He saluted. "Corporal Evans, sir," he said crisply. "The ship is under control. No Polig-Grug."

Cool Evening Breeze nodded. "Snake Squad, forward," she ordered.

"Holy shit," Corporal Evans said. "They really do look like snake-men."

"Operative word is *men*," Cool Evening Breeze said firmly. "Speaker, you know what to do."

The Alsoo speaker waved his hands, and twenty Alsoo sidewinded into the ship. Cool Evening Breeze and Hendriks, along with their handpicked squads of marines, followed closely.

"I'm kind of surprised that there were no Polig-Grug on board," Cool Evening Breeze said to Corporal Evans. "Have you searched the entire ship?"

"Not yet, ma'am," Corporal Evans admitted. "We haven't been able to get into the main cargo hold."

"Five gets you ten it's full of Polig-Grug," Hendriks said in dry humor.

"No bet," Cool Evening Breeze replied. "Bird Squad," she barked. "This ship is, to put it bluntly, a trap," she said. "How do I know it's a trap? Mainly because it is filled with bait. Whether the Polig-Grug think we consider the Alsoo food like they do or whether they somehow figured out we're trying to save them, I don't know, and I don't care." Her crest flared. "What I do care about is that there are bugs to squash."

"Oo-rah," grunted Bird Squad.

"What I also care about is that, as far as we know, the Alsoo on this ship represent the sum total of all existing Alsoo," she said. "And that pisses me off. Does that piss you off, Corporal Evans?"

"I'm a marine, ma'am," Corporal Evans replied. "Everything pisses me off."

"Oo-rah," grunted the marines.

"Marines!" Cool Evening Breeze yelled. "Are you pissed off?"

"Yes, ma'am!" the squads returned loudly.

"You don't sound pissed off," Cool Evening Breeze sneered.

"Yes, ma'am!" the squads shouted.

"Better," Cool Evening Breeze replied. "And what do marines do when they are pissed off?" she asked.

"They fight!" the squad shouted.

"Damn right," Cool Evening Breeze chirped. Her face blurred for a second, and then she was wearing her red and black "demon" war paint. "Snake Squad, go with Hendriks and his squad and get your people to safety," she snarled. "The rest of you, let's go squash some bugs."

"Oo-rah!" came the cry, and it sounded like a single enraged animal.

Hendriks watched as Cool Evening Breeze and her marines jogged off. "Don't you dare get yourself killed, Feather Head," he said under his breath. "Crystal will kill me if you do." He took a breath. "Okay, Snake Squad. Let's move." The Alsoo warbled and followed in Hendriks' wake.

They reached the first of the holding areas, and Hendriks stuck his head inside. There were no Polig-Grug in the room, but there was plenty of evidence that something else was. The Alsoo squad side-winded inside, and the speaker warbled, "Split-tails Eaters/not. Here/this place safe not. Safe place split-tails/have."

There was an answering warble, and suddenly dozens of Alsoo were peeking out from behind every possible hiding place. "Eaters/not they question."

"Eaters/not," the speaker replied. "Fast/fast safe place go/you," he ordered. "Mothers first, hatchlings first." He stamped the butt of his spear on the floor. "Fast/fast."

"Marines, set up a safe corridor," ordered Hendriks. "Speaker, make sure no one stays behind," he said. "Now move it."

It started as a trickle as Alsoo left their hiding places cautiously. They ruffled their feathers as they passed under the eyes of the humans and Rynn. But the trickle quickly turned into a stream and then a torrent as Alsoo after Alsoo left whatever hiding places they had claimed.

Snake Squad kept the Alsoo refugees moving, occasionally physically dragging one reluctant and frightened Alsoo from hiding and pushing it into the ever-growing throng of escaping creatures.

"Shuttle One, you have incoming," Hendriks said over his Torque.

"Roger, Lieutenant," responded the shuttle.

"Speaker," Hendriks shouted. "Keep 'em moving, keep 'em in line, and for the spirits sake, don't let them stop."

"Fast/fast," warbled the speaker to the fleeing Alsoo.

"We're moving the Alsoo, Feather Head," Hendriks said. "How's it going with you?"

"We were right: the cargo hold was packed with bug-lizards," Cool Evening Breeze replied, and Hendriks could hear her breathing heavily. "Spirits, there must be hundreds of them."

"Just keep 'em busy until we get the Alsoo to safety," Hendriks responded. "No need to take chances."

"That's no fun," Cool Evening Breeze replied.

"Do you want me to tell Momma on you?" Hendriks said.

"That's cheating," Cool Evening Breeze chittered. "Don't worry, I'll keep my head … oh shit."

"What?" Hendriks said in alarm. "Breeze? What?" Hendriks started running when Cool Evening Breeze did not answer. "I'm coming, Breeze."

"Negatory, Hendriks," Cool Evening Breeze replied breathlessly. "We're pulling out," she said. "Remember what they said about linked Polig-Grug?"

"They get smart?" replied Hendriks as he ran toward Cool Evening Breeze and her squad.

"Smart, and they act like a single organism," Cool Evening Breeze replied. "Move it, move it!" she suddenly shouted. "Escobar, move your fucking ass or so help me, I'll feed you to those bugs myself."

Hendriks turned a corner and found himself face to face with the retreating Bird Squad. Right behind them was a group of linked Polig-Grug. Hendriks immediately understood why Cool Evening Breeze sounded retreat. Individual Polig-Grug were barely above eating machines, but a linked cluster was powerful and above all acting intelligently. Hendriks pulled out his battle mace. "We gotta stop'em here," he shouted.

"Tell me something I don't know, Fuzzy Butt," Cool Evening Breeze snapped. "Suppression fire," she ordered.

"Shuttle One, status report," Hendriks said at the same time.

"I got a full load and heading out now," the shuttle pilot replied.

"Outstanding," Hendriks said. "Not that you weren't gonna do it anyway, but hurry," He broke communication and concentrated on the oncoming linked Polig-Grug.

The battle between the human/Rynn squads and the linked Polig-Grug seemed to go on forever. Every so often, the shuttle would break in with arrivals and departures. Hendriks and Cool Evening Breeze's initial squads got rotated out of the battle to get some food, and fresher squads got rotated in. And even though those squads that got rotated out could have taken a spot on a shuttle to safety, it was a measure of their commitment that none did. One squad became two, which became a company, and still the battle remained a stalemate.

"How many more Alsoo do we have to ferry off?" Cool Evening Breeze asked after she and Hendriks finished another shift at keeping the Polig-Grug at bay.

"Last report was about four hundred," Hendriks replied. "And Snake Squad is still finding stragglers." He wiped at his face. "*Nieth* says they already have more than the two thousand we originally estimated." He smiled tiredly. "That's actually good news."

"How about the invasion force?" Cool Evening Breeze asked a few minutes later.

"Oh right, the invasion force," Hendriks chuckled. "Forgot about that." He shrugged. "If there was a problem, I think someone would have told us by now." He turned as something rubbed against his leg. An Alsoo was prodding him with his short staff. "Shouldn't you be helping to get your people loaded up, Speaker?" Hendriks asked. His Torque warbled the translation.

The speaker warbled back. "Neuters/they remain/they," he said in some satisfaction. "Breeders burrow/safe/they." He looked past Hendriks to where the marines were keeping the Polig-Grug pinned down. "Eaters." He ruffled his feathers.

"Yeah, Eaters," agreed Cool Evening Breeze.

Speaker First-Son-First-Born ruffled his feathers again and then warbled loudly. From the direction of the shuttle bay came a large number of Alsoo—far more than there were in Snake Squad. The speaker started to warble. "Split-tails/they protect People/we. Truth/oath," he said. "Split-tail/they oath keep/they." He raised his sharpened staff. "This time, People/we warriors/be. This time, people/we Eaters/they fight/we."

"Hey, there's no need," began Hendriks as he deciphered what the Alsoo was saying.

"Need," warbled the Alsoo. "Long time People/we hide/we, scared/we." He shook his staff. "Speaker/me say this time not hide/we, not run/we. This time hatchlings/ours see/we warriors/see."

Hendriks was about to say something when Cool Evening Breeze placed a hand on his arm. "He's right. They need this, Hendriks," she said. She looked at the little Alsoo. "See those rope things that connect the Eaters to each other?" she said. The Alsoo waved its arms in agreement. "Cut them," she said. "And we'll do the rest." She reached to her belt and pulled out her utility knife. "Use this."

The rest of the humans and Rynn listening nodded, removed their own utility knives, and handed them to the closest Alsoo.

The speaker took the knife, which he held like a broadsword, and raised it. The surrounding Alsoo raised their own knives. "Warriors/we this time fight/we," he warbled loudly. "Go/we." A wave of Alsoo side-winded directly toward the Polig-Grug.

"Suppression fire," yelled Cool Evening Breeze.

With the humans and Rynn giving them a chance, the Alsoo reached the first of the connected Polig-Grug. They dodged the slashing legs and biting jaws and swarmed up the bodies of the insect-like creatures.

"Halt suppression fire," yelled Cool Evening Breeze.

The humans and Rynn watched in horrified fascination as the tiny Alsoo hacked and cut madly at the connecting nerve bundles that united the Polig-Grug into a single entity. Jaws would bite down on a screaming Alsoo, claws would rip into their bodies, but still they continued with their suicide mission.

"They're doing it," a marine shouted in excitement. "Go, you crazy sons of bitches."

"Oo-rah!" shouted a number of the marines, and they charged. The Polig-Grug were so distracted trying to contend with the Alsoo that they didn't realize what was happening until the humans and Rynn were already upon them, maces and battle axes swinging.

"Shuttle One to Bird Company!" came over the Torques. "Recall. Recall."

"Everyone on the ship?" Cool Evening Breeze grunted between strikes.

"Everyone but you guys," came the response.

"Speaker!" Cool Evening Breeze shouted. "Speaker!" she repeated several times before the Alsoo leader turned to her. Even across the ten meters or so that separated them, she could see that the little Naga-form was in the grips of a battle frenzy. "Get your people to the shuttle. Now." The alien looked her blankly. "You've won," she shouted. "Now get your people to the ship."

The little Alsoo shook itself and then began warbling to his remaining fighters. In ones and twos and then in small groups, the remaining Alsoo started to retreat. The marines started giving them covering fire. The last to begin his retreat was Speaker First-Son-First-Born. He pushed, prodded, and even hit some of the more recalcitrant Alsoo to get them moving before turning to leave. It was at that very moment that he was grabbed by a king Polig-Grug.

"No!" shouted Hendriks and Cool Evening Breeze in horrified unison as the insect-like creature bit the little Alsoo in half. The speaker didn't even have time to scream before he died. Without thinking, Hendriks and Cool Evening Breeze charged the Polig-Grug and swung their battle maces. They did not stop until they had smashed the legs of the king and the creature was writhing helplessly in pain. Cool Evening Breeze looked at the creature. "I know you can understand me," she snarled. "We are going to exterminate your race," she growled. "We will not stop until there is not a single one of you left."

The creature clicked and whistled. "Old are we," came the translation. "Others have said the same, meat they were. Meat you will be."

Hendriks leaned closer. "Not this time," he said. "Let's go, Breeze."

"One second," Cool Evening Breeze replied. She raised her battle axe and brought it down on the creature's head with every ounce of her hate-fueled strength. The creature's head exploded under the impact. She then picked up the mangled remains of First-Son-First-Born. "Marines, collect our dead and let's go."

The squad searched through the bodies and collected every dead Alsoo they could find. When they were sure they had all of them, they began their slow retreat.

"Hey, are you guys still on the *Silent Shadow*?" came Joseph Franklin's voice just as they were approaching the shuttle.

"Just leaving now, Joseph," Hendriks replied.

"Wait ten, okay?" Franklin said. "I got something to do."

Cool Evening Breeze and Hendriks looked at each other and shrugged. "We'll wait," Hendriks said.

A couple minutes later, Franklin floated into the ship. His floater was piloted by the Alsoo neuter Second-Daughter-Fifth-Born. "Make this fast, Franklin," Hendriks growled. "I want to get the stink out of my nose."

"You and me both," Franklin replied. He pointed to a large bundle hanging off the side of the floater. "You mind getting that out of the bag and attaching it to the nearest power outlet?"

"I got it," said one of the marines. He removed the bundle and pulled a torpedo-shaped object out of the bag. It was less than a meter long and had two flat circular pads on one side.

"Those pads are magnetic. Use them to attach it to a wall or something," Franklin said. "Once you connect it to a power source, press the red button."

"Done," said the marine a few minutes later.

"Okay, we can leave now," Franklin replied. "See you back at the *Nieth*," he said, and Second-Daughter-Fifth-Born started piloting the floater away.

"Hey, you can't just leave without telling us what you just did," complained Hendriks.

"I didn't tell you?" Franklin replied in shock.

"Maker/he dizzy think/he," complained Second-Daughter-Fifth-Born.

"Probably," agreed Franklin. "It's a little gift for the Polig-Grug." He smiled. "We found their home world," he shrugged. "It won't destroy them, unfortunately, but it will send a message."

"Boom," warbled Second-Daughter-Fifth-Born. "Big/big boom."

"And that's just going to be the first," Franklin said cheerfully.

"Eaters/they lots big/big boom get/they," warbled Second-Daughter-Fifth-Born in satisfaction.

Hendriks and Cool Evening Breeze looked at each other

and grinned. "Looks like you're gonna keep your promise to the Polig-Grug."

"Looks like," agreed Cool Evening Breeze. "We should go," she said. "You know how Momma worries when we're gone too long."

"Yeah," agreed Hendriks. He and Cool Evening Breeze entered the shuttle.

"Back to the Shrike, Core Sister," Joseph Franklin said to the Alsoo. Second-Daughter-Fifth-Born warbled in amusement and piloted the floater back to Shrike One. Once he was safely back in the Shrike, he had Black Rocks pilot the fighter craft a few hundred meters away. Joseph spoke to his Torque and reviewed the results that were displayed to just his eyes. He nodded and then spoke a command.

The derelict ship slowly turned until its prow was pointed away from the sun. The Shrike drones detached and shot away as the *Silent Shadow*'s main engines powered up. The ship began to glow brighter and brighter, and then with a soundless roar, the ship seemed to stretch—and then, like a soap bubble, it vanished as if it never was.

"Hey Franklin," Hendriks' voice came through the Torque. "Just wondering, how come you used the *Silent Shadow*? That was a pretty small bomb. You could have used a Shrike."

"Killing two birds with one stone, Hendriks," Franklin replied. "I figured a rogue black hole would be better off among the Polig-Grug than here."

"Ah, good point. Thanks," Hendriks replied. "Hendriks out."

Captain Kasumi checked the status reports as they flowed past her vision via the Torque. "Looks like we got them all," she said in relief. "Still, I'll advise all governments to keep an eye out for unusual disappearances or sightings."

"Agreed," said David Eisenstadt. "I'm still surprised at how crude their attack was."

"I wouldn't call using a singularity crude," disagreed Mel.

"I was speaking about their tactics," Eisenstadt replied. "It was barely above throwing rocks. It was crude and obvious and not what I would have expected from a spacefaring race," he said in complaint. "A five-year-old would have come up with something more sophisticated."

"I think you've put your finger on it, David." Jeremy Blunt rose from his seat and walked over to a wall where there was a life-sized image of a Polig-Grug. "Kings may be intelligent, but according to the records we have, their tactics are almost instinctive. They try to overwhelm their prey's defenses."

"But doesn't that mean that once they realize they've failed, they'll just try again?" Mel suggested. "Only with even more ships?"

Eisenstadt nodded. "Most likely," he agreed. "But now we know where they live," he said with satisfaction.

Bright Sunlight listened as humans and Rynn discussed the possible future. He looked at his daughter with understandable pride. *You've done more in the past few sun paths than your entire species has been able to accomplish in the previous one hundred,* he thought. He turned his head to look at Jeremy, only to find the older human looking directly at him. Bright Sunlight briefly covered his eyes in respect. He stood.

"Well, Daughter, you seem to have everything under control," he said. "Now it is my turn to do the same."

"Father?" Kasumi asked in surprise.

"We can't let the humans be the only ones doing all the fighting." He waggled his crest in amusement. "I need to get back to Nest and convince the other powers that we should be building our own Hunters." He briefly covered his eyes. "I do hope you will visit the home of your birth sometime soon."

Kasumi stood. "I was told that seeing my home may be all I will ever be able to do." She walked over to her father, placed her hands on his shoulders, and touched her forehead to his. "Spirits protect you," she said earnestly.

Again, Bright Sunlight briefly covered his eyes. "The truth that you are is like the sun," he said solemnly. "At first I refused to see that truth and was indeed blind." He smiled. "The truth that you are will illuminate the path that we must travel," he said. "Your name will live forever, Kasumi Blunt of the Forest Cabin Clan."

42

To Be Tall

First-Son-Second-Born was now the speaker for the Alsoo. He was young to be a speaker, but the eyes that looked out at the world were old. With the aid of the split-tails and their magic, a new burrow had been dug in a single Light. Already the females were making the bare chambers more habitable. He side-winded up the ramp that led to one of the guard towers. The split-tails had offered to build the towers and citadel as well, but the speaker had convinced them to just provide the building materials.

The speaker slithered along the walkway that led to the first and only completed tower. The second was still being built. From his vantage point, he could see most of the compound. Big split-tails and small split-tails were everywhere, and while the split-tails would look toward the burrow and towers frequently, few would approach. Speaker warbled quietly when he saw one of those few who did approach.

It was one of the big split-tails—the one the previous speaker had called the spirit speaker. It was difficult to tell one big split-tail from another, but he had no difficulty recognizing this one. The big split-tail halted just at the boundary. The split-tail grunted and hooted. "Greet/me Speaker/you," said a second voice.

"Greet/me Spirit Speaker/you," the speaker replied.

"Short time big talk/you me question," the spirit speaker said. "Big talk/you me warrior/you warrior path/you." The spirit speaker held a long pointed stick, very much like the one the speaker himself carried.

The spirit speaker executed a number of moves that the speaker could recognize as being for fighting, and a few he did not but could almost see the sense of them. Regardless, what he saw impressed him. *Warrior/he*, the speaker decided.

"Spirit Speaker/you teach/we question," the speaker asked and repeated a number of the moves.

"Alsoo/you two-hand-one hands of warriors/you teach/you me," replied the sprit speaker. "First sun step here/me."

"Two-hand-one hands of warriors/we. First sun step here/we," agreed the speaker. "Pledge/oath." He slapped his chest.

"Pledge/oath," agreed the spirit speaker. The big split-tail slapped his chest and then walked away.

The speaker watched him go, and then he walked away himself. He had much to do before the following morning—the least of which was to find twenty-one warriors willing to fight alongside the split-tails.

Jeremy walked back to the administration building in the compound. As expected, Morning Stars Fade was waiting patiently. "He agreed to the training," Jeremy said.

"I had no doubt that would be the case," Morning Stars Fade replied. "Emily has already spoken to Raindrops in a Tide Pool," he said. "They will give the Alsoo a wide berth during training."

"Miss Fields seems most competent," Jeremy observed with a smile.

"Very competent," agreed Morning Stars Fade. He tilted his head slightly. "When did you know, Teacher?"

Jeremy chuckled. "Everyone has potential, Disciple," he said. "It's just more obvious with some." He added, "Miss Fields will be a good companion to you and whomever you choose to complete your core."

Morning Stars Fade briefly covered his eyes. "I think so too, Teacher," he agreed. Morning Stars Fade looked toward where the Alsoo were building their sanctuary. "Will they survive, Teacher?"

Jeremy's expression became somber. "I don't know, Disciple," he admitted sadly. "The odds are against them," he said. "What I do know is that we must do what we can to improve those odds."

The princess walked through the city and came upon the Temple of Light. With her were her longtime companions: the mist, the faceless one, and the stone giant. Curled around her neck was her newest companion, a little crystalline red and green snake. The princess stopped at the steps of the temple and knelt. She clapped her hands together twice.

"I am the princess. I who have thirsted have learned there are those for whom thirst is all they have known. I who have hungered have learned that there are those who have never once known what it is like to not be hungry. I have stood before you naked, but it was by my hand and not thrust upon me by another," she said. "I never expected to walk this path, and I fear I will fail."

"Failure only exists if you let it," came a familiar dry voice. "Failure is only when you give up." The old monk walked down the stairs. "The path forward is hard, and there is no guarantee that you will succeed, but not trying leads only to darkness and extinction." The old monk smiled. "Remember, you do not walk this path alone," she admonished. "You have forged an alliance that, even if fate deems otherwise, will shake the foundations of heaven."

She placed a hand on the princess's head. "Do not worry about a failure that may be and instead focus on what is." She looked past the princess and directly at the companions. "Morning Mist," she said to the mist-like being. "Remember, keep your vow and seek out all who threaten."

"I will, Grandmother," the mist-like being replied in a faint voice.

"David," she said to the stone giant. "The giant must wake or it will be destroyed." There was a sound like stone on stone as the giant nodded.

"And you who bear my name, I charge you with the most difficult task." The old monk reached out with a hand and touched the faceless figure. "You will forever be her shield and her shadow," she said. "But know this and hold it as truth: you are my granddaughter, my blood, and I could not be prouder."

"Thank you, Grandmother," the faceless being replied. "I wish I had known you."

"No more than I you," the old monk replied. "Now go. You have more tasks to perform." She turned and started back up the stairs. Then she stopped and turned back. "And tell that old fool that he still has work to do as well."

Mel opened her eyes in the darkness. "Oh lord, now I'm starting to have dreams where my grandmother speaks to me."

"Me too," Morning Mist said in a tiny voice. "She said I must seek out our enemies."

"The giant must wake," David Eisenstadt said in a hushed voice.

Kasumi sat up and smiled. "The path will be difficult, but for the first time, I truly have hope," she said. "We might as well get up. We have work to do."

43

War Paint and War Drums

"Probe has entered the Polig-Grug system, commander," reported the drone operator. "Running self-checks."

"How long before we start getting data?" asked David Eisenstadt..

"Twenty Earth minutes, commander," replied the drone operator, a Rynn by the name of Meadow Flower. "Assuming the Polig-Grug don't destroy it first."

"Understood," Eisenstadt replied. "Keep me updated."

"Of course, commander," replied the drone operator.

Eisenstadt nodded and turned his attention to other matters. Being commander of the human/Rynn war fleet consumed much of his attention. There were status reports to review, expenditures to approve, and tactics to devise. But the commander's attention kept being drawn back to the still blank display screen. The Rynn designer who had built the war room had questioned the need for a central display, as the Torque would provide just as much if not more detail, but he had acceded to David's request. After a while, David stopped pretending to work and locked his gaze on the display screen.

"First data coming in," the Rynn drone operator finally reported.

"Onscreen," the commander ordered. The drone operator chirped, and an image formed. The commander frowned. "What in blazes am I looking at?" he asked. "Where is the Polig-Grug home world?"

The Rynn drone operator chirped to her Torque, as did several other technicians. For several minutes, that was all that could be heard. Eisenstadt continued to stare at the screen. He had reason to be confused. Instead of a planet, he was looking at something that looked like an orange slice—even more so since the object was orange-ish in color.

"The object is approximately 225,000 kilometers in length and 75,000 kilometers at its widest point," a technician reported.

"It has an atmosphere," another technician reported in tones of surprise.

"Life signs," reported a third.

"Commander, I think we're looking at an artificial habitat," the drone technician said.

"Artificial?" the commander said in disbelief. "It's five times the size of Earth."

"Artificial," confirmed the technician. "What we are looking at is, I believe, what remains of the Polig-Grug home world and probably all the planets, asteroids, and everything else that was in that system."

"It's a Dyson Ring," the commander breathed.

"That would not be an entirely accurate description," said the drone technician. "But technically correct." Her crest lowered but did not flatten. "That's even beyond Rynn technology."

"Something does not add up," the commander said. "If creating that is beyond Rynn technology, it should also be beyond Polig-Grug technology." He looked at the image. "Meadow Flower, get as much data as possible. See how close you can get the probe to that." He leaned back in his command chair. "Something does not add up."

The speaker for the Alsoo led his select group of warriors to the training ground. The sun was just peeking over the distant hills, but the spirit speaker was already waiting for them. "Greet/me you, Spirit Speaker," said the Alsoo speaker.

"Greet/me you, Speaker," the white-furred split-tail replied in the strange double voice that all split-tails used. "Greet/me you, warriors." He pointed to the drawn circle that enclosed most of the training area. "Start/we."

The split-tail spirit speaker walked to the drawn circle and waited for the Alsoo warriors to form into lines. When they were assembled, the spirit speaker picked up his staff. "*Lau*/move called/this." He said and demonstrated. His staff swept upwards. "*Sot*/move called/this." The staff swept downwards. "Hand of hand *Lau*/move, hand of hand *Sot*/move. Begin."

The twenty-plus Alsoo repeated the moves under the watchful eye of both the spirit speaker and the Alsoo speaker. The spirit speaker had the warriors go through the sequence a hand more times before he gestured for them to stop. The split-tail walked over to a spot directly in front of all the warriors, and then he lowered his body over his two tails until he was resting on his tails. The spirit speaker's face set in a stern visage, and he did the lao/sot sequence. The spirit speaker then raised halfway up on his tails and did the lao/sot sequence again. The spirit speaker took a breath and then surged all the way to his full split-tail height and did the sequence. Every warrior's feathers fluffed out before each returned to the normal flattened state when the split-tail reversed the process. Still lowered down, the spirit speaker looked at the gathered Alsoo. "Warriors that/do/you."

The twenty-one assembled Alsoo looked at each other in consternation. Then one warrior, Fifth-Son-Eighth-Born, slapped his chest. "Warrior/me tall/be/me." A look of great concentration appeared on his owl-like face. The assembled warriors' feathers fluffed in response. Fifth-Son-Eighth-Born did the sequence and, with a barely suppressed pained warble, rose up higher on his tail and repeated the form.

The split-leg speaker walked over and stood behind

Fifth-Son-Eighth-Born. "Great warrior/you, rise/you, tall/be you," intoned the spirit speaker. Fifth-Son-Eighth-Born warbled in effort as he rose up higher on his tail than he, and possibly any Alsoo, had done before. As Fifth-Son-Eighth-Born went through the sequence, the spirit speaker stood on his split-tail just behind him with his hands on either side of the Alsoo warrior. Fifth-Son-Eighth-Born did the lau/sot sequence and then all but collapsed to the ground.

The surrounding Alsoo warriors, including the speaker, warbled in excited approval. "Fifth-Son-Eighth-Born, Fifth-Son-Eighth-Born, Fifth-Son-Eighth-Born!" the warriors chanted.

Fifth-Son-Eighth-Born raised his body up fully though tiredly. "Tall/be me short time. Short time short time tall/be me long time," he said in tired resolve. "Good/be tall/be me." Then his expression became fierce. "Warriors/you brothers/me. Know/me Spirit Speaker/he want/we/he."

Fifth-Son-Eighth-Born suddenly stood high on his tail—not as tall as before, but much higher than any warrior would normally rise—and did the lau/sot sequence. Fifth-Son-Eighth-Born remained balanced high on his tail and gestured. "Brothers/me Eaters eyes high/they Eaters eyes see/me."

The surrounding Alsoo started warbling excitedly as they rose higher and higher on their tails and did the lau/sot sequence. An impromptu contest among the Alsoo warriors broke out. The split-tail spirit speaker looked on approvingly and let them continue for most of the morning before clapping his hands together.

"This time, warriors/you learn/you truth/new," he said. "This time warriors/you learn/you tall/be you truth/new learn/you tall/be you truth/old. Truth see/you not." He raised both his hands to the side as if lifting something, and the Alsoo warriors all stood higher. "Truth see/you warriors/tall, Alsoo/you, Alsoo tall." He slapped his chest. "Pledge/oath truth/oath."

The Alsoo warriors rose up even higher on their tails. Some even executed all or part of the lau/sot form and warbled in approval.

Kasumi could barely suppress her own triumphant chitter. "Spirits and ancestors, I know exactly how that feels," she breathed.

"Yeah, me too," Mel replied. "Remind me to tell Grandmother that Gramps may be delayed a few more years."

"I don't think she'll mind," Kasumi replied cheerfully. She nodded at the relayed image displayed via her Torque. "They're going to hate the spirit speaker," she chittered.

"Whatever happened to, 'I'd never hate Germy'?" teased Mel.

"I've trained with him," Kasumi replied. She and Mel looked at each other with exactly the same expression and burst into laughter.

Morning Mist waggled her crest in amusement and returned to trying to make sense of all the Polig-Grug data that had been vacuumed out of the Polig-Grug ships' data banks. "Spirits, this wasn't programmed, it was … grown," she finally said after trying to find some more appropriate description. *Grown* seemed the closest. Morning Mist sat up and frowned. "Torque: assume the following conditions are true. The Polig-Grug are a hive mind but not all the time. Assume that normally two or three—a king and two favorite queens, I suppose …" She paused. "What would cause kings to share queens?"

"Resources," the Torque replied almost immediately. "The more kings that cooperate through their queens, the greater the resources they would be able to control."

"Of course, and competition would eventually lead to larger and larger collections of … kingdoms." Morning Mist paused again. "There must be a limit," she frowned. "Is there a limit?" she asked.

"Unknown," replied the Torque.

"Of course," muttered Morning Mist.

"David, status?" Kasumi asked. This was the daily briefing, and Kasumi's inner circle was assembled in the main conference room in the main building of the colony. While these meetings usually were held with only the inner circle, there were exceptions, and today was one of them.

"I'm going to let Meadow Flower brief you on what we've discovered about the Polig-Grug home ... system," David Eisenstadt replied.

Meadow Flower's crest flicked nervously as she became the center of attention. However, as a senior member of Eisenstadt's command crew, she was becoming used to providing intelligence to the upper echelon of the Rynn/human hierarchy. She chirped to her Torque, and the Torques of all those attending displayed the same image. "This is, as the commander said, the Polig-Grug home system." She chirped again and the image rotated. "When we first began receiving data, we found what appeared to be a single artificial habitat, what we've dubbed 'the orange slice.'" She chirped again and the vantage rotated. "Since then, we have found a second orange slice. It sits 180 degrees opposite the first."

"Is this right?" Kasumi said in disbelief. "Both are over 200,000 kilometers in length?"

"Yes, Captain," Meadow Flower replied.

"Impossible," objected Morning Mist. "The Polig-Grug are incapable of creating anything of that order."

"I have to agree," Meadow Flower replied. "However, the predominant life-forms found on both megastructures are Polig-Grug."

"Predominant?" echoed Morning Mist. "Meaning that there are other life-forms?"

Meadow Flower nodded grimly. "The good news, I suppose, is that none of those other life-forms are human, Rynn, or Alsoo." Her crest fluttered for a moment. "But that does not mean they are not sentient."

"Considering the Polig-Grug penchant for predating on sentient beings, the chances are good that they are," Eisenstadt commented. "Why sentient?" he added in an undertone.

"Unfortunately, there is an easy answer to that one, commander," Meadow Flower replied grimly. "They're more adaptable and therefore more likely to survive," she said. "The more adaptable, the longer they will survive as a food source." She chirped to her

Torque. "There is some evidence that the Alsoo have been predated upon for nearly three hundred of your human years," she said. "And they are nowhere near as adaptable as humans or Rynn."

Kasumi nodded grimly. "And with the Alsoo nearing extinction, the Polig-Grug will …" She broke off. "Have you been able to estimate the population size of the Polig-Grug?"

"We're still refining the data," began Meadow Flower.

"Best guess," ordered Kasumi sharply.

Meadow Flower's crest dropped, and she covered her eyes. "I apologize," she said. "Best guess is somewhere between eighty and one hundred billion," she said in a quiet voice.

Kasumi nodded. "I suspected it would be something like that," she said. "Each one of those megastructures has four or five times the habitable surface area of Earth."

"Closer to eight or nine," corrected Morning Mist. "Maybe more."

"Plus virtually unlimited energy from their home star," Kasumi continued.

"That would be the expected situation," agreed Meadow Flower. "However, that does not appear to be the case. Analysis indicates that there is a heavy reliance on fusion reactors."

"Unlimited solar energy, and they are using fusion reactors?" Morning Mist asked in surprise. "The whole point of creating megastructures like that is to use solar energy."

"Since when have the Polig-Grug done anything rational or logical?" Kasumi returned in annoyance. "Nothing they do makes sense," she said. "They live on an artifact that should be able to easily handle their population size, yet they continue to expand. They use fusion reactors instead of the solar energy that is abundant. They predate instead of domesticating a sustainable food source."

"They use a computing method that appears more junk than logical," added Morning Mist. "They really should not be spacefaring at all," she pointed out. "Joseph Franklin says that their ships are actually organic shells that were grown around engines and other technological instrumentality."

"And their tactics are absurdly simple," Eisenstadt pointed out. "None of this adds up."

"Let's look at this another way," Kasumi said. "The Polig-Grug are not acting intelligent," she said musingly. "Maybe it isn't acting," she suggested. "I know Cool Evening Breeze said she spoke directly to a king and it responded, but …" She waved a hand. "As David keeps saying, this does not add up." Kasumi sat back. "We need more information. Meadow Flower, thank you for your report. It was more than expected in such a short time, but not enough." She smiled apologetically. "I hate to add more work to your already busy schedule …"

"I don't mind," Meadow Flower replied with a smile. "It's certainly more interesting than doing a cost analysis."

"I'm sure," agreed Mel. "I'd like to recommend that Meadow Flower take command of Polig-Grug analytics and further, that she be included in all future general staff meetings."

"Seconded," Eisenstadt said immediately.

"Objections?" asked Kasumi. She looked around. "As there are no objections, Meadow Flower is now officially a member of the general staff," she said. "I'd say congratulations, but the job comes with a lot of added responsibilities."

"And one added perk," Mel added with a grin. "You get to speak to my grandfather," she said. "Or rather, he gets to speak to you."

Meadow Flower covered her eyes. "I will strive to provide competent service," she said in serious tones. "And while I consider it a great honor to speak to the Teacher, I will hope it does not occur too frequently."

Kasumi and Mel laughed in response.

44

Jamal

"You do not have an appointment," Raindrops in a Tide Pool said in mild tones.

"Do you have any idea who I am?" snapped the man. He was a clean-shaven white man in his mid-fifties. His white hair was recently cut, and he wore a crisp gray suit. He might have been considered handsome except for the scowl on his face.

"Not really," replied Raindrops in a Tide Pool. Actually, he did, but he wasn't going to give the man the satisfaction of admitting that. "The captain is a very busy woman, and I can't let just anyone in to see her."

"I am not just anyone," the man said impatiently. "I represent the rightful government of the United States of America, and I demand to see this Captain Kasumi."

Raindrops in a Tide Pool chittered in amusement. "Rightful government? There was just an election, and I don't remember seeing anyone resembling you being declared the winner," he said. "In fact, I seem to remember President Newgate winning another term."

"Do not play with me, alien," snarled the man. "The only reason Newgate won was because you aliens stuffed the ballot boxes." He waved a finger under Rain Drops in a Tide Pool's nose. "And don't pretend otherwise."

"I pretend nothing," replied Raindrops in a Tide Pool. "The New Christian Party received exactly 10 percent of the popular vote," he said. "I fail to see how that makes you the representative of the rightful government, Mr. Sawyer."

"So you do know who I am," Mr. Sawyer accused.

"I didn't recognize the face, but that annoying voice is hard to forget," replied Raindrops in a Tide Pool. "No matter how hard I try." He matched the man's glare with his own. "The vote was validated and certified," he continued. "If you had any evidence of voter fraud, you should have presented your evidence," he said. "As it is, there was ample evidence of your party attempting to suppress votes."

"How dare you," snarled Mr. Sawyer.

"Shut up!" Raindrops in a Tide Pool returned. "In my years living on Earth, I have met humans who have inspired me, made me question my beliefs, and made me try to be better," he said. "And I have met humans who have made me want to, what's that word? Oh yes, *puke*." He stood with his crest at full extension. "You make me want to puke," he growled. "I saw what people like you are capable of. I have seen the result of those policies. Polig-Grug only eat people. Your kind denies them *being* people." If possible, Raindrops in a Tide Pool's crest went even higher. "You represent nothing except the worst of humanity," he said. "Now get out." He chirped to his Torque, and a door opened.

A young black man, at most nineteen years of age, walked in. "Did you need me, Raindrops Drops in a Tide Pool?"

"Yes, I did," Raindrops in a Tide Pool replied. "Mr. Sawyer, this is Shadowed Heart," he said in introduction. "He was born Jamal Johnson. He was renamed Jehoram by his so-called master when the CSA was attempting to … what was that term, Shadowed Heart?"

"'Return order to America,'" replied Shadowed Heart. He stared balefully at Mr. Sawyer.

"Shadowed Heart was among those we recovered," Raindrops in a Tide Pool said. "His parents were murdered. His rights were taken.

Do you want him to show you his slave brand?" Raindrops in a Tide Pool almost purred. "No?" He almost smiled. "Maybe another time," he said. "He told the Teacher that Jamal was dead with his parents, and that he would not ever be Jehoram."

"Raindrops in a Tide Pool was kind enough to provide me with a new name, a Rynn name," Shadowed Heart added. "And a new family." He smiled warmly at the Rynn. His scowl returned as he turned his attention back to the visitor. "I am also a member of colony's security force."

"Which is why I called you," Raindrops in a Tide Pool said. "Please escort Mr. Sawyer back to his vehicle, and then make sure he and his entourage leave."

"It will be my pleasure," Shadowed Heart replied. "This way," he said to the man. When Sawyer refused to budge, Shadowed Heart said, almost conversationally, "I would leave if I were you. As a member of colony security, I am authorized to use lethal force." He added, "Please give me a reason to."

"Stay away from me, boy," Mr. Sawyer said.

"Boy?" Shadowed Heart replied. "I was expecting another word." He smiled coldly. "That would have been a reason."

"I would have considered it a valid one," Raindrops in a Tide Pool commented. "Goodbye, Mr. Sawyer. Don't bother coming back."

Meadow Flower chirped, and the display she was reviewing vanished. She chirped a sigh. "It makes no sense," she grumped.

"Talk it through," said a voice at her elbow.

Meadow Flower's crest snapped open in shock. "Teacher!" she gasped. She hastily covered her eyes in respect.

"Enough of that," Jeremy Blunt said. "Talk it through," he ordered.

With some effort, Meadow Flower got control of her trembling crest. "Yes, Teacher," she said. "The more we learn about the

Polig-Grug, the less sense it makes," she said. "They are spacefaring, and they should not be. They live on an artificial habitat that they cannot have built. They use fusion reactors when they could be using the nearly unlimited power provided by their home star. They somehow are able to capture or create a mini-singularity, but they don't use it except as a weapon."

"How would you use it?" asked the old man.

"I'd use it the way we do use it, as a power source," Meadow Flower returned instantly. "Or to create a local gravity well." She chirped, and an image of *Safe Haven* appeared. A circle appeared outlining a section of the trading ship. "That's how Bright Sunlight uses it."

"Interesting," commented Jeremy. "What else is confusing?"

"They do not domesticate animals and instead rely on the survivability of their prey," Meadow Flower continued. "Even the Alsoo had, at one time, domesticated a food animal," she added. "The Polig-Grug do not do anything a sentient and sapient being would do," she complained. "Yet all evidence points to them being both."

"What have you learned about the other life-forms found on the megastructures?" asked Jeremy.

"Not a lot," admitted Meadow Flower. "There seems to be whole sections of the habitats that are free of Polig-Grug and populated by …" Suddenly, Meadow Flower broke off and started chirping. An image of one of the megastructures appeared. Meadow Flower chirped some more and a section, almost a third, was outlined. "That's where the other life-forms live," she said.

"And no Polig-Grug live there?" Jeremy asked. Meadow Flower nodded. "What keeps them from invading?"

"Unknown, Teacher," Meadow Flower replied.

"Maybe we should find out," suggested Jeremy. "The Alsoo mastered domestication?" he said in musing tones. "Interesting."

"I want to commend you on your self-control, Shadowed Heart," Raindrops in a Tide Pool said. "I would have understood if you had …" He pursed his lips in thought. "Reacted," he said finally.

"Reacting is what he and those like him want," the young man replied after a moment. "Crying, laughing, arguing—anything would bring punishment. And if you reacted to the punishment, you'd be punished some more."

Raindrops in a Tide Pool forced his crest to remain in a friendly position when what he really wanted to do was scream. *How can a species that produces someone like the Teacher produce that?* he thought in horror. Outwardly, he kept his expression calm. "I see," he said in noncommittal terms. "The Teacher has, again, expressed interest in training you," he said.

"I know you consider him some kind of holy man, but …" Shadowed Heart looked down and shook his head.

"Holy?" Raindrops in a Tide Pool chittered a laugh. "Hardly that," he said. Shadowed Heart looked up in surprise. "He is a wise man and a compassionate man, but certainly not holy."

"But you all treat him as if he was a holy man," Shadowed Heart said. "Everyone defers to him. Everyone covers their eyes whenever he says anything. Hell, the Alsoo call him the spirit speaker." He pointed when Raindrops in a Tide Pool briefly covered his eyes. "See, all I have to do is mention him, and you all will do that."

"He is deserving of our respect, but he'd be the first to scold us if we attempted to treat him as anything more than he is," Raindrops in a Tide Pool replied seriously. "He is like all the great teachers in our history," he said. "He has an awareness, a knowing, that is beyond what even the best of us can hope to attain, yet he …" Raindrops in a Tide Pool stopped. "Did you know he savagely killed two men?" he asked.

Shadowed Heart's eyes widened as he shook his head.

"He had good reason for his actions, but it still was an act of savagery," he said. "And did you know that his adopted granddaughter is herself a killer and was trained to be one by the Teacher?"

Again the young man shook his head.

"All members of the Forest Cabin Clan are killers: Teacher Jeremy, Captain Kasumi, Melanie Blunt, David Eisenstadt ... even gentle Morning Mist will kill if necessary and will do so with no hesitation, no mercy." He chittered softly. "Maybe it's for the best that you do not train with him. He'd turn you into a killer as well."

45

A New Student

"He's still there, Teacher," Morning Stars Fade said. "Emily noticed him first," he said proudly. "He's been there since this morning. Watching."

"And what have you learned?" Jeremy asked.

"He fights himself," said Morning Stars Fade. "He seeks something, but sometimes when he looks at you …" His crest flattened.

"He is full of hate, fear, and anger," Jeremy said. "His name is Shadowed Heart, and he is one of the rescued." Jeremy frowned. "I have tried to get through to him before, but I look too much like those who took from him."

"Maybe Sergeant Major Stilson," Morning Stars Fade suggested.

"No, you would have already considered that." He frowned. "What would get through to him?" he asked in concern.

"A friend," Jeremy said quietly. "It will be hard, and he will challenge you every step of the way. Even Emily will face his anger." He sighed. "Especially Emily." Jeremy briefly covered his eyes. "The path will be difficult, and success is not certain, but the rewards of success will move planets."

"Is he my destiny, Teacher?" Morning Stars Fade asked.

"Not unless you become his friend," Jeremy replied.

Shadowed Heart watched as the one they called the Teacher trained the snakelike Alsoo. *Look at them. They'd throw themselves off a cliff if he told them to*, he thought in contempt. "He's just another full-of-himself white man."

"The view is better from the cabin," called a female voice. He turned and found that somehow a white girl with reddish hair and freckles and a Rynn male with a bluish crest had snuck up on him. "Hi, I'm Emily. This is Morning Stars Fade."

"Go away," growled Shadowed Heart.

"Since I live here when I'm visiting that's not gonna happen," Emily Fields said. "Look, you're obviously interested in training. You've already taken most of the self-defense classes offered in the colony. It's kind of a given you'd want to learn more."

"I said go away," Shadowed Heart nearly screamed.

"Not happening," Emily replied tartly. "What is gonna happen is that my boyfriend is gonna kick your butt."

"Boyfriend?" Shadowed Heart asked. "Him?" Emily nodded cheerfully. "You've gotta be kidding. I'd tear him a new asshole without breathing hard."

"You can certainly try," Morning Stars Fade replied. He closed the distance between himself and Shadowed Heart. "You win, and Emily and I do whatever you want for a week. I win, and you do what Emily and I want for a week."

"What if I told you to kill yourself?" sneered Shadowed Heart.

"That would last longer than a week, so no," Morning Stars Fade chittered in amusement.

"Okay, what if I wanted the white chick to blow me?" Shadowed Heart asked.

"You win, and I'll suck your cock right here," Emily replied. "Lose, and your ass belongs to Morning Stars Fade." She grinned. "And despite their height, Rynn men are big enough that you'll know it when he's inside," she giggled. "More than big enough."

"Speaking from experience, cunt?" Shadowed Heart asked nastily.

Emily smiled coldly. "Yeah, and we can compare notes afterward," she said. "So, we gotta deal?"

"Better get down on your knees, bitch," Shadowed Heart said and took a ready stance in front of Morning Stars Fade. "Fighting makes me horny."

"Me too," agreed Morning Stars Fade. "Call it, Emily."

Emily put her hand between the two fighters. "And ... fight." She quickly pulled her hand away and stepped back. As if there was a vacuum created, the two combatants filled the space immediately.

As Emily had mentioned, Shadowed Heart had taken nearly every self-defense class the colony offered. He had trained with Sergeant Major Stilson, he had trained with Summer Rain, he had even trained, once, with Lieutenant Hendriks. More often than not, Shadowed Heart would be found in a training hall or practicing alone. He was confident that he'd quickly defeat Morning Stars Fade and claim Emily as his prize. That confidence lasted exactly ten seconds, after which Shadowed Heart found himself flat on his back.

"What the fuck?" he said in shock and sprang to his feet. He barely dodged a roundhouse kick that was aimed at his head. He could not dodge the follow-up kick that buried itself in his gut. He shook himself and concentrated on defending himself. Now that he was paying attention, he was able to block the follow-up kicks.

"Uh-oh, looks like he figured you out," Emily called. For some reason, she sounded cheerful.

"No one ever said he was stupid," Morning Stars Fade called back. "Just angry." He easily evaded the increasingly wild swings. "You know, if you'd actually hit someone, it would probably hurt."

"Stand still and find out, you fucking chicken," Shadowed Heart panted.

"Now, now ... my ancestors only had *some* avian traits," Morning Stars Fade replied. "Feathers, for example." He surged forward and kicked Shadowed Heart in the shins before dancing out of reach. "Our bones aren't all that hollow, though."

"And he has a dick," Emily said. "Nice one too."

"Why thank you, Emily," Morning Stars Fade replied. "And I've always ... oops." Morning Stars Fade had to evade as Shadowed Heart made a sudden attack. For a moment, it looked as if Shadowed Heart was going to get the upper hand, but Morning Stars Fade was eventually able to get out of arms' distance. He eyed Shadowed Heart. The youth was beginning to stumble as well as breathe heavily from the exertion.

"I think he's almost had enough," Morning Stars Fade said.

"Oh good." Emily walked over to Shadowed Heart, grabbed him by the shoulder, and spun him around. "Night, Shadow," she said and punched him in the jaw. The young man blinked in surprise and then collapsed.

Shadowed Heart struggled up from the darkness of unconsciousness and found himself face up on a very comfortable mattress and covered by a blanket and two arms. His head swiveled back and forth. On his right was Morning Stars Fade, and on his left was Emily Fields. "Hey!"

"Not so loud," groaned Emily. "It's the middle of the night."

"You hit me," complained Shadowed Heart.

"Well ... yeah," Emily replied. "You picked a fight with my core brother," she said. "Cores protect each other."

"You hit me," repeated Shadowed Heart. "And why the fuck am I in bed with you? Both of you."

"You lost, remember?" Emily giggled. "Just be glad Morning Stars Fade is a gentleman."

"Gentleman?" echoed Shadowed Heart.

"I think you must have hit him harder than you thought, Emily. He keeps repeating everything you say," Morning Stars Fade said.

"Yeah, gentleman," Emily said. "He could have claimed his prize while you were out." She giggled again. "I told him to go ahead, but …"

"You just want to see two men having sex," Morning Stars Fade accused cheerfully. Emily nodded rapidly. "We really should let him recover. You did hit him pretty hard," Morning Stars Fade continued.

"Yeah, and my hand still hurts," Emily complained. "You owe me for that, by the way." She propped herself up on one elbow. "I'm going to make this simple for you. Despite that oversized chip you have sitting on your shoulder, both Morning Stars Fade and I think you're a pretty decent guy."

"All your instructors have nothing but praise for you," Morning Stars Fade added. "As does the Teacher."

"You're smart, talented, not bad looking—when you're not scowling, that is," Emily said. "And you're brave."

"You're also easily provoked, quick to anger, unfocused, and irritable," Morning Stars Fade added. "And despite that, we're still willing to consider you as a member of our core."

"Which is why you're here," Emily continued. "You lost, and you owe us a week," she said. "One week to convince you to stay."

Shadowed Heart remained silent throughout the verbal double-teaming. "This is weird," he finally muttered. "Where is *here*, exactly?"

"You're in the guest room in the cabin," Morning Stars Fade said. "The same room that Kasumi stayed in." His crest fluttered. "It's a great honor to be allowed to sleep here," he said. "The Teacher has no time for fools or slackers, and he offered us this room for the week. Think on that."

Shadowed Heart shook his head. "This is weird," he repeated. "Couldn't you have just …?" He trailed off. "No, I guess not," he said. "What's stopping me from just leaving?" he asked.

"Nothing except your own sense of honor," Morning Stars Fade replied. "And don't bother denying you have honor," he said. "The First Teacher said hands do not lie, and the Teacher Jeremy says that if you truly want to know someone, fight them," he chittered. "I gave you a lot of chances to take a cheap shot, and you refused to exploit them. You fought me fairly and honorably—viciously, but honorably."

"And despite your crude talk, I got the distinct impression that if I had said no, you would have accepted it," Emily added. "Was I wrong?"

Shadowed Heart sighed. "No," he admitted.

"I'm still a little annoyed with you," Emily said. "I'm going to make you ask for that blow job," she giggled. "For someone like you, asking is probably going to be the hardest thing you've ever done." She lay back down. "Now, let's get some sleep," she said. "We have a long day ahead of us."

"You guys are weird," complained Shadowed Heart.

"We know. Now go to sleep," Emily said. She and Morning Stars Fade lay back down and placed their arms across Shadowed Heart's body. They fell asleep within minutes. Shadowed Heart remained awake for some time before he too fell asleep.

Shadowed Heart woke the next morning lying on his side and bracketed between two warm bodies. To his initial consternation and confusion, the person he was cuddled up behind turned out to be Morning Stars Fade. For a moment, he panicked.

"You snore," grumbled a voice from behind.

"I do not snore," protested Shadowed Heart.

"You snore," confirmed Morning Stars Fade. "We'd better get up before the Teacher wakes us." He wiggled. "Or we could 'fool around,' as Emily puts it."

"I'm up," Shadowed Heart said quickly. He blushed when Emily giggled and Morning Stars Fade chittered. He sat up ... at which time he realized he was naked. "Where are my clothes?"

"Being washed," Morning Stars Fade replied. He got out of bed, as did Emily. Shadowed Heart's blush deepened when he saw that both Morning Stars Fade and Emily were as naked as he was. Morning Stars Fade went over to a dresser and pulled out a wrapped package. He tossed it to Shadowed Heart. "Wear that."

Shadowed Heart unwrapped the package. Inside was a tunic and drawstring pants of a burnt orange color. "What is this?" he said in confusion. "I've seen something like this before." Shadowed Heart trailed off as a childhood memory intruded. His father had taken him to a kung fu movie.

Shadowed Heart's expression suddenly broke. The next thing he knew, Emily was holding him. Shadowed Heart wiped at his eyes angrily. "You gonna tell me everything's gonna be all right?" he forced out.

"No," Emily said simply. "'Cause that wouldn't be true." She tightened her hug. "I have no idea what you went through, and the Teacher said I can never know."

"He got that right," mumbled Shadowed Heart.

"He gets most things right," Morning Stars Fade said. He sat down on Shadowed Heart's free side and put an arm around his waist. "Talk to us, Core Brother."

Shadowed Heart was silent, but he also did not shrug off the arms that were holding him. "I was ten when they came for us," he said in a near whisper. "My dad ... my dad tried to stand up to them, and ... and ... they just shot him. Like he was a dog." He closed his eyes. "I can still smell the blood, and sometimes I hear my mother screaming. The screaming went on for a long, long time." Tears fell, and Emily and Morning Stars Fade just held Shadowed Heart while he cried. The tears finally stopped, and Shadowed Heart shook himself.

Morning Stars Fade stood. "Come, Core Brother," he said firmly. "You need to hit something." He chittered quietly. "Preferably not me," he added. "But there are plenty of things in the dao chung that you can." He and Emily pulled Shadowed Heart to his feet and got him dressed. Once all three were dressed, they left the cabin and headed toward the training hall. Shadowed Heart was silent during the short walk.

The training hall was dark when they entered. Emily turned on the lights while Morning Stars Fade grabbed a broom and started sweeping the floor. Shadowed Heart slumped down against one wall. He didn't notice when someone sat down next to him.

"I had a wife," said a voice. Shadowed Heart turned to see Jeremy Blunt sitting next to him. The old man was looking at the ceiling. "Her name was Mei Lin, and I thought she was the most beautiful thing I had ever seen," he said. "For some reason, she decided to marry me." He smiled slightly. "We had a son. His name is Brandon," he said. "Brandon was eight when it happened. Two men broke into the cabin." He closed his eyes. "They raped her and cut her throat," he said. "Brandon hid in his room." He turned to look at Shadowed Heart, and Shadowed Heart had to fight the shiver that the look engendered. "Mei Lin lived long enough to tell me who did it," he said quietly. "I was able to avenge her death, but I lost Brandon."

"What happened to your son?" Shadowed Heart asked in a whisper.

"Nothing happened," Jeremy replied. "But I lost him anyway," he said. "He blamed me for her death." He closed his eyes again. "To this day, I cannot say he was wrong to do so."

Shadowed Heart looked at the old man. "Why?" he asked in the same whisper.

"I am an arrogant old man who once was an arrogant young man," Jeremy replied. "My arrogance led to her death." He turned to look at Shadowed Heart again. "I refused to bow down to those who claimed they were my superiors, and she paid the price."

Shadowed Heart swallowed in a suddenly dry throat. "My father refused to bow down," he said. "And they killed him and raped and murdered my mom." Jeremy just nodded. "The only thing that kept me going in the months that followed was the hope that somehow, some way I'd get my revenge." He shook his head. "It was never going to happen."

"No," agreed Jeremy somberly. "I spent the following ten years in prison for manslaughter. I got my revenge but lost my son and my freedom." With a grunt, he got to his feet. "I don't know about you, but I need to hit something."

Shadowed Heart nodded and got to his feet as well. Shadowed Heart licked his dry lips. "Sir?" he said hesitantly. "How do you get past something like that?"

Jeremy smiled sadly and shrugged. "I have no idea," he said. "If you learn how, please let me know." For the first time, he looked directly at Shadowed Heart. "I speak to her every night," he said. "Sometimes she even answers."

Shadowed Heart found it was difficult to meet the old man's eyes, and he covered his for a moment.

"You do realize that I am probably insane," the old man said.

Shadowed Heart barked a short, sad laugh. "Maybe, sir, but I would give anything to hear my mother's voice, even if it wasn't real."

"Brandon said the same thing," Jeremy replied. "Morning Stars Fade, Emily, we have training to do," he barked. He turned to Shadowed Heart. "You're welcome to join us."

"I'd like that ... Teacher," Shadowed Heart replied.

"My god, how does he do it?" complained Shadowed Heart. "I'm exhausted, and he looks like he can go on for another hour." He, Emily, and Morning Stars Fade had been training nonstop for almost three hours. The old man may have been sympathetic and understanding before the training started, but that sympathy and understanding apparently was unimportant where training was concerned. "The man is worse than the slave master."

"Shadowed Heart, twenty roundhouse kicks against the wooden dummy," barked Jeremy.

Shadowed Heart groaned, went over to the dummy, and started

kicking. Emily walked over to the old man. "Thank you, Teacher," she said. "He's almost cheerful." Jeremy snorted in response. She pursed her lips. "I should start breakfast."

"Shadowed Heart will make breakfast," Jeremy said firmly. "Every day for the rest of the week." He smiled. "And the bathroom needs cleaning."

"You're a hard man, Teacher," Emily said with an amused smile. "Thank you."

"And tell him to call Raindrops in a Tide Pool," grunted Jeremy. "He worries."

"Yes, Teacher," Emily replied, and then she leaned over and kissed the old man on the cheek. "Thank you," she said again. Then Emily turned. "Shadowed Heart, you're making breakfast," she ordered loudly. "Move it."

"Better get going, Core Brother," Morning Stars Fade said cheerfully. "I think our core sister is in a mood." He shuddered theatrically.

Despite everything, Shadowed Heart had to smile. "I guess I better make breakfast," he said and, with a quick bow to Jeremy, headed back to the cabin.

"Spirits and ancestors," Morning Stars Fade breathed. "He smiled."

"Morning Stars Fade, go with him," ordered Jeremy. "I doubt he knows how to cook."

The week went quickly for Shadowed Heart. Every morning, they'd wake before dawn and spend the next two or three hours training in the dao chung—after which Shadowed Heart would make breakfast. The rest of the day was spent doing chores around the cabin, doing homework (Shadowed Heart was working on his GED), and taking long walks. Three times during the week, the Alsoo came to train, and Jeremy banished the three young adults from the cabin. They'd usually borrow Jeremy's truck and head over to the colony.

It was nighttime that was difficult for Shadowed Heart. Emily and Morning Stars Fade insisted they sleep together, with Shadowed Heart sleeping in the middle. He wouldn't have minded sleeping with Emily—she was beautiful and had a wicked sense of humor that would somehow get through Shadowed Heart's defenses and, while he still wouldn't laugh, get him to smile. She was obviously interested in him, but she would always rebuff attempts to get her alone.

"Come on, Emily," he pleaded near the end of the week. "I know you like me. You keep telling me you like me. So why?"

"And I keep telling you, cores sleep together, and that includes sex," Emily returned. "Me and Morning Stars Fade are a package deal."

"But I'm not gay," complained Shadowed Heart.

"Neither is Morning Stars Fade," returned Emily. "That term is meaningless to a Rynn," she pointed out. "Let me ask you something: do you like Morning Stars Fade?"

"Well, yeah," Shadowed Heart replied slowly.

"Do you think he'd back you up in a fight?" she asked. "Or do you think he'd just let you get your ass handed to you?"

"I don't know," complained Shadowed Heart. "I mean, I think he'd back me up, but …"

"You know damn well he would," Emily interrupted. "Just as he knows damn well you'd back him up," she said. "And you do know that, don't you?" She walked over and poked Shadowed Heart in the chest. "Don't you?" She waited until Shadowed Heart nodded. "Exactly," she said. "He's probably the one person on this whole planet who you can trust completely," she said. "So trust him, goddammit." Without another word, she spun around and walked away.

Shadowed Heart sat on the steps of the cabin and watched the sun set. He sensed more than saw someone sit down next to him. "Hey, Morning Stars Fade," he said in greeting without turning his head.

"I'm always amazed when humans do that," Morning Stars Fade

said. "And yet you all claim you don't read minds." He chittered. "Teacher Jeremy says it's just that humans are naturally paranoid."

"He's probably right," agreed Shadowed Heart. "Mind if I ask you a personal question?"

"Shadowed Heart, who I wish to call Core Brother, you may ask me anything you wish," Morning Stars Fade replied. "If the question is what I think it is, then the answer is yes."

"And you think humans read minds?" Shadowed Heart said in dry amusement. "Don't tell Emily, but I've only had sex a couple times," he said after a long silence.

"I don't know why you don't want Emily to know that, but if that is your wish, she won't hear it from me," Morning Stars Fade replied. He looked at Shadowed Heart's profile. "Rynn are raised in groups—what you call crèches," he said. "We're used to sleeping with other people. Male and female." His crest rose slightly. "By the time we become fully mature, we've probably already had several sex partners of both sexes."

Shadowed Heart turned. "How do you prevent having babies and stuff?"

Morning Stars Fade pointed to his left wrist. "I got my birth control implant just before puberty," he said. "And Rynn are given a basic sex training class about the same time." He added, "Humans are plagued with sexually transmitted diseases. Rynn are not." Morning Stars Fade smiled slightly. "Mainly because sex isn't hidden." His smile became proud. "And in those rare instances when there is something wrong, we deal with it immediately, honestly, and without being shamed."

Shadowed Heart nodded in response.

"I want to tell you something," Morning Stars Fade said. "As part of my training with the Teacher, he asks me to look at someone and tell him what their face is saying."

"Neat trick," agreed Shadowed Heart.

"It would be if I could actually do it," Morning Stars Fade said. "Half the time when I think someone is angry or pensive, they usually end up just having indigestion." Morning Stars Fade looked at Shadowed Heart. "Then Teacher asked me to look at you." He put a hand on Shadowed Heart's shoulder. "And all I could see was someone who needed ... me." His crest flattened. "It wasn't sex or attraction, it was this odd certainty that you and I were destined to be friends." His crest rose to a more neutral position. "When I discussed it with Teacher, he told me something strange. He said that success was uncertain, but that if somehow I could succeed in getting through those walls you've put up, then together we'd move planets."

"Weird," Shadowed Heart said. "Move planets, huh?" He narrowed his eyes. "Just you and me, or you and me and Emily?"

Morning Stars Fade smiled. "One omits Emily from one's calculations to one's peril," he said. "As you should know."

Shadowed Heart rubbed his jaw. "Yeah, no kidding," he said. "That girl has a heck of a punch." He sighed. "I dunno. I mean, I like you. You've been ... heck, you've been a better friend than I've ever had." He paused. "Well, you and Emily," he chuckled. "Funny to think of a white girl as a friend," he said. "The only white girls I saw were the daughters of the slave owners, and they were just as bad as their parents."

"Emily is Emily," Morning Stars Fade replied. He stood. "I don't know about you, Core Brother, but I'm getting hungry." He extended a hand to Shadowed Heart. When Shadowed Heart took it, he pulled the human to his feet. "I think it would be most difficult to move planets on an empty stomach."

YEAR 13

46

Battle Lines

"This is DefSat Ten. We have an incursion," a cool and professional voice reported. "Identity confirmed as Polig-Grug." There was a pause. "DefSat Fifteen and Sedona station are responding."

"On screen," ordered David Eisenstadt. Despite the fact that everyone on the bridge, and anyone else with a Torque, could see the battle, Eisenstadt still preferred to see it on the large monitor in the command center.

"DefSat Ten, please route all sensor data to my station," Morning Mist said crisply. She watched as the data started running in front of her eyes. "Negative on Alsoo bio signs. Negative on Rynn bio signs. Negative on any non-Polig-Grug bio signs altogether."

"That's the third incursion without any bio signs other than Polig-Grug," Captain Kasumi said in thoughtful tones. "Meadow Flower, your last report mentioned some instability at the border points. Is it possible that the Polig-Grug are … weakening?"

"With a population in excess of eighty billion, weakening is relative," Meadow Flower replied. "The total number of Polig-Grug that we've eradicated over the past three years is not even a thousandth of a percent of their total population." Her crest flicked. "However, something is certainly happening," she chirped, and the megastructure that was the Polig-Grug home world—or rather, one of them—was displayed. Approximately a third was outlined in blue. "That blue line represents the border separating the Polig-Grug from whatever is keeping them at bay." She chirped again, and a second outline, this one in red, appeared. Most of the outlines overlapped, but some sections showed that the area controlled by the unknowns had grown. "The Polig-Grug have lost approximately 5 percent of their territory over the past year."

"They're starving," said a gravelly voice.

"Grandfather?" Kasumi questioned.

Jeremy Blunt sat back in his chair. "Meadow Flower, have there been any attacks on Nest?"

"No, Teacher," Meadow Flower replied. "And with the new Hunter-Killer ships protecting our fleets, the number of fatalities has plummeted." Her crest snapped open. "Of course!" she exclaimed. "They still don't know where Nest is. The Alsoo have become scarce or are extinct, and humans have been successful in keeping the Polig-Grug from establishing a colony here on Earth." Her crest fluttered excitedly. "I believe Teacher may be correct," she said. "The Polig-Grug predate on intelligent, often technological species. Unchecked, they will eventually consume an entire species." She smiled. "But what if they are not unchecked?"

"We keep assuming we're the only players in this conflict," Jeremy pointed out.

"Yes, Teacher," Meadow Flower agreed excitedly. "Even though we know we are not," she said. "We keep forgetting about the Zaski and the Graz'to." The outlines on the image of the Polig-Grug megastructure blinked several times. "And whatever is inside those boundaries."

"I am not going to recommend an alliance with the Zaski," Kasumi said in disgust.

"No need, Granddaughter," Jeremy said. "All you really have to do is make Earth and Nest ... unappetizing."

"If we're lucky, the Zaski and the Polig-Grug will cancel each other out," Eisenstadt said in approval. "We need to send a ship out to contact the Zaski and convince them to seek easier prey." He smiled. "When was the last time you took the *Nieth* out ... Captain?"

"Take the Alsoo warriors with you," Jeremy said.

"We'll take Ape and Bird Squads as well," Eisenstadt said.

"I'd like to go as well, Commander," Meadow Flower volunteered. "We'll be passing close to the Polig-Grug home system, and I may be able to insert a few extra probes."

"It will be dangerous, Meadow Flower," cautioned the commander.

"I think she should go," Jeremy said. "And take those three kids who have been camping in my cabin with you."

47

Hatchlings

"What's going on?" Shadowed Heart asked a passing Rynn. He, Morning Stars Fade, and Emily had returned to the colony only to find themselves in the middle of some event. Most of the colony was decorated with pink and blue streamers and banners, and a military band was playing "Ode to Joy." It looked like a child's birthday party on steroids.

"The Alsoo eggs have hatched," the Rynn male said in excitement. "The mothers are bringing the hatchlings out of the burrow for the first time."

"Oh my god, we have to see this," Emily said in excitement. "Do you know how many eggs hatched?"

"No, but I hope it's a lot," the Rynn said. "Spirits weep, but they could use something to celebrate."

Emily, Morning Stars Fade, and Shadowed Heart all covered their eyes briefly in response. The three started running toward the citadel. They made it just as a roar erupted from the surrounding crowd. They pushed their way to the front. The crowd was kept a good distance from the citadel by the presence of a good number of Alsoo warriors. By their taller posture, it was obvious these were the warriors trained by Jeremy Blunt. The three friends even recognized a few of them.

"Greetings, Warrior Third-Son-Third-Born/you," Morning Stars Fade voice translated by his Torque into Alsoo. "This time/good question."

The warrior waved his free hand in the Alsoo equivalent of a nod. "This time/good truth/oath." He slapped his chest. "Women/they speak big/big number hatchling. Big/big strong hatchling." The Alsoo warrior rose higher. "Hatchlings/they see tall/me. See tall/they be."

Morning Stars Fade, Emily, and Shadowed Heart all nodded in understanding. "Tall/be you, warrior," Shadowed Heart said. "Hatchling proud/they be."

"Truth/oath," Morning Stars Fade and Emily said, and the three of them slapped their chests. The Alsoo warrior rose another centimeter. Morning Stars Fade, Emily, and Shadowed Heart looked around with growing hopeful anticipation—an emotion apparently shared by everyone else currently present in the colony.

Even the colony's chief scientist, Joseph Franklin, and his core were present. Joseph Franklin's floating mobility suit was piloted, as usual, by his Alsoo associate, Second-Daughter-Fifth-Born. The Alsoo neuter sat on Franklin's shoulder with her tail wrapped loosely around his neck, one stubby-three fingered hand playing over the suit's control panel, the other waving animatedly toward the citadel.

"Here they come," someone squealed excitedly.

Morning Stars Fade, Emily, and Shadowed Heart all looked toward the citadel. An Alsoo female was at the top of the ramp, and they could see a cluster of fluffy down-covered hatchlings huddled against her lower body. She started wriggling down the ramp, herding her hatchlings before her. Another female appeared at the top before the first had completed her trek. And then it seemed as if there was a river of females and hatchlings flowing down the ramp. The Alsoo started to warble.

"How many?" Emily demanded. "Someone get a count."

"I'm pretty sure there are a large number of people doing just that, Em," Shadowed Heart said. "But it's gotta be hundreds." A shadow caught his attention, and he looked up. "Oh shit," he exclaimed. He pointed. "Hawks," he shouted. He started running toward the swarming Alsoo hatchlings. Alsoo warriors started warbling in anger and fear.

Shadowed Heart looked over his shoulder and saw the hawk, and his mind's eye traced the swooping bird's path. One hatchling had apparently wandered away from the group and stood alone. The hatchling was looking at the sky with a look of terror on its tiny face. Shadowed Heart shifted his path and sped up as much as possible.

Franklin looked up at the shout. "Hawks? Where?" He looked toward the sky and quickly saw the circling birds. He saw where Shadowed Heart was running and came to the same conclusion. He tapped his Torque. "This is Joseph Franklin. On my authority, raise colony shields. Now!" he snapped. "There are hungry hawks circling."

Whether his warning came in time or not did not matter, as one hawk was already below the shield and was headed directly toward the hatchling, claws extended and ready. Those claws impacted on the back of the human who was suddenly between the hawk and its prey. Shadowed Heart yelped in pain, and the hawk screeched angrily and leaped to the sky, only to be transfixed by an Alsoo spear. The dead hawk crashed to the ground just a few feet from Shadowed Heart.

For a moment, there was complete silence over the colony. The moment shattered into screams, shouts, chitters, and warbles. Emily and Morning Stars Fade raced to the bent-over form of Shadowed Heart. "Core Brother," Morning Stars Fade yelled in worry.

When they reached Shadowed Heart, the back of his jacket was torn completely through, and there was blood oozing from deep scratches that could be seen through the wide rents. Morning Stars Fade tapped his Torque. "Medic!" he requested urgently as he knelt down. "Core Brother?" he said to Shadowed Heart. "Core Brother?" he repeated more urgently when there was no answer.

Finally, Shadowed Heart groaned. "I'm ... okay," he said. He groaned again as he sat up, his hands cupped together. He raised his hands and slowly opened them. A tiny Alsoo hatchling was nestled in his palm.

"Are you okay?" he said to the hatchling. The hatchling rose up partly and warbled at him. "The Torque's not translating," he said in worry.

"That's because it's a baby," Emily said softly. "You saved it," she breathed. "Spirits and ancestors, you saved it." She turned to see a half dozen of Jeremy's specially trained warriors sidling over with their spears raised. "It's okay ... he w ..." She stopped as one warrior raised his spear sharply.

An authoritative warble rang out, and the Alsoo warriors slithered backward a meter. Another Alsoo warrior slithered toward them. He carried a spear that held the dead hawk. He started warbling to the warriors. One by one, the warriors grounded their spears and looked at Shadowed Heart and the Alsoo hatchling.

"See/me all," came the translation as the warrior spoke. He raised the spear with the dead hawk. "Sky eater/he hunt/he hatchling," he said. "Split-tail/he—" he pointed to Shadowed Heart. "Cover/he hatchling. Save/he hatchling." He pointed to the hawk. "Spear/mine, sky eater kill/he me." He slapped his chest. "Truth/oath." He slithered to stand between Shadowed Heart and his fellow Alsoo. "Kill/you he. Kill/you me," he declared. "Speak/me Fifth-Son-Eighth-Born."

"There will be no killing," Captain Kasumi ordered sharply. She strode forward. "Fifth-Son-Eighth-Born speaks the truth," she said. "Forgive us for trespassing, but as you can see, Shadowed Heart would defy anything to save even one Alsoo hatchling." She waited as her Torque translated, as best it could, her statements into the Alsoo warble.

Another authoritative figure came over. This time it was the Alsoo speaker First-Son-Second-Born. "Kill not," he ordered. He slithered over to Shadowed Heart. "Big/Big good/all, split-tail." He warbled, and another Alsoo slithered over. This one was accompanied by a small clutch of five Alsoo hatchlings. She chirped to the hatchling still held by Shadowed Heart. 'Hatchling/mine First-Daughter-Second-Born/she," she warbled.

The hatchling in Shadowed Heart's hand warbled back and wiggled. Shadowed Heart lowered his cupped hand, and the little hatchling wiggled off and wriggled quickly toward her mother. The fuzzy little hatchling was mobbed by her mother and siblings.

Kasumi raised a hand, and a medtech hurried over. "I leave Shadowed Heart in your care," she said. "I expect a full recovery."

"So do I," the medtech returned tartly. "Don't worry, our hero will be properly taken care of, Captain."

Kasumi briefly covered her eyes. "I apologize for questioning your competence, medtech," she said contritely.

The medtech nodded and then leaned over. "Sun-Warmed Boulder, may the spirits shun him, would never have apologized," she said. She covered her own eyes briefly and then turned her attention to treating Shadowed Heart.

Shadowed Heart looked up at Kasumi. "I'm sorry for causing all this trouble," he apologized. "But …" He stopped when the Alsoo female and all her hatchlings, including First-Daughter-Second-Born, slithered over. The Alsoo female placed a stubby-fingered hand on Shadowed Heart's knee.

"Long time mothers/they two hand, three hand eggs have/they. Eaters/they two hand, three hand hatchling/eat they one hatchling, two hatchling live/they." She warbled. "Bad time no hatchling live/they." She placed a stubby hand on the head of one of the fuzzy hatchlings. "Long time hatchling/they die/they mothers/they cry/they." She fluffed her feathers. "This time mothers/they cry/they not." She herded her hatchlings closer to Shadowed Heart. "Protect/they long time split-tail/you pledge/oath question."

Shadowed Heart slowly ran a finger over the tiny down-covered

Naga-form child who he assumed was First-Daughter-Second-Born. The little hatchling warbled happily. A half-smile formed on Shadowed Heart's face. He nodded. "I will protect them. Pledge/oath," he vowed and slapped his chest.

Year 15

48

Sad Soul

Captain Kasumi went over the final checks before departure. "Engineering," she said firmly. "What's the status, Franklin?"

"Singularity generator is humming away, Captain," Joseph Franklin reported cheerfully. "We've got power enough and to spare," he said. "Thrusters are ready. Hyperdrive is ready."

"Weapons," she said next. "How are we doing, Mel?"

"Franklin was right. There was a misaligned energy feed," Mel replied.

"Told ya," Franklin broke in.

"I just said you were right," Mel shot back. "Some people just can't help themselves," she complained lightly. "I got the Terrible Three working on it," she said. "They should have it clean and green by the time we get to Zaski space."

"Plus it will keep those three out of trouble in the meantime," Kasumi said in an undertone.

"If we're lucky," Mel replied with a laugh. "Now let me get back to work."

"Tactical," Kasumi said.

"Sensors are hot," Morning Mist replied. "Shields are online and solid. I'll see them long before we need the shields," she said in assurance. "And those shields should handle anything we've seen to date."

"Weapons control is on line," David Eisenstadt broke in. "Bridge is go."

"Bridge is go," Kasumi responded. "Earth Command, this is *Nieth*."

"This is Earth Command, *Nieth*," came the response.

"Request permission to disembark," Kasumi requested crisply.

"Permission granted, *Nieth*," Earth Command replied. "Good hunting."

"Thank you, command," Kasumi replied. "Nieth out." She turned her head to look at the man in the seat next to hers. "Take her out, David."

"Course laid in," Eisenstadt replied. A huge grin appeared on his face. "Engage."

"One day you're going to have to explain why you and Mel think that's so funny," Kasumi grumbled good-naturedly.

"Don't tell Crystal, but damn, it's good to be deployed again," Captain Hendriks said to his diminutive though lethal Rynn partner.

"Yeah, and in three months, you'll be wishing you were home," Captain Cool Evening Breeze replied. She grinned at her human partner and core brother. "And in Momma's arms," she chittered. "Or maybe Burl's."

"I wouldn't talk, Feather Head," Hendriks shot back good-naturedly. He tapped his Torque, and he and Cool Evening Breeze watched a 3D recording of the last time they were with the rest of their core. Crystal was nursing baby Sofia, with 3D3B sitting on her shoulder and singing softly. Seven year old Jesse was sitting at her feet. Burl could be seen setting the dinner table. And Cool Evening Breeze and Hendriks were sitting next to each other on a sofa. The two fighters had matching contented expressions on their faces.

Hendriks and Cool Evening Breeze exchanged a look that said,

This is what heaven looks like. This is what I fight for. This is what I will die to preserve.

Hendriks tapped his Torque, and the recording stopped and vanished. He tapped his Torque again. "Ape Squad, Bird Squad, inspection in ten minutes. Snake Squad, you have the gym for the next hour. Hup." He tapped his Torque again and stood. "Zaski, huh?" he said.

"Zaski," replied Cool Evening Breeze.

Emily Fields, Morning Stars Fade, and Shadowed Heart entered the gym. "I still don't know what we're supposed to do on this trip," complained Shadowed Heart. "We're not marines. We're not part of the command crew, engineering, science, or anything. We're just … passengers."

"I'm sure the Teacher had a good reason for insisting that we go," Morning Stars Fade replied. He gave Shadowed Heart a lopsided grin. "I just wish I knew what that reason was."

He stopped speaking as he realized the gym was already occupied. Twenty-one Alsoo warriors were going through a series of drills. They too had stopped when the three had entered. Morning Stars Fade covered his eyes briefly. "Please excuse us. We did not realize the gym was in use," he said. "We can come back later."

One of the warriors slithered over and then rose up on its tail. "Know/me you." He pointed to Shadowed Heart. "Hatchling/she save you." He slithered closer. "Hatchling/my save you."

"You're First-Daughter-Second-Born's father?" Shadowed Heart said in surprise.

"Hatchling/my," repeated the Alsoo. "Fifth-Son-Eighth-Born/me."

Shadowed Heart briefly covered his eyes. "Greetings, Fifth-Son-Eighth-Born. I am Shadowed Heart," he said.

"Save hatchling/my question," said the Alsoo.

"Question?" Shadowed Heart echoed in confusion.

"I think he wants to know why you saved his hatchling," Emily suggested.

"Save hatchling/my question," repeated the Alsoo.

Shadowed Heart looked down at his feet. "I don't know," he replied. "I just had to." He took a breath. "She looked so scared," he said. "It's how my face must have looked," he said in a near whisper.

The Alsoo waved his hand in the Alsoo equivalent of a nod. "Spirit Speaker/he say/he, seek/we sad soul split-tail. Sad soul split-tail trust/we." He ruffled his feathers. "Hard trust/we split-tail."

"Sad soul split-tail?" Shadowed Heart repeated quietly.

"That sounds like you, Core Brother," Morning Stars Fade said. "The Teacher has given you a difficult task, Core Brother." He turned to the Alsoo warrior. "Yes, he is a sad soul." He waited for the Torque to warble in translation. "His soul is sad because he saw so much pain." He looked at Shadowed Heart for a moment and then looked back at the Alsoo. "He knows your pain, warrior." He slapped his chest. "Truth/oath."

Again the Alsoo waved his hand in agreement. "Hard trust/we split-tail. Trust/we sad soul split-tail/he." He slapped his chest. "Pledge/oath."

Shadowed Heart hesitated for a moment and then slapped his own chest. "Pledge/oath."

"They want what?" exclaimed David Eisenstadt.

"They want the Terrible Three to train with them," Mel said. "Apparently, Gramps had something to do with this."

"Of course he did," agreed Kasumi in amusement. She ran her long-fingered hand through her crest. "What is he thinking?" she asked no one in particular. "They're starting to show initiative; that's good. But why did he point them to those three?"

"Knowing Gramps, he must believe that there is something to be gained." Mel pursed her lips. "Morning Stars Fade is one of Gramps' special students," she pointed out. "He never said so, but I got the impression that Gramps played matchmaker and got those three together." She shrugged. "I really can't think of a good objection," she said. "Not to mention it solves the problem of what to do with them."

"Morning Stars Fade, Emily Fields, Shadowed Heart," Captain Hendriks said sternly. "As of this moment, you all have the brevet rank of ensign," he said. "That rank will become permanent if Captain Kasumi is satisfied with your actions during this voyage." He paced in front of the three. "Much as I do not approve, the three of you will train with the Alsoo—and, in the event there is military action, you will muster with the Alsoo," he said sternly. "Are there any questions?"

Morning Stars Fade, Emily, and Shadowed Heart exchanged looks. "No sir," Morning Stars Fade answered for all of them. "Thank you, sir."

"Thank me if none of you get yourselves killed," snapped Hendriks. "From 0900 to 1200, the three of you are going to be taking classes on tactics. You will train with the Alsoo from 1300 to 1500. From 1530 to 1800, you will report to the bridge as observers," he said. "The rest of the day is yours."

He blew out a breath. "Listen, you three, this is serious business. The Alsoo expect to fight, and now they expect the three of you to fight with them. Tell me now if you can't do this."

"Sir," Morning Stars Fade replied for the three of them. "We wondered why the Teacher insisted we come; we had no role, no true reason for being here," he said. "I don't know if this is what the Teacher had in mind, but I feel that it is so." He briefly covered his eyes. "We will do the best we can—that we can promise."

"I'm going to hold you to that, Ensign," Hendriks replied. "Dismissed."

He watched the three newly commissioned ensigns leave. He shook his head. "Whatever your plans are, old man," he said quietly, "I hope you are right."

"They still act more like individuals than a fighting force," Morning Stars Fade commented.

"They're too brave for their own good," Emily agreed.

"Brave?" Morning Stars Fade replied. "They're anything but," he said. "What they are is driven," he corrected. "You saw the recording of that fight against the Polig-Grug unity." A *unity* had become the accepted term for a linked group of Polig-Grug. "They were in a berserker rage," he pointed out. "The speaker died because he was too frightened to think straight."

"He didn't look frightened," Shadowed Heart disagreed. "He looked …" He paused. "Well, maybe he was frightened."

"'Scared stupid' is how the Teacher would describe it," Morning Stars Fade said. He briefly covered his eyes. "Somehow we have to get them to keep their heads while in battle or none of them will survive."

"Why don't we just tell them the 'spirit speaker' wants them to … no, that wouldn't work, would it?" Shadowed Heart said. "He's not here."

"And he wouldn't and couldn't order someone to be brave," Emily agreed. She pursed her lips in thought. "The Teacher already figured out a way to make them … man up," she said. "So how do we build on that?" There was a thud, and a book appeared in front of them. They looked over to where Captains Hendriks and Cool Evening Breeze were standing. "Sirs?"

"That is a book on Roman battle tactics. Read it," Hendriks ordered. He and Cool Evening Breeze turned and left before the three could respond.

Emily picked up the book. It wasn't that thick—at most a hundred pages—but the print was small. She leafed through the book. "It has illustrations," she said. "They were probably listening in and decided to give us a hint," she said to Morning Stars Fade.

"That would be the logical assumption," agreed Morning Stars Fade. "I still think humans read minds." His amused chitter was echoed by Emily's and Shadowed Heart's laugh. He pointed to the book. "Let's see if there is anything in there we can use."

49

Centurions

"Warriors/you hear/you me," Shadowed Heart's translated voice said to the assembled Alsoo warriors. "Warriors/you truth/oath," he said. "Short time warriors/you centurions/be."

"Centurions question," asked Fifth-Son-Eighth-Born.

"Big/big warrior centurion/be," replied Shadowed Heart. "Sprit Speaker/he say/he Alsoo tall/be." He waited as the sudden ruffling and warbling greeted his words, and the Alsoo warriors rose higher on their tails. "This time, warriors/you learn/new warrior/think." He tapped his Torque, and an image appeared on a large monitor. The image was of a Polig-Grug unity. "Learn/new attack/you strong hand fight." He raised his right arm. "Warrior/you speak/you 'Strong hand fight.'"

"Strong hand fight," the Alsoo warriors repeated dutifully.

The image, which turned out to be a computer-generated animation, started to move. A double squad of Alsoo warriors formed into a triple phalanx in front of the unity. One CGI warrior shouted, "Strong hand fight!" and the right-hand phalanx suddenly broke off and attacked the unity's left side. As the unity turned to face the threat, the remaining warriors charged. The Alsoo warriors watching warbled in excitement as the CG warriors overwhelmed the unity.

Shadowed Heart repeated the animation several times.

"Warriors/you learn/you strong hand fight," he said. "Warriors/you be/you centurions." He slapped his chest. "Pledge/oath."

"Pledge/oath," responded the Alsoo warriors.

Captain Kasumi chirped in approval. "That was good thinking, Hendriks," she said. She had watched the Alsoo training through her Torque.

"Thanks, Captain," Captain Hendriks replied. "They call him *protector*, you know."

Kasumi nodded. "I heard." She leaned back in her chair. "Well, that will keep all of them occupied," she said. "In the meantime, Meadow Flower, we will be making our closest pass to the Polig-Grug home system in two sun steps," she said.

"I have five probes ready to go at your command, Captain," Meadow Flower replied. "Spirits willing, I will get at least one into the territory held by the unknowns."

"Good," Kasumi replied. "You were wasted as a budget analyst," she added. "The more I live around humans, the more I am reminded of the First Teacher's story of the farmer's daughter who wished to be a stone artist." She briefly covered her eyes. "Sometimes I wonder if she was speaking to us today and not to her followers in the past."

"Sometimes I wonder if the Teacher Jeremy is in truth the First Teacher reborn," Morning Mist replied. She and Kasumi briefly covered their eyes.

"Probes away," Meadow Flower reported.

"Anything from the Polig-Grug?" asked Captain Kasumi.

"No response," Morning Mist replied. Her crest lowered slightly. "Correction. Polig-Grug fighters have moved to intercept."

"Franklin thrusters activated," Meadow Flower said in response. "Probe shields up."

"Polig-Grug are firing," Morning Mist reported.

"Captain, something is happening on Polig-Grug Megastructure One," Mel reported.

"The unknowns?" Kasumi asked.

"Probably," Mel replied.

"Polig-Grug fighter destroyed," Morning Mist said in excitement. "Some kind of beam weapon from the megastructure."

"I think someone wants our probes to make it through," Kasumi said.

"Second Polig-Grug fighter destroyed," Morning Mist reported.

"Probes are about to enter megastructure atmosphere," Meadow Flower reported. "Probe One in atmosphere, probe braking." Her crest lifted to its fullest. "Telemetry coming in," she said and chirped to her Torque. Immediately, everyone on the bridge could see the relay from the probe via their Torque. "Something is coming up to meet the probes," Meadow Flower said, and the viewers could see three objects approaching.

"Those look very, very familiar," Kasumi said. The objects resolved into three classic flying saucer shapes. "Graz'to!" she exclaimed.

"Those ships may be Graz'to," Morning Mist said, and her crest flicked. "But the life signs on those ships are not." Her eyes moved as she started to scan the data. "Those ships are newer than the ones on Earth too."

"Graz'to ships have reached the first probe," Meadow Flower said, her voice rising with excitement. "Probe One has been captured."

"Now … we wait," Kasumi said. "David, get us out of here."

"Resuming course to Zaski space," David Eisenstadt responded crisply. He waited until they had been traveling for a couple hours before clearing his throat. "Why didn't you wait for a response?" he asked.

"Would you want to remain in Polig-Grug space longer than

you had to?" Kasumi replied. "Besides, I doubt we'll get more than an acknowledgement, if that, for a season."

David nodded. "About what I figured, but I wanted to hear it from you." He nodded again. "There is an Earth saying: the enemy of my enemy is my friend," he said. "I always thought it was a very foolish saying." He rolled his eyes. "Don't you cover your eyes at me, young lady," he said. "You may be captain of this ship, but that doesn't mean I can't spank you."

Kasumi smiled. "I'm sure there is some Earth regulation that forbids the spanking of a ship's captain," she chittered. "But feel free to spank Morning Mist."

"Oh good!" Morning Mist said.

"I'd say spank Mel too, but I think she can hurt you," Kasumi said.

"I know she can hurt me," Eisenstadt replied.

Meadow Flower smiled as the command room rang with laughter. She had seen this a number of times before—Kasumi and her core joking with each other after a stressful event. *What a strong core*, she thought in envious approval.

Meadow Flower's own romantic forays had been less successful. She had been invited into a number of cores, but always as an associate. Most of the time, being an associate suited her temperament and the situation at the time, but there were times when she longed for the intimacy of a solid core. *I wish I had someone to laugh with*, she thought. She sighed and went back to work analyzing the Polig-Grug.

50

What's In a Name?

Shadowed Heart, Emily, and Morning Stars Fade—sometimes referred to as "the Terrible Three"— watched intently as the Alsoo split into three phalanxes. "Keep those lines straight!" Shadowed Heart barked. "Eighth-Son … I mean, First-Son-Second-Born, you're in the wrong phalanx," he grumbled. "Spirits and ancestors, I don't know if he's in the wrong phalanx because he forgot or because I used the wrong name when assigning positions. And it's most likely I used the wrong name."

"So what's stopping us from giving them better names?" Emily asked in reasonable tones.

"Getting them to use them," Shadowed Heart replied.

"Good point," Emily replied. "But I think I may have a way to convince them."

"If you can convince them, I'll … do something," Shadowed Heart said doubtfully.

"Too easy," Emily said to Morning Stars Fade. "Tell you what: if I come up with some names and convince them to use them, you can decide what my reward will be. Okay?" Emily said in teasing tones.

It was two days later when Emily outlined her plans. Shadowed Heart made a single addition, and they unveiled their plans during the next training session.

"Warriors, form phalanx!" ordered Shadowed Heart. The Alsoo warriors immediately formed into three double lines of six Alsoo per phalanx. The three extra Alsoo took position at the head of each phalanx. "Warriors, you've worked hard and learned much," he said in approving tones. "But you are not yet centurions." He nodded to Emily.

"Warriors," Emily said, "when the split-tail Kasumi first came to Earth, she was alone, without friends, without family. She was like the Alsoo, expecting to die." The Alsoo ruffled their feathers in response. "She was saved by the spirit speaker," she said. "And the first thing the spirit speaker did was give her a new name."

The Alsoo warbled in confusion.

Emily went on, "The spirit speaker says that when one who has been defeated wishes to rise again, to be tall again, they must first lose everything." She swept her gaze across the assembled Alsoo warriors. "You have lost much, that is true, but you have not lost everything," she said. "Warriors, if you wish to become centurions, you must give up what you have not yet lost. You must give up your names."

"Lose/we names question," Fifth-Son-Eighth-Born questioned. More often than not, he spoke for the Alsoo, and this time was no exception. "Know/we question."

"We will give you new names," Emily replied. "Better names. *Centurion* names." She tapped her Torque and spoke quietly. An image appeared on the overhead monitor. It was of an Earth rattlesnake—a sidewinder rattlesnake. The image moved, demonstrating why it was called a sidewinder. The Alsoo all warbled. "We call you Snake Squad, and that is why." Emily pointed to the image. "On Earth, snakes are great hunters. There are many snakes, but the sidewinder is one of the greatest. Snake Squad is no more. You are now

Sidewinder Squad." The Alsoo warbled and stamped their spears in approval. "Fifth-Son-Eighth-Born, come forward."

The Alsoo slithered forward. The image on the screen changed to that of a Cobra with his hood flared. "Fifth-Son-Eighth-Born, you are now Cobra," Shadowed Heart declared. He knelt in front of the Alsoo and pressed a device he held against the Alsoo's chest. There was a hiss, and when he removed the device, there was an image of a sidewinder imprinted on the Alsoo's chest. "Stand tall, Cobra of Sidewinder Squad!" He covered his eyes briefly.

"Second-Son-Third-Born," Emily said. "Come forward."

The image changed to that of a boa constrictor, a large animal held in its coils. The called Alsoo changed places with Cobra. "You are now Boa," declared Shadowed Heart. He repeated the imprinting of the sidewinder image and the covering of his eyes. "Stand tall, Boa of Sidewinder Squad."

Emily repeated the call for each member of Sidewinder Squad, and Shadowed Heart renamed them Mamba, Cotton Mouth, King Snake, Copperhead, and so on until every Alsoo was renamed and tattooed.

Morning Stars Fade stepped forward. "Sidewinder Squad, stand tall!" he called, and the newly named Alsoo warriors rose high on their tails. "You are no longer warriors. You are now and forever centurions." He slapped his chest. "Truth/oath."

"Truth/oath," warbled the Alsoo proudly.

Like any military unit that ever existed, the soldiers of the *Nieth* needed a place to unwind free of commanding officers and the restrictions of rank. They had received permission to install and maintain what they called the Enlisted Man's Club. Despite the name, officers were often there; not all the soldiers were men; and more than half were not even human.

For example, holding down a table on this evening were Hendriks and Cool Evening Breeze. Both held the rank of captain, but only one was either male or human. But it would have been a very foolish Rynn or human who would object to their being there. They both looked up curiously as the door to the club opened. They frowned as no one appeared to be in the doorway; then they looked down. A number of Alsoo clustered hesitantly in the doorway. Hendriks nodded in approval. "Someone find a free table and a pitcher of beer. We've got some thirsty soldiers."

Cool Evening Breeze beckoned the Alsoo into the club. "I don't think you boys ever drank Earth beer before." She raised her own glass. "It tastes like piss, but it gets the job done." She turned to Hendriks. "They can drink beer, can't they?" she questioned in a quiet aside.

"According to Medical they can," he grinned. "I asked. I wonder what a drunk Alsoo is like."

An hour later, they found out. It turned out that inebriated Alsoo were indistinguishable from inebriated soldiers anywhere. Some became friendly, some became taciturn, and a couple were seen weeping in a corner. Then one Alsoo climbed onto his table and started warbling. It didn't take the Torque to realize that the Alsoo was singing.

It was a simple song, and it seemed to have dozens of verses, but all the verses were followed by the same refrain: "Cry/we die/we short time sing/we." By the third or fourth verse, the humans and Rynn were joining in. When the song finally ended, the humans pounded their tables while the Rynn trilled their approval.

Finally, like all soldiers anywhere, the Alsoo finished their beers and staggered out of the club and back to their own quarters. Hendriks and Cool Evening Breeze watched as the last Alsoo weaved out the door. "Poor bastards," Hendriks said quietly. "Poor, brave bastards."

The following morning, Shadowed Heart, Morning Stars Fade, and Emily were faced with nearly two dozen Alsoo with hangovers.

Morning Stars Fade shook his head. "They're definitely soldiers," he said in mock disgust. "Any excuse to get drunk."

"Twenty laps around the gym," barked Emily. With a warbling groan, the Alsoo started slithering around the perimeter of the gym. "Spirits, but I am so damn proud of them," she said. "Look at them, hungover and dehydrated, and they showed up anyway."

"Spirits and ancestors, don't let them know that," mock-cautioned Morning Stars Fade.

Between Emily, Morning Stars Fade, and Shadowed Heart, they coaxed, cursed, and goaded the Alsoo into sweating out most of the alcohol in their system. By the end of the first hour of training, the Alsoo were almost their normal selves.

"Centurions!" Emily called. "Line up and stand tall." The Alsoo formed into their triple ranks. Emily walked over to a table where there was a number of cloth-covered objects. "Yesterday we named you, but that is only half of being a centurion." She removed the cloth covering the objects. She lifted one up. It was dome-shaped with a wide metal flap on one side and a thin one on the other, and it was topped by a crest of stiff fur. "This is a helmet," she said. She lifted another object. "And this is armor. Each of you will be provided with your own helmet and armor," she said. "You will not share. You will not trade. You will keep both clean and polished."

She pointed to one Alsoo. "Boa, advance and stand tall." The Alsoo Boa side-winded closer. Emily placed the helmet over the head of the Alsoo and adjusted the chin strap. She did the same with the armor.

"Hot," complained the Alsoo.

"Get used to it," Emily said without sympathy. "It can and will save your life," she stated. "The armor will protect you, and the helmet will allow you to talk to each other even in the cold dark," she said, using the Alsoo term for space. "Now, everyone line up and get their own helmet and armor."

They spent the next hour having the Alsoo practice putting on and taking off the helmet and armor, and then another hour learning how to use the simple controls in both. When they were confident the Alsoo understood the basics, they had them return to formation. "From now on, you will report to the gym in armor. You will not take off the armor until you return to your quarters. You will clean the armor before you eat, sleep, or do anything. Understood?" Emily asked.

The Alsoo waved their hands in acknowledgement.

"Good, now twenty laps," she ordered. "Go."

51

Zaski

"Approaching Zaski space," Morning Mist reported. "All sensors at maximum."

"Thank you, Morning Mist," Captain Kasumi replied. She chirped to her Torque, and her vision was overlaid with a representation of local space. "Not much here," she commented.

"We're pretty far down the galactic arm," Morning Mist replied. "The stars are more spread out."

"And I thought Earth was in the boonies," David Eisenstadt said.

"Sensors are picking up an approaching ship," Morning Mist said.

"Ship matches known Zaski craft," Meadow Flower said almost immediately. "It's one of their hunter/killer ships," she said in identification.

"Perfect," Kasumi purred. "Let's show the Zaski what it's like to be prey," she said in hungry anticipation. "This is the captain. Battle stations! Battle stations! This is not a drill. I repeat, this is not a drill."

"Weapons ready," came the report.

"Shields ready," came the next report.

"Assault team ready," came Shadowed Heart's voice. "Sidewinders are ready when you want them, Captain."

"Ape Squad and Bird Squad ready to back them up, Captain," reported Captain Cool Evening Breeze.

Kasumi's face blurred for a second, and then she was wearing her war paint. She looked around, and the rest of the bridge crew were also in war paint. "Hail them," she ordered.

"They are responding, captain," Meadow Flower replied. "And demanding we drop shields and allow a boarding party."

"David, answer them," Kasumi barked. "Loudly."

Eisenstadt smiled. "Weapons, give them a warning shot, right through their engines." He looked at the overhead monitor and watched as a graphic showed a missile track and the Zaski ship. He pumped his fist when the graphic showed a hit. "Good shooting, Weapons."

"They are responding with their own barrage," Meadow Flower reported crisply.

"Defense," Eisenstadt barked. He stared at the monitor. The incoming missiles were angry red dots—dots that vanished one by one as the ship's defenses eliminated each. "Weapons, they still can maneuver."

"On it, Commander," replied the weapons master.

"Boarding party, get ready," Kasumi ordered.

"Yes, Captain," Shadowed Heart replied. He turned to the assembled and armored Alsoo. "Sidewinders, helmets on," he ordered. The Alsoo quickly donned their helmets. "Voice check." Each Alsoo made sure that the communication system was active and functioning. Shadowed Heart tapped his Torque. "Sidewinders ready, Captain."

"Ape Squad ready," Captain Hendriks said a beat later, followed quickly by Cool Evening Breeze for Bird Squad.

"Load them up," Kasumi said. "And spirits and ancestors watch over you."

"Thank you, Captain," Shadowed Heart replied. "You heard the captain, Sidewinders. Load up."

"Spirits, but even I wouldn't want to tangle with someone

looking like that," Hendriks said as the armored and helmeted Alsoo boarded the shuttle. The last Alsoo got on board and strapped himself in. "Okay, Ape Squad, load up."

Hendriks observed the Alsoo out of the corner of his eye. Except for the occasional ruffling of their feathers, the Naga-forms seemed one and all outwardly calm and confident. He then glanced over to the trio everyone now referred to as the Terrible Three. This was the first time he'd had an opportunity to see the three of them together for any period of time. Emily, sitting between her two core brothers, was talking quietly to Morning Stars Fade, but Hendriks noted that she had one hand resting on Shadowed Heart's shoulder.

"They're a strong core," Cool Evening Breeze chirped softly.

Hendriks chuckled. "And Rynn think humans are mind readers," he said in amusement. He leaned closer to his core sister. "And don't ruin it by telling me you were observing me observing them. Let me keep some illusions." Cool Evening Breeze chittered.

Overhead lights started blinking. "Well, showtime," Hendriks said and stood. "Okay, ladies, if you haven't peed yet, you're going to have to hold it until this mission is over." Chuckles, chitters, and warbles greeted this sally. "ROE is as follows: quarter will be granted if and only if an enemy combatant removes itself from the conflict. In other words, if they run away, do not chase. If they drop their weapons, do not kill," he said. "Since this is the first time we will be meeting the Zaski in force, if you are not sure if they are surrendering or not, assume not," he said firmly. "Any questions?" His question was greeted with silence.

There was a jolt. Cool Evening Breeze stood and walked over to a hatch and opened it to reveal the metal hull of the Zaski ship. "Kind of rude of them to not allow us to dock," she said cheerfully. "Oh well." She pulled a pen-like device from her belt and ran it along the outline of the hatch. "Knock, knock!" She hit the hull with her fist, and the section of metal hull fell inward, accompanied by a puff of air. "Air pressure is higher than we're used to," she reported. "Sidewinders, you have point," she barked.

"We have point," replied Shadowed Heart. He stood, followed by Morning Stars Fade and Emily. "Sidewinders, advance and secure." He stepped aside as his Alsoo centurions flowed through the makeshift hatchway.

Once through, the Alsoo formed into a triple phalanx of seven Alsoo per column. Shadowed Heart, Emily, and Morning Stars Fade followed and took up position at the back of each phalanx. Shadowed Heart looked around. "We seem to be inside some kind of cargo bay," he reported over his Torque. "Centurions, advance at deliberate speed." The triple phalanx started moving at a slow, steady pace.

"Hey, we can't let Slytherin have all the fun," Cool Evening Breeze chirped. "Bird Squad, forward," she ordered and she and her squad went through the portal.

Hendriks waited until the last of Bird Squad exited the shuttle and got into formation before ordering his own squad forward. "Anything?" he asked via his Torque.

"Still quiet ... oops, spoke too soon," replied Cool Evening Breeze as a door opened at the far end of the bay and a number of creatures started entering quickly. "Zaski," she said in unnecessary identification.

If the Polig-Grug were bug-lizards, then the Zaski could best be described as mushroom-sharks. They had wide flaring heads that resembled a mushroom cap. Instead of distinct eyes, there was a dark band that stretched along a third of the mushroom cap. The creatures had no visible nose or any form of breathing system, and dominating the "head" was a wide sharklike mouth. Each Zaski had two tentacle-like arms that carried what was obviously a weapon. There were no visible legs; instead, the creatures advanced like a snail on a rubbery single foot. In color, the Zaski were a mottled gray.

"Spirits, but they're ugly," Cool Evening Breeze chirped in disgust.

"Centurions, Iron Flower!" barked Shadowed Heart. With a smoothness that spoke of long hours of practice, the Alsoo Centurions suddenly raised their spears and presented the oncoming Zaski with three columns that bristled with sharp points.

"Nice move," Hendriks muttered in appreciation.

The Zaski stopped and started firing their weapons. Apparently they used projectile weapons, but the metal slugs bounced off the shields of the centurions. The shields stopped the bullets, and the sharp points of the Alsoo spears promised pain and death. The Zaski tested the defense anyway as they suddenly extruded extra tentacles—tentacles that extended toward the Alsoo, tentacles that began to probe for weaknesses in the Alsoo's defense.

"Bird Squad, battle maces!" ordered Cool Evening Breeze. "Advance."

"Ape Squad, battle maces," echoed Hendriks. "Advance."

"Sidewinders, Iron Flower. Advance," ordered Shadowed Heart.

The three squads advanced slowly and deliberately. The projectile weapons may have been useless, but the Zaski were neither helpless nor cowardly. They met the alliance's advance with their own. The shields could stop a bullet, but the Zaski could and did use their tentacles as bludgeons that stopped the advance.

"Ugly and strong," Cool Evening Breeze grumbled. "And spirits weep, what are they made of?" she snarled. She had reason for her frustration. Blows from her mace that would have killed a Polig-Grug were shrugged off. The combatants were in a stalemate.

Shadowed Heart was worried. His Alsoo centurions were holding their own, but, like the humans and Rynn, they were no longer advancing. His eyes narrowed as something fought for his attention. The humans and Rynn were using their battle maces, but the Zaski were shrugging off the blows; meanwhile, his Alsoo centurions were using spears, which were successfully keeping the Zaski at bay. His eyes widened.

"Centurions, slow advance," he ordered. "On my count," he said. "One." The Alsoo warbled and side-winded forward one body length. The Zaski resisted for a moment and then retreated. "Two."

The Alsoo moved forward another body length. Again the Zaski retreated.

Shadowed Heart quickly tapped his Torque. "Captain Breeze. Captain Hendriks. The Zaski don't like getting punctured."

"Ape Squad," barked Hendriks. "KA-BARs out."

"You heard the man, Bird Squad," Cool Evening Breeze shouted. "KA-BARs."

In moments, the humans and Rynn in Ape and Bird Squad exchanged their maces for their fighting knives. It quickly became apparent that the Zaski had good reason for avoiding sharp objects, as a large enough puncture caused the mobile mushrooms to start "leaking" uncontrollably. Zaski could be seen retreating and frantically applying adhesive patches. Even after being patched, the wounded Zaski would not return to the battle.

A sudden thrumming filled the air. "Vibrations indicate language," reported the Torques. "Best guess translation: desist, stop, cease."

"Torque, translate: throw down your weapons," snapped Cool Evening Breeze. "I will start counting. If you have not thrown down your weapons when I get to ten, you will be destroyed." The translation was barely out of her mouth when the Zaski started divesting themselves of their weapons.

"Wusses," Hendriks said in derision.

"I am disgusted," Cool Evening Breeze replied. "And ashamed," she said in self-reproach. "All this time we were afraid ... for nothing."

"I wouldn't say *nothing*, Breeze," Hendriks disagreed. "Even humans would think twice about taking on a four-foot-tall ambulatory mushroom," he said. "With teeth." He put a hand on Cool Evening Breeze's shoulder. "And if the kid hadn't figured out their weakness, we'd still be fighting them."

There was another thrumming. "Translate," ordered Cool Evening Breeze.

"What do you want?" came the translation.

"We want you to stop attacking our ships and eating our people," snapped Cool Evening Breeze. "We are not food."

"You are animals," came the translated reply. "Animals are food."

"We eat mushrooms," Hendriks replied. "Especially with butter and garlic." He grinned mirthlessly. "So if you don't want to end up as a menu item, you will look elsewhere for your meals." He put his hand on Cool Evening Breeze's shoulder. "Rynn are a bit squeamish about eating something that talks back, but humans are not." He shrugged. "I'm not sure about the Alsoo."

"Mushroom/they eat/they we," an Alsoo broke in. "Hungry/we this time."

"You'll have to forgive our Alsoo friends," Hendriks said. "They have a very high metabolism." He smiled at the amused warble that greeted his comment. "Here's the deal. You don't eat us, we won't eat you," he said. "You will not attack our ships. You will not impede our ships' progress. Your ships will be inspected to ensure that no other sentient creatures are being exploited as a food source."

"We must eat," the translation came back. "Our population is large; our food production does not keep up."

"Ooh, now that sounds like an opening," Cool Evening Breeze chittered. "We may have a solution," she said to the Zaski. She chirped, and an image of a Polig-Grug unity appeared. "There are about 80 billion of these creatures," she said. "They're tough and mean, but if you want to try eating them, be our guests," she said. "We'll even give you the coordinates."

An hour later, the boarding party was back on the *Nieth*, and the *Nieth* itself was heading home. "All in all, it was a pretty easy operation," Captain Hendriks was reporting to Captain Kasumi. "No one died, and injuries were light—a couple broken arms and a large assortment of bruises—and we vacuumed their database," he reported in satisfaction. "So, if they break the agreement, we know where they live."

"And we made sure they know we know," Cool Evening Breeze added. "Spirits, but I'm still disgusted," she chirped. "And if it wasn't for you humans, we'd still be running from them."

"Maybe, maybe not," David Eisenstadt replied. "The Rynn have always been brave. You just didn't know it," he said. "I think you would have eventually figured that out on your own."

"You have more faith in my people than I do, Commander," Cool Evening Breeze replied.

"That's what friends are for," the commander replied. "Now get out of here," he ordered. "And send in the Terrible Three."

Eisenstadt and Kasumi watched their two top soldiers leave the conference room with proud smiles—smiles that widened when Shadowed Heart, Emily, and Morning Stars Fade entered. The three lined up in front of Eisenstadt and Kasumi and waited alertly. "Give me your honest assessment of how the Alsoo performed," Kasumi instructed.

The three looked at each other. "Go ahead, Shadowed Heart," Emily said. Morning Stars Fade nodded.

Shadowed Heart took a step forward. "They held up their end of the job," he said. "Better than I expected. Heck, better than I think they expected." Kasumi nodded and beckoned Shadowed Heart to continue. "When I left them in their quarters, they were doing two things I never saw them do before: bragging and telling each other jokes."

"Dirty jokes," Emily amended.

Shadowed Heart nodded. "One other thing, Captain," he said. "They haven't said anything, but their mood is different. It's hard to explain, but …" He paused as he tried to organize his thoughts. "I was listening to Cobra, and he said something interesting. He's Little Bit's dad, you know."

"Little Bit?" questioned Kasumi.

Shadowed Heart blushed. "First-Daughter-Second-Born. I call her Little Bit," he explained. "Anyway, he was talking about Little … his daughter and … he was making plans for her, Captain. You should have heard him. It was like he had won the lottery, and … it's hard to explain."

"I think you just did a fine job of explaining," Kasumi disagreed. "Well done, Ensign." She smiled. "Well done, all of you." She briefly covered her eyes. "The truth of what you are is like the sun; it blinds as well as illuminates. And sometimes it shines a light where no light has been before." She smiled warmly. "Now get out of here. I have work to do."

***

"Spirits and ancestors, but it is good to be home," Shadowed Heart said as he exited the shuttle. The *Nieth* had returned to Earth the previous day, but it had been nearly twenty-four hours before they were able to get a shuttle ride to the colony. They might have been able to go earlier, but Shadowed Heart, to his own surprise, had insisted that his Alsoo centurions go first. He took a deep breath. "The air on the *Nieth* may be filtered and clean, but it sure doesn't smell like this." He turned at Emily's giggle. "What?"

"Just wondering who you are and what you have done with Shadowed Heart," she said with a grin. "And how do we keep him from coming back?" she added with another giggle.

Shadowed Heart blushed. "Yeah, well …" he began. He was interrupted by a high-pitched warble. He turned to see a tiny feathered Alsoo hatchling heading toward him as fast as her little snakelike body could propel her. "Little Bit!" he exclaimed happily. The next thing Shadowed Heart knew, there was a foot-long Alsoo hatchling curled contentedly around his neck. "You've grown!" Shadowed Heart exclaimed. He rubbed the little Alsoo's head. "Have you been a good girl?" he asked. The Alsoo hatchling just warbled.

"I think you're going to have to wait another year or so before she can answer," Emily said. She walked over and caressed the little Alsoo. "As pretty as ever," she cooed. "You really should not run off without your parents," she scolded the hatchling.

"And here they come now," said Morning Stars Fade. He pointed to where two adult Alsoo and a group of five hatchlings were approaching. One adult Alsoo sported a tattoo on his chest. "Greetings, Centurion Cobra," he said respectfully. "Greetings, Cobra family."

"Greetings, Centurion Split-Tail Mor'ing Sta' Fa/you," replied the Alsoo warrior. "Greetings, Centurion Split-Tail Em'ly Fee/you." He covered his eyes. "Greeting Protector/you." He wrapped the end of his tail around the Alsoo female with him. "Female/she mate/me she," he said in introduction. "Question have/me."

"Question?" Shadowed Heart asked. He smiled. "A centurion does not need permission to ask questions."

The Alsoo waved his hand in acknowledgement. "Name/new/you Cobra/me," he said. "Give/you mate/my name/new question."

Shadowed Heart blinked. "Did he just ask me to give his mate a name?" he whispered.

"That's what I heard," Emily replied in the same hushed voice. "Spirits, but this is new." Her voice was filled with awe.

Shadowed Heart nodded slowly. He looked at the Alsoo female for a long moment and then knelt down in front of her. He tapped his head. "Who answers when you speak to yourself?"

The Alsoo female ruffled her feathers but remained silent. Shadowed Heart was about to try asking the question differently when the Alsoo female leaned forward and started to draw something in the dirt in front of her. Shadowed Heart tilted his head and tried to guess what was being drawn. "A flower?" he said. "No, that's … that's the sun, isn't it?" The Alsoo female waved a hand and then drew a line upwards. "Sunrise?"

"That's a beautiful name," Emily said quietly.

Shadowed Heart nodded. He slowly reached out and placed his hand over the female's head. "A beautiful name for a beautiful woman," he said. "Greetings, Sunrise."

The Alsoo female ducked her head behind Cobra's body. "Greetings, Protector," she said in a hushed voice. "This time all time Sunrise/me be," she declared shyly.

"Now and forever, you are Sunrise," agreed Shadowed Heart.

"Now and forever," Emily and Morning Stars Fade repeated. All three covered their eyes briefly. The two Alsoo adults repeated the gesture and started to move away.

Sunrise warbled, and the hatchling around Shadowed Heart's neck warbled back. Little Bit patted Shadowed Heart's face and then slithered down his body. With a lot of backward looks, the hatchling followed her parents.

"We must tell the Teacher," Morning Stars Fade said. He was about to say something more and stopped. "Core Brother?"

"I was Jamal once," he said and wiped at his eyes. "My parents gave me that name." He looked at the retreating Alsoo. "Every time I thought of that name, I would remember," he said. "It hurt." Both Morning Stars Fade and Emily nodded in understanding but remained silent. "I hope Raindrops in a Tide Pool will understand."

"Compromise, Core Brother, and honor both," Morning Stars Fade suggested gently. "I think Jamal Shadowed Heart is a good name," he said. Jamal nodded. "Let's go to the cabin, Core Brother, and tell the Teacher ..." He paused and then smiled sympathetically. "Everything."

The princess approached the Temple of Light. Unlike the previous times she had been there, the old monk was at the bottom of the steps and waiting for her. The princess covered her eyes. "Forgive me for not visiting sooner, Grandmother," *she said contritely.*

The old monk smiled. "You apologize when you are not even sure this is real?" *she said in amusement.*

"Knowing something and believing something are two separate things, Grandmother," *the princess replied.* "And while you have taught me that belief may be a trap, that does not mean I should not believe in anything," *she said.* "I do not know if this is real, and I may never truly know, but every part of me wishes to believe it is." *She looked down.* "Not because I fear death, but because I would rather believe I am talking to a wise counselor and friend than to believe I am speaking to myself."

The old monk laughed. "Don't you trust your own counsel?" she teased.

"In some things, but I am still young and have much to learn," the princess replied. "The Teacher would scold me for refusing to acknowledge that."

"He has taught you much, and there is more you must learn," the old monk replied. "But you must accept that there will not be enough time for him to teach all that he knows."

The princess bowed her head. "There are some things that are difficult to accept, but none more so than that," she said. "Will it be soon?" she asked in a whisper.

"Time is meaningless to one such as I," the old monk replied. "Time is an illusion that only the dead do not share." She lifted the princess's chin with one finger. "Take heart in this one truth: he was old and bitter and believed he was beyond redemption," she said gently. "You not only showed him that redemption was possible, but you put his feet on the path to being redeemed."

The old monk looked into the princess's eyes. "I am Mei Lin Blunt. How or why I am here I do not know, nor do I care. What I do care about is that the man you call Teacher has learned how to care—no, to love—again, and that is because of you." She placed a hand on the princess's head. "His time is soon, but not yet," she said. "And when he does pass, sing for him."

"Every night, Grandmother," the princess promised with tear-filled eyes. "I promise."

Kasumi woke with a start. "Spirits," she whispered.

"The dream?" Mel asked sleepily.

"Yes," Kasumi replied in a hushed voice.

"Grandfather is going to die soon, isn't he?" Mel asked quietly.

Kasumi chuckled sadly. "And humans continue to insist they do not read minds," she said. "Yes."

"I had the feeling that would be the case," Mel said. "How soon?"

"Grandmother said it was soon but not yet," Kasumi replied. "I had the feeling that he is supposed to do something first."

Year 18

Kasumi Blunt of the Forest Cabin Clan, captain of the *Nieth*, leader of those Rynn who were part of the colony on Earth, Rynn ambassador to Earth, and Rynn ambassador to the Alsoo, sighed as she reviewed yet another report. "When Grandmother said the way would be difficult, I didn't think she meant paperwork," Kasumi grumbled. She grimaced when her muttered comment was met with laughter. "It wouldn't be so bad if most of these documents were useful." She sat back. "But most of them are just petty nonsense."

She lifted a sheet. "Take this one, for example," she said. "It's from Senator Sawyer." She smiled sourly as the majority of those in the room groaned. "Demanding, yet again, that we allow evangelist missionaries into the colony."

"The man is incompetent," Morning Mist replied. "He knows that no missionaries from any group are allowed in the colony. He knows, because I told him that personally."

"Which he claims is a lie, since Teacher Germy is allowed in the colony," Kasumi replied in annoyance. She read from the document: ' ... the presence of the charlatan, Jeremy Blunt, who professes and promotes belief in the false doctrine of Ancestors and Spirits, has been allowed free access to the childlike Alsoo and is condemning their souls to the fires. Common decency requires that they be exposed to the TRUTH—' he capitalized it 'before it is too late.'"

"He actually called the Teacher a charlatan?" Morning Mist said in disbelief.

"Several times," Kasumi chirped in disgust. "He also makes mention of Germy's time in prison and even suggests that it was the Teacher himself who murdered his wife." She tapped the document. "'Whose wife was killed under mysterious circumstances while her alleged murderers were conveniently silenced.'" Her crest angrily snapped open and closed several times.

"This cannot go unanswered," Morning Mist said angrily. "It is one thing to ..." She stopped at Kasumi's raised hand.

"You know what the Teacher would say," Kasumi said gently.

"You cannot allow the Teacher to be insulted," Morning Mist returned.

"I have no intention of allowing Germy to be insulted," Kasumi replied. "Nor do I intend to accede to Sawyer's demands," she said. "But I can't ignore it." She chirped to her Torque. "Ophelia, we need to talk."

52

The Ophelia Winslow Interviews, Part One: The Terrible Three

"Good evening, darlings," Ophelia Winslow boomed to her audience. "You don't know how happy I am to put aside being the oligarch and go back to what I love doing best: talking to all you wonderful people," she gushed. "We have an exciting lineup for our first show."

Her expression became serious. "But first, I have a personal message." She turned to face a camera. "Aliens have been living among us for more than a decade now, and, for the most part, relations with the Rynn and the Alsoo have been friendly and respectful." She frowned. "I said 'for the most part' because there have been incidents of intolerance and even hatred—and, I am ashamed to say, all on the part of humans."

She shook a finger at the camera. "Humans are now exploring the stars. Humans are now living longer than ever. Unemployment, world unemployment, is at historic lows, and yet some of you out there are willing to jeopardize all that we have gained solely because your personal philosophy has not been adopted by our friends from the stars," she said. "I am speaking to you, Senators Seasons, Sawyer, and Coolidge." She smiled. "We'll be right back."

The director pointed to Ophelia. "And, we are back," she said. "My first guest is actually three guests. I met them during my last visit to the colony, and I was so impressed with them that I just had to have them on the show."

She stood. "Ladies and gentlemen, I am so proud to introduce Morning Stars Fade, Emily Fields, and Jamal Shadowed Heart."

She applauded along with the audience as three young adults walked onstage. A more unusual and diverse trio would be hard to imagine: one was a young black man in his early twenties, another a young white woman of about the same age, and the third a young Rynn male with a pale blue crest.

Ophelia waited until everyone had seated themselves. "Before we get started, I'm going to give a little background on my guests. Morning Stars Fade is, obviously, Rynn. He is a member of the combined Rynn-human tactical force and hold the rank of ensign. Emily Fields and Jamal Shadowed Heart are also members of the tactical force, and both also hold the rank of ensign," she said. "It is also my understanding that all three are the youngest members of the tactical force."

She looked at Jamal. "Jamal Shadowed Heart? That seems to be almost a Rynn name."

"Not almost," Jamal replied. "I was adopted by a Rynn core group and was given a Rynn name." He chirped for a moment. "That's how it's pronounced in Rynn."

"I see," Ophelia replied. "It's unusual for a Rynn to adopt a human, is it not?"

Jamal nodded. "I'm the only one that I know of," he said. "My adoptive father is Raindrops in a Tide Pool, and my adoptive mothers are Night Storm and Dierdre McIntosh."

"Oh, so Dierdre McIntosh was why you were adopted," Ophelia stated.

"Not really," Jamal replied. "I like Dierdre, but she is not really very maternal." He smiled briefly. "It was really Raindrops in a Tide Pool who insisted," he said. "I was considered unadoptable, you know."

He didn't wait for a response before continuing. "I was one of the rescued," he said. "And I had some trust issues." He turned to the murmuring audience. "A lot of the rescued have trouble readjusting to normal life. Most of us saw our parents murdered."

Morning Stars Fade put a hand on Jamal's shoulder. "Thanks, Core Brother," Jamal said quietly.

"We'll be right back," Ophelia said to the audience.

"And we're back," Ophelia said after the break. "While we were on break, we started receiving comments on social media." She shook her head. "Apparently, some people do not believe that the CSA had reinstituted slavery."

Jamal stood and removed his coat, and then he turned his back on the audience and removed his shirt. There was a collective gasp when his naked back was displayed. It was a mass of thick, angry white and red scars. Jamal quickly put his shirt back on and turned back to the audience. "The Teacher Jeremy says that there will always be people who will deny even in the face of incontrovertible evidence." He, Morning Stars Fade and Emily all briefly covered their eyes. He looked at the camera. "To those who deny, I say this: deny all you want, but belief is not truth, no matter how much you want it to be."

"You mentioned the Teacher Jeremy," Ophelia said. "There are some who consider him a vicious murderer."

"They're pretty much the same people who don't believe the truth about the CSA," Jamal said. "Did you know that Senator Coolidge is related to the two men that Teacher Jeremy supposedly murdered?" he asked. "And did you know that Senator Coolidge and Senator Seasons were both members of the CSA leadership?"

"My core brother is being very circumspect," Morning Stars Fade interjected. "Since I'm not a human, I think I can be a little more blunt." He grinned at the implied pun and then sobered. "There are a number of human politicians in a number of countries who the Rynn consider criminals. Senator Coolidge and Senator Seasons are at the top of that list."

"Criminals?" gasped Ophelia.

"Criminals," asserted Morning Stars Fade. "Subject to arrest, imprisonment, and possible execution if they are found on Rynn territory."

Ophelia paled as the interview took this sudden and unexpected turn. "I didn't … I never …" She stopped. "Execution?"

"The Rynn are very similar to humans—we're vain, quarrelsome, and, at times, selfish and violent—but we've never had slaves," Morning Stars Fade said. "When we learned about slavery and that humans believed you could own other humans, we nearly abandoned our trade mission here."

"I remember that," Ophelia replied. "But … execution?"

"From our way of thinking, slavery is as … evil as predating on a sapient being," Morning Stars Fade replied. "It is considered a level of incompetence unparalleled in Rynn history," he said. "And the punishment for such incompetence is death or banishment."

Ophelia swallowed, and with some desperation turned to Emily Fields. "And you, Miss Fields? What do you think of all this?"

"My core brother—" she placed a hand on Jamal's arm "—will never be whole. Sometimes he cries in his sleep. Sometimes he can't sleep," she said angrily. "Sometimes he doesn't have to be asleep to cry," she said. "There are times when he looks at me like I'm the enemy."

"Em," protested Jamal.

"Don't pretend, Jamal," Emily said. "The only good thing is that those times are becoming rarer as time goes on." She looked at the camera. "But he will never be whole," she said. "Do you know what the Alsoo call Jamal?" she asked rhetorically. "They call him the 'sad soul.'" She smiled grimly. "He's one of the few humans or Rynn that the Alsoo are willing to spend any time with, and possibly the only human or Rynn they fully trust. And do you know why?" she asked. "Because he's the only human or Rynn they've ever met who has suffered anywhere near as much as they have."

She tightened her hold on Jamal's arm and turned to the camera. "To all you deniers out there: my contempt for you cannot be put into words. Stay away from me and my core," she snapped. "Or else."

"That … that sounded like a threat, Miss Fields," Ophelia said faintly.

"Good," Emily replied. "I wouldn't want anyone to have gotten the wrong idea."

53

The Ophelia Winslow Interviews, Part Two: Warriors Go to Hell

"Good evening, darlings," boomed Ophelia Winslow. "Hard as it may be to believe, I think tonight's guests may be even more exciting than last week's interview with the Terrible Three," she said to her packed audience. "Not only are we going to meet with another human/Rynn core, we are going to meet an actual Alsoo."

The crowd started murmuring excitedly enough that Ophelia had to raise her hands to get them to quiet down. "Thank you," she said when the crowd finally settled. "Tonight, we are going to meet the second oldest human/Rynn core, and one that contains someone very, very familiar to all of you." She smiled. "Ladies and gentlemen: Captain Hendriks, Captain Cool Evening Breeze, Crystal Chandler." She paused as the crowd erupted in shouts of surprise. "And with them is their children; two-year old Sofia and ten-year old Jesse and the core's two associates, Burl and 3D3B.."

Ophelia stood and applauded along with the crowd. The applause went on for a bit and then died down when no one came onstage. "Honestly," scolded a voice, and then two figures—one human, one Rynn—half-walked and half-stumbled onstage. The crowd laughed and then started applauding again as the very familiar face of Crystal Chandler followed the stumbling figures. Crystal carried two-year old Sofia in a baby carrier; a small figure of a second Rynn followed close by holding the hand of a ten-year old boy who was nearly as tall.

Ophelia waited until everyone was seated. She frowned. "I thought 3D3B was with you." she began. She stopped as a snakelike figure crawled out of the carrier, climbed up Crystal's body, and wrapped itself around Crystal's neck.

"Baby/she new mouth/toy have/she," warbled the Alsoo via a translator. She held up a circular object. "Toy/she lose/she." The crowd chuckled.

"What I think 3D3B is trying to say was that she had to find Sofia's pacifier," Crystal said. "The translator tries, but the Alsoo syntax is confusing even with the Torque." 3D3B warbled in amused agreement.

"I hope you don't mind," began Ophelia. "But there aren't too many Alsoo, and most people will never meet one," she said. "And they're very curious. I know I am." She looked at 3D3B. "You were the first Alsoo adopted into a core," she began.

"Big/big ugly split-tails/they big/big clumsy/they baby/have/they," 3D3B said. "Scared/they."

"Big ugly humans and Rynn are clumsy and afraid of the baby?" guessed Ophelia.

"Close," corrected Crystal. "More like they're clumsy around the baby." She grinned. "But you're right about them being afraid of Jesse."

"Rather face a Polig-Grug," muttered Cool Evening Breeze, "than change a diaper." The crowd started laughing. "Hey, a Polig-Grug can only kill you," she said in defense. "But baby poop is something else."

"We thought about using it to fight the Polig-Grug, but not even bug-lizards deserve that," Hendriks added. The crowd roared.

"Dizzy/think split-tails/they," complained 3D3B.

"Big/big dizzy/think split-tails/they," agreed Burl. "Hi, I'm Burl." He grinned. "Everyone gets that same expression on their faces when I introduce myself."

"Well, we're used to hearing more descriptive names," admitted Ophelia.

"Well, my Rynn name is somewhat untranslatable," Burl replied. "We don't have trees on Nest. The plant forms that fill the same niche are more like Earth succulents, with the green—well, purple-green—part at the base and a tall spike that grows from the center. It's only a superficial resemblance, but my name refers to when the spike sometimes gets a knot in it."

"A burl," exclaimed Ophelia.

"Yep," agreed Burl. "Anyway, me and 3D3B were brought into the core as associates, mainly because those two big bad marines were afraid of changing a diaper."

"Or cooking," added Crystal. "And no one can get Sofia to go to sleep like 3D3B can." She reached up and caressed the little snake woman. "The two of them have been a godsend."

Ophelia nodded. She was about to say something when someone in the audience shouted, "Sinners! Repent!" A number of people booed the shouter and called for the shouter, a woman, to sit down and be quiet.

"No," Crystal Chandler said. "Let her speak. The First Teacher said, 'Truth is like the sun; it can blind and illuminate.'" The entire core, including 3D3B briefly, covered their eyes. "And Teacher Jeremy will often quote Louis Brandeis and add, 'Light is the best disinfectant.' So, let's bring this into the light."

She stood and stared over the audience. "What sin do you think we need to repent?" she demanded. The woman in the audience shrank back and did not answer. "You started this, and I am giving you the opportunity to speak, so speak." She smiled. "What sin?"

She cupped her ear as the woman mumbled something. "Louder. I could not hear that."

"You live in sin," the woman shouted angrily. "You fornicate with animals. God says marriage is between one man and one woman."

"Hmm," Crystal Chandler noised. "Let's take those one by one, shall we?" She smiled. "Live in sin?" she asked. "If by that you mean we're not married … that is what you meant, isn't it?" The woman remained angrily silent. "You know, a dialog usually implies two people talking, but for the moment, let's assume you meant we're not married." She stared coldly at the woman. "Our core was duly registered with the state of California and we had a very lovely ceremony at the colony." She made a tossing motion. "So that's one."

"One man, one woman," shouted the woman.

"Well, that's true for you, I suppose," Crystal replied. "However, the colony follows Rynn traditions. Again, all duly registered with the state of California and the federal government." She made the same tossing motion. "You may not agree, but it is perfectly legal, so that's two," she said. "Now let's talk about the whole bestiality thing. Do you mean Cool Evening Breeze and Burl, or do you mean 3D3B?"

"You fornicate with a beast of Satan." She pointed to 3D3B. "Behold the serpent."

"Big/big crazy think split-tail," warbled 3D3B. "Big split-tail family/they mate/they not."

For the first time, Hendriks stood and walked over to the edge of the stage.

"Lady," he growled, "I want to tell you something. I ran into a whole bunch of yahoos just like you. They quoted the Bible right and left and used it to justify a whole shitload of nonsense." His growl became a snarl. "Slavery, brutality, every crime against humanity possible, all in the name of the Bible," he snapped. "And you have the goddamn gall to come in here and … oh, don't run away, lady, I haven't finished." He tapped his Torque and mumbled something.

The woman who was heading toward the exits suddenly bounced. "Like I said, I ain't done talking yet." He walked to the stage stairs and headed toward the now-cowering woman. "They were just like you, quoting the Bible to justify their worst actions." He now towered over the woman. "Do you want to see a serpent? Then look in the mirror," he declared. "3D3B has more love, more compassion, more … humanity in the tip of her tail than you have in your entire body." He tapped his Torque again and muttered something. "I'm done. You can leave now." Hendriks turned his back on the woman and headed back to the stage.

"God will not be denied," the woman shouted.

Hendriks stopped and turned. "No," he said. "He won't." He smiled coldly. "The Teacher Jeremy says, when you point a finger at someone, remember that there are three fingers pointing right back at you." He briefly covered his eyes. "Now get the …"

"Hendriks!" scolded Crystal warningly.

"Sorry, Momma," said Hendriks. He turned back to the woman. "Just go," he said. "I don't want my kids exposed to your sickness."

Ophelia waited until the woman had scrambled out through the exit. "We'll be right back," she said in a hushed voice.

"We're back," said a very subdued Ophelia Winslow. "I want to apologize," she began, only to stop when Cool Evening Breeze raised a hand. "Breeze?"

"You have nothing to apologize for," Cool Evening Breeze said. "You have always been a good friend to the Rynn."

"Not always, Breeze," Ophelia replied. "To my shame, I was …" She swallowed. "I was just like that woman." She turned when the audience expressed disagreement. "Thank you, my friends, but I am just as guilty," she said. "I may not have ever said or even have thought the same, but in the past, I would have just dismissed her as an aberration and would have said she was not a true Christian." She shook her head. "It's not enough to disavow the individual. If we are truly followers of Christ, we must disavow the poison that courses through the church itself." She took a breath and then clapped her hands together sharply, twice. "Spirits and ancestors of humans, Rynn, and Alsoo, please forgive me. I was silent when I should have spoken," she said.

Cool Evening Breeze covered her eyes briefly. "Spirits bless you," she said. "The First Teacher said the greatest blessing is providing water, food, and shelter unasked, for no other reason than because it is the right thing to do. We often forget the other half of her sermon. She then said, the greatest crime is to not offer water, food, or shelter even when asked, because we are afraid or unwilling to do the right thing." She stood and walked to the edge of the stage. "I was a geologist. I thought my life was satisfying and complete, and then I came to Earth. I became part of colony security, but it was just play-acting. Hendriks taught me what being a soldier, being a warrior, was really about. It's about serving something bigger than yourself. It's about being true to an ideal. It's about finding something to die for."

Hendriks walked over to stand beside Cool Evening Breeze. "All warriors go to hell," he stated bluntly. "It's the price we know we must pay for protecting what's important to us: family, friends, and honor." He placed a hand on Cool Evening Breeze's shoulder. "Breeze and I, we're warriors, and if hell is our destiny, so be it. I'd rather spend an eternity in hell with Breeze than spend one minute in heaven with people like that woman."

54

The Ophelia Winslow Interviews, Part Three: Rocket Man

"Good evening, everyone," Ophelia Winslow said to her studio audience. "There is a common saying, 'Be careful what you wish for, you might get it.' I looked for the origin of this phrase and found that no one knows who first said it." She added, "After last week's show, I am even more hesitant to wish for an exciting show."

She continued, "I have always prided myself on never screening the audience. I want a mix of people. I want a mix of ideas. What I do not want is hatred." She shook her head. "I will continue to allow anyone who wishes to attend my show to attend, but I beg you, be respectful, be kind."

Ophelia put a bright smile on her face. "Our guests tonight are another mixed core of human, Rynn, and Alsoo. They are also, in a word, heroes."

She continued, "*Hero* is an often overused word, but in this case, it fits. All of them have risked their lives more than once, and two of them have been hospitalized with life-threatening injuries. Four of the six nearly died trying to save the people of Atlanta." She stood. "Ladies and gentlemen: Doctor Joseph Franklin, Red Clouds Paint the Sky, Black Rocks, Frozen River, Light of Three Moons, and Second-Daughter-Fifth-Born."

The applause that began died as the core came onstage. The first onstage was Franklin in his floater, piloted by Second-Daughter-Fifth-Born. It was obvious that Franklin needed both the floater and the pilot, as his head was propped up with a brace. Following close behind was the rest of his core. They all checked the floater and Franklin before seating themselves.

Ophelia swallowed a couple times before attempting to speak. Her voice broke anyway. "Good evening," she said.

"Good evening," the core responded.

"I did not realize that Dr. Franklin was so weak," Ophelia began.

"It's his own fault," Light of Three Moons said in tart tones. "He has a habit of pushing himself beyond his limits," she said. "Don't worry. He is much stronger than he appears. He just forgot to eat." Her crest rose. "Again."

"Big think split-tail/he, dizzy/think all time/he," warbled the Alsoo. "Hear/he me not."

"Nag, nag, nag," complained Dr. Franklin. He turned to the audience. "Word of advice: if you ever join a core, keep the number of women down to one," he said. The audience laughed in response. They stopped laughing again when a trembling hand reached up to caress the Alsoo neuter.

"For those who don't know," Ophelia Winslow said, "Dr. Franklin was critically injured during a Polig-Grug attack on Earth—an attack he was directly instrumental in thwarting," she said. "Over the past eighteen years, Dr. Franklin and his core brothers have been in nearly every major battle the combined human–Rynn forces have faced on Earth and in space.

"Frozen River was critically injured in the first battle with the CSA," she went on. "Red Clouds Paint the Sky and Black Rocks have both been injured several times in smaller yet just as important skirmishes. Heroes all of them."

She turned to face a camera. "And yet there are some who would condemn them because of who they love," she said. "One has to ask, considering the amount of hate directed at all of you, why do you continue to protect those who would not do the same?"

"I'm not fighting to protect them," Dr. Franklin returned sharply. "If I could, I'd feed some of them to the Polig-Grug." His hands started trembling more. Second-Daughter-Fifth-Born wrapped her tail around his hands until the trembling eased. "Thank you, Core Sister," he said quietly. "She's who I'm fighting to protect." He nodded toward the Alsoo. "Jamal Shadowed Heart and those like him are who I'm fighting to protect," he continued. "I'm fighting to protect those like me who were forced to live in the shadows—or, worse, forced to deny who and what they were in the name of some deity or other."

He continued defiantly, "As far as I'm concerned, any deity who condemns someone for who and how they love is a deity that is not worthy of worship." He took a calming breath. "There was a story about me on a popular website," he said. "Mostly sympathetic, but they were very critical about a similar comment I had made during an interview. They claimed I was being intolerant of others 'beliefs.'" He smiled coldly. "Damn right I'm intolerant," He said.

"Dr. Franklin?" Ophelia asked in shocked surprise.

"I'm intolerant of intolerance," explained Dr. Franklin. "There are those who consider me and my lifestyle, even my being part of a core, as being immoral." He turned to look directly at the camera. "I reject your intolerance. I reject your hatred. But mostly I reject your right to your intolerance. You and yours are what me and mine consider the true definition of evil. You will soon be consigned to the dustbin of history, and my fondest wish is to see that day."

It started with a single person clapping but quickly swelled, and then the entire audience rose to their feet.

"Spirits and ancestors," Black Rocks said in a whisper. "When our core brother speaks, it's as if his words are more felt than heard." He covered his eyes. "Spirits sing, but he is magnificent."

"We'll be right back," said Ophelia Winslow in a hushed voice.

55

THE OPHELIA WINSLOW INTERVIEWS, PART 4: REDEMPTION SONG

"Good evening, everyone," Ophelia Winslow greeted her studio audience. "And good evening to all those viewing."

She pursed her lips. "Over the past few weeks, we've met three different human/Rynn cores. Each core was unique in its own way, and each core has made comments that were at times thoughtful and at other times almost incendiary," she said.

"After last week's interview with Dr. Franklin and his core, I have received more letters, more emails, more tweets, and more comments via nearly all forms of social media than any two shows combined." She brushed at her hair nervously. "And I have received more death threats and more hate mail than I had received in the last two years," she said. "I have even been threatened with lawsuits if I brought on any more cores."

Ophelia lowered her head and placed her hands behind her back. "I have even lost a couple of longtime sponsors." She raised her head. "Well, to that I say, good riddance," she said sternly. "When Kasumi Blunt revealed herself and the USA split into four, I became the oligarch and did what I could to keep this country together," she said. "When the crisis ended, I gladly gave up being the oligarch and returned to being Ophelia Winslow." She sighed. "But between the split and the reunion, I was the oligarch, and I saw, firsthand, the crimes of the Spencer government. In my arrogance, I did not realize that it wasn't just the Spencer government; it was each and every one of us who remained silent in the face of one of the most monstrous events in our history."

Abruptly, she said, "I have an announcement. This is my last show. After last week's episode, I realized that I wasn't trying to return to my role as a television host but rather trying to hide from my responsibilities. I may no longer be the oligarch, but that does not mean I no longer have any power, any authority. This is my last show, but this is not going to be the last you will see of me."

She smiled. "And speaking of last ... I've saved the best for last. Ladies and gentlemen, I am proud to announce my next guest. It is a single guest. I first met him over forty years ago. He helped start me on my path to fame, so it is only fitting that he be here with me in closing the circle. Ladies and gentlemen, Jeremy Blunt."

There was only a smattering of applause as an old man walked out onstage. He could have been anywhere from sixty-five to ninety-five, but few would have believed he was at the top of that range. In fact, he was less than a year shy of his one hundredth birthday. Despite his advanced age, he was robust and healthy. His hair had been recently trimmed, and he was freshly shaven. He could have passed for a healthy sixty-year-old.

"Ophelia!" he greeted the television host in obvious pleasure.

"Jeremy," returned Ophelia. She led him over to a couple of chairs that flanked a small table. She waited until he sat. "You look wonderful," she gushed.

"Blame the Rynn for that," Jeremy mock grumped. "Damn Omiset," he complained cheerfully. "They promised me fifteen years, and here I am going on eighteen extra years." He chuckled. "Kasumi refuses to apologize too."

Ophelia laughed in response. "Well, I for one am very glad you're still around," she said, and then paused. "It's going to become a common occurrence, isn't it?" she said. "Living and functioning well into what we think of as extreme old age?"

"My granddaughter thinks that the human lifespan will eventually double," he said. "Assuming we don't completely alienate the Rynn." He shrugged. "That, unfortunately, still appears to be possible. I doubt that it will happen, but what may happen will be even worse."

He explained himself. "The more, shall we say, conservative nations are refusing to adopt the use of Omiset and birth-control implants—in fact, most of the purely biological advances being made available—while, at the same time, demanding those technological advances that can be most easily converted to military use."

"Can't you tie them together?" asked Ophelia.

"We are, and that's part of the problem. They are refusing everything, though they are not above stealing what they can." Jeremy sighed. "We're going to see humanity divided into two groups: long-lived spacefaring and short-lived earthbound." He shook his head. "We are already starting to see some instability in a number of nations over it."

"Instability?" asked Ophelia.

"Imagine knowing that there is a cure for your mother's cancer, your child's cystic fibrosis, and then knowing that your country's government refuses to allow the treatments. Or worse, finding that the treatment itself is considered blasphemy," Jeremy pointed out. "The Rynn are quite willing to provide the treatments, but you can't just suddenly double life expectancy and still expect your women to have six or seven children," he said. "And you can't just double life expectancy for some imagined elite. Something has to give."

He rubbed his head. "There have been riots in the Middle East.

Riots in the Near East. And riots on the East Coast," he said. "Remember that woman from your second show?"

Ophelia nodded. "Hard to forget her," she said.

"She tried to burn down a Rynn clinic the following day." Jeremy blew out a breath. "Fortunately, the clinic was protected by a force shield."

"Spirits be praised," Ophelia said. She frowned at Jeremy's chuckle. "What?"

"There is a truism about cultural interaction," he said. "The more advanced culture will tend to replace the less advanced one," he pointed out. "It's a tendency, and it's not always one way, but for some, any indication of cultural … contamination must be stamped out."

"And I just said 'spirits be praised,'" Ophelia said in understanding.

"If things continue the way they are, the events of the last decade are going to seem tame in comparison to what will happen," he said. "At the very least, the Middle East is going to be engulfed in war, half of Europe will devolve into fascism, and the Old South is going to secede, again."

"Surely something can be done," Ophelia protested.

"Oh, there are many things that can be done. The question is, do we have the will to do them?" Jeremy shook his head. "We haven't before, so I am not hopeful we will now."

Ophelia nodded. "We'll be right back," she said gloomily.

"And we're back," Ophelia said. "For those who have joined us late, our guest tonight is the Teacher, Jeremy Blunt," she said. "We have already discussed the somewhat grim future that may be ahead of us. Mr. Blunt, is there anything positive that we can expect?"

"Positive?" Jeremy replied. "Oh, many things—long life, exploring the stars, new worlds, new people," he said. "It isn't that these things *won't* happen, it's a matter of how many will live to see it and share in the bounty that is sure to come. Make no mistake: humanity will colonize the stars. Humanity will experience a golden age that will dwarf anything that has come before. The question is, what will be the price?"

Jeremy stood and faced the audience. "Each and every one of you here and each and every one of you watching has in your hands a choice. You can accept what the Rynn offer or you can reject it," he said. "And there are those, maybe even here in this room, who would deny you that choice. There are those who may tell you that it is a choice between heaven and hell. And they are right." He raised a quelling hand. "Just not in the way they think."

He explained, "Ophelia has introduced you to three different cores. Every one of the humans in those cores chose to accept what the Rynn offered," he pointed out. "You met a young man who was abused by those who called him a slave because of the color of his skin. You met another man who trained to become a killer, and you met a third man who denied who and what he was." He nodded. "Each one, in his own way, considered himself damned." Then Jeremy pressed a hand against his chest. "And me—killer by trade, slave to duty, and one who denied that he was either a slave or a killer," he said. "Damned and thrice damned was I."

Ophelia's hand went to her mouth, and she watched in awe as Jeremy captured the attention of everyone in the audience. If silence was any indicator, the capture was complete and unshakeable.

"The price I paid was my wife, my son, and my freedom," Jeremy declared. "I knew that on the day I died, the gates of hell would open and consume my soul." His voice took on a preacher's cadence. "I knew that there could never be, would never be, should never be redemption for such as I." Jeremy's arms spread to the sides. "And then I found a star child and found in her my own redemption. A star child I almost did not find because I had almost skipped taking my daily walk."

He clapped his hands together twice, sharply. "I am Jeremy Blunt, and I call on our shared ancestors as witness. With the Rynn's help, we saved the Alsoo—but it was close, so close. One day, one single day, and it would have been too late."

He continued. "I know my adoptive granddaughter's people do not believe in fate, but can any of you look at the Alsoo and deny that the hand of fate was involved? Can any of you look at the Alsoo and deny that Hendriks and Jamal and Joseph by their actions were well and truly redeemed?" He lowered his hands. "They were willing to pay the price for their redemption. But I know them, and I know that they would have paid it regardless, even if there were no redemption, because it was the right thing, the only thing to do."

He smiled. "The choice they had was to accept what the Rynn offered or reject it. The choice they had was to save the Alsoo or let them perish. Redemption or damnation. That choice is now yours."

Silence greeted Jeremy's final words, and he turned and sat down opposite Ophelia. It took several moments before Ophelia even realized that Jeremy had stopped speaking and several moments more before she trusted her voice to not crack. "I think this is a good time to take a break," she said quietly.

"Spirits and ancestors," Kasumi whispered. "He truly is the First Teacher reborn." She chirped, and the Torque stopped playing the recording from Ophelia's show. She chirped again. "This is Captain Kasumi: I am placing the colony on full alert," she said. "No one is to leave the colony without fully charged shields. Colony shields to remain at full power and full coverage until further notice. All leaves are cancelled. Recall all colony personnel. We are on full alert. Repeat, full alert."

"Are you sure about this, Kasumi?" David Eisenstadt asked calmly.

"No, I'm not sure, David," Kasumi replied. "But if Germy is truly the First Teacher reborn or even if he is just …" Kasumi paused. "I was about to say, even if he is just a Great Teacher and realized how stupid that would sound," she said. "He is indeed a Great Teacher, and in our history, whenever a Great Teacher issued such a challenge, violence was sure to follow."

"Human history is not much different," Mel agreed.

"I wasn't disagreeing with Kasumi, I just asked if she was sure," Eisenstadt countered. He tapped his Torque. "All stations report on full alert status," he ordered. "I want the location of all off-colony personnel verified, including the Alsoo, and I want retrieval teams on hot standby," he ordered. "High Flyer Command, I want the birds circling immediately."

Klaxons started sounding throughout the colony and on all the defense satellites. The mixed squads of human and Rynn were suddenly wearing war paint, and inside the Alsoo burrow Sidewinder Squad members were donning their armor.

"Go/me this time," Cobra said to his mate, Sunrise. His tail wrapped comfortingly around his suddenly frightened mate. "Safe/be you. Safe/be hatchlings." He put on his helmet and adjusted the chin strap with hands sure with long practice. He tapped the side of his helmet "Sidewinder Squad assemble," he warbled. He grabbed his spear, slithered out of his chamber, and started up the long tunnel to the surface. As he traveled, he was joined by the other members of the Sidewinder Squad.

"Big warning sound," Boa said. "Know/you question," he asked Cobra.

"Know/me not," Cobra replied. "Know/me assemble. Know/me protect/she mate. Know/me protect/they hatchlings."

Cobra and his Sidewinder Squad comrades all waved their free hands in agreement and continued up the tunnel. They exited to find most of the split-tails moving quickly around the colony. Cobra tapped his helmet. "Sidewinder Squad. Phalanx make," he ordered. The twenty-one members of Sidewinder Squad took up position at the border of the burrow.

The speaker for the Alsoo joined the Alsoo centurions. "Split-tails/they worried/they," commented the speaker.

"Truth/oath," agreed Cobra. "Stand/we with split-tails/they. Pledge/oath." He slapped his chest.

"Protector question," the speaker asked.

"Protector/he here not," Cobra responded. "Protector/he Spirit Speaker watch/he."

"Cabin question," the speaker asked.

"Cabin/not," Cobra said. "Far/far big/big split-tail burrow all/be." His expression was grim but determined. "Sidewinder Squad/we protect/we burrow. Sidewinder Squad die/we protect." He slapped his chest, and the gesture was echoed by the entire Alsoo squad.

"Protect pledge/oath," they warbled in unison.

"Hendriks reports that Ape, Bird, and Sidewinder are all ready, Commander," Meadow Flower reported. "High Flyer Squadron has launched. DefSat One green. DefSat Two green. DefSat Three yellow. DefSat Four green. DefSat Five yellow." Her crest flattened slightly. "Commander, DefSat Three just went red." Her crest flattened completely. "Spirits!" she exclaimed. "DefSat Three and DefSat Five are both red. I am getting Torque emergency broadcasts from DefSat Three and Five."

With a visible effort, she forced her voice to remain calm. "Commander, DefSat Three and Five are broadcasting," she chirped.

"... peat. Earth defense satellites have been liberated from the godless heathens who have dared to rebel against God," came the broadcast. "We are the Hands of God, and we call upon our brethren to rise up …"

"Someone block those broadcasts immediately," Kasumi shouted.

"Rise up and take back our countries, our world, our God. Rise up …" The broadcast suddenly stopped.

"Morning Mist, Meadow Flower, someone tell me what's happening," Kasumi demanded.

"Best guess?" reported Morning Mist. "Outside or co-opted agents have taken command of DefSat Three and Five."

"Moles," rumbled Eisenstadt. "Sleeper agents. People placed in position with this takeover as their sole purpose."

"Analysis agrees with the commander," Meadow Flower interjected. "Analyzing recruitment records now."

"Keep us informed, Meadow Flower," the commander replied.

"Not everyone on those satellites are moles," Morning Mist said. She chittered suddenly. "A friend of yours is coordinating a response," she said almost cheerfully. "Relaying."

"Commander?" came a familiar voice.

"Daniels? Is that you?" the commander asked urgently.

"Yes sir," replied now-Colonel William Robert Daniels. "Up until fifteen minutes ago, I was CO of DefSat Five," he said in tones that sounded more annoyed than worried, "when one General Alton Bridgestone came up for a 'surprise inspection.'" You could hear the implied quotes in Daniels' voice.

"Aw shit," the commander exclaimed.

"Sorry, sir," replied Daniels. "I was careless."

"We can discuss that later, Daniels," growled Eisenstadt. "What are your plans?"

"I'd rather not say, sir," Daniels replied. "The wrong people may be listening in."

"You're secure, Colonel," Meadow Flower said. "The only Torques you are now communicating with are here in this room. And if anyone tries relaying what you say, I will know."

"I didn't know you could do that," Daniels said in an accusatory voice. "Never mind," he said crisply. "Bridgestone only controls the bridge and weapons. I control everything else," he said. "And my people think they can detach him from weapons in about an hour. Once weapons are under my control, we will move against the bridge."

"Make it ten minutes, Daniels," barked the commander. "Keep Morning Mist updated."

"Yes sir," replied Daniels.

"That takes care of DefSat Five," the commander said. "Who's the CO on Three?"

"Commander Al-Sadhi," reported Meadow Flower. "He's been with us for almost two years." Her crest suddenly flattened. "It isn't Al-Sadhi, sir," she said. "His Torque just reported his death."

"No!" exclaimed Colonel Bloom in horror. He and his squadron were assigned to DefSat Three, and he had just watched his CO and friend, Commander Sharrif Al-Sadhi, gunned down by supposedly his own men. "What the fuck is wrong with you, you sons of bitches?"

The men in the uniform of Earth Defense turned toward Captain Bloom. "This satellite and all who serve here are under the command of the Hands of God," he said sternly. "Commander Al-Sadhi resisted the lawful order to relinquish command and provide the launch codes." He raised his weapon. "Don't make me shoot you, Colonel."

Colonel Bloom stared at the weapon then raised his eyes to look at his opponent. He made a chirping sound. "Too late," he said.

"Colonel?" replied the man. Suddenly, the man's body jerked and then fell to the ground.

"I said, too late," replied Bloom. His hand held a weapon. He smiled coldly. "About a thousand years too late." His smile got colder and wider. "My name is Alexander Bloom. You killed my friend. Prepare to die." He started walking forward.

A man aimed his weapon and fired at Colonel Bloom. The high-velocity slug should have punched the same baseball-sized hole in Colonel Bloom as it had in Commander Al-Sadhi, but something deflected it.

"My name is Alexander Bloom. You killed my friend. Prepare to die," repeated Colonel Bloom. "Bet you dumb fucks don't even know where that's from, do you?" He aimed his weapon at a second stunned man. He fired, and the man's body jerked and fell to the ground.

"My name is Alexander Bloom. You killed my friend. Prepare to die!" he screamed, and his weapon fired again and again. The rest of his squadron added their own weapons' fire.

Colonel Bloom lowered his weapon when the last of the enemy squad was either dead or dying. He tapped his Torque. "This is Colonel Bloom to Command. Commander Al-Sadhi is dead, and DefSat Three is in enemy hands. I will attempt to make contact and link up with our people and see what we can do about taking back the satellite. Out."

Captain Bloom turned to his squadron. "Okay, boys and girls, let's make some noise."

"Anyone ever tell you, you are a sick fuck, Bloom?" asked his wingman, Lieutenant DuBois, a young-looking light-skinned black woman. "Fuck!" she exclaimed. "Only a sick fuck would quote from *The Princess Bride* and kill someone," she complained. "Normal people quote Tarantino." She checked her weapon and headed for the hatchway.

Colonel Bloom stopped by the dead body of Commander Al-Sadhi. "They're dead, buddy," he said to the corpse. "You can rest easy." He knelt down and covered the man's head with his jacket. Then Colonel Bloom stood. "ROE is as follows: kill them all and let God sort it out," he said. "Let's go."

"Sorry for the delay, Mr. President," David Eisenstadt said to the image floating in front of him. "We had a few situations to handle."

"No doubt," President Newgate replied dryly. "I assume those situations have been handled?" he asked in the same dry tones.

"Not completely, sir," replied the commander. "But they are contained."

"Thanks the spirits for that," muttered the president. "It's a madhouse down here. The only good news is that hardly any of those countries prone to launching weapons have rebuilt even a fraction of their nuclear capabilities. So all the fighting is conventional."

"Fighting?" Eisenstadt asked in dark tones. He looked at Morning Mist.

"Mostly minor skirmishes," she replied to his unasked question. "Closer to police actions," she added.

"Those police actions are causing casualties," President Newgate snapped. "If I had known that Mr. Blunt's appearance would have caused this, I would have stopped him."

"Would you have really, sir?" asked Eisenstadt. "To be fair, I doubt he expected this either." He rubbed his close-cropped scalp. "Sir, my priorities at this moment are regaining control of all of Earth Defense satellites and maintaining control of everything else up here," he said almost apologetically. "The only ground forces I can spare are Ape, Bird, and … Sidewinder Squads."

Captain Hendriks and Captain Cool Evening Breeze walked deliberately to the Alsoo colony. They stopped at the border of Alsoo territory. Usually if someone came near the border, a guard would approach and both warn them off and ask why they were there. Depending on the circumstances, either more Alsoo would arrive or the visitor would be escorted to a specified location. This time, neither of those things occurred, as Sidewinder Squad was already waiting and in full gear.

The two captains slapped their chests. "Pledge/oath," they chorused.

"Pledge/oath," responded the Alsoo. Cobra, Boa, and Mamba side-winded forward. "Eaters question," asked Cobra.

"Not Eaters, centurion. Something far worse," replied Hendriks.

The Alsoo squad leader tilted his feathered head. "Split-tail fight split-tail question," he warbled.

Hendriks smiled wryly. "You weren't supposed to get it in one,

Cobra," he complained. "I had a whole bunch of ominous-sounding things I was gonna say."

The Alsoo leader warbled in amusement. "Crazy/think split-tail," he replied. "Think/me split-tail crazy/think this time Alsoo crazy/think." The rest of Sidewinder Squad warbled their own amused responses.

"I think he just said we're rubbing off on them." Hendriks smiled. "But then again, all warriors are crazy." He stopped smiling, and his posture became more rigid, more official. He pointed to the Alsoo citadel. "The women and hatchlings will be safe inside the colony. Pledge/oath," he said. "You don't have to come with us, but we really need every warrior possible."

"Sidewinder/we fight/we bad split-tail/they question," asked Cobra.

"They're not bad split-tails, but we do not think the same way about some things," Cool Evening Breeze replied. She waited for the translation to complete. "We must fight them, but not as enemies but as … help me out here, Hendriks." Cool Evening Breeze struggled to find a way to explain.

"Brothers time time fight/they," said Cobra. "Time time want/they same female/they, same burrow/they. Split-tails brothers/they," Cobra warbled.

"Exactly," Cool Evening Breeze exclaimed. "These split-tails are our brothers, and we must treat them that way even though we are fighting."

Cobra turned to the two Alsoo flanking him, and they warbled at each other. Occasionally, one of the other Alsoo warbled a comment from the still-maintained phalanxes. The discussion didn't last too long, but it felt as if the matter was being discussed in great detail. The translators didn't try translating what it considered a private conversation.

Finally, the Alsoo waggled their arms at each other and turned to Hendriks and Cool Evening Breeze. "Bad time brothers fight/they. Tribe/we make peace brother/they. Big split-tail, little split-tail,

Alsoo/tribe be/we. Tribe we make peace." He slapped his chest. "Pledge/oath."

Hendriks and Cool Evening Breeze braced to attention and slapped their chests. "Pledge/oath."

56

And in the End

Jeremy Blunt gazed pensively out of the window of the limousine that was taking him and his three students to a local airfield and the Rynn shuttle that was waiting for them.

"Teacher," Morning Stars Fade said urgently. "We are still being followed."

Jeremy nodded. "And what does that tell you, Disciple?" he asked.

"That someone we trust has broken that trust," Morning Stars Fade replied. "I cannot believe it would be the oligarch."

"It isn't," Jeremy replied. "A pawn can take a king just as easily as a queen." Jeremy pointed his chin at the driver. "Isn't that so, Mr. Owens?"

The driver looked at his passengers via his rearview mirror. "When did you catch on?" he asked. "Just out of curiosity."

"You did quite well hiding what you were doing," Jeremy said calmly. "But you should have been able to shake the car tailing us when my student first alerted you." He smiled slightly. "What was it: money, position, power?"

"God," replied the driver.

"Ah, of course," Jeremy replied.

"I hope you aren't going to do something foolish," the driver said somberly.

"Foolish?" Jeremy laughed. "No, I don't think we'll do something foolish," he said. "However, what we will do will be very violent," he said. "Disciples."

Jamal pulled his weapon and shot the driver in the back of the head while Emily expanded her personal shield to cover Jeremy, Jamal, and Morning Stars Fade. The car started to sway now that no one was steering the vehicle. Jamal tapped his Torque. "Emergency pickup requested," he said. He leaned across the front seat, pushed the body of the driver away, and grabbed the wheel. It was fortunate that they were on a more isolated stretch of road—though it was quite likely that fortune had nothing to do with that. Jamal scrambled into the driver's seat.

"They're firing at us," reported Emily calmly.

"We need to get out of this car," Jeremy ordered. "There's a good chance that our actions were anticipated."

"Maybe not, Teacher," Morning Stars Fade replied. "There does not appear to be a bomb or any other devices that could affect the car."

Jeremy raised an eyebrow. "I think I'm disappointed," he said. "No. I'm insulted," he corrected himself.

"Most think you are just an old man, Teacher," Morning Stars Fade chittered. "They have a reason to believe you are harmless. But it bothers me that they would think the same about us," he noted. "As you humans say, I have half a mind to complain."

"Never interrupt your enemy when they are making a mistake," Jeremy said. "Nor let them know that they are making a mistake."

Morning Stars Fade and Emily briefly covered their eyes. Jamal just laughed.

"If this is supposed to be either a kidnapping or an assassination," Jeremy said in the tones of a professional lecturer, "there should be at least one more vehicle. Preferably at a blind intersection," he added.

"And the number and nature of the other vehicle will inform us as to their intentions."

"Don't you ever stop teaching, old man?" complained Jamal.

"Teachable moments like this are few and far between," Jeremy said cheerfully. "We should seize the opportunity that presents itself."

"Teacher," Emily said urgently. "A second SUV and a panel truck have joined the one that's been following."

"A kidnapping then," Jeremy nodded. "Jamal, expect them to try cutting you off."

"ETA on shuttle is five minutes, twenty seconds," Emily reported.

"Well done, Emily," Jeremy praised. "That was going to be my next question."

"Both SUVs are speeding up, sir," Jamal reported. "We're coming to an off-ramp," he said. "Town of Mountaindale. Population 32." He chuckled. "Looks like they got at least one thing right," he said derisively.

"Let's play along for now," Jeremy said. "Maybe if we let them kidnap us, we'll learn who our mastermind is."

'Teacher, you may think this is fun, but your granddaughter will skin me alive if anything happens to you," growled Morning Stars Fade.

"Which one?" Jeremy asked in curious tones.

"Does it matter, Teacher?" replied Morning Stars Fade.

Jeremy chuckled. "I suppose not," he said. "Oh well, if there's going to be gunplay, we should do it someplace like Mountaindale." He leaned back in the seat. "Remind me to tell you the story of when Mei Lin and I were in a similar situation."

Two pairs of eyes swiveled to look at Jeremy, and three pairs of ears pricked up. In the case of Morning Stars Fade, the pricking was literal. "Was Mei Lin a part of your ... previous life, Teacher?" Morning Stars Fade asked cautiously.

"She giggled the entire time," Jeremy replied. "She later told me it was the best date she had ever been on."

"Yes, Teacher," Morning Stars Fade replied with a smile. "I

wonder if Emily will think this was the best date she has ever been on," he teased.

"Depends on if we get out of this alive or not," Emily replied. "Three minutes before shuttle arrives."

"SUV is going to try cutting me off, sir," reported Jamal. "Big house nearby," he said in interested tones. "Mr. Big?"

"Probably not so big," Emily countered "Two and a half minutes."

"Hang on," Jamal ordered as he applied the car's brakes to avoid the car that suddenly cut them off. He spun the wheel, hit the gas, and shot around the car. "Here comes number two," he warned and hit the brakes again. He stopped the car, quickly put it into reverse, and backed away. He spun the wheel and hit the brakes again to spin the car around. He jammed down on the accelerator.

"Forty-five seconds," Emily reported. "Well hello, Dr. Franklin," she said.

"Sorry we're late," came the voice of Joseph Franklin over the Torques. "Traffic, you know," he said. "We have the two cars and the van on lock."

"Just pick them up and put them down somewhere else," Jeremy ordered. "Jamal, let's pay a visit to that house we just passed."

"Yes sir." Jamal slowed the car just as the two SUVs and the lone panel truck were pulled into the air as if by an unseen hand.

"Right on time," Emily reported. "Care to join us, Dr. Franklin?"

"I have an Alsoo neuter telling me in no uncertain tones that I am a 'crazy/think big split-tail/me,'" replied Franklin. "So yes, I would love to join you," he said. "Frozen River and Black Rocks will stay with the Shrike."

"And that's only because we drew the short straws," Black Rocks cut in and complained.

"And Red Clouds Paint the Sky, Light of Three Moons, and Jana will come with me," Franklin continued.

"Jana?" asked Emily.

"Second-Daughter-Third-Born," replied Franklin. There was a crash as the two SUVs and the panel truck hit the ground hard.

"Picked up. Put down," Franklin's voice said cheerfully. "You started something, Jamal Shadowed Heart," he continued. "Or rather, Sunrise did, which impresses me no end, by the way."

A shuttle appeared a safe distance away and hovered just above the ground. A hatch opened, and three figures emerged— two Rynn on their own legs and one human in his personal support pod that floated a foot above the ground. The pod was tilted forward, and since it outlined his body from his feet to his chest, he looked more like he was inside an anime-inspired mech-suit. The idea that anime had a great influence on the design of the pod was enhanced by the control blister on his shoulder. The blister contained a visibly excited Alsoo manipulating a set of controls. "Anyway, I found, believe it or not, a Naga name generator."

"Jana new/call me," agreed the Alsoo. "Pretty."

"Yes, it is," agreed Franklin. "Aren't the three of you supposed to keep Jeremy out of trouble?" he complained lightly. "You know Kasumi is going to have words with you regardless of how this plays out."

"Yes sir," agreed Jamal. "However, I doubt the captain would have had better success getting the Teacher to do anything he does not wish to do."

Dr. Franklin grinned. "Be sure to mention that to her," he encouraged. He made a chirping sound. "Black Rocks, have you completed a scan of the surroundings?"

"Just updating the information now," replied the voice of Franklin's core brother. "That house has been reinforced with armored plate, with a section that has double the reinforcement," he said.

An image appeared in front of several people.

"Safe room," Jamal stated.

"And?" asked Jeremy.

Jamal tilted his head and examined the image. "Tunnel entrance," he said. "Probably booby-trapped," he said in observation. He whistled. "They've got shields. Heavy-duty ones."

"Agreed," said Franklin. "Who owns this place?"

"An old friend of the Teacher," Emily replied. "A former US senator by the name of Malcolm Coolidge."

"How disappointing," said Jeremy.

"Disappointing, Teacher?" asked Emily, her freckled face scrunching up cutely in confusion.

He waved an all-encompassing hand. "All this. All the deaths. All the wasted time and effort on a meaningless war. To Senator Coolidge, none of that is as important as getting the last word," he said. "He used the renewal of civil war to hide a simple kidnapping," he complained. "I have half a mind to just ignore the idiot and go home."

"You can't let him get away with all this," Jamal objected forcefully. "You can't do that."

"I said 'half a mind,' Jamal," chided Jeremy "But any response we make must have the required effect," he said. "What says, 'Do not bother the Forest Cabin Clan' in language the senator would understand?"

"How about carving 'Do not bother the Forest Cabin Clan' on his forehead?" suggested Emily.

"Tempting," agreed Jeremy. "But no." He looked at the house. "Let's make him use that safe room," he said. "Joseph, could you please have the Shrike demolish that house?" he said. "But not all at once. After all, we want him to make it to the safe room."

Franklin chirped. "Did you get all that, Black Rocks?"

"Targeting program is locked and ready, Joseph," Black Rocks replied. "Just say the word."

"The word," Franklin replied with a wide smile.

"Humans are so weird," complained Black Rocks. "Launch."

There was a boom, and the upper left part of the large house exploded. Ten seconds later, the upper right side exploded.

"He's moving," Emily reported. "Better take another shot; they're starting to slow down." The middle of the building exploded a second later. "And they're moving."

"Finish the job just as they get inside the safe room," Jeremy ordered.

"And they're in," Emily reported. The sound of a double boom followed. "Nice shooting, Black Rocks."

Malcolm Coolidge wiped his sweating jowls. Eighteen years older, forty pounds heavier, he remained the same bombastic figure who had propelled himself into politics. He had amassed great wealth and great power despite losing his senate seat some years earlier. All losing that seat had done was free up some time that he had better use for. "It's been quiet for the past fifteen minutes," he said. "Maybe they think I'm dead and left."

"Maybe we should show them a body so they can be sure," said a sour female voice. A woman in her late thirties sat in a chair possessively hugging the pale and quiet twelve-year-old boy in her lap. "How dare you involve Alexander in one of your schemes."

The preceding eighteen years had been kind to Denise Coolidge, at least physically. The young boy on her lap was all that remained of a happy marriage cut short by a misguided civil war. She had lived for the past fifteen years in this house, one of a number of properties owned by the Coolidge family. It had two redeeming virtues: it was free, and normally, it was far away from her father. "I should never have let you in the front door."

"Shut up, Denise," snapped Malcolm Coolidge. "I'm thinking."

Denise bit down on the obvious retort and hugged her son tighter. She'd known something was wrong when her father had suddenly shown up two nights ago. Maybe *wrong* was not the right word, she considered now, but something was going on, and now her home of the last fifteen years was destroyed. *Someone will pay for that*, she vowed.

She looked up at the sound of a jarringly prosaic knocking on the door to the safe room.

"Who ... who's there?" she called.

"Denise!" Malcom Coolidge snapped angrily.

"Are you all right, Mrs. Edwards?" called a gravelly voice. "Is Alexander all right?"

"We ... we're fine," Denise called back.

"Excellent," replied the voice. There was a humming, and then the door crashed inwards. A moment later, a young black man walked into the room holding a ready weapon. He was quickly followed by two other young adults, one female and human, and one male and Rynn. She swallowed when the fourth person entered. "Mr. Blunt."

"Mrs. Edwards," the old man said gravely. "Alexander."

"Be polite, Alexander," Denise said firmly.

"Yes, Mother," the young boy replied. "Greetings, sir."

Jeremy nodded and walked over to where Denise and Alexander were now standing. He knelt down a little to look into the eyes of the young boy. "I know you are too young to truly understand what is going on, but I must speak to you about something very important." The boy seemed to be about to say something, but then he nodded. "Good," said Jeremy. "A long time ago, even before your mother was born, a feud started." He frowned. "Do you know what a *feud* is, Alexander?"

"Yes, sir. It's when families fight," replied Alexander.

Jeremy nodded in approval. "Exactly," he agreed. "Your family and my family are feuding."

"It is a stupid feud," snapped Denise. "Senseless and futile," she said angrily. "If I had my way, I'd be done with it all."

"Unfortunately, and may I add stupidly, it is not your decision," Jeremy replied. "It is, however, Alexander's."

"Don't say anything, Alexander," ordered Malcolm Coolidge. "I'm still in charge."

"For now," agreed Jeremy. "But one day, Alexander will be," he said. "And it is to that future authority that I am speaking."

"Don't say anything, Alexander," repeated Malcolm Coolidge sharply. "Nothing."

The young boy swallowed nervously. "You're right, sir, I don't really know what's going on. But I do know that my mom doesn't want this feud to continue. It makes her cry, and I don't like that," he said. "And if I can stop it, I will."

Jeremy smiled and stood. "Thank you, Alexander," he said in satisfied tones. "Mrs. Edwards, if there is anything you need, anything at all, please don't hesitate to ask."

"I need a new house," Denise said sourly.

"That goes without saying," Jeremy replied. "I meant if you needed something difficult to obtain," he said. "In the meantime, and only if you wish, I can offer you a ride. It would be to the colony at first, but only until we replace your home." He leaned forward. "By your son's words, the feud is over. You have nothing to fear from me," he said quietly.

Denise nodded. "I think we will take you up on that offer," she said.

"Emily, why don't you escort Mrs. Edwards and Alexander to Light of Three Moons and Red Clouds Paint the Sky," Jeremy said. He looked at Alexander. "Have you ever met an Alsoo, Alexander?" He smiled as the boy slowly shook his head. "Her name is Jana, and she's a very fine lady."

"Come along, Alexander," Denise said, and she led her son over to where Emily waited. Soon, they were gone.

Jeremy turned. "Your life is literally in my hands," he said somberly to Malcolm Coolidge. "I lost my grandfather at eighteen, and that was difficult enough. I shudder to think what it would be like to lose your grandfather at twelve."

"It sucks," Jamal muttered.

"Yes, you would know," Jeremy said. He pointed a finger at Coolidge. "And you were partially responsible for his knowing that," he said in his gravelly voice.

Jeremy reached out and grabbed Coolidge by the throat. Pain blossomed under those fingers. "I want to make something very clear to you," Jeremy said. "First, this is the only time I will tell you this:

leave me and mine alone. Second, the reason why it will be the only time is that any provocation will result in your death."

"You can't threaten me," wheezed Coolidge. "When I am done, you won't even have that stupid cabin you're so proud of." He tried to pry Jeremy's fingers off his throat. "I'm a former US senator and you're just a hired killer. Who do you think would be believed?"

"Teacher, I believe the man is mentally ill," Morning Stars Fade said in amazement. "Does he truly not know who and what you are?" He turned to Malcolm Coolidge. "Sir, you are speaking to the head and founder of the Forest Cabin Clan."

"So he's the head of some big family," Coolidge replied, still trying to remove Jeremy's fingers from around his throat.

"Spirits, you truly do not know," Morning Stars Fade said. "Sir, to a Rynn, a clan is not just a family. It's more closely related to a country, except that it's a corporation—and even that's not all of it. A clan is businesses and property and all that belongs to the common economy," he said almost pleadingly. "Clans that are competently run grow, and clans that are incompetently run disappear—their assets and people absorbed by another clan."

He continued, "The Forest Cabin Clan is most competently run. By your reckoning, it's worth is somewhere around twenty trillion American dollars." He looked into the man's eyes. "Twenty trillion dollars that the Teacher can draw upon at will," he said.

Malcolm Coolidge stopped struggling and stared at Morning Stars Fade in disbelief.

"For example," Morning Stars Fade said, "the ship that destroyed this house is owned by the Forest Cabin Clan."

"I thought it was owned by the colony," wheezed Malcolm Coolidge.

"Sir, the Forest Cabin Clan *is* the colony," Morning Stars Fade said in emphasis. "The Forest Cabin Clan owns the *Nieth*. The Forest Cabin Clan owns DefSat One and commands all five of Earth's defense satellites. It part-owns the space dock. It owns the *Seeker*.

Right now, the Forest Cabin Clan is approximately the tenth largest economy on Earth. And growing."

He walked over and gently removed Jeremy's fingers from around the senator's throat. "Do not bother the Forest Cabin Clan again," he said softly and then turned. "We should go, Teacher."

Jeremy nodded and started walking away.

"One more thing, sir," said Morning Stars Fade. He leaned forward. "It won't be the Teacher who executes you. It will be me," he whispered into the senator's ear. Then he smiled and turned away.

Jeremy returned to the shuttle to find an entranced Alexander talking to the Alsoo neuter Jana. Denise Edwards looked at Jeremy. She must have seen what she was looking for in his face and nodded. "I would not have mourned," she said. "You're kinder than he deserves."

"For Alexander's sake," Jeremy replied. "And for yours."

The following evening, Jeremy was on the front porch of his cabin in the woods. He finished his one allowed cigarette and carefully stubbed it out. "It's over, Mei Lin," he said to the night sky. "The world is still having its problems, but this one thing, at least, is finally done." He levered himself to his feet and walked into the cabin.

The princess looked at the Temple of Light. It seemed somehow festive. She clapped her hands together twice. "I am the princess," she said. "I have thirsted and learned the true value of water. I have hungered and learned to appreciate what I eat, and I have been naked and learned to be comfortable in my skin." She knelt at the foot of the stairs. She heard someone approaching and looked up with tears in her eyes. "Have you come to say goodbye, Grandfather?" she asked.

An old monk sat down on the bottom step and placed his hand on the princess's head. "It's you who needs to say goodbye, Granddaughter," the monk said in a gravelly voice. "I have kept Mei Lin waiting long enough."

"I will sing for both of you every night," the princess promised. "Goodbye, Grandfather."

Kasumi opened her eyes—eyes that were damp with tears. A hand reached out and took hers.

"He's gone, Mel," Kasumi said.

"I know," Mel whispered back. "I was there."

"We all were," David Eisenstaft added in dazed tones.

Kasumi sat up and rubbed her face tiredly. Her hands came away wet. She took a breath and began to sing.

Epilogue

Jeremy Blunt was dead. It was doubtful that four words had meant so much to so many ever before. Jeremy Blunt was dead, and in an assault shuttle on its way into potential conflict, twenty-one Naga-like Alsoo wept. Their sad warbles filled the ship. Nor were they the only ones on the shuttle to grieve. Captain Hendriks wiped away a tear with one big hand.

"Should we abort the mission?" the tiny humanoid with the bird-like features sitting next to him asked.

Hendriks took a breath and then stood. "What is wrong with you ladies?" he sneered. "So the old man is dead. What did he say about dying?" he asked.

"That dying was easy—any fool could do it," Cool Evening Breeze replied. She briefly covered her eyes in respect.

"That's right." Hendriks locked gazes with the various soldiers seated in the shuttle—human, Rynn, and Alsoo. "Any fool could do it," he said. "He also said it isn't the dying but the death that counts," he added. "He was an old man, and he died quietly and peacefully." He shook his head. "And in bed." He smiled slightly. "He must have been disappointed."

"Dizzy/think split-tail/you. Sad Spirit-Speaker not," Cobra warbled dismissively. "Spirit-Speaker die/he safe/warm in burrow/he."

"Do you expect to die in bed, Cobra?" Hendriks replied. "Safe and warm and surrounded by your wife and hatchlings?" he asked. "Or do you expect to die sticking that toothpick you call a spear up the butt of some Polig-Grug bastard that's attacking your burrow?" Hendriks asked derisively.

The little Alsoo waved his hand in agreement. "Crazy split-tail/yes. Dizzy think/not," agreed Cobra. "Spirit Speaker warrior/he," he warbled to his fellow centurions. "Hen'riks speak/he truth. Warrior/we die/we fighting. Die/we protecting." He slapped his chest. "Truth/oath."

Hendriks slapped his own chest. "Truth/oath," he returned. "The old man was a warrior, and he'd be the first to tell you that you're all acting like hatchlings," he said. "Yes, he's dead, and yes, we miss him. But you shame him and all he's done by crying."

"Truth/oath," Cobra agreed. He rose up as high as he could in his specially designed seat. "Warriors tall/be," he warbled loudly. The rest of the centurions rose up. "This time fight/we. Fight done cry/we."

"Now that sounds like something the spirit speaker would say." Cool Evening Breeze covered her eyes briefly. "We got a job to do. We'll cry later," she said. "That's what warriors do." Her face blurred, and she was wearing her red and black war paint.

"Oo-rah," grunted the human, Rynn and Alsoo fighters.

One Alsoo warrior started warbling a familiar tune, one that the fighters—Rynn, human, and Alsoo—had adopted as their semi-official camp song. It had dozens of verses, and humans and Rynn had started adding their own. Despite the verses, though, the chorus was the same: "Cry/we. Die/we. Short time sing/we." Though it was not always sung in the same language.

"Okay, ladies," Captain Hendriks said as the shuttle landed. "It's showtime." He waved over Cobra and Cool Evening Breeze. "Cobra, I need your boys to set up a perimeter. Nothing gets within twenty body lengths without you knowing about it," he ordered. The Alsoo warrior waved his arm in agreement and turned and side-winded back to the Alsoo centurions.

The Naga-forms slithered out. Hendriks watched them go for a moment and then nodded. "Looks like they're settled down," he said in approval. He turned to Cool Evening Breeze. "You okay?" he asked.

"I'll cry later," Cool Evenng Breeze replied.

"You and me both," agreed Hendriks. "We got a job to do."

As news of Jeremy Blunt's death spread, the world held its collective breath, wondering what the Rynn response would be. To the joy of most of the world and the profound disgust of much of the rest, the Rynn declared their intention to continue their technological transfer.

By tradition, Rynn funerals were quiet affairs. Family, friends, and—especially in the case of a clan leader—notables would come to pay their respects and provide some anecdote about the deceased. There was no viewing of a body or gathering around a grave. But like humans, Rynn needed to gather together, share their grief, and provide support.

Mel and Kasumi went to the cabin and spent the evening together, just the two of them. They sat on the porch next to Jeremy's chair and watched the sky slowly darken. Mel reached into her tunic and pulled out a pack of cigarettes. She lit one and placed it in the ashtray next to the chair.

"Thank you," Kasumi said quietly. They waited until the cigarette burned out on its own, and then they carefully made sure it was completely out before placing the butt into the can under the chair. Kasumi looked at Mel. Mel smiled and nodded. Kasumi cleared her throat. "Good evening, Grandfather, Grandmother," she began. "It looks like the South is starting to settle down, but there are still a few hot spots. We sent the entire Zoo to deal with the worst ones." Kasumi, with Mel adding comments every so often, recited the news of the day. After which Kasumi sang.

Glossary of Rynn Terms

Alsoo: an owl-faced Naga-form alien

associate: an interim, temporary, or conditional core brother or sister

clan: the basic Rynn socio-economic-political unit. Rynn clans are a collective, led by a hereditary clan leader who acts as CEO, spiritual leader, and political leader.

core: Rynn are polyamorous and normally form unions of three adults, though cores of four or more are not unusual. Members of a core are referred to as core brothers and core sisters.

Graz'to: secretive alien race that corresponds to the Grays that humans have reported seeing.

kip: the round and concave Rynn bed

Light: an Alsoo day

Omiset: Rynn biological treatment capable of forcing the body to repair itself at high speed

pedin: a Rynn standard distance measurement; approximately half a meter

Polig-Grug: a carnivorous alien that has characteristics of insects and lizards; aka bug-lizards

Rynn: a birdlike spacefaring race

spirits: Rynn do not have religion as humans understand it but are very spiritual.

sun step: a Rynn hour, approximately the same as a human hour

sun walk: a Rynn day; approximately 26.5 hours

sun path: a Rynn year; approximately 330 days

Torque: Considered the ultimate Rynn technological achievement, it is a high-powered computer, analytical, communication, and diagnostics system. It is a toroid that is worn around the neck.

Zaski: carnivorous alien species that resembles mushrooms; actual biological classification unknown

WITHDRAWN